The Ultimate Trial

By

T.D. Maughold

Published by Infopath (IOM) Ltd

The Ultimate Trial

First published in Great Britain in 2007 by Infopath (IOM) Ltd.
Web Site: www.infopath.co.im

ISBN 978-0-9552330-1-2 (From Jan 2007)
ISBN 0-9552330-1-1

Printed in the Isle of Man by
Mannin Printing.

Acknowledgements

To my wife, Sue, who was the inspiration for the character Louise Templeton; thanks for all your help and support. Many thanks to Stuart Neale for reading and checking the manuscript. - TDM

Front Cover: Brandish Corner – Courtesy of the Author

Inside Front Cover: TT Trophy – Courtesy of Mannin Printing

About the Author

T D Maughold graduated in Medicine from University College London and followed a career in surgery, working in a number of hospitals across the north of England. He first visited the Isle of Man over thirty years ago and has been a passionate follower of motorcycle racing in general and the TT Races in particular ever since.

He has long held the annual pilgrimage he makes to the Island for the last week of May and first week of June to be sacrosanct and has missed only three TT meetings in the last twenty years. Over the years he has known many great riders and has been personally and practically involved in supporting the races in a number of different capacities.

He has ridden motorbikes since he was seventeen and currently owns a Triumph Daytona.

T D Maughold is now retired from medical practice and lives in the Isle of Man.

The Isle of Man

Chapter One

Early February – Saturday Night/Sunday Morning

Midnight. The soft chimes of a distant grandfather clock cut through the silence of the darkened old house as if to gloomily proclaim the demise of another day. Outside, the wind slackened and its howling voice fell silent. The sheets of black February rain which had hammered against the window panes since before dawn eased and the sharp rattle of water impacting glass faded and died. Suddenly the cold black droplets and streaks were no more. In their place, a silent flurry of soft white flakes and smudges clinging stickily and greedily to everything they touched.

A cold easterly gale had battered the cliff top for most of the previous day, but the last house in Onchan had been constructed in the latter part of the nineteenth century and had weathered such winds for well over a hundred years. It remained pleasantly cool in the hottest days of summer and comfortably warm in the coldest depths of winter. The Victorian builder had known his job and the owner, who had spent most of the evening dozing in his favourite armchair as was his custom when the long winter nights set in, was blissfully unaware of the weather outside. The chair was old and battered, but comfortable and stood in the middle of his favourite room, a large, high-ceilinged, but spartanly-furnished chamber with pastel blue walls. By daylight, the mullioned windows commanded a breathtaking panorama across Douglas Bay, but the heavy velvet curtains had long been drawn and the lights were dimmed. The embers of a coal fire burned low in the grate bathing the room and the face of the sleeping man in a dull red glow. The face, like the furniture, looked old and tired, set in the firelight against a background of silhouettes and dancing shadows.

A flicker of bright orange flame burst from the sleeping fire, momentarily lighting the room and revealing the collection of motorcycles which stood in the background, famous machines with pedigree and history, iron trophies brooding silently in the company of their owner, the collector. The flicker faded and the silhouettes and dancing shadows returned.

Outside, the moaning wind had died and the snow began to fall silently and heavily from a leaden, moonless midwinter sky.

1

Suddenly, the urgent bleat of a telephone sounded somewhere in the house, not near, yet not that far-off. The sleeping man stirred and opened his eyes. He blinked, then glanced at the clock on the mantelpiece. Two am. The telephone continued to ring. The man struggled to his feet and groaned; a call at that time could mean only one thing and could not possibly be ignored. The telephone was in the front hallway, alongside the grandfather clock; he slowly made his way out of the blue room and along the corridor. He picked up the receiver and answered:

"Good evening; Quayle and Son, Funeral Directors."

"Richard?" the voice on the other end of the line asked. It was the undertaker's assistant.

"Ernie?" the undertaker replied sharply, "...Yes, of course it's me. Who else d'you think it'd be at this time in the morning?...What's the problem?" The man on the other end of the line spoke and the undertaker, for once listened. As he listened, a frown passed over his face.

"Okay, sound's like there's no alternative. You say they won't wait 'till the morning?...No...I see. Leave it to me then...the old Quilleash place, you say?...and Dr MacDonald's issued a certificate?...okay you just ring them back and say I'm on my way...probably be at least an hour in this weather. I'll meet you there." He listened for a reply, but heard only the buzz of the receiver. For some reason, his assistant had rung off, either that or for some technical reason the call had become disconnected. The undertaker dialled his assistant's number, but the line was now engaged so he put down the 'phone and went to his room to change into his working clothes. Outside, the snow continued to fall.

Fifteen minutes later the undertaker emerged from his dressing room and made his way to the large garage and workshop which adjoined the rambling house. Dressed now in a formal black suit, he stepped into the hearse and started the engine; the V-eight burst into life with a muted roar and the undertaker pressed the remote to open the garage door. It swung upwards slowly and silently and the car moved out into the cold white night.

It was rare enough for snow to fall anywhere on the Isle of Man, warmed as it is by those diverted flows of the Gulf Stream which made their way up the Irish Sea. Occasionally the summit of Snaefell, the

Island's highest peak, glinted white in the cold mid-winter sun and the Mountain Road rejoiced in the lightest dusting, but for snow to fall this low down, in the coastal parish of Onchan, was almost unheard of. It was a bad sign and one which boded ill for conditions further inland. A journey at night in the snow was not one he had desired or expected, but the undertaker had his job to do and with little enthusiasm for the task in hand, he set about it.

"Bloody snow!" he swore.

There had been a death in an outlying farmhouse in the south of the Island. The bereaved family had asked for Quayle and Son. It was a natural enough request, for Quayle and Son was the oldest and best known firm of undertakers on the Island. The undertaker's assistant had taken the call that night, but he lived in a remote spot himself and the snow was now drifting deeply. He had tried to get his hearse out of his garage, but the task had proved impossible. He would be able to get there in his Landrover, but something more appropriate was needed to collect the body.

The undertaker drove slowly along Douglas Promenade. Two o' clock in the morning in early February was not a time when much traffic could be expected, but the handful of cars that would normally have been abroad had vanished and the road was deserted. The wipers worked overtime to produce a clear black arc in the white windscreen and through that arc the undertaker saw that the tarmac was already covered in a white carpet which was getting thicker by the minute. Passing the Sea Terminal, he crossed the harbour bridge and drove along South Quay, before moving off into the dark Manx countryside. The heavy snow-laden cloud cast a thick veil over the town, dulling even the twinkling street lights and, away from those reassuring sentinels of the night, the night seemed blacker than any he could remember. The headlights of the car were powerful, but that night they struggled to pick out the road through the gloom. Out in the country the snow lay deeper. After a mile or so he passed the Okells brewery, but although he was moving at little more than a snail's pace, his tyres were fighting for grip. At the roundabout, he turned left onto the main road south and wondered how much worse things would get, regretting already his decision to take the job. Visibility had fallen to little more than a few yards when he saw blue flashing lights a short distance ahead. It was a police car and was blocking the approach to Richmond Hill. The undertaker pulled up and got out, leaving the V8 still running. He walked over to the police car and rapped on the driver window; it descended silently.

"Evening Sir," the officer said, "hope you're not thinking of going south tonight; nothing's going to get up this hill at the moment and there are pretty deep drifts further on."

"What about the other roads south, I mean through Foxdale or St Marks?" the undertaker asked. The policeman shook his head.

"Dunno, no reports on those, but if the main road's out of action, I can't see it being any better out there. Where are you trying to get to?"

"Got a bereavement down near Port Erin," the undertaker replied, "and I really do need to collect the deceased tonight." He emphasised the word "do", but he was tired and sensed that his voice lacked commitment. The policeman looked at him curiously for a second then smiled.

"Sorry Mr Quayle, I didn't recognise you...mind you hardly surprising in this, is it? Where d'you need to get to?" The undertaker told him the address.

"Old man Quilleash?" the officer retorted, "poor old sod...mind you he's had a good innings, must have been ninety..."

"Ninety two," came the reply.

"I'll see what I can do."

The policeman spoke into his radio. It was silent for a few seconds then hissed and crackled in reply. All roads to the south were considered impassable and the weather was expected to get worse before it got better. No-one should attempt to travel, even if their journey were really necessary, until conditions improved. The undertaker heard the message and smiled grimly.

"Better tell the Bereaved then, so they don't wait up," he said.

"Looks that way, Mr Quayle," replied the policeman. The undertaker returned to his vehicle and punched a short sequence of numbers on his car-phone. It was his assistant's mobile; he was somewhere out in this and the sooner he knew what was going on, the sooner they could both be back in their respective homes. His assistant knew the 'phone number of the Bereaved and he could break the news.

A second or two later the number he had dialled began to ring…and ring and ring. Strangely enough the voicemail did not cut in. The undertaker rang off and shook his head in disgust.

"Bloody telephones," he swore and with some difficulty punched a text message onto the keypad then pressed the "send" button. His assistant would get the message. They would do the job later that morning. Now it was time to go home.

It was very late (or very early) when the undertaker finally reached the last house in Onchan. The journey back from Richmond Hill had been a painfully slow one and he resolved never to attempt to drive a hearse or indeed any rear-wheel drive vehicle in such conditions ever again. Douglas Promenade had resembled some sort of venue from the winter Olympics, albeit a nocturnal one. He pulled onto his drive and pressed the remote for the garage…nothing happened, so he pushed it again. Still nothing.

"Bloody electric doors, must be snow in the mechanism," he muttered to himself. He turned off the car engine, got out and made his way to the door. It was then that he noticed his assistant's battered green Landrover parked in the shadows by the side of the house. The undertaker shook his head, thinking that his assistant must have misunderstood the text. He walked over to the vehicle, but as he expected it was empty; Ernie had a key to the house; the house would be warm and only a fool would sit out in the cold on a night like this.

The key turned in the lock and the undertaker stepped into the hallway; he reached to his left and flicked the light switch, but nothing happened. He tried the switch again…still nothing. Probably the result of a power cut brought on by the snowstorm, but there was a back up generator in the workshop to keep the fridges running. Strange, though, that it hadn't come on automatically when the mains supply failed.

"Ernie!" he shouted into the darkness, "you in there?" The front door swung to behind him and closed with a heavy thud. The silence of the house was oppressive, claustrophobic even, broken as it was only by the ticking of the clock and the undertaker began to feel the hackles on the back of his neck rising.

"Come on Ernie, I know you're here, your bloody car's outside. Now stop messing about and help me get the power back on!" The house screamed silently back at him and he knew that something was seriously wrong. Returning to the hearse, he slipped into the driver seat and gathered his thoughts; the process was aided by a small bottle which made its way from its secretive resting place to the undertaker's lips. In reality, there was only one choice open to him: he picked up the torch he always kept in the glove compartment and turned it on. The light it emitted was less than satisfactory; no doubt the batteries needed replacing, but it was better than nothing so he made his way back to the house, retracing footsteps which had even in that short space of time almost been obliterated by the falling snow. Once inside the house, he tried the light switch once more; yet again nothing happened so guided by the feeble yellow beam of the torch he went in search of the workshop, the generator and his assistant.

Some time later the undertaker re-emerged from the front door; the house was still in darkness and the snow still falling, but the man seemed to give little thought to either as he lurched almost drunkenly across the driveway, opened the door of the car and fell into the driver seat. In the pale interior lighting of the hearse, his face looked waxy and devoid of expression, but his breathing was laboured and those short staccato intakes of breath were the tell-tale signs of fear. He started the engine and the car moved off.

The snow was falling less heavily now, but the wind had returned, gusting strongly and blowing the cold white powder into deep unpredictable drifts all over the Island. In the pale half light of dawn, Constable Quilliam surveyed the wintry scene from the warm comfort of his patrol car. He had parked by the roadside on Onchan Head and was contemplating breakfast; not the meagre continental version, of course, one glance at him would reassure the onlooker that croissants and fresh orange juice rarely passed his lips, but the full blown English (or more correctly Manx) dish: fried eggs, bacon, sausage, mushrooms, tomatoes...Suddenly the radio crackled and the vision was gone.

"Delta Uniform to Nineteen, come in, over." The policeman reached for his receiver, acknowledged the call, gave his position and listened to his instructions. The job sounded routine: a missing person. An undertaker's assistant who had been called out in the night and had not yet returned.

"Probably stuck in the snow," was his response, "anyway, if he told his missus he was going down south, why do you want me to look for him up here?" He then learned that the man had 'phoned his wife and told her that he had been summoned to his employer's house in Onchan. As the hours had gone by, she had grown increasingly concerned and had tried to 'phone her husband on his mobile and then on the employer's home number, but there had been no reply on either. Control wanted Quilliam to pop round.

"He'll just have stayed overnight there; more sense than to try to drive in this, probably sleeping," the policeman muttered to himself, but started the engine and gingerly moved off through the virgin snow.

He had driven past the house more times than he could remember and like everyone was familiar with its owner, the undertaker Mr Quayle. Some called the man eccentric, others used harsher epithets, but he was respected in a Manx sort of way and was rumoured to be fabulously wealthy. The house was old, sprawling and rather dilapidated. It stood in grounds well set back from the road, some distance from its nearest neighbours and clung limpet-like to the cliff top at the far end of the village. PC Quilliam pulled off the road and entered the driveway which descended steeply between two groves of tangled and overgrown trees. The patrol car's wheels slipped and spun as it made the tricky descent before finally coming to rest in a wide courtyard beside the house. The policeman opened the car door and swung round, testing the crisp deep snow with his foot before risking his weight on it; his foot sunk an inch, maybe two, but it seemed firm enough so he pulled himself out and stepped boldly forward. The test had been rather deceptive; his first full-blown step took him rather deeper and the heavily-built, middle-aged constable swore silently as several inches of his blue serge trousers disappeared below the surface, an icy wetness suddenly clinging to his legs. It was too late now to have second thoughts so he struggled on through the snow and a few seconds later had reached the front of the house; it was then that he looked around and took stock. The courtyard was empty save for a motor vehicle of some description parked by the side of the building; it had evidently been there for some time and was covered in deep drifts, but Quilliam hazarded a guess that it was a Landrover (colour unknown). Control had told him that the missing man drove such a vehicle and it was the first sign that he was on the right track. It was time to try the house.

PC Quilliam turned to the door. His preliminary inspection revealed a button on the left-hand side of the frame; he pressed it and waited. After a time, he pressed it again. Nothing stirred within so he pulled himself up to his full six foot frame, coughed and in his best official manner rapped firmly on the woodwork. The door moved silently inward; it had not been locked. It was then that the policeman's suspicions began to become aroused. He pulled the baton from his waistband and cautiously prodded the door fully open. Dawn had broken and the seagulls had begun their morning chorus, but the interior of the house still basked in a gloomy, silent shadow. Something did not feel quite right, but Quilliam was not a man to shirk his duty; he pulled out his torch and stepped forward. Inside the house, his senses seemed heightened. The door creaked to behind him, damping down the noise of the seagulls with a dusty silence, broken only by a metrononomous ticking. He panned the torchlight around and saw the antique grandfather clock and then he saw something else.

It was a line of footsteps passing along the corridor to the front door, partial footsteps, as if made by someone running, but ruddy-brown in colour and embossed on the pale wooden floor by a sole which had been dipped in blood. Quilliam felt his muscles tensing as he followed the footsteps towards their source. They led him along a tall and lengthy corridor, through an open door and concrete-floored garage to another door and thence to a broad, but windowless chamber. Quilliam flashed his torch around the room and realised that this was the place where the undertaker stored and prepared his customers. A row of stainless steel doors covered one wall and a table such as that Quilliam had seen at his thankfully infrequent attendances at post-mortems took centre stage. It was that table which now attracted the policeman's eyes, for on it lay a body, the fully-clothed body of a man; a man with a long, cruel knife protruding from his chest.

Chapter Two

Early February – Sunday Morning/Sunday Afternoon

"Richard, what in the hell are you doing here at this time of the night?...sorry morning...it's nearly five...don't you have a home to go to?" Louise Templeton was not amused; she had been representing a client in the police station until after midnight herself and had not got to bed until nearly two. To be woken at 4.50am by an elderly undertaker was not something she had expected or desired.

"Never mind all of that," he replied, "can you let me in? I need to speak to you now and in case you hadn't noticed it's like the arctic out here." There was something about the tone of the man's voice that told her the matter was serious and without further word, Miss Templeton pressed a button on her entryphone. Three floors below, the entrance door to the apartment block opened with a metallic buzz and click. A few minutes later there was a soft knock at the door and she let the undertaker into her home.

The apartments were the newest in Douglas. Built in the middle of the Promenade, on the footprint of a collection of derelict hotels, they boasted luxury, practicality and, above all, location. When Miss Templeton had seen them, she had fallen instantly in love and had bought a 999 year leasehold interest. She was one of the first occupants of the block and had moved in only a couple of weeks before. Indeed, so recently had she taken possession, she had not yet had time to fully unpack. She wondered how the undertaker had known she was there, but only for a second, reasoning that he tended to know these things; how, she could not possibly guess, it was just one of the peculiar characteristics of Richard. She knew him well enough to know that he was not his normal self that night though; he was visibly cold, wet and shivering and there was something else; if she wasn't mistaken he looked shaken and, maybe, rather scared.

"Sit down Richard, you're soaking; do you want a towel...No?...well knowing you, I suppose you want a drink?" The man shook his head; Louise Templeton raised her eyebrows, such a response from Richard was without precedent. She sat down and continued: "Now that you've got me out of bed, do you mind telling me what it is exactly that you want?"

"I think I might need an advocate," he replied, "I, er, have a feeling that the police will be wanting to see me in the very near future." Louise smiled grimly and nodded, thinking that she knew what was coming next.

"So that's why you don't want a drink, is it? I've warned you before about that bottle you keep in the hearse; you haven't been drink-driving in this weather, have you, for God's sake?" The man shook his head and grimaced.

"Drink-driving? No, well I might have had a couple of small ones to keep the cold out, but that's not it…it's a hell of a lot more serious than that…it's my assistant Ernie Quine…he's dead, murdered and I have an awful feeling that the police will think I had something to do with it." The advocate's face dropped; this was not what she had been expecting.

"I think you'd better tell me the full story, Richard, from the beginning please, and maybe you'll want that drink after all."

It had taken an hour for the undertaker to tell his story, but that was due in no small part to the advocate's insistence that no small detail be overlooked. She took detailed notes, her mind already thinking forward to the inevitable police station interview and even, as a worst case scenario, the trial. Some parts of the story she needed to hear repeated.

"So you're absolutely sure you didn't speak to Ernie after the police told you the road was closed?"

"Positive. Like I said, he wasn't answering his mobile; it rang and rang so I gave up and sent him a text."

"A text?" Miss Templeton was amazed that the undertaker was capable of such a technical feat. "Can you show me your message?"

"Well, I can, but the mobile 'phone's outside in the hearse; it's on a hands free set up, you see."

"Never mind, we'll look at it later; what precisely did you say?"

"Oh just something like `Driving impossible, cant get to deceased u ring bereaved to tell them will come morning returning home see u then`

"So you told Ernie to meet you at your house?" Miss Templeton asked.

"Of course not, why would I want to do that? Like I said, I would see him at the Quilleash place in the morning."

"That's rather open to interpretation, Richard, Ernie might have taken `returning home see u then` quite literally as a message for him to meet you at your house. Anyway, when you got to the house, the lights were out. You told me that you went in and turned on your torch. Why did you go straight to the workshop?"

"Because that's where the generator is. I wanted to get the lights on. I shouted for Ernie a couple of times, but when he didn't reply, I didn't want to go wandering about looking for him with a pocket torch whose batteries were about to expire."

"So the workshop...that's down the corridor, into the garage and then through...it's an adjoining building, isn't it?"

"Yes, that's right. My father had the garage and the workshop built back in the 1960s; they weren't too fussy about planning then. I went through the garage; the door into the workshop was closed, but unlocked so I went in and that's when, that's when I...I..." the undertaker stuttered, "I saw him, lying there on the table..." his voice tailed off.

"Did you touch anything? I mean, did you touch the knife?"

"No, I don't think so, I mean, well, I can't remember."

"Did you see anything, anything at all that might help the police find out who did it?"

"I didn't hang around, Louise. Somebody had stabbed Ernie Quine through the heart and I didn't want to bump into them."

"Do you think they were still there?" the advocate cut in sharply, "you told me that the door was locked and there weren't any vehicles outside apart from Ernie's Landrover. How do you think the murderer got in?"

"I haven't a clue how they got in. They might have come with Ernie for all I know, but I had a feeling that somebody else was still there and I didn't want to meet them."

"So you came straight here?"

"Yes, of course I did. What am I going to do, Louise?"

The advocate had heard the undertaker's story and had given him her best advice. She had told him that things looked rather bad, but that his best option would be to attend the police station and give a voluntary statement.

"Of course, I don't mean now, Richard," she said. "Once you're there, they'll probably want to interview you for hours and they won't let you go even when you've answered all their questions."

"Won't let me go," the undertaker exclaimed, "what d'you mean?"

"Richard, can I put it very simply to you," the advocate explained patiently, "you are probably (and she emphasised the word) their prime, if not their only suspect, so they'll arrest you as soon as you turn up and they won't give you police bail and they will strenuously object to the court giving you bail once they've charged you with the offence."

"Charged, why should I be charged?" the man exclaimed in total disbelief.

"Richard, think about it; you're an intelligent man. Your assistant has been found on your embalming table with a twelve inch knife sticking out of his chest. Earlier in the evening he was supposed to meet you. You have no alibi to cover the time of the murder. This is the Isle of Man: murder is not exactly common, so who exactly do you think the police will suspect?" Miss Templeton did not mince her words, but she was an experienced practitioner in the criminal courts.

"So what do you think I should do?" the undertaker asked meekly.

"Get some sleep; take my spare bedroom. You've had none and once the police get hold of you, you'll get even less. It's now six-thirty; take six and a half hours. I'll wake you up at one and we'll go down to Police Headquarters, but I warn you, that could be the end of your freedom for several months."

Finally, grudgingly, after a great deal of persuasion, the undertaker retired to Miss Templeton's guest bedroom and lay down on her spare bed, an oasis amongst the unpacked boxes and cases. A short while later, she heard musical snores which confirmed her earlier suspicion that, despite his protestations, the old man was desperately tired. It was now time for the advocate to take some action herself. Louise was tired, of course, but her former life as a staff nurse and then sister on a busy medical unit had trained her to ignore such feelings and go without sleep if it was inconvenient. Years before she had covered double shifts when colleagues were absent and the stamina so-gained had stood her in good stead. She made her way to the underground car-park and started the engine of her four wheel drive; it was an extravagant tool, but for once, in these conditions, it could prove more than useful.

At seven o' clock Miss Templeton drove past the last house in Onchan. The presence of half a dozen police vehicles, together with several hundred yards of blue and white scenes of crime tape confirmed her worst fears, but she had to check as Richard had been known in the past to exaggerate. She pulled into the roadside and punched a number on her mobile 'phone. After a few seconds it was answered. Miss Templeton smiled sweetly as she spoke, although the recipient could hardly see her body language and it soon became apparent that at least some of what the undertaker had told her was true.

"Morning Louise," the custody sergeant replied pleasantly, "you're up bright and early; I see from the board that you were here until after midnight last night. I would have thought you'd have wanted a lie in!"

"Well, you know what it's like," she said, "if I'd stayed in bed, one of you lot would have been on the 'phone by now. Anyway, what's cooking? Any interviews lined up yet?" The sergeant laughed.

"Can't keep you away, can we? Nothing for you yet, you'll be pleased to hear."

"Nice quiet Sunday morning then, eh?" the advocate probed gently.

"Wish it was. Truth is we're all a little busy," he confided, "bit of a bad business up in Onchan in the night."

"Oh really," she yawned, showing little interest, "is it likely to come my way?"

"That depends on whether we catch the fella who done it," he replied, continuing, "he's not in the house, but he won't get off the Island."

"So what's he done then?" she asked, hoping that her voice carried a contrived degree of boredom."

"Shouldn't really tell you, Louise," the sergeant continued in tones which had now dropped to little more than a conspiratorial whisper. He was bubbling over with suppressed excitement and desperate to tell someone his secret. The advocate knew that he was going to tell her; the trick now was to pretend that she didn't want to know.

"Whatever it is Ken, if you haven't got a suspect in custody awaiting interview, then it can wait. I'm going to cook myself a hearty breakfast.

"It's a murder, Louise," the policeman announced triumphantly, "and a really nasty one. If you'd heard what I've heard, you wouldn't be able to face that breakfast. Well known local fella, knifed through the heart and in an undertaker's parlour at that!"

At half-past one the advocate and the undertaker walked into the reception of Police Headquarters, Douglas. The advocate rang the bell and waited, but as usual no one rushed to answer and after a few minutes she rang again. A door behind the counter eventually opened and a middle-aged woman, who Louise took to be one of the civilian staff, made her way over to the glass partition. Her forehead was creased and she looked rather flustered. Miss Templeton could not remember seeing her before and the woman obviously shared the same feeling.

"Yes," she barked, staring at the advocate, "can I help you?"

"Louise Templeton, Advocate. I would like to speak to the duty inspector, please. I have a client who wishes to make a statement regarding an incident which took place in Onchan this morning involving Ernest Quine." The receptionist stared at the advocate and then at the elderly man who stood beside her and then at the advocate again.

"You...your client wants to make a statement about the murder?" she stammered, the assertiveness of a few seconds earlier had gone.

"About an incident in Onchan involving a Mr Quine," Miss Templeton corrected her, "could you please ask the inspector to come down?"

"I...er...I don't know if I can do that. I'm afraid I'm rather new here; I'll have to go and ask." She turned around and ran off like a frightened rabbit. There was a commotion somewhere in the background and suddenly the door leading from the reception waiting area to the interior of the police station burst open and two uniformed policemen appeared.

"Mr Quayle," the elder and taller of the men announced, "*just* the man we've been looking for!" He clapped his hand on the undertaker's shoulder and continued, "I'm arresting you on suspicion of murder. You do not have to say anything, but if you fail to mention when questioned facts that you later rely on in court..." As the policeman recited the caution, the undertaker stared at the advocate, his eyes conveying desperation, terror and...could it be just a little guilt?

The police investigation had moved on. A Home Office forensic team had landed at Ronaldsway Airport and had been ferried to the crime scene without delay. Such expertise was not to be found on the Island, but procedures were in place so that it could be summoned at very short notice. Clad in white protective suits, the experts measured, logged and photographed every inch of the workshop before the body of the late Mr Quine was allowed to be removed. By that time its clothed exterior had already been carefully examined by the pathologist, Dr Stopps. Core temperature had already been taken to allow for calculation of the time of death and the hands had been bagged in clear plastic to preserve any evidence that later examination might reveal. The cause of death looked pretty obvious, but a full post-mortem was scheduled for later that evening and Dr Stopps was not prepared to commit himself about anything until after that time. To the investigating officers, however, it looked like a pretty open and shut case.

"How long am I going to have to stay here, Louise," the undertaker whined. It was early evening and the advocate and her client were seated by a bare table in one of the interview rooms which formed part of the custody suite. It had been recently repainted and no longer stank of vomit, cigarettes and stale beer, but it was an uninviting place to spend more than the briefest amount of time. The two police officers had left the room and the tapes were no longer running, but Miss Templeton knew that the three hour interview her client had just endured was hardly likely to be the last. Things were just beginning.

"They can't charge you yet, Richard," the advocate advised, "because once they do that, they can't ask you any more questions and they will want to ask you a lot more questions, believe you me, but not yet. There'll be a post mortem and forensic evidence to sift through and they'll want to take witness statements from anyone who is remotely involved. They'll have to review your detention after twelve hours and then again after twenty-four hours. Under the Act, they're not supposed to hold you for more than twenty-four hours without charge, but a chief inspector can authorise your continued detention if he has reasonable grounds."

"Reasonable grounds, what reasonable grounds?" the undertaker moaned. "This place gives me the creeps. How much longer do you honestly think they'll keep me here?"

"I couldn't say, Richard, but I think we'll know more by tomorrow morning. In the meantime, is there anything you can think of that would give us a clue about why Ernie was killed or who might have killed him?"

"I don't know. Louise, really I don't. You heard me tell the police that Ernie called me; he told me about the call from the Quilleash place and I was going to meet him there. I never expected to find, to find..." His face fell into his hands and Louise realised that the man was silently crying. They had all rather overlooked the fact that the dead man had been his assistant and probably his friend for a number of years. Louise gave her client a hug and told him that it was time for her to go.

It was dark when the advocate walked out of the police station and a cold easterly wind was blowing in from the sea. The temperature had fallen considerably and the snow crunched softly beneath her feet as she made her way back to the car. Once again, she had spent an entire Sunday afternoon at work. A wry smile passed across her face as she reflected on that decision, taken a decade or so earlier to retrain as a lawyer after her earlier career as a nurse. She certainly earned more money now, but the perceived easier life had been a pipe dream. The hours were longer, the responsibility heavier and the work she had to do harder, but she didn't regret it for one minute. Her life had changed for the better and she had changed with it. Finishing an early shift on a Sunday would once have meant rushing home to change and then rushing out again so as not to miss out on the hectic social life which had accompanied her duties as a staff nurse at the large district general hospital. The cares and worries of that shift would have been left behind with her uniform. Parties, pub-crawls, a succession of good-looking, but insincere and self-opinionated boyfriends, had all been left behind from the day she enrolled as a mature student at the northern red brick university and began to study law. Now things were different: her work meant everything, was never forgotten and the task she had taken on that day could prove her toughest challenge yet.

Chapter Three

Early February - Monday Morning

The piercing cry of a mobile 'phone rose above the moan of the wind and crash of the sea and Louise Templeton opened her eyes. That she had managed to fall asleep that night had been nothing short of a miracle. The winds had reached gale force and the surf had battered the promenade since the early hours. The windows of her apartment were double-glazed, but that had not been enough to dampen the fury of the storm or the frightening bangs and crashes which had punctuated the tempestuous night. The pale luminosity of the mobile display showed the time, six am and the identity of the caller, Police Headquarters. She was still on call so she answered.

"Sorry to wake you, Miss Templeton," the police officer spoke, "but we've got a couple of customers who we want to interview for suspected theft offences and they've asked to see the duty advocate. Are you able to come up to Police Headquarters now?" Miss Templeton let out a silent, long-suffering sigh.

"If I must; can't you interview them later?" she asked, but the officer had an excuse already prepared.

"The arresting officer is on night duty, Miss Templeton and he goes off at seven; he doesn't mind staying a bit longer, but if we don't do it now, he won't be available until tonight."

"Very well, give me half an hour and I'll be with you," she said, putting the phone down and getting out of bed. She moved over to the window, drew the curtains and gazed down to view the promenade through the half-light of early dawn. The storm had been a loud one, but nothing had prepared her for the spectacle which now lay before her eyes.

Palm trees had been uprooted and thrown onto the beach, cars swept from their parking places to lie at crazy angles across the street, carefully-tended flower beds washed away and everywhere, atop everything lay streamers of kelp and a grimy layer of sand, shingle and mud. She remembered now that the local radio had warned of a high Spring tide that night, but the onshore gale had taken the waves several feet higher still, over the sea wall and onto the road. It had melted the snow on the promenade, if nothing else, although she noticed that higher ground was white and the clouds were still ominously heavy. She turned from the window, quickly showered and pulled on her clothes.

It was a short descent in the lift to the underground communal garage; Louise had pressed the button without thinking, but as the lift door began to open she realised her mistake. A powerful jet of icy black water shot through the widening gap and as the opening grew wider, the jet became a wave, filling the elevator cage almost to her knees. Shuddering as the freezing liquid soaked through to her skin, Louise waded forward into the garage. It was dark and bitterly cold, illuminated only by those pale shafts of light which managed to filter through the pavement level ventilation grills. The electrical lighting had failed, fused no doubt by the influx of sea water during the night, but even in that dim light, Louise could see that the garage had become a vast subterranean lake, bobbing with flotsam and jetsam, the detritus of the promenade. Fortunately her 4-WD was unscathed and was standing close at hand. She struggled over to it, unlocked the door and climbed in. The engine burst into life and the car moved slowly through the water, up the ramp and onto the street. Louise was soaking from the knees down, but she decided against going back to change; the sooner she got to the police station the better, the day had started badly and she had an awful feeling that it was going to get worse.

Miss Templeton's instinctive feelings were proving to be correct. She had driven slowly and carefully along the wreckage-strewn promenade, passing a fire engine which had begun to pump out the flooded basement of one of the hotels. On pausing to advise the firemen standing by the appliance of the state of the garage she had just left, she was acerbically reminded that garages were accorded a very low priority in the overall scheme of things and that it would be some time before her subterranean lake was drained. Suitably chastised for airing her own selfish wishes, the advocate carried on to Police Headquarters where she was kept waiting in the cold, draughty area outside reception until the arresting officer was located. When she learned his identity, her heart sunk. He was an odious specimen of humanity, an arrogant and overbearing police constable who had evidently graduated from the same charm school as members of the Gestapo and she knew that he disliked advocates in general and her in particular. The interviews were unlikely to be pleasant.

The two suspects were well-known to the police as indeed they were to the advocate. Darren Finch and Jason Quiggan were still young men, but already habitual offenders whose place in the criminal pecking order lay somewhere towards the bottom of one of the lower divisions. Louise had represented each of them many times before and found them pleasant enough rogues who accepted her advice without question and when convicted, as almost inevitably they were, accepted their sentence without complaint. On this occasion the alleged offences were of theft and burglary, committed over the previous two nights. The snow and then the storm had created havoc and the police view was that the two men had taken full advantage of the darkness, power cuts and shrieking alarms; it was Darren's lot to be interviewed first.

The interview began with the usual formalities as the rasping voice of Constable Kermode read out the caution and asked the suspect to confirm that he understood it and was aware of his rights. Another policeman accompanied Kermode, but other than identifying himself as PC Lee, he remained silent throughout. The twin deck cassette recorder rolled slowly on, preserving for posterity Darren's protestations of innocence and wildly unlikely explanation of the sequence of events which had led to his and his friend's arrest. Kermode listened in silence to the rambling story of a midnight search for a missing dog. When Darren's story came to an end, Louise felt like giving applause; you had to give the young man some marks for imagination, if nothing else, and the slightest flicker of a smile had begun to creep over Kermode's colleague's face, but Kermode had never been known to smile, ever. Holding Darren in an icy stare, he began:

"So the various items that were found in your possession when you were arrested earlier this morning, the DVD player and the digital camera, how do you account for them?"

"Borrowed them from a mate, was just on our way to take them back to him," Darren replied smugly.

"At one o'clock in the morning in that weather?" Kermode asked contemptuously, continuing, "you really think we're going to believe that? and I suppose you'll be able to give me the name and address of this mate of yours and he'll be able to confirm this story, will he?"

"Yeah, he will," Darren said, nodding and smiling.

"And this mate of yours, he'll be able to provide proof of ownership, will he?"

"What d'yer mean?"

"You know, receipts from the shop where he bought them, that sort of thing?"

"Dunno. Maybe."

The policeman moved onto another item which had been found on the suspect.

"What about the mobile?"

"Me mobile, what about it?"

"Not your mobile, Darren, that was turned on; the other one, the one in your pocket that was turned off. Surely even you don't need two mobiles?" Darren looked mystified so Kermode refreshed the young man's memory. "This is the 'phone I'm talking about," he said, plonking the telephone, now duly ensconced in a clear plastic evidence bag, on the table in front of him.

"Oh that. I found that."

"Where and when did you do that Darren?" But of course Darren couldn't remember. The interrogation carried on in this vein for some time until eventually the policeman had had enough and brought the proceedings to a close. It was then the turn of Jason Quiggan to experience the friendly face of Constable Kermode, but Kermode had become bored with the affair and after a cursory ten minutes or so of questioning, brought the interview to a close and turned off the tape.

The two men were released on police bail pending further investigation; there was no other alternative in the circumstances, but the advocate could see that Kermode could barely disguise his contempt at having to let them go. They thanked Louise, collected their possessions and walked out of the police station whistling defiantly. The advocate glanced at her watch: it was nine am and time for her to go to work. She walked towards her car which was parked in its usual spot by the entrance to the park. The clouds had lifted a little and a few rays of thin February sunlight fleetingly cut through the grey morning. To her surprise, the clients were waiting by her vehicle.

"Any chance of a lift into town, Miss Templeton," Darren asked cheekily.

"I suppose so," the advocate replied wearily, "get in."

They had just moved out of sight of the police station when Darren dropped his bombshell.

"If we were to tell you something, in confidence like, you wouldn't tell the police, would you?" he began.

"Is this connected with the interviews this morning?" Louise asked warily.

"It might be," the young man answered.

"Anything you tell me is privileged, Darren, you should know that. I've acted for you enough times before, haven't I? but I should warn you that if you tell me something and then want me to say something at odds with that in court, then I can't. I wouldn't tell the police what you told me, but I couldn't act for you any more. You'd have to find yourself another advocate." Darren looked at his friend and the other man nodded.

"Tell her," he said.

"It's like this, Miss Templeton," Darren began, "I do know where I got the mobile from and some other stuff that the police don't know about."

"The police searched your flat after you were arrested, didn't they," the advocate cut in.

"Yeah, but I don't keep anything there; first place they look, see Jason and I were out on Saturday night, well more like early Sunday morning and we broke into this house. We got a pile of good stuff and I found that mobile lying on the floor, like somebody had dropped it. Anyway, the place was empty, there was no-one there or so we thought until…" he dropped his voice almost to a whisper.

"Go on," the advocate said encouragingly; she was interested now.

"Until we looked in this room, big room with a funny sort of table in the middle and lying on the table there was this dead fella."

"Dead, you were certain he was dead?" Darren looked at his friend as if seeking corroboration.

"He was stone dead, Miss T," Jason confirmed, "and there was a bloody great knife right through his heart."

It was evidence that could be of crucial importance. The two young burglars had stumbled on the corpse of Ernie Quine and they had left the house before the undertaker had returned. She took them back to her office and went through the whole thing again, jotting down notes as they spoke, but try as she might to persuade them, they would not agree to give statements and they would not speak to the police, at all, ever.

"They'd just try to put the blame on us," Darren explained, "they'd say we'd broken into the house and killed this fella when he caught us at it; I ain't going down for life for something I ain't done." So the advocate was now faced with a double dilemma; she knew something which she could use to save one of her clients, but couldn't use it without breaching the confidence of two others. And the week had just begun!

Chapter Four

February - Tuesday Morning

As Miss Templeton had suspected, the police had held Richard Quayle for a further night without charge, but by Tuesday morning preliminary forensics were back and the undertaker faced another interview. Miss Templeton arrived at the police station and found her client in a state of some distress; two nights in a comfortless cell had done nothing for his appearance or disposition and she was now required to go through half-a dozen witness statements with him, explain the implications of the scientific tests and take the man's instructions before proceeding to what would be a lengthy interview under caution.

"How are you bearing up Richard," she began gently.

"Bearing up, how d'you think I'm bloody well bearing up," the man replied angrily, "this place is a hell-hole; the noise goes on all night and whenever I do manage to doze off, someone comes and wakes me up again. The food isn't fit for a dog to eat, let alone a man, I've not had a bath or a shower and I need a drink, a bloody stiff drink. You've got to get me out of here Louise; do something, do anything, just get me out. I don't care what it costs." Miss Templeton muttered sympathetic noises, but explained that there would have to be another interview before she could do or indeed try to do anything. She explained what was in store and then started on the statements.

The first had been made by Kenneth Quilleash, son of the old man who had died. It supported the undertaker's story about a death in the south of the Island, but other than that it was unhelpful. According to Mr Quilleash, Ernie Quine had 'phoned shortly after two am to say that he was on his way to pick up Mr Quayle and would then drive south. He had never rung back. Mr Quilleash had stayed awake half the night waiting for the men to arrive; he had tried calling Mr Quine and the listed number for Quayle and Son several times, but the undertaker's assistant had not answered and the other number reached an answerphone. Eventually, he had given up and gone to bed. When the morning came he had called another firm of funeral directors who had responded speedily and efficiently. Needless to say he was less than impressed by Quayle and Son. Even the murder of Ernie Quine and the arrest of Mr Quayle set against the backdrop of a blizzard, seemed, as far as he was concerned, to be inadequate excuses for what he described as an inept and incompetent level of service.

The second statement came from Ernie's wife, Maureen. She confirmed that her husband had received a call from Mr Quilleash, had tried in vain to get the hearse out of the garage and had then 'phoned Mr Quayle, but she again was under the impression that her husband was to drive to Onchan and meet Mr Quayle there. She had seen him leave their house at a little after two and had never seen or heard from him again. She had little pleasant to say for her husband's employer and had her own ideas about possible motive.

"Mrs Quine suggests that Ernie was thinking about handing in his notice, Richard; say's that you were paying him well below the going rate. What do you have to say to that?"

"First I've heard of it," the undertaker replied brusquely, "Ernie always seemed happy enough with the job; mind you, Maureen's a moaning bitch, always has been. I paid him what I paid him; If he'd wanted to go elsewhere, I wouldn't have stood in his way and I certainly wouldn't have killed him; the woman's crazy suggesting that."

"She says that you've got a terrible temper, Richard and that you can be violent."

"Bloody rubbish."

There were further statements, from the police officer who had spoken to the undertaker at the bottom of Richmond Hill, from Constable Quilliam, from Police officers who had been first on the scene and had taken samples for forensic analysis. That took them on to the interview and whatever the police were prepared to say about the results of the forensics.

"So Mr Quayle, as you know we took away the clothes you said you were wearing on Saturday night and we ran some tests." The usual formalities had been completed and the interviewing officer, a Detective Sergeant from the Serious Crime Unit, had skipped the statements and launched straight into the science. It suggested to the advocate that they had found something.

"What sort of tests?" the undertaker demanded.

"Fingerprints, DNA, fibre analysis," the Detective Sergeant replied calmly, "the usual sort of things that we do in a serious crime and guess what we found?"

"Nothing," the undertaker asserted angrily, "your tests won't have shown anything on my clothes, 'cause as I keep on telling you, I didn't do anything. Now when are you going to stop all of this and let me go. I found Ernie's body, but that's all I did; you should be out there looking for the killer, not harassing me. You're just wasting time."

"Mr Quayle," the policeman continued, "we found nothing on the clothes you were wearing when you were arrested, but we didn't stop there. We went through your dirty laundry and we found a shirt and trousers with bloodstains, fresh bloodstains, of the same blood type as Mr Quine so we ran a DNA test and that showed that the chances of the blood not being Mr Quine's is about 1 million to one. How do you explain that, Mr Quayle?"

"I, er that's impossible, what clothes are you talking about?"

"Officer," the advocate interrupted, "you do need to provide rather more information, these clothes may have had nothing to do with my client; they may have been discarded by the real killer." The officer glanced at Miss Templeton, as if until then unaware of her presence.

"Your client is the one expected to answer questions, Miss Templeton, not you," he said coldly, "You will have the opportunity to advise him when this interview is concluded." He turned to his colleague who produced an A4 size colour photograph of a white shirt and dark grey trousers. The Detective Sergeant placed the photograph on the table in front of the undertaker. The bloodstains were obvious, even to the untrained eye. "Do you recognise these, Mr Quayle?"

"No," came the firm and unequivocal reply.

"Then can you please explain why analysis of hair fibres found inside these items of clothing have shown your DNA?"

"I can't, I mean…"

"And whilst you're at it Mr Quayle, can you tell us why your fingerprints were found on the murder weapon?"

The interview had gone badly for Richard. He had blustered and shouted, but he had been unable to come up with a satisfactory explanation for any of the seemingly damning forensic evidence against him. The only thing that the police case was weak on was an explanation for the bloody footsteps. They did not match the shoes Richard had been wearing or indeed any others within the house. The police view was simple, he had thrown the bloodstained shoes away which was rather at odds with him not doing the same with the clothing.

Miss Templeton was alone with her client once more. He had been charged with the murder of his assistant and would appear before the High Bailiff the next day. She told Richard that she would apply for bail, but that it would be refused and he would be remanded in custody to the gaol. She felt that this case was slipping away from her. She would need to instruct experts of her own and, more importantly, she would need some help. Richard wrung his hands and cast her a look of despair.

"Anything, Louise, whatever it costs, just do it."

Chapter Five

February - Tuesday Evening

By the time dusk fell that February evening, the police had withdrawn from the last house in Onchan, their examination of its interior now substantially complete. A patrol car standing on the road outside the house and a blue and white ribbon hanging forlornly across the entrance to the driveway marked the property as a crime scene, but the house was silent, its rooms empty and still. In the distance, the lights of Douglas promenade twinkled invitingly. The heavy layer of cloud had lifted and the stars shone again in the deep velvet curtain of the night.

A small boat bobbed along in the dark waters by the foot of the cliff. It bore no riding lights; the two shadowy figures within knew where they were going and did not want to be seen. The low hum of an electric outboard was all but lost against the sound of the waves breaking on the rocks, but as the boat rounded a point, its engine cut; a second later there was a deep scrunch as the vessel beached on a steep shingle bank at the head of a tiny hidden cove. One of the men was already out of the boat and moving quickly up the bank towards the foot of the cliff. It was a moonless, dark, dark night, but the starlight would have to suffice, the figure could not risk using his torch. He soon found the path and the steps and began to climb.

The steps were old, older than the house and belonged to the time of a flourishing trade in rum and tobacco, a time when men had willingly risked the dangers of a starlit voyage to the Cumbrian coast for the money that was to be made avoiding the Revenue men. Hewn out of the wet and slimy rock, the steps climbed steeply upwards until they reached the bottommost terrace of a garden. The figure passed silently through the garden until he reached the house. There was a faint tinkle of breaking glass, but it was a noise that no-one heard save for the man who made it. In the house now, he risked the torch and as he passed from room to room, the faint glimmer of its beam darted nervously about as he searched carefully for that which he sought. He opened a door which had been closed and suddenly felt that he was no longer alone. Flashing the torch around, he saw why and smiled. He had found what he had been looking for. Dropping the heavy rucksack from his back, he knelt down beside the dark object, pulled out his tools and began slowly and furtively to undertake his task.

An hour passed, two; the job was taking longer than he had hoped, but he was not worried, for the night was long and the room faced east, overlooking the sea. The curtains were open, but no-one would look through those windows tonight; the policeman would have no reason to forsake the comfort of his patrol car to brave the cold darkness. The operation had entered its critical stages, but the man kept his nerve; his hands did not tremble or shake and the delicate pieces gradually fell into place. At last it was done. He took a deep breath and smiled again; his masters paid him well, but sometimes he wondered whether they paid him enough.

He made his way back through the house, treading softly and slowly until he reached the conservatory door. Looking down at the slivers of broken glass, he shook his head; a little messy, perhaps, but would anyone notice? And if they did, what would they deduce? That the house had been broken into whilst guarded by the police? He passed through the garden and began the long steep descent down the cliff.

Louise Templeton had reviewed the statements again and the evidence that the police had been prepared to disclose. The expert reports were short enough, but heavy on jargon and technical detail; she would need help with interpretation, but she got the gist of what they said. Ernie Quine had been killed by a single knife wound to the chest; the blade had passed through the third intercostal space, had notched a rib and had pierced the ventricle. Death may have been instantaneous, but the pathologist was of the opinion, given the quantity of blood in the pericardial sac that it was not and that the undertaker's assistant had remained conscious for a few seconds before succumbing to cardiac tamponade. The advocate's medical dictionary lay open beside her; it had seen plenty of use that evening. The pathologist opined that there would have been some bleeding externally, but not much. Most of the bleeding was internal and when the heart stopped, the bleeding would have ceased. So why were there bloody footsteps leading from the workshop to the front door? Louise looked again at the DNA report. It dealt with the bloodstains on the clothes and the floor and confirmed that the blood came from the corpse. But why would Richard change his clothes, but not hide or destroy them? And if Darren and Jason were telling the truth, Ernie had been killed before Richard had returned, unless, of course, Richard had set the whole thing up, had lured Ernie to the house, killed him and then drove off into the night seeking an alibi, but no, surely, he would have... She put down the reports and shook her head. The case needed a more experienced head than hers, but who could she go to? She had never defended a homicide before; that particular crime was thankfully rare on the Island.

Suddenly, she had a flash of inspiration. She recalled an inquest which had taken place the year before, a most *unusual* inquest and one with, to her way of thinking, a very unsatisfactory outcome. She recalled the death of a rider in the motorcycle races, the arrest of a doctor and a story she had found hard to believe, even at the time. She had acted for the doctor...and funnily enough Richard had been involved in that case too...yes he had...she thought back to the events of the previous June and then tried to recall the name of the pathologist they had instructed. He had been good, very good; the Coroner had adjourned the matter and had eventually entered an Open verdict, but the pathologist had convinced her that it should have been one of unlawful killing. Now what was the pathologist's name? Unfortunately, she could not remember. It would be on the file somewhere in her office, but she was impatient now and could not wait. The doctor would know and she certainly remembered his name.

"Is that Dr Price?" she asked tentatively, "Dr Jonathon Price?"

"Speaking," the voice on the mobile answered.

"This is Louise Templeton," the advocate continued, "the advocate from the Isle of Man."

"Louise," the voice exclaimed heartily, "its great to hear from you, how is everybody...I mean how are you?

"I'm fine Jonathon, absolutely fine, look I'm sorry for ringing you at this time, but.."

"This time? Its only ten o'clock, the night is young," the doctor interrupted cheerfully, "and how is my friend Richard: still up to no good?"

"Er, I think I'd better tell you something, Jonathon. You may want to sit down."

"I don't believe it," the doctor said finally, after he had heard all that the advocate had to say. "Richard's not like that; grumpy old man maybe, murderer, never. There must be some mistake. Could the samples have been contaminated or something like that?"

"I agree, Jonathon," the advocate replied, "I know Richard better than you and believe me, he just isn't capable of this, but the police are certain that he's the man."

"Humph," Price responded, "I don't have that high an opinion of your police; if you remember…"

"Yes, Jonathon, I know," she cut in tetchily, "I remember as well as you do, I was your advocate, don't forget, but they're usually pretty good and this time they *do* have some pretty strong evidence against him."

"So what do we do?"

"We, Jonathon?" she asked.

"Well, er, I do rather owe the old boy, you know; he saved me, I've got to help him."

"I need a pathologist, Jonathon, someone whom I can rely on and I need one fast. That friend of yours, the chap we used last year…"

"Professor Clarke," Price interrupted, "I'll get him, but it sounds to me like you could do with some help on the ground."

"What do you mean?" she said.

"You need an investigator, someone who can find out who really did it; if I know the police, they'll rest on their laurels now they've got a suspect and the real killer will be sitting back laughing. It'll cost Richard a few quid, but he can afford it; I'll send over my old friend Roy Love."

Chapter Six

February - Thursday Morning

Thursday morning brought clear skies, bright sunshine and a welcome rise in temperature after the cold snap of the previous few days. The snow had now all but gone, save for that lying on a few north facing slopes on the range of hills that ran down the spine of the Island. The wreckage that had strewn Douglas Promenade had largely been cleared and the basements and underground garages pumped free of water. For once, Louise Templeton had not spent most of the previous night at Police Headquarters and this morning she felt refreshed, recharged and ready for anything the day had to throw at her. It was just the sort of morning, she thought, to pay a visit to her client who, as she predicted, had been remanded in custody to the Island's Victorian prison.

HM Prison Isle of Man stood a mile or so from the centre of Douglas and was an elderly red-brick establishment, ill-suited to the modern day prison regime with its emphasis on rehabilitation and human rights. A new facility was under construction out in distant Jurby, but completion was not envisaged for a year or more and in the meantime, the Island had to make do with the old. The advocate reflected, as she parked her car, that there was a certain practical advantage in having a prison close to the town. It was convenient for the courts and convenient for the lawyers visiting their clients; the new facility would be neither, but such practical considerations would not have been considered important when the decision was made to relocate.

Miss Templeton walked up the short path from Victoria Road to the main entrance and pressed the bell. It was answered quickly and the small door within the heavy wooden gates swung inward. The prison officer knew her well.

"Morning, Miss Templeton," he greeted her cheerfully, "who is it today?"

"Quayle, Richard Quayle, remanded by the High Bailiff yesterday," she replied walking behind the officer into the small office which stood on the left hand side of the entrance arch. The man looked in a ledger, confirmed that the visit had been booked and then took the advocate's 'phone, keys and bag. "Where are we today?" she asked, "legal visits?"

The man nodded. He picked up the telephone which stood behind the counter and spoke to one of his colleagues.

"Can you bring Quayle down to legal visits? His advocate's here." The advocate walked back out into the archway inside the main gate. It was separated from the prison courtyard by a gate of iron bars. After a short wait, another prison officer appeared in the courtyard with her client. The iron gate was unlocked and the advocate passed through to join them. 'Legal visits' comprised a small shed (Louise could think of no more accurate description) located to the left of the courtyard and no more than a dozen yards from the main gate. She followed her client in and behind her, keys jangled as the officer turned the lock. The undertaker and his advocate were now alone.

Louise had told him the previous day about Professor Clarke, but their conversation had by necessity been brief, held as it was in a cell beneath the courthouse. She had time now to expand on her plans; that her client was not reliant on obtaining legal aid was a distinct advantage.

"I told you Louise," he said, "I don't care what it costs. You get hold of this Professor and get the private eye as well. I remember them both. I picked up the pathologist from the airport and he struck me as pretty clued-up; same with Jonathon's friend. I need to get out of this place as soon as possible. I've got things to do, things to arrange and I can't do anything whilst I'm stuck in here."

The advocate was curious.

"Things to do Richard, you mean your business?" She asked.

"To hell with the business," he responded fiercely, "it's less than sixteen weeks to the beginning of Practice and I have a rider and a machine entered in every event; I need to be out there getting engines tuned, getting suspension set up, getting..."

"But Richard," the advocate interrupted, "you have been charged with murder; isn't that just a little bit more important than the TT races?"

"A little bit more...a little bit more important than the TT races," the man said echoing the words as if almost unable to comprehend what his lawyer had said, "Louise, these aren't just any old TT races, these are the Centenary races, they'll be the biggest, fastest, richest TT meeting ever, in fact they'll be...," he struggled for the correct superlative.

"The Ultimate Trial?" his advocate suggested.

The advocate had obtained her client's instructions and now had to act. Professor Clarke was contacted and agreed to travel to the Island and perform a second post-mortem the following day. He said that he would be able to give some pointers on the other forensic evidence, but that other experts may prove necessary; he would be able to say more when he saw exactly what the police had. Roy Love had been easy to track down and had agreed to take on the case. He too was available immediately and would make the necessary arrangements and get back to Miss Templeton within 24 hours. He rang back within the hour and told her that he would be on the boat that night. Louise put down the 'phone and sighed with relief; there were certain elements to this case which did not add up, but she had assembled her team and hopefully things would soon start to seem clearer. She put away the undertaker's file and turned to her other work.

The white-walled Italianate crematorium basked in the bright morning sun. Inside, the mourners paid their last respects and filed out to the waiting cars. It was a Thursday morning and a funeral had taken place, the funeral of an elderly farmer from the south of the Island who went by the name of Quilleash. He had been an old man, but had been hale and hearty until the last few days of his life when he had succumbed to a short and unexpected illness. The doctor had been called and a diagnosis of influenza made. The influenza worsened, bronchopneumonia set in and within days the end had come. The doctor had explained how difficult it could be with influenza, particularly in the elderly…and had issued a certificate and the family, none of whom had wanted a post-mortem, had been content, all, that is, bar one of them.

Seth was the youngest of the four sons and although fast approaching early middle age had made little of his life to date. He had walked away from education the day he turned sixteen and had struggled to hold down a succession of low-paid, uninspiring dead end jobs, interrupted by short periods of incarceration at HM Prison before finally admitting defeat and drifting back to work on the farm a decade or so earlier. He knew that the rest of his relations cared little for him and his elder brother, Kenneth, now head of the family, held him in a special type of derisory contempt, but unlike all of the others he had loved his father and unlike all of the others he knew that something was wrong.

Seth had been drinking heavily the night before. He had been drinking alone, as usual, but it was, he had reasoned, his own personal wake. His relations had been far too busy to contemplate such a thing. He had drunk until he lapsed into unconsciousness and he had been topping up since the moment he awoke. A hip flask had carried him through the funeral service and the alcohol had served only to fuel his fires of anger and despair. The family had now returned to the farmhouse above Port Erin where an event, the only event that would have brought them there, was about to take place. Drinks had been poured and pleasantries exchanged (except with Seth who had sat scowling in a corner of the room); it was now time for Kenneth to take command. He banged the base of his glass sharply on the dining room table and the chatter faded and died.

"Ladies and Gentlemen," he began, "members of the family, we have said our farewells to the old man. Now it is time to move forward…" There was an air of expectation in the house and Seth could almost feel his greedy relations inch forward in anticipation of what was to happen next. "…so I would like to ask the family advocate, Mr Gruber to read out my father's last will and testament."

A slightly-built man stood up. It was difficult to determine his age, but Seth guessed somewhere in his fourth decade. The lawyer wore an expensive suit and an expensive smile; in fact everything about the man was expensive. He had attended the funeral and had now attended the house; an invoice of breathtaking magnitude would no doubt soon be on its way. Why this man had been instructed Seth had never been able to fathom. Bradley Fitzgerald had always been the old man's advocate. He had been the old man's friend and had managed to successfully guide him through the various legal obstacles that life threw up without fuss, without drama and more often than not without even charging a fee. But Bradley was an old fashioned advocate and Kenneth had badgered and nagged and cajoled the old man until finally he had relented and agreed to instruct someone new. A fresh will had been prepared and Seth had little doubt how it would read; he poured himself another drink and stared at the man with contempt.

The last will and testament of Kenneth Quilleash (Senior) was a short one. Gruber explained that he had been appointed executor and that legal formalities required him to obtain a grant of probate and to make certain enquiries as to the old man's creditors. It would be some time before the estate could be distributed, but when it was there were to be certain pecuniary legacies (Gruber read these out; most members of the extended family got a few thousand, some more, some less, Seth's name was not mentioned), but the bulk of the residuary estate would pass to Kenneth (Junior). So that was it. Seth stared at the bottom of his empty glass. Kenneth was to inherit the money, the land, the lot and Kenneth was an accountant, not a farmer. Kenneth would sell and Seth would lose his home and his job. He looked up from the glass and glared at his elder brother, but Kenneth was in deep conversation with the lawyer and saw nothing of the look. Seth put down his glass and slipped out of the house; he needed to think, he needed to plan and he needed to plot. No one seemed to notice him leave and the conversation between Gruber and the Kenneth continued to flow.

"A tidy portion of land, Ken," the advocate said, "and you can give vacant possession?" Quilleash nodded. "Then I think that you and my client can do business; you're still keen to sell?"

"As I told you months ago," Quilleash replied, "this place means nothing to me. Nothing, but bad memories, but I expect this client of yours, this Russian chap, to pay the full market rate."

"Oh he will, Ken, you needn't worry about that."

Chapter Seven

February - Thursday Night/Friday Morning

It had been a long and exhausting day. The traffic had eased once he had passed the motorway intersections outside Preston, but the grey-haired private detective was now struggling to keep his eyes and his concentration on the road. A straggling line of red tail lights marked the inside lane of the northbound carriageway ahead of him. On the other side, headlights appeared from out of the darkness, flashed past and were gone. A brightly illuminated sign came into view advising that the turnoff for Lancaster and Heysham lay one mile ahead. Roy Love glanced at the clock on the dashboard: one am; he would be at the ferry terminal by one-thirty; the boat was due to leave at two-fifteen and all vehicles making the crossing were required to be ready to load at least an hour before. It would be tight, but with a bit of luck they would let him on. He eased back into the driver's seat and relaxed. The journey from Cardiff had taken longer than he thought, but he should make the boat. Two hundred and forty miles: M4, M5, M6. He had left his native city after the rush hour and had confidently predicted reaching Heysham by eleven, but the motorways of England were now congested by night as well as by day and the profusion of speed cameras meant that time lost in a traffic jam could no longer be made up. Still, he would soon be off the motorway and when he was on board the ferry he could rest and leave traffic jams, congestion, speed limits and cameras behind him. Junction 34 loomed into view; he indicated left and slowed. The slip road veered sharply round in a tightening anticlockwise spiral. It was a tighter bend than he recalled and he trod heavily on the brakes. At that instant a black van shot past him; its driver, too, had misjudged the curve and for a moment Love thought there would be a crash. He braked harder and braced himself, but the van held its line…just…reached the T junction, went through an amber light, turned right without slackening its pace and sped up the road towards Lancaster. It all happened in an instant, the van had appeared from nowhere and had now disappeared into the night, its driver obviously in a great hurry. The incident woke Love up. He stopped at the red lights, waited for them to change and then turned right himself.

The road approached the ancient city of Lancaster, crossed the River Lune and then followed the river towards the sea. The traffic was quieter now and the private detective finally began to relax. The Port of Heysham was well signposted and a few minutes later he was there. It was a smallish harbour, as harbours go, lying beneath the two towering, ugly, slab-sided concrete power stations. Love recalled that they were Advanced Gas Cooled reactors; built over thirty years ago at the height of the nuclear boom, they had long dominated the flat skyline of the south-eastern rim of Morecambe Bay, but were now aging and fast approaching the end of their working lives. Decommissioning was a word he had often heard used, but what did it really mean? Would the now rather dreary coastal hinterland be put back into its original state or would the buildings just be left to moulder and decay? The road swept round to the right and the detective turned his gaze from the surreal landscape of reactors, pylons, transformers and steam to the collection of dark warehouses, cranes and ships that lay ahead.

There was a short queue of traffic waiting to board the ferry. Love pulled up at the end of the queue and fumbled in his pocket for his e-ticket. It was only when he had found the document and placed it on the seat beside him that he noticed the other vehicles. There was a Mercedes saloon directly in front of him and in front of that a black van. He had not caught sight of the number plate of the van that had passed him on the slip road from the motorway, but he had a feeling that this was the same one. It was a long-wheel base Ford Transit and looked new; a fact confirmed by the registration number. Love saw the shadowy face of the driver reflected in the offside wing mirror; the ferry terminal was poorly lit, the gloom a stark contrast to the bright lights around the nearby power stations, but even in the half-light the face had seemed hooded. The face moved back out of view, perhaps its owner had realised that he was being watched. Love toyed with the idea of getting out of his car and stretching his legs, but the line of traffic had started to move. He put his car in gear and trickled forward to the booth where he handed his ticket to the smiling lady in the Steam Packet Company uniform.

It was precisely half-past one and the ferry had started to load. Fortunately, the lady had taken Love's ticket, but after doing so and handing him his boarding card, she closed the booth and lowered the barrier behind him. He had made it in the nick of time and his was to be the last vehicle allowed onto the boat. Little traffic seemed Douglas bound that night and after driving at crawling pace past a deserted railway platform and down a steep ramp he found himself on board the bottom vehicle deck of the Ben My Chree. It was a large vessel and the vehicle deck no more than a quarter full. He managed to successfully interpret the waving hand signals of one of the orange-jacketed Steam Packet employees, pulled over to the side of the lofty, but dimly-lit hold, applied his hand brake, killed the engine and got out. The black van was now some way ahead of him; vehicles had been loaded in tranches of three or four and the van had been part of an earlier tranche. By the time the detective got to it, the driver and any passengers had disappeared. He peered through the windscreen at the darkened interior of the Transit. There were shapes covered in what appeared to be tarpaulin; he couldn't be sure, but they looked like motorcycles. Funny time of year to be taking bikes to the Island, he thought, but maybe they were being delivered to someone. The van had obviously been rushing for the ferry, nothing more than that and Love mentally castigated himself for being too suspicious. He walked over to the stairwell and began the steep climb to the passenger deck. Behind and below him, the clang and hiss of hydraulics echoed around the car deck as the sea doors of the ferry began to close.

The passenger deck was even quieter than Love had expected, but the small hours of a February morning were not a popular time for travel to the Isle of Man. The bulk of the vehicles below were commercial, but the trailers which supplied the Island made the journey alone. The drivers brought their wagons to Heysham, dropped off a full trailer, picked up an empty one and then drove back to whence they had come. Drivers from the Steam Packet shuttled the articulated loads onto and off the vessel with skill and surprising speed. When the Ben My Chree docked in Douglas, the whole process would be repeated: a nightly performance, scarcely noticed or appreciated by the public except of course on those rare occasions when because of bad weather or mechanical failure the ferry did not sail and the shelves of the Island's supermarkets told their own story.

The private detective was hungry, more than that he was starving. He never ate breakfast and the commitments of his work diary meant that lunch had been forgone that day. The last thing he had eaten had been dinner almost thirty-two hours before. He made his way over to the cafeteria and scrutinised the 'specials' board before deciding on chilli con carne and rice and a cold beer. The crossing would take three and a half hours, but the forecast was good and the sea was expected to be calm. He would try and get some sleep as soon as he had finished his meal. The waitress poured his drink and took his money, telling him his food would just be a few minutes and she would bring it over to him. He sat down at one of the empty tables and gazed around; no-one else seemed to be there. The food quickly materialised and he tucked in, eating ravenously until the plate was empty and the beer was gone. Sitting back and contemplating sleep, he looked around the cafeteria again: this time he was no longer alone.

Over in the far corner of the room, four figures sat huddled together; if they were talking at all, it was in whispers, but if they had tried to mark themselves out, they couldn't have done so more effectively by shouting out loud. Roy Love stared in disbelief; the men wore long monks' habits of coarse brown woollen cloth and their hoods were pulled up obscuring their faces from his sidelong gaze. He caught the flash of a pair of dark eyes, but that was all; he wanted to get a closer view so he moved back to the counter and ordered another beer. When he turned back, the figures were gone. He sat down at his table and sipped the beer, thinking. Thoughts of sleep had evaporated, replaced by the burning question of why four monks would be travelling to the Isle of Man in the middle of February in the middle of the night.

The private detective knew that something was not quite right; a civilian would shrug his shoulders and think that the men were simply visiting a monastery or a church on the Island, but if that were so, they would surely travel by plane. Monk's habits were not something Love had ever really thought about before; did different orders wear different types? If so, were these Benedictine or Cistercian or Franciscan or some other order that he couldn't recall. He finished the beer and decided he had to find out.

Wandering around the interior of a moving ship was not a venture to be undertaken lightly. Even though conditions were relatively good, this was still the Irish Sea and in February it was never flat calm. The vessel had been at sea for nearly an hour, had passed the Lune Deeps and was now charting a straight course towards the Island. Outside, the bright orange flares of the Morecambe Bay gas rigs punctuated the intense blackness of the winter night and the engines of the Ben throbbed and pulsated as the ship ploughed forward through the cold dark waters. Love thought he had gained his sea legs, but a sudden swell caused the ferry to lurch to one side and he fought to keep his balance. A stewardess looked at him with more than a touch of concern.

"It really would be best, Sir, if you stayed in your seat," she advised.

"Its okay," Love replied, smiling, "I think that wave caught me by surprise, but I'll be ready for the next one." The expression of concern melted and she smiled. Love ventured a question. "I don't suppose you noticed a...(he struggled for the correct collective noun)...er...(suddenly he remembered)...abomination of monks come this way a short while ago? The stewardess frowned.

"I'm sorry, Sir?" The collective noun was correct, Love was pretty sure of that, but it was one of the lesser known ones and it did, to the uninitiated novice (no pun intended) sound rather insulting.

"It's the proper name for a group of monks," the private detective explained, "and there is such a group on board."

"I'm not sure if I can..." she began.

"Police," Love explained, flashing his warrant card; it was a desperately old one, stemming from his secondment to Greater Manchester Police a good fifteen years before, but the trick was to never give the person you showed it to long enough to have a good look. The stewardess, who was young, slim and extremely pretty became putty in his hands.

"They...they went forward," she stuttered nervously, "I think they went to a cabin on the next deck."

"D'you think you could find out which one?" Love asked gently. The young woman nodded.

"Wait here," she said, "I'll only be a moment." She disappeared through a door marked 'staff only', but returned within a few minutes. "They are in number 800," she said, a little breathlessly, "there won't be any trouble will there, only the Captain..." Love shook his head.

"I just want a quiet word with the Brothers, Miss, now could you tell me where cabin number 800 is exactly?" The stewardess gave him directions.

"Do you want me to show you the way, Sir?" she asked, but Love politely declined the offer; it was a decision he was soon to regret. He moved forward, compensating now for the gentle roll of the boat and climbed the stairwell to the next deck. A corridor ran off to his left, at right angles to the axis of the vessel and cabin 800 was the first door on his left. He knocked and waited. After what seemed an age a disembodied voice within answered.

"Enter!" It was an English word, but the voice that uttered it was not English, although its ethnic origin he was at that moment unable to place. Love turned the handle and opened the door.

Chapter Eight

February - Friday Morning

The private detective opened his eyes and stared upwards; at first he saw nothing but blurred light and heard nothing but the distant throb and hum of machinery. He felt light-headed and more than a little sick and as his senses fleetingly returned the feeling of nausea deepened. He closed his eyes and unconsciousness supervened.

A three tone bell sounded, bringing him back to his senses. It sounded again and was followed by a disembodied voice instructing all drivers to return to their vehicles. Love was lying on his back, but he seemed unable to remember where. He tried to get up, but his head throbbed and ached and his limbs seemed as if they were made out of lead.

When he awoke again, someone was shaking him and not too gently. He opened his eyes to see the frowning face of a young man in a Steam Packet uniform bending over him.

"Come on Sir, ferry docked ages ago, you may have had a little too much to drink, but I'm afraid you're going to have to disembark."

Love's eyes remained open this time; with some difficulty he struggled to sit up and when he did realised that he was in a small cabin, a cabin filled with the almost overpowering smell of booze with a hint of something else, but he could not say precisely what. The steward helped him to his feet.

"Hope you're going to be able to get off the ship, Sir," he said in a strong South African accent, "looks like you've been having a bit of a party!" Love looked around, saw the empty bottle of whisky on the bunk beside him and tried to explain.

"I've not been drinking, I mean not in here; I was looking for some men in monks habits..."

"Yes, Sir," the South African steward smiled, "whatever you say, now if you could make your way ashore, I have to get this cabin ready for the next sailing." Love looked at the man's face; it was patently obvious that he didn't believe a word that Love was saying. Memory had started to return, in particular, memory of the conversation he had had with the stewardess. The local constabulary might take a rather dim view of impersonation of a police officer so Love thanked the man for waking him and wobbled unsteadily out of the room.

Love took the precaution of asking one of the Steam Packet drivers to bring his car out of the hold and park it by the Sea Terminal. It was a request backed up with a ten pound note which the man gratefully accepted. It had been a prudent step for as Love staggered off the ship, he noticed that the port police were watching him closely. His head was a little clearer now and he recalled the tantalising scent of something that his nose had detected in the cabin despite the whisky fumes. It brought back memories of hospitals and anaesthetic; could it have been chloroform or ether? A vague memory of cold wet cloth held against his face by powerful hands surfaced fleetingly and then was gone. That he had been drugged, he was certain, but his story was not likely to be believed and an arrest for driving under the influence would hardly have been the best start to his investigation. He would make his own enquiries about the mysterious monks, but that could come later. What he needed now was coffee and fresh air and a chance to clear his head. He glanced at his watch: it was now six-fifteen and a pale light had already begun to creep into the eastern sky. The articulated trailers were being brought out off the vessel, all other vehicles, apart from his car, having long since gone. Fortunately, he had taken a note of the registration number of the black van, or at least…He checked his inside pocket and breathed a sigh of relief when he felt the slim notebook he always carried. Just to be sure, he removed it and flicked through the pages. The handwritten notes he had made about the investigation he was to conduct were still there, but a page had been removed; it was, of course, the page he had been looking for. The detective frowned. He checked his other pockets, but his keys, his wallet, everything else was there.

The post-mortem had been scheduled for ten am and five minutes earlier Professor Clarke and Miss Templeton had arrived at the unmarked, windowless door which stood on the right hand side of the corridor leading towards the rear of the hospital. Louise pressed the bell and they waited. Whether by accident or design, when the new hospital had been constructed the mortuary had been placed next to the kitchens and a pungent aroma of hospital food drifted past them. After a minute or two the door opened to reveal the clean-shaven, pale face of a young man: it was the new mortuary attendant. Louise had heard that his predecessor had retired some months before. The new man was pleasant enough, but his complexion seemed unhealthy to start with and the advocate wondered whether he had really chosen the right job. They followed the man along a short corridor to an office where three men were sitting, drinking coffee and chatting about the mid-week football results.

"Morning Paul," Professor Clarke greeted one of the seated men cheerily, "Miss Templeton, this is Dr Paul Stopps who, as you know, performed the first post-mortem on behalf of the Crown.

"Morning Charles," the other pathologist replied, perhaps not quite as cheerily. The two other men were detective constables whom Miss Templeton knew well enough. Introductions were made and without further ado, the Crown Pathologist started to go through booklets of photographs taken at the murder scene and then at the first post-mortem on the deceased. His comments were directed at Professor Clarke, his opposite number, instructed on behalf of the Defence. Occasionally one of the police officers ventured a question which he deigned to answer with a condescending and very superior smile, but his facial expression and manner made it quite clear to all present that this was to be a meeting between and for the benefit of the two *experts* and whilst those of a more humble station were permitted to be present, it was by favour rather than as of right. The man took arrogance to dizzy new heights. Louise was a woman and a lawyer and was condemned on both counts to be totally ignored.

"Don't appear to be any significant bloodstains in the workshop, Paul," the Defence pathologist pointed out, "are you sure he was killed there? I mean if we assume he died from acute cardiac tamponade, he might have struggled for a minute or two before he expired and if so you'd expect a bit more blood around the room; also, doesn't it look a bit, well staged to find the body lying there on top of the preparation table and one small pool of blood on the floor for the murderer to conveniently, conveniently for the police, that is, step in and leave a trail of bloody footsteps leading to the door."

"It fits in with the findings," Stopps retorted rather frostily, "the fingertip bruises on the upper arms of the deceased are consistent with him being forced onto the table and..."

"But wouldn't the person doing the pushing then have to let go of the deceased in order to grab the knife and inflict the fatal injury,"

Professor Clarke interrupted, "otherwise Mr Quine would have got up again and surely resisted?"

"...And, as I was saying before you interrupted Charles, may I remind you that the SOCOs did find bloodstains on the suspect's clothes and his fingerprints on the murder weapon. If you have an alternative explanation, I would be more than pleased to hear it," the Crown Pathologist responded testily.

"Looks to me like there could have been two assailants, one pushed Quine onto the table and held him down whilst the other knifed him through the heart, either that or he *could* have been killed elsewhere and brought back to the undertaker's house...anyway, that'll be for a jury to decide. Let's go and see the body."

The two pathologists, policemen, advocate and mortuary attendant trouped out of the office and along the corridor, where they donned gowns and plastic overshoes before making their way into the autopsy suite. It was a large and brightly lit room, functional rather than aesthetically pleasing, Louise thought to herself, but nevertheless extremely modern in design. Dr Stopps led his opposite number to a stainless-steel table which stood on one side of the room and flung back the white cloth to reveal the body of the late Ernie Quine. The police officers and mortuary attendant followed at a distance and the advocate brought up the rear. It was not Miss Templeton's first post-mortem, but she had never found the experience to be a satisfying one and attended only because she felt she owed it to her client.

The pathologist's knife had been to work at the original post-mortem and on this occasion, all that was necessary was for the young mortuary attendant to undo the rough darn of heavy twine. When this was done, the skin edges fell apart, exposing the inner chest wall. Stopps' gloved fingers darted about pointing out where the knife had entered the chest: it was a narrow, clean wound, little to speak of, but then his fingers lifted the ribs and sternum clear of the body and the damage wreaked beneath was clear enough. Louise had seen enough and looked away leaving the two experts to argue the finer points. Turning her head she noticed that the body they had come to see was not the only one on display that morning. Another human form lay beneath a white shroud on the table on the other side of the suite. She had no real desire to find out more, but the Crown Pathologist had already noticed her gaze and had detected her lack of enthusiasm for the morning's activity. Dr Stopps was a sadist who took a perverse delight in shocking others. Breaking off his conversation with Professor Clarke, he moved across the room to the other table and whipped back the cover.

"Came in this morning, Charles, you and, er, your lawyer might want to have a look, just for interest, of course, nothing to do with the other case."

"What is it, Paul?" Professor Clarke asked with professional interest.

"Washed up on Douglas beach, but it's certainly not a textbook drowning and the body may not even have originated here. The tide could have carried it from almost anywhere around the Irish Sea. Haven't opened him up yet, but I'll be doing that when I've finished with Quine. If you want to take a look Charles, I wouldn't object, in fact it does help to have another pair of eyes check one's findings. If you look at the neck you can see a tight band of polythene that has cut in to the tissue. I haven't removed the object yet, but it looks like a common or garden plastic bag, twisted into a band and then used as a ligature. What do you think?" Professor Clarke peered at the cadaver. It's neck was mottled and swollen, but there, biting into the rotting flesh was a makeshift cord of rolled-up plastic. He could just about make out an inscription on the bag.

"Ramsey Bakery," he read out triumphantly, "it's a bread bag and a local one at that. I don't think you'll need to look beyond the Island to identify this body. How long d'you think it's been in the sea?"

"Well developed washer-woman skin, but no signs of adipocere," Stopps replied, "so won't have been in the water that long, certainly no more than three or four weeks and I would hazard a guess that it's a lot, lot less, but you can see that decomposition has started to set in and the fishes and the crabs have already been-a-nibbling." Stopps grinned with macabre delight as Louise found herself looking down at the empty eye sockets of the weed-festooned corpse. It was time, she decided, to leave.

Professor Clarke found her waiting in the car.

"I'm sorry Louise, I really must apologise for Stopps, he goes too far sometimes. There is a certain breed of pathologists who love to show off and demonstrate how well they can cope with the gruesome and gory side of it all. It's a form of exhibitionism really and not at all healthy. Are you alright?"

"I'm fine, Professor, did you find out anything helpful? I mean, I got the drift of your points about the bruises and how it would have been difficult for one man to kill Ernie without there being more of a struggle and more blood, but are you sure?" Professor Clarke smiled.

"I'm more than that young lady, I'm absolutely certain. Now let's go and meet that private investigator of yours and I'll tell you both what I think."

Chapter Nine

February - Friday Afternoon

Louise had arranged to meet the private detective in his hotel room that afternoon rather than at her office, partly because she couldn't be more specific about the time, having no idea herself how long the post-mortem would take and partly because she wanted to keep Roy Love's presence on the Island as quiet as possible. She arrived at the hotel with Professor Clarke a little before two. It was a large flat-roofed establishment in the middle of Douglas Promenade, of typical and now rather dated, nineteen sixties design, but it was reported to be comfortable, reasonably priced and boasted a large rear car park which would allow the detective to come and go as he pleased. The receptionist smiled pleasantly when told who they had come to see and telephoned his room; the detective answered immediately and told them to make their way straight up.

"Pleasant trip over, Roy?" Louise began. It was the wrong question to ask the detective, given the events of the night, but those events could hardly have any bearing on what he was being asked to do here and certainly need not be mentioned in the presence of the professor so he merely grinned and answered meekly:

"Night crossings of the Irish Sea in the middle of February are not exactly my cup of tea, Louise, but I'll get over it. Whilst we're on the subject of tea, would either of you like a cup of tea?...or coffee for that matter?" His two visitors expressed their preferences and Love picked up the 'phone to order room service. When he had finished, he sat down and invited the advocate to explain what exactly she wanted him to do.

"I think I'd better go through the client's story in some detail first; I realise that you both heard it briefly when I telephoned yesterday, but if I can put a little more flesh on the dry bones, it might help us get to grips with the case. I'd like to go through the witness statements that the police have disclosed and then I'd like Professor Clarke to let us have his thoughts and observations so far. Professor, your flight back to Manchester is at seven so we've got plenty of time. Are you happy for me to deal with the evidence that way around or would you like to go first?" The pathologist shook his head and smiled.

"Sounds sensible to deal with things in the order you suggest, Louise and it's Charles, by the way, I think we can dispense with formalities, don't you?"

Louise began from the beginning and related the story Richard had told her five days before. From time to time, one or other of her companions interrupted, seeking clarification of some point or other, but the interruptions were infrequent and did not serve to slow down or stifle her flow. She moved on to the interviews, to the statements of witnesses and finally to the forensic and medical evidence as the police had outlined it to her.

"Which brings us to you, Charles," she concluded, "what are your thoughts after examining the evidence and the body this morning?"

"Well I stand by what I said to Paul Stopps earlier," the pathologist began, "Quine certainly had fingertip bruising to both of his upper arms, entirely consistent with someone standing facing him, holding his arms forcibly like this…" he demonstrated on an imaginary model, "and then pushing him backwards onto the table. Whoever did it would have been powerfully built and with fairly large hands as Mr Quine wasn't by any stretch of the imagination a little man. I remember our undertaker quite well. If you remember I spent some time with him last year and I don't think that he was big or strong enough to do that. Then *either* the individual restraining Mr Quine took their right hand off the victim's left arm, seized the knife and stabbed him *or* someone else administered the fatal wound. My vote is for the latter; as I said to Paul, if the attacker relaxed his grip on Quine, then the man would hardly have just laid there and waited for whatever was coming next. Even if Quine had just found himself with one arm free he would have struggled, lashed out, done something and if that had happened the entry wound would probably not have been as clean. Which brings me to the weapon. First of all, where was it when the assailant was holding the victim? The knife was found in situ and Stopps showed me it this morning; it's a fairly standard pattern that you could probably buy in half a dozen shops on the Island, but it is quite large with a blade about thirty centimetres long. Our attacker would have had to pick it up from somewhere, again suggesting that he would have had to let go of Quine to do that. He certainly couldn't have gripped the man and held the knife at the same time. The anatomical track of the wound is instructive; the knife entered the left side of the chest through the third intercostal space between the mid-axilliary and anterior axilliary lines and the wound goes downwards and inwards notching the upper border of the fourth rib and puncturing the left ventricle. There was a considerable quantity of blood clot in the pericardial sac which means that his heart continued to beat for a few seconds until Mr Quine died of acute cardiac tamponade."

"What does that mean in English, Charles?" Louise asked. The pathologist laughed.

"It means that the victim was stabbed by someone standing in front of him and slightly to his left and that person brought the blade down violently from above their head; the usual stab wound to the chest is made from a much lower starting point, a quick horizontal thrust like this..." he demonstrated on the imaginary model again, "rather than an overarm swing. The fact that Quine took some time to die, it could have been seconds or even as long as a minute or two, suggests to me that the wound was made by a second assailant whilst the first held the victim still until he had stopped struggling and expired. That would explain the lack of blood about the place and the track of the wound. It wouldn't be possible to stab in the usual manner because the first assailant would have been in the way. The knife had to be brought down from above and through the space between the two men...oh.. and the man wielding the knife was almost certainly right-handed, which lets off your client. I seem to remember him telling me last year that he was left-handed."

"It sounds good," a quiet voice said. It was Roy Love and it was the first time he had spoken for a good while, "but knowing the police, they won't let go. They've got DNA and you know that they love DNA, it's their philosopher's stone: they think they can prove anything with it. How would you explain that?"

"Simple enough," the pathologist replied, "contamination, either accidental or, as seems more likely here, deliberate. The murderers decided to put Richard in the frame and made sure that some of the victim's blood found its way onto one of Richard's suits." Roy Love shook his head, long years as a police officer had made him rather sceptical.

"Maybe, but that's something you'll have to convince a jury; I can't see the prosecution dropping their case."

"Which is why you're here, Roy," Louise Templeton cut in, "we can't just rely on expert evidence; not before a jury, it's far too risky. What we need to do is find out what really took place last Sunday morning. The police have made an arrest and they've charged our client; you can guarantee that they won't be looking for anyone else as they've already made up their minds. If Richard didn't kill Ernie, then who did and why? Any suggestions?"

"I suppose," the private detective began, "that the best explanation would be the simplest, "let's suppose a couple of burglars had broken in..."

"The police said that there was no sign of a break in and there didn't appear to be anything missing," the advocate interrupted.

"They *say* there was no sign of a break in," Roy continued, "but maybe they just didn't look hard enough. As for nothing being missing, well I would have thought that only Richard could answer that, but let's say the police are right. The burglars could have been surprised by Eddie before they had taken anything so they killed him and made their getaway before Richard came back." Two names, suppressed for some time, crept back into the advocate's mind. Darren Finch and Jason Quiggan, but surely those two weren't murderers? She said nothing.

"But Roy, it was freezing cold and snowing hard," the pathologist argued, "Surely any sensible burglar would have realised that the house was likely to be occupied; I mean it was only chance that Richard had been called away. Burglars tend to prefer empty properties don't they?"

"Most do," the detective confirmed, "but Richard told me last year that lots of his neighbours go away for part of the winter, at least and February is a pretty bleak month here, so I'm told. Maybe the burglars thought the place was empty? Anyway, I think that should probably be our working hypothesis. I shall need to examine the house. Can you get us in?" Louise Templeton nodded. She had already spoken to the officer in charge who had confirmed that the police had finished with the house. They could go there in the morning.

They discussed the case for a little longer, but by four-thirty had all said enough. The pathologist told Louise that he would e-mail his report the next day and begged her to keep him informed of developments.

"After all," he said, "I rather liked your client when I met him last year and this case is interesting. Stopps is a decent enough fellow when you know him, but has a number of faults. You've seen one or two of them today, Louise, I mean his arrogance, his ego, that sort of thing, but far more worrying to my way of thinking is the fact that he makes his mind up far to quickly and then refuses to reconsider his opinion or shift his position, even when faced with strong conflicting evidence."

"A bit like the police, you mean," Louise said laughing. The pathologist smiled again.

"A bit like the police."

The taxi had departed bearing Professor Clarke back to the airport. It was too late in the day to start any real work and, after all, it was Friday so the advocate and the private detective made their way to one of the hotel bars. Louise knew that this particular establishment was favoured by neither the police nor other members of her profession and it would be possible to have a quiet relaxing and private drink and chat without being overheard or disturbed. After a few opening pleasantries, she brought up the events of the previous year.

"I keep reading about Vladimir Illosovich in the newspapers," she began, "he seems to have rather fallen from favour. Did we have any part to play in that?" Roy Love grinned mischievously.

"You could say that. You remember Mike Smith, the Pinkerton guy? Well he put in a report to his firm and they disclosed it to the FBI, the CIA, the DOJ, the lot. The legislative environment has changed since 9/11 and with their Patriot Act, the Yanks don't need proof beyond reasonable doubt anymore when it comes to terrorist activity, they just need reasonable suspicion. It's changed from a criminal burden to a civil burden and the human rights brigade reckon it's not even that. Anyway, the result was that Illosovich found himself Public Enemy Number One as far as Uncle Sam was concerned and probably even less popular than Mr Bin Laden. The Department of Justice got worldwide freezing orders on his assets; they took his property, his money, his shares, you name it, and rightly or wrongly the rest of the world meekly complied. The Russians, who prefer to stay on the right side of the Americans these days, charged him with fraud, money laundering and a whole range of other offences up to and including treason. Mike tells me that he skipped Russia, didn't turn up for his trial and was found guilty in his absence. He owns nothing now: the Russian Courts appointed a Receiver to run Petromax and his other businesses and Mr Illosovich is definitely on the run. Some say he's holed up in one of the former Soviet Republics, one of the more dodgy ones that doesn't kowtow to the Kremlin, but in reality nobody knows where he is. I think that you can be pretty certain, though, that neither you nor I will ever set eyes on his face again."

Chapter Ten

February - Saturday Morning

Louise arrived at the hotel shortly after eight and found Roy Love waiting by reception. He had breakfasted early and was keen to make a start on the day's work.

"My car or yours?" he asked cheerfully.

"We'll take mine," the advocate replied, "the police know I'm going to the house so they'll expect to see my car in the driveway; I didn't tell them I'd have company and if they happen to pass by and see an unfamiliar vehicle, particularly one with UK plates, they're bound to check it out."

"I'll get my stuff then, it's still in the back of my car," Love said, "are you parked behind the hotel?" Louise confirmed that she was and followed him out of the rear entrance to a dark blue BMW saloon which stood nearby. The detective opened the boot and removed two matching attaché cases.

"My scenes of crime gear," he explained, "well, as close as it comes to that when you're in private practice." He shut the door and they walked across the car park to the four wheel drive.

The promenade was still quiet as Louise turned left out of the car park and began the short drive to Onchan.

"No horse trams yet?" the detective asked.

"They only run through the summer season," Louise replied, "for the benefit of the tourists; we, er, don't get too many of those at this time of the year." Love looked at the cold grey sea over to his right and shivered.

"No, I suppose not," he agreed and asked about their client, the undertaker.

"He's not taking it at all well," the advocate said, "in fact they've put him on suicide watch."

"I'm not surprised, it's not a pleasant thing for anyone, particularly someone of his age and I suppose he's worried that his business will go to pot?"

"Funnily enough, he doesn't seem to give a damn about that, all he keeps going on about is the TT."

"But that's not until June, is it?" Love enquired, "a lot could happen before then."

"It's only three and a half months off, so we'll be lucky if we can get a trial by then, but it's not the trial that he seems worried about. You see he has a rider entered in every solo race; that's, as he tells me every time I see him, two superbike races, a supersport and a superstock: a total of three bikes to tune and prepare."

"Can't his riders help?"

"Well, he only has one rider, Rorletski, the Russian who won last year and he has a full-time job on the Island down at the motorcycle dealers in Castletown; I seem to spend a lot of my time relaying messages to him from Richard, hardly the role of an advocate, but there's no point telling Richard that. I think Rorletski's got everything under control, but that doesn't stop Richard worrying."

"He takes the racing very seriously then?" Love asked, "I remember his collection of motorbikes, but I assumed he was just that: a collector."

"Take it seriously?" Louise exclaimed, repeating the words as if unable to believe what her companion had said, "you don't know the meaning of the word, he's a fanatic. He didn't enter any machinery at all last year and I think he missed the involvement, the buzz, but this year it's the centenary of the races so he's determined to enter…and to win. To make matters worse his great rival, the chap who owns the motorcycle dealership in Castletown has entries and wants to win as well."

"Isn't that where you said Rorletski is working?" Love asked, a little puzzled. Louise laughed.

"It is, but don't worry about that, Colin Desmond, the owner is Richard's best friend as well as his greatest rival. Rorletski needed a job and was far too squeamish to get involved in Richard's line of business; he's a skilled mechanic so Colin employed him. I don't know how they got around the work permit people, but they managed somehow…Anyway, this is the house," the conversation about motorcycle racing came to an end as she turned off the main road and took the four wheel drive down the steep driveway to the courtyard at the front of the last house in Onchan.

The police had removed their scenes of crime tape and to the uninformed observer the place looked like any other large detached house. To Roy Love's trained eye, however, there were certain signs that marked this particular property out from its neighbours.

"I see they've searched the garden," he muttered, more to himself than anyone, but Louise heard the words.

"Whatever for?" she asked, "they've already got the murder weapon."

"Well, they haven't found the shoes," he replied, "the shoes that made those footprints and they have to do a comprehensive search in any event, just in case something turns up. Let's go in, shall we?" He had removed a small, but impressive-looking digital camera from one of the attaché cases and had been taking both stills and video of the garden and the outside of the house. Louise unlocked and opened the door and the detective filmed the hallway carefully before allowing her to enter. He took the same precautions and followed the same routine with every room. It was only when he had filmed the entire house that he began his slow and meticulous search. It soon became apparent to the advocate that this was not going to be a quick job. By one o' clock Roy seemed to have made little progress and Louise was getting tired and rather bored.

"Would you like to go for some lunch?" she asked. They were now in Richard's Blue Room and the detective had been examining one of the undertaker's motorcycles with even more than his usual care. He looked up with an expression of intense concentration on his face.

"I don't want to break off just at the moment, Louise," he replied, "but I could do with a coffee and maybe a sandwich. Why don't you pop out and get the refreshments in? Don't hurry back as what I'm doing at the moment may take quite a long time." Louise found the suggestion rather appealing; she did have one or two other things to do and so she took her leave and told him that she would be back in an hour.

It was a quarter-past two when she returned to find the detective in the conservatory at the rear of the house. It looked out over a small garden which sloped down to the top of the cliff. Roy was examining the door. Hearing her come into the room, he stood up.

"The middle pane has been broken and recently," he explained, "classical way of gaining entry. People don't seem to realise that burglars love glass and they love conservatories hidden away at the back of the house, out of the sight of prying eyes. Somebody came through the garden, broke the window, reached in and turned the key which had been left in the lock, opened the conservatory door and they were in."

"They came through the next door neighbour's garden then, or they climbed the cliff," the advocate remarked, "but surely the police spotted this."

"Well, if they did, they didn't bother to tell us about it, did they?" Love commented, a little sourly. "Come on, let's have a look at the rear garden."

The garden was roughly triangular in shape and dropped steeply from its base at the rear of the house to a rickety fence which marked the edge of the cliff. A couple of terraces had been cut into the ground years before in an attempt to minimise the slope and make upkeep a little easier, but the garden was as wild and overgrown at the back as at the front. It was quite clear that gardening had never been one of the undertaker's pleasures or priorities. A well maintained brick wall ran down one side of the triangle and separated the plot from the neat and tidy garden of the neighbour who lived to the south. To the north, the cliff edge, bounded by the rickety fence rose and cut back until it encroached on a wing of the house. An intruder could not have gained access easily from either side. The detective and the advocate followed a rough path down through the terraces until they reached the apex of the triangle. The fence came to an end a few feet before the neighbour's wall and there they found the first step.

Roy Love stared at the step for a moment and then turned and asked sharply:

"Did you know about this?" The advocate shook her head.

"I've been to the house plenty of times, but I don't think I've ever been out of that conservatory door. Richard isn't really, well *keen* on gardens, but I suppose you've gathered that by now. Strange he's never mentioned these steps before, but then again maybe he didn't know they were here. The place is so overgrown that you can't tell they're here until you get right to the cliff edge. I suppose they go down to the sea?"

"It looks that way," Love replied, "but there's only one way of finding out." He pulled the camera strap around his neck and, both hands free now, rather gingerly began the descent.

"Be careful," she shouted after him, but his head had already disappeared from sight.

Louise waited anxiously for a good fifteen minutes before she heard signs of him returning. There was a crackle of breaking twigs and the swish of bracken being pushed aside and then a minute or two later his head appeared above the edge of the cliff. He seemed rather breathless and his face was a little red, but for the first time that day it wore a triumphant smile.

"What did you find?" she asked excitedly.

"Let's go back to the house and I'll show you," he replied.

They made their way back to the kitchen; it was time for a break and Louise produced a large brown paper bag from which she withdrew two cardboard cups of coffee and two freshly made baguettes.

"There's an excellent delicatessen just round the corner from my flat," she explained, almost apologetically.

"Thanks Louise, I think I need that. If you don't mind I'll just take a swig of that coffee before I say another word." He drank noisily and took a large and hungry bite from the baguette. "I had the camera on camcorder mode all the way down and up so hopefully I've got a visual record of the staircase and where it goes. Let's take a look." He switched the machine onto playback mode, but a tiny red light suddenly started flashing. "Damn!" he said, "battery's just about flat. The recording should be okay, but I think we'll have to play it back later."

"So what did you see?" the advocate asked again.

"A steep, very steep winding staircase," he replied smiling, "which goes backwards and forwards down to the base of the cliff. It seems to have been carved out of the rock and looks like it's been there for ever and a day. I'd guess that smugglers made it centuries ago… and its slippery and dangerous, I lost my footing and nearly fell a couple of times.

"So what's at the bottom?"

"A little cove and, I think a very steep shingle beach. The tide looks like it's in at the moment and the waves are lapping the base of the cliff, but I could see the shingle through the water and I'd guess that at low tide there'd be enough of a beach to land a small boat. Anyway, I saw enough signs on the way down there and the way up to convince me that someone's used those steps pretty recently. I think that's the way our men gained access to the house."

"Pretty daring for Manx burglars," the advocate suggested. Roy Love shook his head.

"I don't think that these were common or garden local burglars, Louise," he said, "whilst you were getting our refreshments, I did find something out."

Chapter Eleven

February - Saturday Afternoon

"You found something? What?" Louise asked. Roy Love smiled and answered the advocate's question with a question.

"You remember the Petromax motorbike, the one that we had all the fun and games with last year?"

"Of course I do; I don't think any of us are likely to forget that in a hurry. I noticed that you were looking at it earlier. That can't have any bearing on Ernie's murder, can it?" The detective shrugged his shoulders.

"I can't say for certain; I looked at everything in the house, but given that particular machine's history I looked at it rather closely. Come with me, I want to show you something." Louise put down her coffee and followed the detective out of the kitchen along a short corridor and into the Blue Room. The black and gold Petromax machine still took pride of place in the undertaker's magnificent collection. Other motorcycles stood about the room, each representing a little piece of history, in one or two cases, a history that was rather more tarnished than the gleaming paint and sparkling chrome would outwardly suggest, but the Petromax had a past that was darker still, it had led to the murder of at least two men. Was Roy suggesting that the two could now be three?

"What is it you wanted to show me?" Louise asked after staring at the machine for a long minute. Love knelt down and pointed to the tiny hexagonal bolts which held the fairing in place around the engine.

"These Allen bolts have been removed since I was last here; the metal's shiny on the inside of the socket."

"Are you sure?"

"Pretty sure. If you look over there..." he pointed to the tail unit, "...the metal inside the sockets is slightly tarnished; as you would expect when they haven't been touched for a long time. The front fairing has been removed. You would only do that to get to the engine."

"But Rorletski took the engine apart last year, when we found the camshafts were missing. Wouldn't that account for the difference?" The detective shook his head.

"No, I don't think so, the metal tarnishes quite quickly. There are other signs...Richard keeps his bikes immaculately clean, doesn't he? polishes them every week. I know, he told me. Someone has left a couple of marks on the fairing...here," he pointed to a greasy finger print, one that was so obvious even the advocate conceded he had a point. "It's the sort of mark you would make putting the fairing back on. You might have clean hands when you start to take the thing off, but if you then start working on the engine, it's not long before you get a bit of oil or grease on your fingers. When you put the thing back together again, you get the dirty marks. Now if Richard had done it or, more likely, someone had done it for him, he would have polished the fairing afterwards." The advocate frowned.

"But if, as you seem to be saying, someone else took the fairing off, surely they would have done the same thing. I mean, the fact that they put the thing back together does tend to suggest that they didn't want anyone to know what they'd done. These marks are, as you say, pretty obvious; why didn't they wipe them away?"

"Pretty obvious to you and me, in broad daylight, but if you're working by torchlight and you're in a hurry,"

"And you've just killed someone'" Louise added, reading his thoughts, "yes, I can see your drift, Roy, but why? I mean why take the bike apart? We did that last year and we found nothing. We never proved that there ever had been anything; it was just a theory, when all said and done."

"It was a theory which fitted all the facts," Love pointed out, "And not everyone in the world is as well-informed as us."

"What exactly are you suggesting?"

"It's just an idea, but what if someone else knew about the special engine parts, knew that they had been installed in that particular machine, but didn't know they had been removed."

"Surely they'd have made a move long before now?"

"It's only been eight months; it may have taken them that long to track the machine down and to formulate a plan."

"So you're saying that our burglars..."

"Weren't casual or opportunistic local villains; they came here with one aim in mind, to get whatever they thought had been hidden inside that bike and they didn't want anyone to know what they'd done; that's why they put the bike back together. They planned this carefully and I don't think they expected to find anyone at home. When they found Ernie, they panicked and killed him."

"So they knew that Richard would be called out?" the advocate asked, raising her eyebrows.

"They must have done; I just don't think they had counted on the snow. If it had been a normal February night, Richard would have gone with Ernie and by the time he returned the mysterious engine parts and his uninvited guests would be gone and he would never have known." Louise shook her head.

"That's not quite true, Roy," she countered, "Ernie took the call, but he couldn't move his hearse because of the snow; that was the only reason he called Richard." The detective shook his head..

"Did he try to get his hearse out or did he just look at the snow, think 'I haven't a chance in this' and call his boss? We don't know and unfortunately we probably never will, but my guess is the latter. I reckon they sabotaged the hearse and if Ernie had tried to move the thing, it wouldn't have started...but we can check that. Alternatively, of course, they might have just assumed Richard would go himself, after all the name 'Quayle and Son' is in the telephone book; if somebody had rung that number, they wouldn't have known that on some nights the call was diverted to Ernie and at other times went through to Richard's home. You realise what this means, of course?"

"It means, Roy," the advocate replied, "that your investigation is going to take a little longer than we initially thought. I think you're going to have to look into the circumstances of the death of the late and, I assume, much lamented old Mr Quilleash."

"What do we know about the man?" the detective asked.

"At this exact moment, nothing; from what Richard told me, the doctor, I think it was Doctor Macdonald issued a death certificate straight away so he can't have been too concerned. I can't say I know anything about the family, but I'll make some enquiries." Louise shook her head and frowned, continuing, "It's going to be difficult, without anything more in the way of evidence, to suggest that the old man's death was suspicious. If we're lucky, he'll have been buried, but at the moment we've absolutely no chance of getting an exhumation order. The police and the Coroner would simply think we were mad. Let's say you're right and someone killed him, how could the killer know that he would die in the middle of the night and how could they know that the family would call Richard's firm?"

"Lots of questions, Louise and I'm afraid I don't know the answers, but I do think that's what happened. Anyway, it's nearly half-past three. I've finished here; why don't we take a little drive down to the south of the Island and see what we can find out?"

It made a pleasant break for both of them. The advocate sometimes felt that her entire life involved no more than a seemingly endless oscillation between her apartment, her office, the police station and court; this was the first time she had left Douglas for months. Her companion's lifestyle was similar, but different. At times, he almost lived on the road, but no longer took pleasure in the thousand odd miles he covered in his average seven day working week. For once he was able to sit back, let someone do the driving, admire the scenery and relax. It was some time before either of them spoke.

Louise followed the promenade back to Douglas Harbour, crossed the swing bridge and then took the old Castletown Road. She passed through Port Soderick village and had driven a good few miles further before she finally broke the silence.

"Is there a Mrs Love, Roy?" It was a simple enough question, but tentatively, almost reluctantly put. The detective was surprised by her manner: from the little he had seen of the advocate, forthright and assertive questioning was what he had come to expect. Was she embarrassed or perhaps worried about the answer she might get?

"There were...well actually there still are two of them," he replied with a mischievous grin, "Don't think either of them have changed their names since the decrees absolute, but I'm not currently married, if that's what you mean. Twice bitten, definitely third time shy. What about you?" The advocate shook her head.

"Never found the right man," she replied, "there was once..." she began, then hurriedly changed the subject "...here's the main Castletown Road. We'll be at Ballasalla in a minute and then passing the airport..." A door had drifted open for a moment to reveal a faint glimpse of the person behind that ice-cool exterior, but the door drifted shut and the emotionless, efficient Miss Templeton had returned.

When they reached Castletown, Louise turned left off the main road, crossed the little bridge by the picturesque harbour and took the four wheel drive along the narrow little street beneath the magnificent medieval castle. She slowed for a moment and pointed out a door to one side of the castle's main gate.

"Must be the only castle in Europe where they still have a working court."

"Working, you mean they still have trials in that place?"

"Oh, yes," she replied quietly, "it's where I did my first. It was a 'Taking without consent', the theft of a motor vehicle. I was desperately nervous and got here ages before I should. The caretaker had to let me in and there was a cat, a big fat tom cat that we had to get out of the courtroom before the trial could begin," she mused, her eyes a little misty at the reminiscence, "It was before the High Bailiff, but anyway I lost," the door snapped shut again and the reminiscence came to an end.

They had left Castletown and rejoined the main road to the south. The road passed through a landscape of farms and little green fields, before it climbed a gentle hill then dipped suddenly to reveal a panorama of sea and cliffs and sky. There, a few miles ahead of them, stood the Meayll Peninsular, a hilly outcrop of land lying between the coastal villages of Port St Mary and Port Erin. It stood apart from the range of southern hills which ran down the west coast and formed the most southerly point of the Island. Beyond it lay the Calf and beyond that mile after mile of empty sea. Louise Templeton pointed out the geography and asked the detective where he thought they should start.

"I had a look in Richard's telephone directory," he replied, "and there is a Quilleash listed at Cronk Ny Arrey Farm, Cregneash. Do you know where that is?" The advocate reached into the pocket of the door beside her and pulled out an ordinance survey map. She passed it to her companion.

"Cregneash is a tiny village between Port Erin and Port St Mary. It's a folk museum owned by Manx National Heritage, but I suppose some people must live there and "Cronk" is the Manx name for "hill"; have a look at the map and see if you can find the farm." Love carefully unfolded the map and spread it out on his knees. He soon found the name Cronk Ny Arrey. It was a hill between Cregneash and Perwick Bay.

"We'll take a look," the advocate suggested, "The farm can't be that far away and if we can't find it, I'm sure there'll be someone we can ask." The road now followed the coast, passing through a straggling collection of dwellings which went by the name of Gansey. A branch forked right and was signposted Port Erin, but the advocate ignored it and carried on. A short distance later the coastal road pulled inland itself; they came to a cross roads.

"Port St Mary is over there," she pointed to her left, "but we go straight across and up." She followed her own directions and the road turned sharply to the right and climbed steeply. It was narrow, but not unduly so and passed by a smattering of cottages and small farms. Love looked closely at the names, but did not see the one he was looking for. Suddenly they were in open country again and the buildings disappeared. As the detective gazed at the fields beside the road, the sun emerged fleetingly from behind the scudding grey clouds to cast a golden beam from low on the western horizon. As it did so something to his left glimmered and shone. Love squinted and stared.

"What in the hell is that?"

Chapter Twelve

February - Saturday Afternoon/Evening

Louise pulled the four wheel drive over to the side of the road and stopped.

"Over there," Love exclaimed, "look." She stared in the direction of his pointing finger. The sun had gone behind a cloud again, but a second or two later it emerged and she could see its golden rays reflecting off something over to their left.

"You see it?" he asked. The advocate nodded.

"I do, Roy, but I haven't a clue what it is. Looks pretty futuristic though; not really the sort of thing you'd expect near a folk museum." The structure lay several hundred yards away from them and formed the summit of a low hill. As far as Love could make out from the map, that hill was Cronk Ny Arrey.

"It looks a bit like the UFO from Close Encounters," he suggested and Louise agreed. "Probably some sort of military thing," she added, "you know an early warning station, like Fylingdales in the North York Moors or a communication installation like Menwith Hill near Harrogate, it has that sort of air about it."

"You seem pretty knowledgeable on such matters, Louise," Love commented in tones of some surprise. The advocate laughed.

"Sorry officer, just a few lingering memories from my student days when I belonged to CND. We used to hold protests at those sorts of places so I got to know where they all were. Never heard of this one though. Still, it's nothing to do with what we came here to find, let's carry on, shall we?"

They reached the brow of a hill and Louise pulled off the road into an old quarry which lay on the right.

"This is the car park for Cregneash Village, Roy," she explained, "the road gets pretty narrow and they don't exactly encourage vehicles so I think from here on we'll walk." They climbed out of the four-wheel drive and made their way across the road and down into the pretty collection of thatched-roofed cottages that comprised the hamlet of Cregneash.

"It's like stepping back in history," the detective exclaimed, "I didn't realise that there were still places like this left, outside film sets, that is." The advocate laughed.

"Well they do use it as a film set as well," she commented, "have you ever seen *Waking Ned*?"

"Can't say as I have," Love admitted, "did they make it here?"

"It's supposed to be a village in the south of Ireland," Louise explained, "but they filmed part of it in Cregneash and some of the rest in the studios up near Ramsey. They make quite a few films in the Island nowadays; I think the Isle of Man Government makes it financially worth their while."

"Interesting," Love said, "have you met any film stars then?"

"I once sat opposite John Malkovich in a coffee shop in Douglas," Louise admitted, "trouble was I didn't recognise him and only found out after he'd gone and someone told me who he was." They both laughed and Love changed the subject.

"Any idea where this farm might be then?" The advocate looked at the map.

"My guess is through the village and somewhere along this track." The detective peered over her shoulder and looked at the lines on the map which came to an end somewhere between the village and the sea.

"Can't be more than half a mile long," he said, "let's take a look."

They walked through the village and along the little track. Love felt relaxed and happy: a pleasant country walk with a charming and attractive young lady made a welcome change from the sort of work he normally undertook. The surroundings hardly suggested a connection with murder, or indeed any sort of crime. He suspected this trip would prove fruitless, but suddenly he stopped in his tracks.

"What is it Roy?" the advocate had noticed that something was wrong and she followed the detective's eyes to the van that lay ahead. It was an unremarkable sort of vehicle: a black Ford Transit with English plates, but something about it had caused her companion's mouth to drop.

"Shhh," he whispered, holding his finger to his lips. "I'll tell you why later, but I think I know that van. God knows what it's doing here, but take care; if it belongs to who I think it does, then it's up to no good." They approached the vehicle slowly. It was facing the opposite way so they had no idea whether it was empty until they reached the front. When they got to the van, Love indicated to the advocate that she should stay at the rear whilst he tiptoed forward. Suddenly, the tension which she could see in his face disappeared and he visibly relaxed.

"It's empty," he called, "and locked," he added after trying the door. "Strange place to abandon a vehicle, though. Look, it's completely blocking the road." The advocate moved forward to his side and looked inside the van.

"Probably just some tradesmen over from England," she said, "doing some work at one of the farms." She looked around as if seeking confirmation for her statement. Sure enough, a few yards ahead of them a metal gate hung open to reveal a rough and rutted track. Beside the gate, stood a faded wooden sign; it was in need of a lick or two of paint, but they could both read the words.

Cronk Ny Arrey Farm

Louise and the detective looked at each other.

"What now?" she asked.

"Now," he replied, "we go and see if there's anyone at home."

They started up the track and saw the farm immediately ahead of them. It was a traditional Manx farmhouse, built from whitewashed local stone and looked, even from this distance in a state of some disrepair. The building stood on the south facing slope of a hill, the very same hill that they had seen from the road leading to Cregneash.

"Looks like that radar installation, or whatever we think it is, was old Mr Quilleash's nearest neighbour," the detective observed. The advocate remained silent, but as they approached the house she thought she saw the net curtain in an upstairs window twitch. Any further signs of life were notable by their absence so Roy Love strode up to the door. There was no obvious electric buzzer, but the front door bore a traditional and rather rustic knocker which the detective rapped loudly. Nothing happened so he rapped again and they both listened for a response.

Silence.

Love rapped a third time, but again no-one came. He turned to Louise.

"There's no one here, least no one who's willing to see us. I suppose we could look around the place, but we haven't a clue what we're looking for and if the owner finds us we'd have a hell of a lot of explaining to do."

"What do you suggest?"

"What I always suggest in these circumstances. Let's go to the Pub!"

As they drove back from Cregneash to Port St Mary, Love explained about the van.

"Dressed as *monks?*" Louise retorted in tones conveying a certain degree of incredulity, but the detective stood by what he said he had seen. "Are you sure it wasn't some fancy dress stunt or something?" she suggested, "I mean we do get a lot of stag parties coming to the Island." Love shook his head.

"They saw that I was looking at them and there was something about one of them: I think I've come across him before and I'm sure he recognised me."

"What did he look like?"

"That's just it, I can't say. He had eyes that were as dark as coal, but that's just about all I could swear to, I went to the food counter to try and get a better view, but when I turned around to look they had all gone."

"So you went to look for them. Did you find them?" the advocate asked.

"Well, er, sort of." The detective's face assumed a downcast and rather sheepish look.

"Meaning?"

"I looked around all of the passenger areas; I even went out on the deck, but there was no sign of them anywhere. I even wondered whether they'd gone back down to the vehicle deck, but before I went down there, I thought I'd ask one of the crew. So I spoke to one of the stewardesses…"

"And she told you?" Louise interrupted in tones of some surprise.

"Well, I did, er, tell her that I was a policeman and showed her an old warrant card."

"*Roy,*" the advocate rebuked him gently, "as an officer of the court, I'm not sure that I want to hear any more."

"She told me that they were in one of the cabins so I thought I'd go and have a look," he continued, telling Louise about his knock on the door, him hearing the command 'enter' and then him recollecting nothing more. "And I remember that voice from somewhere, but I just can't put my finger on where. I was going to tell you this as soon as I met you, but with Professor Clarke there, I didn't really…and then I forgot all about it until just now," he concluded lamely.

"You're sure it's the same van?" Louise enquired.

"Can't be a hundred percent certain," he replied telling her about the missing piece of paper with the registration number, "but I think it is." The advocate shook her head.

"I don't know what to make of it Roy, but I'll see what I can find out. There aren't any monasteries on the Island and I think a collection of monks would rather stand out. Which pub do you want to go to, by the way, one in Port Erin or Port St Mary? It's easy enough for us to go either way."

"The ones where we're most likely to hear something about old Mr Quilleash," Love replied, "and any other useful gossip or local skeet."

Louise tried the nearest, but Roy's subtle questions elicited no more than blank looks and shaking heads at the Railway in Port St Mary so she decided to carry on to Port Erin, but enquiries at the first two licensed establishments they entered revealed little more of any substance. They drove down the promenade and in some desperation Louise stopped outside the Bay Hotel.

"I don't think this place would appeal to an old farmer," she explained, "but the landlord's pretty knowledgeable and he might be able to point us in the right direction, at least." They stepped through the door and walked up to the bar. It was now a little after five and the sun had finally sunk beneath the western horizon, its golden light replaced by a gathering gloom. A few early evening drinkers were already in what Louise took to be their usual seats and the advocate directed her question at them as much as at the man who was serving their beer.

"I'm an advocate," she began.

"I know who you are Miss Templeton," one of the regulars cut in, "you got me out of a bit of bother a year or two ago; what can we do for you?" Louise decided to tell them the truth.

"I'm representing Mr Richard Quayle," she began.

"The undertaker who murdered his assistant?" another voice piped up.

"who is *accused* of the murder of Mr Ernest Quine," she continued firmly, "and this is my colleague, Mr Love. We are looking for information about the death of Mr Kenneth Quilleash, of Cronk Ny Arrey Farm, Cregneash.." A man who had been sitting silently at the corner of the bar slammed his empty pint glass down violently and stormed out of the room. There was silence for a couple of seconds and then the landlord spoke.

"That's Seth Quilleash," he explained, "old Ken's youngest son; bit of a ne'er do well, I'm afraid, but he's taken the old man's death pretty hard. He might be able to help you, but then again he might not. I'd try and get him sober, though, because you don't want to know him when he's drunk. Trouble is, he's drunk most of the day at the moment; maybe if you tried first thing in the morning, you might have half a chance."

"Where does he live?" Louise asked.

"Place you've just mentioned," the landlord replied, "the old man's farm, but not for that much longer. His elder brother inherited it under the terms of the old man's will. He's got it up for sale and rumour has it he's got a buyer so that means Seth'll have to move out. He's none too happy about that, as I'm sure you can understand."

Chapter Thirteen

Sunday – Late February

They had arranged to meet at the old quarry that was the car park for Cregneash and Louise Templeton arrived a little before nine. Roy Love was pacing up and down impatiently and by the look of things had been there for some time.

"About half an hour," he said in answer to her question, "and there's something going on. Did you notice anything unusual on the way here?"

"A couple of police cars passed me on the Castletown Bypass," she replied, "lights on and going at a fair lick. I assumed there'd been an accident somewhere. Why?"

"They went down there," he pointed to the village, "hold on here's another one, they really have called in the cavalry, I wonder whatever for." A white police Transit roared past the car park and they heard a screech as brakes were heavily applied. "Let's go and take a look," Love suggested, "then we'll try and have a word with Seth Quilleash." The advocate agreed and they walked out of the car park, down the hill and into the narrow village street.

The scene was a stark contrast to the one they had witnessed the previous day. Then, it had seemed deserted, but this morning was thick with people, standing around, talking, walking. Louise was puzzled for a moment, the suddenly realised why.

"It's a film crew," she explained, "and it looks like they're packing up for the day. I know they try and do these scenes before the general public arrive. That wouldn't explain the police, though, unless they were part of it, extras or something."

"They'd hardly be passing you at high speed near Castletown if they were supposed to be here," Love pointed out a trifle sarcastically. I know you told me that the Manx Government like to encourage the film industry, but I think that'd be taking the spirit of cooperation a little too far. Those were real police and they were heading for a real incident; I know, I've been to enough in my time."

"Where are they then?" the advocate asked. She had looked carefully around the village and had not seen anyone even resembling a policeman. Love shrugged his shoulders.

"Dunno," he replied, "but I don't think there's anything else to see here. Lets go to the farm and try and find Seth."

They walked out of the village, up the short steep hill and were soon by the gate to Cronk Ny Arrey. It had rained heavily in the night and the potholes of the farm track had been transformed into stagnant pools of dirty brown water. Between those pools, the sticky wet earth told its own story.

"Tyre marks," Love remarked, "lots of them...and there...are your police." Louise looked up. They had passed a slight kink in the track and the farm buildings were now in sight. A fleet of police vehicles stood in a haphazard formation outside.

"Burglary?" the advocate ventured, but her companion shook his head.

"You wouldn't get this many coppers at a burglary, Louise, even in a place like the Isle of Man and look, one of the uniforms is putting out scenes of crime tape. This doesn't look good. Do you think we should go back?"

"We've come this far," the advocate said resolutely, "so we might as well go on. I know most of the police on this Island and I'm sure they'll give me the low down on what's going on."

"It's your party, Louise," Love replied with a smile, "lead on."

They continued up the track towards the farm. The uniformed police constable remained focussed on the difficult and dangerous task of securing the scene and didn't look up from his blue and white tape until the advocate and the private detective were almost on top of him.

"Can't come here," he snapped, angry that he had not noticed their approach. "It's a crime scene; now, can you please return the way you came."

"What's going on, Neil?" the advocate asked. The policeman gave a start.

"Sorry Miss Templeton, I didn't recognise you there. I don't know if I should really tell you, nothing's public yet."

"Come on, Neil. Anyway, who's in charge?"

"It's a murder, Miss Templeton," the constable whispered, "and DS Blackburn is leading the team."

"Mike Blackburn, in charge of a *murder*?" the advocate retorted.

"Until someone a bit more senior gets here anyway," the constable admitted, "it *is* Sunday morning and we only got the call forty minutes ago."

"And I suppose most of the senior officers are still at home in bed, or off Island on the usual management courses," Louise interrupted scornfully. "Anyway, who is the victim?"

"Fella by the name of Kenneth Quilleash, Junior, that is. He's an accountant from Douglas."

The advocate frowned; this was not quite the news she had expected.

"We had come to see someone who lives at the farm," she explained.

"And who might that be, Miss?" the constable enquired.

"His brother, Seth," the advocate explained, "is he around?" the policeman shook his head.

"Seth Quilleash is missing," he replied grimly, "and is now wanted for questioning in connection with the death."

Detective Sergeant Blackburn was honest enough to realise that he was a little out of his depth, but he approached the task in hand calmly and, as was his trademark manner in such circumstances, insisted in sticking to the book. When told of the arrival of an advocate, he shook his head and swore beneath his breath.

"What's she doing here?" he asked, "and who's the man?"

"Says she's looking for Seth Quilleash," Neil Quigley replied, "but she didn't say why. The other one's a private detective. She wants to speak to you." Blackburn shook his head again.

"Most irregular; doesn't say anything in the book about speaking to advocates, leastwise, not until we've arrested someone. What does she want?"

Why not ask her, the constable felt like saying, but he controlled the impulse. "She says she was here yesterday. Maybe she noticed something? Will you have a word?"

"If I must," the sergeant responded, "I'll come out. The SOCO boys will be here any minute and they'll go mad if we let anyone else contaminate the scene."

He walked out of the house and over to join the advocate and her companion. Louise introduced the two men.

"We were looking for Seth," she explained, "it's sort of in connection with the death of his father."

"Good god," Miss Templeton," DS Blackburn exclaimed, "you're not making something about that, are you? I would have thought you'd have had enough on your plate defending that undertaker. Ken Quilleash, Senior died of natural causes. Doctor Macdonald issued a certificate; nothing suspicious there."

"There was no post-mortem, though, was there?" the advocate said.

"No and there won't be one, either; the old man was cremated and his ashes scattered in the sea."

"Anyway," she continued, "we came here late yesterday afternoon and knocked on the door. No-one answered, but I'm pretty sure someone was watching us from up there." She pointed to the upstairs window where she had seen the net curtains twitch. "Then we went around the pubs in Port Erin seeing what we could find out."

"Find out about what?"

"About old Ken Quilleash."

"And did you?"

"We went in the Bay Hotel down in Port Erin, said that we wanted to ask questions about old Ken Quilleash and this man slammed his pint glass down and stormed out of the bar. The landlord told us that it was Seth Quilleash."

"What time would that be?" Blackburn asked, interested now, despite himself, in the information the advocate had just imparted.

"Just after five. Why? Any idea when he was killed?" she motioned towards the house.

"You know I can't tell you that, Miss Templeton," the sergeant replied, "even if I knew which I don't. Local Police surgeon's in there now, but just about all he'll tell us is that the man's dead. We'll have to call in a pathologist from England to get any real answers." He had lied; the police surgeon was a perfectly competent local general practitioner who took a keen interest in the science of forensic pathology. He had observed that rigor mortis was well established, but not yet beginning to pass off. That fact coupled with the degree of cooling of the body had enabled him to tell Blackburn that the victim had been dead for between twelve and fourteen hours.

"Who found the body?" The advocate tried another question. Blackburn thought for a moment before he replied.

"No harm in telling you that, I suppose; news'll be all around the Island in another couple of hours. It was the victim's wife; she drove down here first thing this morning looking for her husband. Seems he came here last night to meet someone, but he didn't tell her who. When he hadn't returned by this morning, she tried ringing, but there was no reply so she came down here herself."

"You're going to have to find out who he was supposed to be meeting then." They were the first words the private detective had uttered and a dark scowl flashed across Blackburn's face.

"We think it was probably Seth," he said frostily, "the victim was going to sell the place and Seth would have had to leave. The victim's wife told us that her husband had mentioned that he needed to speak to his brother. He didn't say he was going to do it last night, but it gives us a pretty good motive for murder, doesn't it?"

"So he could exchange these comfortable lodgings for Victoria Road gaol?" the advocate replied, "surely no-one would be that stupid; like you say, he's the obvious suspect."

"We know Seth Quilleash pretty well, Miss," Blackburn explained, "and he isn't too well endowed with brains. Battering someone over the head with a blunt instrument doesn't strike me as a particularly planned or thought-out crime. More like the sort of thing someone would do when prone to a violent temper and told something they really didn't like. Seth, as I'm sure you're quite aware, fits that description rather well, but he won't get far: we've already notified the Sea Terminal and the airport and I'm sure we'll have got him before the end of the day. I'm sorry you had a wasted trip, Miss Templeton, but if you don't mind, I have things to do" Having said rather more than he had intended, he brought the conversation to a sudden end, turned and walked away.

The advocate and the private detective slowly made their way back to the car park, discussing their plan of campaign.

"Blackburn isn't what I would call a dynamic thinker," Louise began, "but he does have a point. Seth looked pretty drunk when we saw him and if his brother told him he was going to have to leave…"

"I thought he knew that already," Love said.

"Maybe the vague suggestion transformed itself into something more concrete," she suggested, "maybe his brother had found a buyer and gave Seth a date by which he had to get out?"

"Possible," he agreed, "but how does this fit in with our problem?"

"It doesn't," Louise replied, "it's just an annoying, irritating coincidence and it means we'll never get the chance to speak to Seth."

"What do you suggest we do next?"

"You poke around and see what you can find out here, but don't spend more than a day or two on it. Have you kept in touch with that Pinkerton guy?"

"I have."

"Then let's not lose sight of what we're investigating. Tell him about what you found at Richard's house and in particular about that Petromax bike. You never know, he might have some ideas."

"What about you?" the detective asked.

"I'm going to see Richard tomorrow," the advocate replied, "to ask him if he's touched the bike recently and if he has ever had the slightest connection with this family who go by the name of Quilleash. We can't really do much more at present." They parted company and left in their respective vehicles; the advocate heading back to her apartment, the private detective to spend a bit more time in the south.

It was twelve noon before a detective more senior than Sergeant Blackburn arrived at the murder scene. Inspector Davies was accompanied by the forensic pathologist and was less than enthusiastic about the task to hand.

"Bloody nuisance," was his only comment when Blackburn had filled him in, "don't know why the hell you had to call me for a cut and dried thing like this. Seth Quilleash will have done it, I agree with you on that. Get a team of men looking for him, but I warn you he can be a bugger to find. He knows this island like the back of his hand and when he goes to ground, he goes to ground."

"We're watching the Sea Terminal and the airport," the sergeant responded. Inspector Davies laughed.

"You're wasting your time there," he said, "to the best of my knowledge Seth has never been off this Island in his life. He'll be in a hut or on a hillside somewhere, but he won't leave the land of his birth." He turned to the pathologist. "Thanks for coming again Dr Stopps," he said, "you've heard the police surgeon's observations, I take it? Yes, good; I'm afraid this one looks pretty clear cut, but I'm sure every case presents its own peculiarities to a man in your particular trade."

"*Profession*, if you please Inspector," the pathologist replied icily, "and I prefer to start every examination with a completely open mind so with all due respect to the local general practitioner, I intend to disregard his observations until I've made my own."

Chapter Fourteen

Monday Morning – Late February

For the second time in under a week, the mortuary at Nobles Hospital had borne witness to a forensic post mortem. Dr Stopps pulled off his thin latex gloves and stepped back from the shiny steel table. His face wore a slightly dejected look.

"I'm afraid that your local general practitioner was quite correct," he began, "and I have little to add to his observations. Quilleash was battered to death with the proverbial blunt instrument. Hit from behind and no-doubt by someone he knew."

"Knew?" Inspector Davies asked. Stopps scowled at the interruption.

"Multiple fractures to the occipital bone with contusions and haemorrhage within the cortex. There were absolutely no other signs of injury so he didn't try to defend himself. That and the fact that he had turned his back to his attacker means he wasn't expecting the blow so it was probably someone he knew. The first blow would have knocked him unconscious, but the killer added quite a few more; I'd say he died within a few minutes and would put the time of death at between six and eight on Saturday night."

"It was a frenzied attack then?"

"Oh yes and the killer was quite strong. The occipital bone is one of the thickest in the skull and it normally takes a fair old whack to break it."

"A fair old whack by someone strong," Davies voiced his thoughts out loud, "and someone he probably knew. His brother Seth is a farm labourer."

"Sounds suspiciously like your man," the pathologist said in a rather patronising manner, "now if that's all, I'd like to be taken to the airport please. There's a flight in a couple of hours and I'll let you have the written report tomorrow."

Detective Inspector Davies drove the pathologist back to the airport himself; he wanted to go back to the scene of the crime and Ronaldsway lay on the most direct route to the Meayll Peninsular. Dr Stopps was not among his favourite pathologists, being rather aloof and conceited. The man had given his opinion on the murder and gave the distinct impression that pleasant small talk with a member of the constabulary was beneath him. The journey was therefore a silent one and to Davies seemed to pass painfully slowly. At last they reached the airport and the Inspector brought the car to a halt by the door leading to Departures. Stopps got out, muttered a curt word of thanks and disappeared into the terminal building leaving Davies alone with his thoughts for the first time in over a week. And what a week it had been! Murder was an uncommon crime in the Island, but with the ranks of available officers seriously depleted by sickness and study leave, Davies, as the most senior-ranking detective currently on duty had found himself leading not one, not two, but three homicide investigations. As he drove off, he turned the bare facts of each case over in his mind: the first one, the undertaker's assistant, seemed straightforward enough. They had a suspect and plenty of forensic, but the lack of any clear motive still preyed on his mind. It must have been a spur of the moment thing, he concluded. If Quayle had planned to kill his assistant, surely he could have found a less obvious way to do it. An argument about something, no doubt and Quayle had lost his temper. No reports of any raised voices, but it was a large and thick-walled house standing some distance from its neighbours. The murder had taken place in the middle of the night, when most sensible people would have been fast asleep and the deep drifting snow would have added an extra layer of sound insulation. Quayle was the man and he would probably come clean and admit it when it came time to enter a plea.

The second case was rather different. The victim had still not been identified and as to the killer, no-one could even begin to guess. The body of man aged somewhere between thirty and forty had washed up on Douglas beach. The man was Caucasian and of slender build, but his clothes bore none of the familiar high street labels. If the cause of death had been drowning there would have been nothing to form even a tenuous link with the Isle of Man. Corpses washed up on the Island's beaches fairly regularly and every now and then were borne by the currents and the tide from the other lands that surrounded the Irish Sea. In this case, though, Dr Stopps confirmed that the man had been strangled and that a most unusual weapon had been used. The rolled up plastic bag had indeed come from Ramsey Bakery and the sell-by date and bar code had still been visible and had told them that the body had been in the water for rather less time than the pathologist had first thought. The man had been killed sometime between Saturday and

Tuesday night and analysis of the currents and tide flows around Douglas over that period suggested that it was unlikely that the body had drifted more than six or seven miles. That gave them a semicircle centred on Douglas and extending roughly from Laxey down as far as Santon or from a boat anything up to the same distance out to sea. They had started to make enquiries, but no-one had seen anything suspicious in that area and, so far at least, no-one had been reported missing. It was going to be a long hard struggle and Davies thought privately that they would never get to the bottom of the case.

Finally, there was the accountant; the eminently respectable Mr Kenneth Quilleash (Junior). There was a vague link with the undertaker and his assistant, of course, but the Island was a small place and coincidences were surprisingly common. That was all the link was, a coincidence. It was common knowledge that the old man had left the farm to his eldest son and equally common knowledge that young Kenneth was going to sell. Seth was notorious for his temper and was the killer, without the shadow of a doubt. The problem in this case would be finding, not identifying or convicting him. Teams of men were searching, but previous experience told Davies that Seth could be rather hard to trace.

As Detective Inspector Davies was driving south, the advocate was in conference with her client. She had arrived at the prison a little before ten and had been escorted through the inner gates a short while later. The undertaker was already waiting in the familiar little hut known as *legal visits* and as soon as the prison officer shut the door and turned the key, he began to speak.

"Well?" he demanded impatiently, "what did the professor and your private detective find out?"

Louise told him about the post-mortem and that Professor Clarke had concluded that he could not have been the killer. She had just begun to explain why when her client interrupted.

"Surely you can get me out of here on the strength of his report alone," he said excitedly.

"The other pathologist takes a different view, Richard," she pointed out, but her client was having none of that.

"He's just a *Doctor*, our expert's a *Professor*; you tell the Deemster what you just told me and he'll have to throw the case out...won't he?" The undertaker's voice conveyed an air of desperation.

"It hasn't got to the Deemster yet, Richard," she explained, "you've been remanded by the High Bailiff and you won't be before the Deemster until after committal. Once you've been committed to the Court of General Gaol Delivery, you'll be able to enter your plea. We could try to go for "no case to answer" at committal, but I can tell you now that we wouldn't be successful. There are two conflicting expert opinions and that means they'll have to go before a jury. I'm afraid you're going to be in here for a little bit longer than you seem to think."

"How long?" he demanded.

"Well, realistically, I can't see a trial much before September," she replied.

"*September!*" he shouted angrily, "I can't wait that long. I can't do anything in here, anything at all... and the TT's only three months off. How am I supposed to prepare."

"There are more important things than the TT, Richard," the advocate replied, "anyway, shut up for a minute and let me tell you what Roy Love found when he went through your house." Her client bit his lip and stared at her sulkily, but for once did what he was told and said nothing, allowing Louise to finish what she had come to say.

"'Course I knew about the steps," he said when she asked him, "I've lived in that house nearly all my life. Used to run up and down them when I was a young fella, but I haven't been near them now for a good number of years. Roy's right about the beach at the bottom; it's a short steep bank of shingle and it completely disappears when the tide's fully in. You could land a boat at low water, but it'd be a bloody dangerous thing to do in the dark unless you really knew what you were doing. The beach is very short and it's surrounded by jagged rocks; if there was any sort of swell you'd soon be in trouble. As for the bike, no, I haven't touched it, apart from to clean it, since young Rorletski took the covers off the top end last year. I clean all the machines in my collection at least once a week and if someone else had tried to do anything to it, I would have known."

"So you didn't try to strip it down and have a really good look at the engine?" the advocate asked. Her client shook his head.

"Not a lot of point when we found out it was a fake," he replied, "with a lead engine case and no camshafts. Just a vehicle to smuggle plutonium, that Pinkerton 'tec said."

"So why on earth did you keep it?" she said.

"It cost me a lot of money," he replied defensively, adding, "and it does look rather nice."

Louise asked him about the Quilleash family, but he shook his head.

"Can't say as I really know them," he said, "think I might have met the old man a couple of times and I believe my father buried his father, but I wouldn't even have remembered the name if it hadn't been for that 'phone call a couple of weeks ago."

"*What 'phone call?*" the advocate demanded, astounded that her client had neglected to mention this little fact before.

"Oh, didn't I tell you?" he replied, shifting a little uncomfortably, "I had a 'phone call from the son Kenneth, the one you tell me's been murdered."

"*And?*" she prompted him, "what did he want?"

"He told me that his father was dying and, er, he just wondered if Quayle and Son could make the necessary arrangements when, er, the time came."

"*He asked you that? Before his father was even dead?*" Louise spat out the questions angrily, astounded that anyone could be so callous.

"Well, it's not completely unheard of," the undertaker replied defensively, "some Manx families just like to see a bit of continuity and to make sure they know who to go to when the unpleasant, but inevitable finally occurs."

"So you agreed to take the job on?" she asked.

"I said we'd be available and I told him I could be contacted day or night."

"Did he give you any idea when this event was likely to happen," she asked, anger now giving way to curiosity as her view of the late Mr Quilleash (Junior) began to change.

"He said it wouldn't be more than a week or so," the undertaker replied, "told me that the old man had taken bad with the 'flu and bronchial pneumonia had set in. Dr MacDonald had told him that bronchial pneumonia was 'the old man's friend' and he should prepare for the worst; old man Quilleash was over ninety, when all's said and done."

Louise had arranged to meet Roy in a coffee shop near the old market in Douglas. He remembered it from his meeting with the Pinkerton man the summer before and recalled that it served excellent home-baked cakes as well as a wide range of beverages. He ordered a couple of Danish Pastries, a latte and a mocha and followed the advocate down into the basement, agreeing with her suggestion that it would be a little more private there.

"So someone did know Richard would be available," he said when she had told him her story "and knew it would be a way of getting him out of the house. I take it that Richard didn't say he'd normally leave it all to Ernie? No, he wouldn't would he? Wouldn't really fit with the old family undertaker image. Ken Quilleash Junior would have been left under the firm impression that a call to Quayle and Son, day or night, would result in Richard's attendance." He shook his head grimly and continued, "it does tend to confirm what I have been hearing."

"Which is?"

"That old man Quilleash was hale and hearty; his sudden illness, deterioration and death seems to have perplexed many of his friends and there have been some dark mutterings down in Port Erin and Port St Mary."

"So you managed to find some people who knew him?" the advocate asked.

"I did," he replied, "we went the wrong way on Saturday, we should have turned right and gone into Port St Mary. It didn't take me long before I found the right place; Pub called the Bay View. One of those places that is stuffed with locals, you know what I mean: you walk through the door and they all stop speaking and just, well, *stare* at you. It's probably okay in the middle of summer, but at this time of year strangers just stand out like a sore thumb. Anyway, I'd put my thickest skin on and just smiled back at them; told them that I was looking into the death of old Ken and gained their trust and confidence with a few strategically ordered rounds of drinks."

"That was generous of you," Louise said genuinely.

"Thank Richard," the private detective replied, "it's on my list of expenses." He continued: "the feeling down there's pretty much against the accountant. They seem to think he had something to do with the old man's death and he deserved what Seth did to him. There is a rumour that young Kenneth persuaded his father to change his will and had already lined up a buyer for the farm, but that's just rumour. I have found out something a little more concrete, however: the name of the old man's lawyer."

"Really?" the advocate asked, "he could prove useful; who is it?"

"Fellow by the name of Gruber," Love replied.

"Oh God," the advocate exclaimed, burying her head in her hands.

"What's up?" Love asked.

"You may not remember," she replied, "but he was the advocate who acted for Petromax at the inquest into the death of their rider at the races last year."

"Ah, Petromax again," he said raising his eyebrows, "you could call me paranoid, but these coincidences are becoming a little too common for my liking. What do you think of this guy Gruber?"

"An odious, oily creep," she said, "but competent enough in a corrupt sort of way. He seems to have an immense income, but where it comes from is anyone's guess. The man seems to have very few clients and do very little work, but he lives in a mansion and drives a Ferrari." Love nodded.

"You needn't say any more, the inference is clear enough."

"I can't understand why a decent old Manx farmer would instruct Gruber," Louise said shaking her head, "in my experience farmers are pretty careful with their money and Gruber will charge the earth."

"Rumour has it that Kenneth Junior was responsible for that," Love replied, "word in the pub is that your old boss Bradley Fitzgerald used to act for the old man, but for some reason Kenneth got the old man to change his lawyer and then change his will. Then the old man rather conveniently died."

"And then someone murdered Ernie Quine and tampered with the Petromax," Louise continued, "before finally Kenneth Junior was killed. We need to find out more about that farm; is it valuable?" The private detective shrugged his shoulders.

"Dunno," he said, "but it's got a few hundred acres of land and you know what property prices are like on the Island nowadays. Looks like mainly rough grazing to me, but maybe someone got planning consent for residential build; that'd make it worth a hell of a lot more, particularly with those views."

"No chance," the advocate replied, shaking her head, "any application would have to be advertised and Manx National Heritage would object. Whoever wants it won't want it for building. Can you have another look at the site?"

"I'll take a walk around the whole area and see what I can find out. Do you want to come?" Love asked. Louise shook her head again.

"No, I think I'd better speak to Gruber. I'm not sure what excuse I'll give, but I'll see if I can extract any information from him. Why don't we meet back at your hotel at eight o' clock tonight?"

Chapter Fifteen

Monday Afternoon/Evening – Late February

The offices of Simon Gruber LLB, Advocate, Solicitor and Attorney at Law oozed leather, chrome and mirrored glass. They spoke of money and presented rather a contrast to the cramped quarters Louise Templeton had taken up when she left Bradley Fitzgerald and set up in business for herself.

"Can I help you?" a waif-like, suntanned receptionist turned her attention from her long red fingernails to the advocate standing before her and smiled. It was an insipid smile that caricatured insincerity. Louise smiled back.

"My name is Louise Templeton and I have come to see Mr Gruber; could you tell him I've arrived?" The faintest of frowns gently creased the girl's perfectly made up face; it was obvious that this was an unwelcome intrusion on her usual afternoon work.

"Are you a client?" she asked, as if a little unsure of what to do next. The pitch and tone of her voice seemed to indicate that clients were infrequent and unwelcome visitors to these chambers.

"No, I'm an advocate and Mr Gruber is expecting me. I spoke to him on the telephone only half an hour ago."

"Please take a seat," the girl waved at the richly-upholstered sofa and comfortable armchairs which stood around a glass coffee table in the corner of the room before pressing a button on the fancy telephone which lay to her right.

"Are you expecting a Louise Templeton, Simon?" The voice of Simon Gruber answered immediately and directed the receptionist to send Miss Templeton straight up.

Louise stepped out of the lift into another world. If the reception downstairs was opulent, Gruber's office was positively decadent. The man himself was sitting behind a polished mahogany desk that seemed almost as big as her office. He stood up and welcomed her with a flash of what must have been the whitest teeth Louise had ever seen.

"Louise, it's absolutely wonderful to see you. Please come in and take a seat. What can I do for you? When we spoke on the 'phone you said something about property, please tell me more."

"I understand, Mr Gruber, that you are one of the executors of the will of the late Kenneth Quilleash?" she said. The row of shining teeth disappeared like the sun passing behind a dark grey cloud and something in the tone of Gruber's voice told her that the question was as unwelcome as it had been unexpected.

"Come, come now Louise, call me Simon, we don't stand on ceremony in this practice. I assume you're referring to the late Kenneth Quilleash Senior?" Louise nodded and he continued, "I only heard this morning about the tragedy which took place over the weekend. Desperately sad for the family, to lose two of its members in no more than a week and one of them at the hands of his own brother, but never mind, these things do happen. Yes, to answer your question I am one of the executors, in fact I'm now the sole executor of the will, seeing as poor young Kenneth was the other. Why do you ask?"

"I have a client," Louise replied, "who may be interested in acquiring Cronk Ny Arrey Farm and I have heard through the grapevine that it may be for sale. Is that true?"

"I'm afraid you're a little late, Louise, it has already been sold."

"What? Surely not? I mean you can't have got Probate yet. Who is the purchaser?" Gruber's sickly smile had come out from behind the cloud and was now shining again like the midday sun. He waved his index finger as if ticking her off.

"Now, now Louise, an agreement for sale has been signed and a substantial deposit paid. This took place before the death of Mr Quilleash (Junior) and as he died after his father and the will lacked any clause requiring the beneficiary to outlive the testator by a particular length of time in order to inherit, the farm, or rather the proceeds of sale of the farm will form part of his estate and the conveyance will go through exactly as he had instructed. As for the purchaser, I'm afraid that little detail is, for the moment, confidential."

"If that's the case, Simon," she said, getting to her feet, "I'll tell my client and I'm sorry for wasting your time."

When Louise arrived at Love's hotel that evening, she found him relaxing in a comfortable corner of the bar. A freshly-pulled pint of the local Okell's bitter lay in front of him and as the advocate approached, he stood up and asked her what she wanted to drink. A glass of Chardonnay was ordered and when it arrived, the private detective told her what he had found. It transpired that he had spent a thoroughly exhausting afternoon tramping around the Meayll Peninsular and had learned a great deal about the geography and history of the area. It was a fascinating and beautiful part of the Island, he told her, but as for economic value, he wouldn't have thought it particularly high.

"There are a number of old quarries," he told her, "and the whole peninsular is dotted with tumuli and relics of previous inhabitants. It's an archaeologist's dream; I mean in a relatively small area you can see the remains of everything from Neolithic burial mounds and settlements to Second World War pill boxes and radar installations. There are old forts and lead mines, but the land itself is rather rough, at best supporting grass suitable for grazing and over much of the rest of it, only a mixture of bracken, gorse and scrub. I did find out what the installation behind the farm is, though, the one that I said looked like a UFO; it's an aircraft directional beacon and apparently it keeps planes on the right track flying between here and the States. Anyway, I wouldn't have thought having that behind your property would add any value at all. If there's no chance of getting planning permission for development, what about alterations? The view's fantastic, but the buildings are rather, well, dilapidated and the whole place needs a lot of tidying up."

"I wouldn't have thought you'd be able to do much." Louise said, considering the question carefully, "as far as I'm aware, Manx National Heritage have a pretty strong influence when it comes to planning applications in that particular part of the Island. They want to keep the place exactly as it's always been so any improvements a buyer wanted to make would be very limited in scale. I think we're missing something, though. If this is all about someone trying to get their hands on Cronk Ny Arrey, surely they wouldn't go to the trouble of killing someone just to get hold of a semi-derelict old farmhouse that just happens to have a couple of rooms with a view. You mentioned the radio beacon. I know it's pretty far fetched, but could someone be planning sabotage?"

"Don't think so," Love said, "it's only a directional beacon and if somebody switched it off there'll be bound to be plenty of back up systems."

"Have you checked?"

"No, but it stands to reason there will be." She stared at him in silence for several seconds before he threw his hands up into the air in a gesture of defeat. "Okay, okay, I'll check, but it's something I'll probably have to do back home."

"That's fine, Roy, you don't need to do it now, but I do think we should cover every possibility. You mentioned lead mines; any possibilities there?" Love shook his head.

"I don't think so," he replied, "they are all boarded up and totally derelict, nothing like the mine in Laxey that Jonathon and I went down last year."

"What about the black van and the monks you told me about?" she asked. He grinned a little sheepishly.

"No sign of them at all; I asked a few of the locals and they looked at me as though I was off my rocker. Maybe the whole thing was a bit of an hallucination; I was rather tired and I hadn't eaten a thing for a very long time. Did you find out anything from Gruber?"

"Only that the rumours are true and the farm has effectively already been sold. Completion can't take place until after the grant of probate and, given the circumstances, that'll take a month or two, maybe even three. Gruber wouldn't tell me who the buyer is, but we'll find out after completion."

"How?"

"The deeds will be filed in the Land Registry and the name of the purchaser published in the local paper so I think for the moment it's just a case of we watch and wait."

They discussed the case for a little longer, but it had become apparent that any breakthrough was still some way off. At the moment, the only evidence that the court would listen to was that of their forensic pathologist. Until something else turned up, they were going to have to make do with that. There seemed nothing more that the private detective could do for the present and, as even the undertaker's resources were finite, Roy Love decided to leave the Island in the morning.

"But if there are any developments, or you need any assistance," he added, "just pick up the 'phone and I'll be there."

As the advocate and the private detective finished speaking, another meeting was taking place in a board room within the newly refurbished Isle of Man Government offices.

"Can't say as I'm too keen on the idea, at all," the Chief Constable said rather sourly. He had just heard the Chief Minister's enthusiastic announcement and although the news was totally unexpected, he had already begun to experience a definite sense of unease. "I mean, what with the current international situation," he continued, "do you think such a visit is really, er, well, wise?"

"Don't be so negative, John," the Chief Minister rebuked him mildly, "nothing could be better for the Island's reputation; it'll lift our profile and it'll certainly do wonders for the races."

"But the security...it'll be horrendous. It's bad enough at that time of year trying to keep an eye on all the visitors. This year, with it being the centenary of the races, it'll be even worse; we are predicting fifty thousand, but there could be even more. How can we possibly guarantee that he'll be safe?"

"He wants to come," the Chief Minister stated emphatically, "his private Secretary phoned me personally and when the President of the United States of America says he wants to visit, I'm hardly going to turn him down."

"But why on earth...?" the Chief Constable began, but the Chief Minister cut him short.

"He's always wanted to see the TT races; when he was younger he was a bit of a biker and he's had someone working on his family tree: turns out he's got some Manx connections. Anyway he's coming. Given the current level of threat in the UK, he doesn't want to travel via England so he'll be flying Air Force One to Shannon in Ireland then by private jet from Shannon to Ronaldsway. As for security; we're on the Isle of Man, for God's sake and what with the CCTV at the Sea Terminal and Airport, we can keep a pretty close eye on who enters or leaves. You're going to have to make any necessary extra arrangements, but the President's men will be in touch with you about that in the next few days."

"Next few days?" the Chief Constable repeated the words, his jaw dropping in amazement, "how long have you known about this, Sir?"

"Well, I got the 'phone call a couple of weeks ago, but I've told nobody, until now, that is and you can be sure that there won't have been any leaks from the President or his men. News will get out, but not for a week or two at least and that'll give you plenty of time to bump up our security and make sure no-one gets on the Island who we really don't want."

Chapter Sixteen

Saturday Morning – Late May – Practice Week

Price arrived at the dock a good three hours before the sailing to Douglas was due to depart and was astounded to find that even at that hour he was forced to join the end of a very long and rapidly growing queue of vehicles. It seemed to begin by the quayside and snake in a disorderly crocodile around and through the fenced off car park that he took to be the ferry terminal. He had never travelled from Liverpool to the Island before, but when he had booked the crossing several months before, this was just about the only boat that had any space left, unless he had been prepared to go even earlier than the first Saturday of Practice which he was not. When Price had first arrived, he had thought that the setting looked impressive enough: the dull brown waters of the Mersey flowed sedately past the Pier head with its imposing Victorian buildings, relics of that great city's long and historic association with the sea. Towering above them all, two huge stone birds gazed impassively down from their lofty perch atop the Royal Liver Building. He had thought the landscape dignified, masterful even, but now he had had the chance to look again, Price felt that something let the whole scene down. That something was the Steam Packet Company. Its terminal building consisted of little more than a collection of shabby portacabins standing in the middle of a car park and separated from the quayside by a steel and wire fence. There was no sign of a proper roll-on, roll-off dock and it looked to Price as though vehicles were expected to descend a steep ramp to a floating pontoon on the river and thence by another ramp to the ferry. The whole thing lacked neatness and style; it looked temporary, amateur and cheap.

The doctor looked at his watch: it was now eight forty-five in the morning and the sailing was due to depart at nine. He peered over to his right and could just about see the mouth of the Mersey from his position in the queue. It would take some time to load all this lot, he thought, but there was still no sign of the boat. The man behind him seemed to share his thoughts.

"Not going to get us off on time today, are they mate?" he said. It was the voice of a cockney and carried with it a sense of cheerful acceptance of the inevitable blended with something of that indefatigable character of the Blitz. Seemingly not expecting a reply he continued: "same every year, ain't it; you'd think they'd have worked it out by now, that the boats are just a little bit busier this fortnight than they are for the rest of the year, but they don't do they? And this year, from what I've heard it's worse."

"Worse?" Price asked. He wasn't really sure what the man meant or where the conversation was leading, but it passed the time.

The man put the crash helmet he was carrying down on the seat of his green Kawasaki and Price realised that he was in for a lecture. His name, the man declared, was Desmond, but most called him Des and the reason why he had put his helmet down had already become apparent. Des used his hands as demonstrative tools; he needed those hands to make his points and of those points, he certainly had more than a few.

"Centenary, init?" Des explained, "not that they've had long to get ready for it, well only a bleedin 'undred years. Massive demand, they said, that's why I'm on this bleedin boat. Normally go over next Friday and come back the Saturday after the Senior; one week on that Island's enough for anyone, but could I do that this year?" Again the question seemed a rhetorical one; Des did not so much as pause for a reply, but carried on with his invective: "naa, too late they said. Come to the TT every year, book regular as clockwork last week every January, just after the date when everyone has to confirm that they're going. Never had a problem before; always got the sailing I wanted, but this year…no chance, bleedin full, every single bleedin boat, apart from this one, of course and y'know why this one's goin' ter be late?" Price shook his head, but suspected he was about to learn. "Because of 'heavier than expected vehicular traffic'. Would you believe it? Guy up there," he waved his right hand towards the front of the queue, "was supposed to be on the boat last night. He'd booked months ago, but when he got here, they told him it was full and he'd have to wait for the next so he's been here for nearly eight hours and he told me that the ferry's been getting half an hour later every single trip. If it goes on like this, they'll be a day behind themselves by the end of the week."

"I thought they were supposed to be fast craft," Price interjected. A second later he wished he hadn't.

"Fast craft!" Des exclaimed, "bleedin horrible things. Give me the old *Lady of Man* or the *King Orry* any time; those were good boats and popular so what did the Steam Packet do? Got rid of them, of course and could I get onto that *Ben My Chree*?…"

"Doktor Price!" a voice behind him cut in to the conversation and Price turned in surprise. It was a voice he had not heard for nearly a year and it made a welcome contrast to Des' cockney twang. "We meet again doktor, you remember us?"

The face was clean-shaven, gaunt and heavily lined. It bore more lines, perhaps than it did a year ago and, if such were possible, was even more cadaverically thin, but Price instantly recognised the face of the tall Russian.

"Mikael Boroweski," he shouted in delight and shook the man's hand, "and Peter, I must say, I didn't expect to see either of you here today." The bearded giant beside Boroweski stepped forward and seized Price by the hand. His hands were the size of dinner plates and the doctor winced for a moment as he felt a grip of iron; Peter saw the expression, laughed and let go.

"It is good to see you again, doktor," he said.

"It is good to see both of you," Price replied. "You are going to the TT, obviously; are there just the two of you this year?" He recalled the former Soviet Army Field Hospital and their ancient Russian bikes. Boroweski shook his head.

"No Doktor, our comrades are already there; they have been on the Island for some time." He said no more and Price sensed from the Russian's grave, unsmiling face that questions such as since when? and why? would have been deemed unwelcome so he let the matter go.

"Where are your motorcycles?" he asked, changing the subject. The two Russians were dressed casually, but smartly and of the kit he had come to expect of them there was no sign.

"We are travelling as foot passengers," Boroweski explained, "our comrades took motorcycles with them in a van."

"Are you camping at Glen Lough again this year?" Price asked. Boroweski shook his head.

"No, we have house in south of the Island this year, Doktor. House with enough room for all of us." Price waited for the Russian to say more, to expand on this statement, to say exactly where the house was, but Boroweski seemed reserved and his companion remained silent. The conversation stuttered and died.

"Here comes the boat, at bleedin' last!" Des announced to the relief of Price and everyone turned to see the blue and white vessel coming up the Mersey. Boroweski looked at his companion and then spoke.

"It is good to see you doktor, but we are foot passengers and we must go now and join queue. Perhaps we see you on board?" With those passing words, he and the giant Peter turned and were gone. Price frowned; the men had seemed friendly enough, but after what they had all gone through the previous year, he had expected a little more. Was it paranoia on his part or did the glances that had passed between the two Russians signify something more than a natural degree of caution and reticence.

The ferry was a high speed catamaran, with vehicle and passenger decks riding high above the water between its twin hulls. It pirouetted slowly in the river and then slipped back gently to its mooring beside the floating pontoon. Warps flew ashore, winches creaked and spun into action and within a surprisingly short period of time the vessel was secure. The rear watertight doors opened and its vehicular cargo began to disembark.

"About bloody time," Des grumbled, but the remainder of his sentence was lost beneath the growl and roar of engines as several hundred motorcycles simultaneously barked into life. They were all far too early, of course and Price knew it would be at least half an hour before they could even begin to board, but he still returned to his machine, pulled on his helmet and turned his ignition on.

Boarding the vessel was a long, drawn out and tedious affair, made worse by the running commentary Price's new found companion seemed duty-bound to provide. The crocodile of motorcycles inched slowly forward as one by one the vehicles made their way down the first ramp, along the pontoon then down the second into the bowels of the vessel. When the doctor finally reached the vehicle deck, he saw the reason for the delay. It was cramped and tightly packed already, but the men in the Steam Packet overalls seemed determined to fill every last remaining space. He was waved forward into a tiny gap which seemed far smaller than his machine. He tried to explain this to the man who seemed to be in charge, but his remonstrations fell on deaf ears.

"Engine off, Sir," the man commanded, "and leave the bike in gear." Price meekly obeyed, climbed off the Triumph Daytona and stood to one side. The foreman pointed at the bike and then at the gap. "In there," he barked brusquely and two fluorescent-jacketed operatives seized the machine and lifted it bodily into place. Price looked on in horror as one of the men looped a coarse and heavy rope around the footpegs, pulled it tight over the pristine paintwork of the shiny new tank and then secured the rope to the neighbouring machine.

"Watch what you're doing," he called out, "that bike's brand new."

"I wouldn't waste your breath," Des advised him gloomily, "they don't care a damn about bikes; just how many they can pack on board, like sardines in a can. Let's go up and get a brew." Another brace of bikes had already been muscled into position behind the doctor's bright yellow Triumph. Des was right, there was nothing he could do so he turned and followed the cockney through a doorway and up the stairwell to the passenger deck. At least, he thought, it would mean a rest and a comfortable seat for a couple of hours. He voiced these thoughts out loud.

"You'll be lucky, mate," came the inevitable reply, "there won't be room to move up there; just listen to that bleedin' din!" They had reached the top of the stairwell and the dull background hum of noise which Price had first noticed when they had started to climb had become louder and its constituent parts more clearly defined. He had at first taken it to be the ship's engines, but as he listened more closely he could hear shouts and laughter. His companion pushed the heavy metal door open and the true source of the noise was instantly revealed. They had reached the passenger deck and a huge party was evidently in full swing. For once Des had not been guilty of exaggeration; room to move would have been a frivolous luxury: here there wasn't room to breathe. There were bodies occupying every conceivable inch of space: heavily built men wearing leathers squeezed into every seat and those without seats lay outstretched on the floor. Tottering piles of helmets, gloves, rucksacks, tankbags and panniers of almost every make, type or description arose from table and floor. There was, quite simply put, no more room...anywhere.

"Let's get out on deck," the cockney suggested, "at least the air'll be fresher; it don't 'alf pong in 'ere." Price sniffed: damp leather, sweat and beer. He nodded.

"You show me the way, I'll follow."

With great difficulty, they struggled through the seething mass, doing their best to avoid treading on those who were lying on the floor. After ten long minutes they reached the doorway leading to the tiny outside deck which lay at the rear of the vessel, outside and behind the bar. Price soon discovered that this was the only place where people could smoke and for that reason it was probably even more crowded than the bar inside, but he managed to find a corner in which to prop himself. As he leaned back the ship's bell sounded, the diesel engines rumbled and the vessel began to make way. A monumental cheer rang out, drowning the emergency procedure announcement and Price, despite the uncomfortable nature of his surroundings, smiled. It would not be the easiest of crossings, but he had begun to feel a little excited: his holiday had begun and he was on his way to the Isle of Man TT.

Chapter Seventeen

Saturday Afternoon – Late May – Practice Week

The ferry was already nearly three hours late when it set out from Liverpool and Price had expected the boat to crank up the engines and at least try to live up to its reputation as a high speed craft. When it left the mouth of the Mersey, it began to make a little more headway, but although the Irish Sea, for once, looked like a mirror, the ferry's rate of progress was far less impressive than he had been led to believe it would be. After a couple of hours staring at the water, he struggled back inside to the bar. He was tired and desperately in need of a coffee, but when he saw the jam of bodies, five deep at the counter, he had second thoughts about the whole idea. He turned and was about to return to the outside deck when his erstwhile companion, the cockney, who had disappeared from sight some time earlier hailed him from the other side of the bar. Price managed to struggle across to join him and found the man deep in conversation with a group of German bikers.

"How's it goin' mate," he said cheerfully, "meet Eric and Stefan and Pete. This is...er, I don't think you told me your first name, but I heard those friends of yours at Liverpool call you Dr Price."

"Jonathon," Price said and shook the Germans' hands. The men were of an age that was hard to estimate with any degree of real accuracy; Price hazarded a guess at somewhere in their mid forties, but accepted that he could be anything up to a decade out either way. All three were clad in similar two-piece leathers which seemed just a little tight around the midriff.

"Good to meet you Jonathon," one of them said in perfect English, but Jonathon had already forgotten which one was which.

"Good to meet you," he replied and then turned to the cockney, "Des, I thought this was supposed to be a fast craft; we don't seem to be moving much faster now than we were in the Mersey, what do you think is going on?"

"Just the bleedin Steam Racket trying to save a few bob on the fuel," was the cockney's reply, but the German with the perfect English answered and seemed rather better informed about the whole affair.

"It is caused by the delay at the Port of Douglas," he explained. "I have spoken to friends who travelled earlier and the boats are taking far longer than usual to unload. In addition there are extra boats this year and so the boats must go slower and wait their turn." Price frowned.

"Wait their turn?" he said, "surely there's plenty of time for each boat to unload before the next one arrives; there shouldn't be any need for the things to have to queue up."

"It is the searches," the man explained.

"Searches?"

"Yes, my friends tell me that everyone leaving the boat is being searched and it is causing considerable delay. I think it is because of the visit of the American President."

"Visit of *whom*?" Price asked, unable to believe what he had just heard.

"The President of the United States of America," the man replied calmly, "have you not heard? I read it in *Die Welt* only the other day." Price shook his head.

"I haven't heard anything; are you sure? I mean why?"

"I understand that he once was a keen biker and the paper said he has distant roots in the Isle of Man. It is the Centenary of the races and he is half-way through his final term of office. I suppose that given the world situation there are very few places now where he can now safely go. *Die Welt* had a very good leader about a man living on borrowed time visiting a race living...but I digress, it probably loses something in the English translation; that, I am sure, is the reason for the extra security. It is inconvenient, but I am sure we shall all learn to cope."

"Island ahoy!" someone shouted and the entire population of the bar stood up and tried to rush outside. After a few minutes most of them gave up and sat down again, but Price persevered and managed to force his way through the crowd to reach the outside deck. The sun was shining brightly from dead ahead of them, but by craning his neck forward and shielding his eyes with his hand, he managed to see the summit of Snaefell above a low-lying bank of early summer mist. It looked just as he had remembered it from the summer before and he smiled. As he stared at the land ahead, he felt a tap on his shoulder and once again heard a familiar voice.

"Doktor Price, I think it is time that we talk."

As the Sea Cat slowly manoeuvred into its berth alongside the Victoria Pier in the outer harbour, Price could see that the Port of Douglas was virtually at a standstill and it was still only Saturday at the beginning of

Practice Week. There were no other ferries in the dock, but the whole quayside seemed to be alive with bikers and motorcycles. It was a seething mass of brightly coloured humanity and at first glance he could think of no reason why the place should be so full. As he focussed on the spectacle, however, he recalled what the German had told him and began to understand what was happening. The people were all part of a gigantic queue which snaked around the whole port area before finally reaching a line of police vehicles which blocked off the exit leading to the promenade. It must be at that exit where the searches were taking place and, if so, taking place painfully slowly for the queue seemed to be moving at little more than a snail's pace. The ship's bell sounded and drivers and riders were told to go down to the vehicle deck, so Price made his way back inside and began his descent into the bowels of the ship. The gangways and stairwells were crowded so the journey took far longer than would have been usual, and when he finally reached the vehicle deck, the scene was one of virtual pandemonium. The outer doors of the vessel had been opened, and, as every vehicle's engine was running, but no-one was moving, the air was already thick with the smell of petrol and toxic fumes. Price found his Triumph Daytona still firmly tied to metal railings which had been wedged in place to secure the bikes for the crossing. If such were possible, the space his motorcycle had been jammed into seemed even smaller than it had been when they left Liverpool and there was absolutely no way he would be able to move the bike on his own. Of the burly seamen and their supervisor, there was, of course, no sign and Price was a little concerned about what he was going to do. Fortunately his problem was solved by Des and his new-found German friends who arrived on the scene a few moments later. They helped him to untie the ropes and, when the traffic started to move, lift his bike out into a space that was clearing. Price pulled on his helmet, started the engine and slowly started to move.

It took three-quarters of an hour just to crawl off the ship and join the beginning of the queue. Price looked at his watch and discovered that it was nearly five pm: at this pathetic rate of progress, he would never make the first evening practice which was scheduled to begin in little more than an hour. Half-an-hour passed and he moved another fifty yards further. He gave up on the Practice and, feeling rather hot, had taken off his helmet when nothing short of a minor miracle suddenly occurred.

"Dr Price?" He looked up. It was a uniformed member of the Isle of Man Constabulary and both the voice and face seemed vaguely familiar. Price had seen the man moving slowly down the queue, making the odd note of something or other on the way and assumed, quite correctly, that he formed part of the search and checking process. The man's name surfaced from the depths of his unconscious memory.

"It's Ken, isn't it?" he said, "I remember, Mad Sunday last year." The officer gave him a broad grin.

"Thought I recognised you there, doc," he replied, "but you were on a different bike and wearing different coloured leathers and, er, you look like you've lost a bit of weight."

"I was on a Yamaha, last year," Price confirmed with a laugh, "a borrowed R6 and if you remember, you gave me a bit of a hard time about my lack of documentation. You'll be pleased to know that the Triumph is mine and this time I can prove it; as for the leathers, they're my old ones: I went on a diet and managed to slim down just in time for the TT. What are you doing down here, Ken, I thought you were in traffic..." he looked around and realised that they were in the middle of exactly that so continued with another laugh, "...well, er moving traffic, anyway." The policeman shook his head and sighed.

"All the goalposts have been moved for this fortnight, doc, duties rearranged and all leave cancelled. Searching and checking all the arrivals has become the number one priority and those of us in traffic get the job of checking over the machines."

"But why? I mean, I know you have to keep a look out for drugs coming onto the Island, but I've never heard of anything like this being done before. What exactly are you looking for anyway?"

"It's because of this high profile visitor who's coming over sometime next week," the officer said, "it's someone who is a potential terrorist target and we've got orders not to let anyone remotely suspicious through."

"Oh, you mean this visit by the President of the United States of America? I thought it was a wind-up, but quite obviously it's true."

"How did you know about that?" the policeman demanded, "his identity is supposed to be top secret."

"Couple of people told me on the boat," Price replied. "A German told me he'd read it in *Die Welt* and a Russian of my acquaintance told me it was in *The Washington Post*." The policeman shook his head in amazement.

"They told us that no-one outside a small and trusted circle knew. So much for the paranoia about secrecy, still, I suppose it'll make it easier for us to explain why everyone's being made to go through this. Are you going to be one of the race doctors again?" he asked, changing the subject.

"I certainly am, but not until Monday. Good job, seeing as I'm hardly likely to see any of the practices tonight."

"Start your engine," Ken said with a wink, "no, don't put your helmet on...everyone is being photographed as they go through the checkpoint...and follow me." He turned around and led the doctor down the outside of the winding queue. At times Price found the gaps he had to squeeze his machine through quite challenging, but after a few minutes they had reached the end. A little knot of harbour police were doing most of the searching accompanied by a couple of uniformed constables. Two men in dark grey suits stood a little apart from the group of searchers: they were wearing dark glasses, but were taking an obvious interest in the proceedings. Price assumed that they were Special Branch at first, but then heard one of them speak to the other. The accent was unmistakably American and Price guessed that they were some sort of secret servicemen, sent over to make sure that the Manx coppers knew exactly what to do.

"This is Dr Price," Ken announced to the harbour police, "he's one of the TT Medical Officers; I know him and he needs to be out on the course for practice tonight so can you let him through now?" The man who seemed to be in charge nodded.

"Can you just look up at the camera, please doc?" Price looked up where he was directed and the man waved him past. He pulled on his helmet and was fumbling with the strap when one of the dark-suited strangers approached and spoke.

"Aren't you gonna search this guy?"

"You heard what the officer said, didn't you?" the harbour policeman said rather rudely, it was quite apparent that he resented being told what to do by a stranger, "this is one of our race doctors and the officer knows him. I don't think we need to search him, do you?" The American shook his head and cast a cold stare at Price; it was the stare of someone devoid of emotion and, despite himself, the doctor shivered.

"No exceptions, that's the rule. When you make exceptions, you make mistakes and someone you don't want is gonna get through." The harbour policeman glared at the suited stranger and then looked at Ken. The Manx policeman looked uncomfortable and Price sensed the beginnings of a minor incident so he stepped in.

"Okay guys, I've nothing to hide; search away, but please make it quick." The tension eased, the harbour police and Ken relaxed and the dark-suited American walked back to his friend.

Five minutes later, Price was waved on his way. He pressed the starter button and the three cylinder Triumph Daytona burbled into life. As he pulled out onto the promenade, he realised how quiet it was: normally when ferries arrived and disgorged their contents, the road would be choked with traffic for half an hour or more, but the search and checking procedure had reduced the flow to a trickle and for once he had an empty road. He thought about checking into his hotel, but after the white lies Ken had told for him, he felt duty bound to watch the evening practice so he turned left onto Broadway and made his way up the hill. Turning right again at the traffic lights, he rode up Victoria Road, then turned left just after the prison to reach Nobles Park and the TT Grandstand just as the first machines were leaving the grid. As he parked the bike in a corner, he heard the roar of a full works Superbike plummeting down Bray Hill; it was a sound that was unmistakable: he had finally made it to the Island and the TT races had just begun.

Chapter Eighteen

Saturday Evening – Late May – Practice Week

"It's great to be back," said Price, "and that first Practice was just sensational; would you believe it? a new unofficial lap record from a standing start on the very first lap." Louise Templeton had arrived and his long, uncomfortable sea journey already seemed a thing of the dim and distant past. It was nine o' clock in the evening and they were sitting by the window of his hotel's promenade level bar. Price had ordered champagne; the first glass had gone down rather easily and the level of liquid in the bottle was already looking disturbingly low, but it was a celebration and the lady with him seemed to share his enthusiasm for the event which had just got underway.

"It's the new Brandish Corner, I think," she explained, "they were working on it all last October and it's really increased the speeds down from Creg Ny Baa."

"You can say that again, Miss," a voice from the adjacent table remarked. Price and his companion turned around to look: Louise recognised the face of a famous racer.

"It's John Bass, isn't it?" she asked. The man in the jeans and tee-shirt nodded; he was on his own and looked a little bored so the advocate asked him if he would like to join them.

"Love to," he replied and moved over. Introductions followed and then the advocate invited the racer to give them his views on the re-jigged Course.

"It's great," he said, then after a moment or two's consideration added, "but I think it's got a little too fast."

"What do you mean?" Price probed. The legendary racer smiled and began to explain.

"Thing about the TT is it's a long race and a fast race; there are only a couple of really slow corners, the Hairpin and Governors and a fair old chunk of the course is flat, or nearly flat out. The lap record's now over a hundred and twenty-nine miles an hour: that's an *average speed* over a lap that's nearly forty miles long. You've got do six of those laps in the big bike races so it's a hell of a long race. In the Grand Prix and Superbike world championships they race around short circuits that are only two or three miles long. The races are about eighty miles long so they do somewhere between thirty and forty laps, but they only have to learn two or three miles of road. Those circuits have miles of run-off and even if you do come off your bike, it's very rare for you to hit anything and get any more than slightly hurt. Despite that fact, the organisers have been trying to make the circuits slower and safer by putting in extra bends, well they call them chicanes, actually. Here, you've got forty miles of road to learn, but instead of trying to slow it down, they iron out the bends and make it even faster. Brandish used to be a tight left-hander: you'd power down from the Creg and then have to cog down to second gear to take it, before winding the bike up again for the run down to Hillberry. I came down that straight to Brandish tonight on the Superbike and hardly even needed to brake, let alone change down. Result was that I arrived at Hillberry a damn sight quicker than I've ever done before and don't get me wrong, Hillberry was a bloody fast corner in the old days, but tonight I scared myself. I made the corner alright, but I was a little bit on the ragged edge. I heard that Rorletski took the lap time up to one twenty-nine point five tonight; he's a good rider, but mark my words, it's getting a little bit too fast and I just hope that someone doesn't pay the ultimate price for it all." The racer stood up and thanked them for their company, but told them he was a little tired and was going to wander back to his room. When he had gone, Price spoke to his companion.

"Interesting story Louise, how does that fit in with the local view of things?"

"Well, as you know, the Manx Government has this rather schizophrenic attitude to it all. They spend a lot of time telling us that they want to cut down on the road fatalities and so last year they ran a big campaign to get people to agree to an all-Island speed limit only…" her sentence tailed off and Price noticed that she was looking closely at someone who had come into the room and was standing at the bar.

"Only what?" Price asked. The man at the bar looked around and then walked out without ordering a drink.

"Only…that's the Minister," the advocate whispered, "…the one in charge of the campaign…only the Government's propaganda was so obviously distorted and biased that it upset even the people who would have welcomed a speed limit and in the end the whole thing was withdrawn. But, quite apart from that, how can you take them seriously when they market the Island as the capital of speed? As John Bass just told us, the way to increase safety is to slow the traffic down and the way to do that is to put in extra corners, but here they just iron the corners out."

"Here's to the absence of corners," Price said raising his glass. The advocate smiled. "Anyway," he continued, "I hear that you've left Bradley and set up in business for yourself; is that true?" The advocate nodded.

"It is; I'm now the Principal and sole employee of *Louise Templeton, Advocate and Notary Public*, sounds good, don't you think?"

"It sounds great, but why did you leave Bradley? Did you fall out?"

"Of course not, Bradley's still one of my best friends, but I needed space. I wanted to do what I wanted to do in the way I wanted to do it. You can't do that when you work for someone; you can't even do it when you're in partnership with someone so I had to go my own way. Bradley was pretty upset about it at the time, but he's come round and we still meet up for a drink on a Friday after work."

"So what are you doing at present?" Price asked.

"Quite a lot," the advocate replied, "but your old friend the undertaker is number one on the list."

"Christ, I'd forgotten all about him. Is that still going on?"

"It is," she confirmed, "we tried to bring a 'no case to answer' at committal, but the High Bailiff threw it out. If the trial had been listed to be heard before the usual Deemster, we would have been talking about another two or three months, but it turns out Richard knows him, so to avoid prejudice we've had to get an acting Deemster from England. We selected a jury the other day and we're due to start the hearing on the Tuesday of Race Week. It's been listed for three days, so Richard might get his wish and be out in time to see his man race in the Senior."

"Does he have much of a chance?"

"He's convinced me that he didn't do it, but unfortunately I can't speak for the jury. It's all going to be about forensic evidence so it's a hard one to call; I'd say its looking like evens at the moment, but you can never tell until the day."

"My old friend Roy didn't turn anything up them?" Price enquired. Louise shook her head and told him the story about the Petromax and the last house in Onchan; it was interesting, she explained, but not something she would dream of putting to a jury without an awful lot more hard fact.

"Have you heard about this visit?" Price asked when she had finished.

"You mean the American President," Louise answered with a yawn, "yes I heard about it months ago, why?" Price told her about his protracted crossing of the Irish Sea.

"I'd heard that the visit was supposed to be secret," he said.

"That's probably why everybody knows about it," she replied, "and it's not exactly popular, from what I've heard on the street. This President Shrub has managed to antagonise just about everyone on the planet, but we welcome him with open arms because our Chief Minister has worked out that this visit is going to do the Island some good. Trouble is, apart from the Chief Minister, no-one can quite work out how."

"Well it's certainly attracted some international attention already; you'll never guess who I met at Liverpool and then again on the boat?"

"Who?" the advocate asked and appeared genuinely interested.

"Mikael Boroweski, with his friend Peter, that's who."

"He knew about the Presidential visit?"

"He told me it had been in the *Washington Post*. Now we know Mikael is not exactly who he professes to be and I did sort of wonder whether I should have tipped off the coppers down at the Sea Terminal, but then I thought about it and remembered that Mikael and his men had done rather well for us all over here. I just can't see them coming here to cause problems, in fact rather the reverse; that's what I'm worried about. Mikael told me something's brewing and he gave me the address where he and his men are staying, a farmhouse down in the South."

"*A farmhouse down in the South*," the advocate echoed his words. That reminds me of something I've not told you, but in the circumstances I probably better had." She explained about the death of Ken Quilleash (Junior) and Cronk Ny Arrey Farm and Price seemed interested, in fact more than that, his eyes lit up.

"Mikael and his men are staying *yards* from there; he told me the place and I looked it up on my ordinance survey sheet. Louise, I know you're a lawyer, but all these coincidences seem far too remarkable for me."

"What are you suggesting?"

"I think I should go and have a word with Boroweski down in their place in the south and I think I should go and do it tomorrow, long before President Shrub arrives with all of his men.

"You think it may help?"

"Dunno, but I have a little more confidence in Mikael than I do in Shrub or the CIA. Mikael has proved in his previous actions that he's a valuable ally and I just can't see any good reason why he should change sides now."

"You think these things are all connected?"

"Let's put it this way, Louise, how many murders do you get here in the average year?"

"We had four in four months a couple of years ago."

"But normally?"

"I don't know exactly, one every two or three years?"

"So this year we've had Ken Quilleash Senior,"

"We don't know that for sure," Louise interrupted.

"Ernie Quine...and Ken Quilleash Junior."

"And the guy who got strangled with the Ramsey Bakery plastic bag."

"You never told me anything about that," Price complained, "explain?" and the advocate did.

"So just before the news about the President broke, Roy tells us that he sees mysterious monks with motorcycles travelling to the Island. Worse than that, he gets drugged or anaesthetised by the same, then I bump into Mikael Boroweski, someone we suspect to be a Russian secret agent, then I get here and find the place thronging with Manx cops and US secret servicemen, all trying to keep the bad guys out. I think they may be a little late, don't you?"

"Well, I suppose if you put it that way Jonathon, you may have a point."

The champagne had come to an end and the bar had begun to get busy and rather noisy. Louise Templeton looked at her watch and told Price it was about time for her to go.

"Let me walk you home," he asked her, but the advocate shook her head and smiled.

"Not tonight, Jonathon," she replied, "I'm in a new flat just around the corner; I'll show you it sometime over the next week or two, but not before I've had a chance to tidy it up a little. I'll meet you in your hotel car park tomorrow at eight and we'll go and see your old friend Boroweski. I'll bring my car, if you want, but I take it you want to ride down there on your bike?"

"Of course I do. It'll be great to have a ride out before the place gets really busy."

"In that case I'll come on my bike too."

Chapter Nineteen

Sunday Morning – Late May – Practice Week

The following morning Price woke early and drew back the curtains from the windows of his sea-front room. The sun was already shining brightly from a cloudless sky and the tide was in, its waves gently lapping at the sea wall across the Promenade from the hotel. Apart from a couple of joggers, the place was deserted and the number of motorcycles that Price could see parked by the roadside seemed far less than he had expected, given the difficulty he had experienced obtaining a crossing that year. As he took in the panorama of Douglas Bay something immediately registered in his mind, there had been a change. It was a moment or two before he realised what it was: the decaying eyesore that had been the Summerlands complex had disappeared. He could see the cliffs behind it and the tramsheds beyond, but the sprawling building itself had been razed to the ground. Not before time, he thought to himself, and turned his eyes to the other side of the bay and the harbour. The blue and white marquee was already in place by the Sea Terminal, but of the promenade's other usual TT entertainment: the funfair, the sideshows and the burger vans, there was as yet no sign. Still, he thought, it was only Sunday and there were a few days yet for them all to arrive. He stepped back from the window, showered, dressed and made his way downstairs.

Price had meant to take the Triumph for a little spin before meeting up with Louise, but he breakfasted lazily and by the time he had finished there really didn't seem the time. He picked up a complimentary copy of one of the Island's local newspapers and made his way back up to his room. As he thumbed through it, he noticed Miss Templeton's name appear frequently as advocate in the Court Crime Reports section, but the short articles seemed to relate to what he considered very minor crimes. Of the forthcoming trial of the undertaker, there was no mention and he was about to put the paper down when a name suddenly grabbed his attention. It was the property Louise had mentioned the previous night.

Cronk Ny Arrey Farm sold to Religious Foundation

He read the paragraph, carefully tore it out of the paper, folded it and placed it in his wallet. Louise had not mentioned this, but perhaps she did not yet know. Looking at his watch, he realised that it was nearly eight so he pulled on his boots and leathers and made his way down to the Triumph which was parked at the rear of the hotel.

Dead on eight o' clock, a blue and white motorcycle pulled into the car park and came to a halt beside him. He had wondered whether Louise would arrive on her Harley or the big Suzuki, but this was neither. The rider wore blue and white full race leathers and a helmet with a visor that was so dark as to make Price wonder how anyone could possibly see through it at all. At first he thought it was someone else entirely, but as the engine died and the visor flipped open, he recognised the advocate. More than that, he thought, no he was certain that he recognised the bike.

"Isn't that?" he began.

"The R6 Yamaha you were riding last year?" she finished his sentence for him. "Yes it is; I sold the Suzuki and the Harley and your friend the Chief Medical Officer let me have this for next to nothing. What with the new flat and setting up in business, I had to make a few economies and, when all's said and done the six hundred is a great little bike for over here."

"I know," Price agreed, "that's why I bought the new Triumph 675, but won't the R6 be a little underpowered for your stunt riding exploits?" The advocate's face flushed.

"You know about that? I thought I'd kept it from you."

"Richard, the undertaker, told me just before I went home last year." Louise shook her head.

"There's no point in telling that man anything; he can't keep even the slightest secret," she muttered, as if to herself. "I've given up stunt riding," she continued, firmly and rather loudly, "now that I'm in business for myself, I just can't take the risk."

"Won't you miss all that action and excitement?" Price teased gently.

"No," she replied emphatically, but it was obvious that she thought that she would.

They moved off and turned right out of the hotel car park. The Promenade was a little busier now and they passed small groups of early-rising bikers admiring the little knots of two-wheeled machinery which stood parked at irregular intervals by the side of the road. Price knew that as the week progressed the knots would begin to merge into a rather more continuous string of shape and colour of bikes of all types and sizes, but realised as he rode why there were so few bikes for the present. Once, when he had first visited the Island, this Promenade had held nothing but hotels. The rival attractions of overseas cheap package deals and reliable warm weather had waged a war of attrition and had caused the number to plummet over the years. He had thought that the numbers had reached an absolute minimum, but could already see that more hotels had been lost and more apartment blocks had arisen since his visit to the Island the previous year.

Louise would normally have followed the old road south and bypassed Santon, but as this was his first full day on the Island, Price had insisted that they ride over Fairy Bridge. That done and the traditional greeting to the little folk made, they turned right at Ballasalla and the doctor followed the advocate through what seemed a complex maze of narrow winding lanes passing through little villages until at last they reached Port Erin. The road descended steeply onto the gently curving promenade which followed the lines of the picturesque semi-circular bay and the two riders brought their machines to a halt outside a large public house next to the harbour whose sign announced it to be *The Bay Hotel*.

"This is the place that Roy and I came to back in February," Louise began, "and saw Seth Quilleash on the very night, it transpired, that his brother was killed. The police are convinced that Seth is the murderer and, given the set of circumstances, I can't really say that I blame them for that at all. The fact that no-one seems to have set eyes on Seth since is, I think, a little disturbing, but the police think he's left the Island or hiding. I disagree, I think he's dead and…"

"I saw something about the sale of the house in *The Manx Independent*," Price interrupted, remembering what he had read and pulling the folded piece of torn newspaper from his wallet. "Here, have a look." The advocate looked at the fragment of newsprint and frowned.

"Can't believe I missed that, Jonathon, I've been looking out for something like it for weeks…so a religious foundation…that would fit in with Roy and his monks."

"But why Louise, I mean can you make any sense of this at all?"

"Not a lot," she replied, "let's go up and take at look at Cronk Ny Arrey, then see if we can find your friend Boroweski. You mentioned that he seemed eager to talk to you; maybe he knows something that we don't."

They started the bikes and turned around. Price followed the advocate back along the promenade and then up the short hill before turning right. The road narrowed and climbed steeply between houses before reaching the rough scrub and gorse of the moor. Louise pulled into the side of the road and opened her visor.

"This road takes us to Cregneash and the Sound. By the way, that hideous monstrosity with the high walls and barbed wire over there," she said, pointing to a large dwelling which lay to her right, "is the former abode of the famous racing driver, Mr Ansell." Price somehow got the impression that she didn't really think much of Mr Ansell, famous or not, but had little chance to reply as the advocate had already put her machine into gear and set off again. When they next stopped it was in the car park at Cregneash. It was empty and the time now was a little before nine o' clock.

They parked the bikes and started off on foot down the road to the village. It was a tiny place and Price recalled seeing larger hamlets in his time. Ahead of them, the cliffs and barren wilderness of an even smaller island formed a spectacular backdrop to the little stone chapel and the green telephone box which seemed to sit in the centre of the place. Around them, he saw the tiny thatched cottages, bleached turf and houses of whitewashed Manx stone. He had to admit that it all looked quite impressive, indeed beautiful in a wild and windswept sort of way.

"Pretty," he said, "does anybody actually live here or is it all for show?"

"Of course people live here," Louise replied, "real people who live real lives. I once acted for one of the residents who...," she was about to tell him a story, but obviously thought better of it. Changing the tone of her voice, she continued, "but that's not important, now where did you say Boroweski said he was staying."

"I think, from what he told me, it's at the end of this lane," Price replied, "and from what you've told me that puts it within spitting distance of Cronk Ny Arrey farm. Shall we proceed, Miss Templeton?"

"Be my guest," she said, "but keep your eyes open; this place may look deserted, but I somehow think that everything we do is being closely observed."

They walked slowly down the winding lane past the houses whose little signs announced their quaint Manx names. When they reached the bottom of the hill another single-tracked road joined from their right, but Louise explained that it was just the other village street. They started to climb and she pointed out the gateway on the left leading to Cronk Ny Arrey Farm. It looked as deserted as ever and as far as any members of the religious order there was no sign, so they continued up the road. It was a fairly steep climb for those wearing motorcycle leathers, but of the dwelling they were seeking, there could be no doubt at all. Two flat roofed, whitewashed low buildings lay to the left hand side of the road on the skyline and when the advocate and the doctor reached them, they realised that it was the end of the road.

"Is this it?" Louise asked and Price nodded.

"The road comes to an end right here, and according to this sign, there's nothing ahead of us but the Chasms, whatever they are. If anything, I'd say these houses are even closer to the radio beacon than the farm. Anyway, there seems to be a bit more signs of life here than in the rest of the village" he added, pointing to a couple of motorbikes that were parked outside. A wispy thread of white wood smoke spiralled upwards from one of the building's chimneys and a brace of powerful Suzuki motorcycles were propped up on their side-stands by the side of the road. "GSXR 1000 race replicas," Price commented, "not *quite* what we've come to expect from our Russian friends, but I suppose even Russians have to eventually move with the times. Shall I knock, or will you?" The advocate said nothing and Price moved to the door. He had just about summoned up the courage to announce his presence when the door opened and a low voice within hissed.

"Come in…quickly, do not stay out there." Price obeyed without question and as Louise followed him in, she raised her eyebrows as if to say 'here we go again'.

Price had immediately recognised the voice as that of his old friend Boroweski, but the man seemed tense and far from his usual self. He was on his own and it transpired that he had followed them with binoculars from almost the moment they arrived on the scene. He showed some discontent about the mode of their arrival so the advocate tried to placate him to some degree.

"Mikael, we're dressed as bikers and for this fortnight that's about as good a disguise as it gets. We're blending in with the local scenery and even here, in Cregneash we'll fit in. What is it that makes you so paranoid?"

"It would have been better, Miss Templeton, if you had just ridden straight here," Boroweski replied, "but to walk slowly through that village without wearing helmets, destroys any possible camouflage that your clothing may confer. Your face and that of the doktor I recognised immediately and if I was able to do this, others may so too."

"No-one was watching, Mikael," she protested.

"How do you know? Did you see me?" She shook her head and conceded that he had a point.

"Mikael, you wanted to see us," Price began, "I assume you're going to say that you're here to watch the races, but I suspect that something else is going on. What is it?" He had agreed with Louise that they would be blunt and open and it seemed to produce the desired response as the Russian smiled weakly for the first time.

"It is bad, Doktor Price, but we know nothing definite, only bare intelligence that there will be a major incident at the TT races this year."

"When you say incident, you mean...?"

"I mean terrorist incident, Doktor; I too will be honest and open with you and must apologise for misleading you last year. It is true that I am doktor, but I am officer with Russian SVR."

"What's that?" Price asked, having never heard of the initials before.

"Sluzhba Vneshney Razvedki," Boroweski replied, "it translates as Foreign Intelligence Service. My men and I are anti-terrorist squad."

"So what do you know about this incident," the advocate enquired, "and how did you find out?"

"I cannot reveal our sources, Miss Templeton, but we heard as long ago as mid-February that a major target would be attacked in a place called 'Mann'. Our intelligence officers were intrigued as they knew of no such place, but a few days later, they heard of the proposed visit of the American President to the Isle of Man. They knew that I had experience of this Island and so the operation was put into my hands. I sent some of my men immediately and as you know, my assistant Peter and I arrived on the same boat as you."

"I can't quite understand, maybe you can explain it to me," Price began, "why an incident involving the US President can be of any interest to you, particularly if it's going to happen here. I mean, without being rude, the Russians and the Americans have never, er, well, got on and the Isle of Man would seem to be just a little outside your jurisdiction." Boroweski's long face creased into a smile again and this time he laughed.

"But that was in the old days, Doktor, now we are best of friends and united in our desire to fight terrorism. In that fight there is no limit to our jurisdiction…and there is a Russian connection, but more than that I cannot say."

"So you knew that something was going to happen on the Island?" the advocate persisted, "are you sure it's going to involve President Shrub and why are you down here in Cregneash?"

"What other major target could there be?" Boroweski replied candidly, "I know of none that could be so described. As for this village, our intelligence referred to a small island off the southern tip of Mann and we deduce that this island must be that one over there," he pointed out of the window.

"It's called the Calf of Man," Louise articulated slowly, "but there's nothing on it apart from one small house owned by Manx National Heritage."

"That was our conclusion too," the Russian replied, "we do not know what is going to happen, or where, but we have chosen this place as our base as we think the incident will take place close to here."

"We might have some information to help you there," the doctor said looking at Louise, "it so happens that we do have some suspicions of our own about your near neighbours." He pointed at the farmhouse just across the hill and told Boroweski all that they knew. It took a long time and the Russian asked lots of probing questions, but at last his narrative came to an end. Boroweski thought silently for a minute then voiced what he had been thinking out loud.

"I agree with your friend Mr Love, the radio beacon is no more than a coincidence. If it were destroyed by explosion or fire, then safeguards exist; it is after all only one in a line of such beacons. The beacon we must disregard, but I am most interested to hear that the Petromax has been tampered with. That machine is, of course, well known to us and it would be prudent for us to inspect it."

"I can't quite see how the Petromax would tie in with an attack on the President, Mikael, but Louise here has the keys to Richard's house so I'm sure that we can arrange for you to take a look at the bike. When would be convenient for you?"

"I will speak to my men when they return. This President is due to arrive a week on Wednesday and leave after the end of the Senior Race. That gives us nine clear days before we expect anything to happen. You have numbers where I can contact you?" They swapped mobile numbers and the conversation came to an end. It was time for the doctor and the advocate to leave.

Chapter Twenty

Sunday Morning (Washington) Sunday Afternoon (Isle of Man) – Late May – Practice Week

President Shrub looked up from his desk in the Oval Office.

"I hear what you're saying, but my mind, like this desk, is resolute; everything's arranged and I sure as hell am gonna go."

"But Mr President, the risk is enormous; this island is extremely close to England and you know how dangerous it is there now. We have men on the ground in this place Douglas and their reports are not very encouraging; the infrastructure is way behind the times, do you know they still use steam trains and horse drawn vehicles for getting around?"

"Well so do I in my ranch down in Texas," the President replied stubbornly, "a horse and buggy anyway and I like steam trains. I've been wanting to see those damn motorcycle races since I first heard about them so your arguments about my own personal safety aren't gonna sway me. My old friend Clint told me it was a fine place and safer than Carmel so if you're telling me that your secret servicemen can't protect me…"

"No, no, no, Mr President, I didn't mean that," the President's Security Advisor added hurriedly, "if you think back to that report I showed you last year."

"Which one was that?"

"The one about the Russian tycoon, Illosovich and the link to Al Qaeda." President Shrub's brow furrowed and he looked a little lost.

"I don't kinda recall it, you show me so many; d'you want to run it by me again?" The security advisor sighed and patiently explained the key points and salient details of the comprehensive document that had been submitted for the President's scrutiny and careful attention in the previous fall. When he had finished the President shook his head.

"Don't remember a thing about it, but you can hardly expect me to remember everything that you put in front of me. Sounds, though that you should be looking at this Russian guy, not trying to blame it on the Isle of Man." The security advisor sighed again.

"We restrained all his worldwide assets, Sir and Illosovich himself is on the run."

"So you don't think he's in the Isle of Man then?"

"No, Sir."

"Well, why in the hell are you bringing it up? You haven't given me one good reason why I shouldn't go."

The President's Private Secretary who until now had said nothing, coughed politely and tried a different tack.

"Mr President," he began, "if considerations for your own safety can't persuade you, do you think on policy grounds, that it would be prudent to give this island the sanction of approval that a Presidential visit would confer."

"What the hell d'you mean by that?" the President demanded.

"Well, I take it that you have read the Senate Subcommittee Report on Offshore Tax Havens and Abuses?"

"I have?"

"I gave it to you several months ago."

"Well I must have read it then; just remind me of its major points again?"

"It suggested that corporate structures on this Island have been used by a number of wealthy US citizens to avoid paying US tax."

"What's wrong with that?"

"It's against the law, Mr President."

"Oh," Shrub replied, not really understanding: like probably everyone else in the world, he hated the whole idea of paying tax.

"Well, if it's anything to do with the Senate, that House is stuffed full of mealy mouthed Democrats and Liberals and I'm telling you now I'm not going to cancel my visit because of anything to do with them. I'm going to watch a motorbike race, not debate national policy and that, gentlemen, is the end of that."

When Jonathon Price and Louise Templeton left Cregneash, she told him that she needed to return to her office, to get on with some paperwork and begin the preparation for Richard's trial. Price took this as his cue to do some sightseeing so he rode back to Port Erin and spent an hour or so walking around. After that, he took the Triumph over the Sloc road to Glen Maye and parked up to have a look at the Glen and its waterfalls, before finally riding down to the western city of Peel. It was called a city simply because it had a cathedral and in terms of size it was particularly small. Price had heard that it had spectacular sunsets, but knew very little else about the place so he decided to explore. He pulled in to an empty space by the harbour and, as it was now five o'clock in the evening, decided to find a pub and have a cold beer. Almost immediately he came across a place he remembered; it was called

The Creek and he had paid a visit in Peter the Russian's sidecar on that memorable Mad Sunday the previous year. He walked into the Lounge Bar and waited patiently whilst a blond-haired lady of indeterminate age finished serving a couple of German bikers. When she turned to him, he remembered her face. He ordered a pint of Okells, adding:

"I'm sorry if this seems a little rude, but do you know a man called Richard Quayle?" The pint glass she was holding slipped out of her hand and fell, smashing noisily into a myriad of pieces when it hit the stone floor. Fortunately, Price noted, it had been empty. She recovered her composure in an instant and, taking a fresh glass, poured a pint of the local beer.

"I do know someone of that name," she replied, "he's an undertaker from Douglas, if that is the man you mean."

"I thought I'd seen you with him last year," Price said cheerfully, "I'm a friend of his, Jonathon Price." They shook hands, but the lady looked at him rather furtively. Price finished the beer and walked back out into the late afternoon sunshine.

Price rather enjoyed himself exploring Peel. It had all manner of unexpected nooks and crannies, narrow little alleys and winding little lanes and, although he had expected nothing to be open with it being Sunday, he discovered that many of the shops were taking advantage of the seasonal tourist trade. When he got back to *The Creek*, he discovered that the sun had still quite a distance further to travel before it descended behind the sea. The beer garden outside the front of the pub suddenly seemed extraordinarily inviting and he decided to leave the Triumph where it was standing, have a few more beers, see the sunset and then take a taxi home. He fell in with a group of visiting bikers who were camping on the edge of the town. They were a pleasant enough crowd and the pints of Okells were flowing freely when a voice called out his name.

"Is there a Doctor Price out here?" It was one of the friendly girls who worked behind the bar so he put up his hand and answered to his name.

"Over here," he shouted.

"Telephone call for you," she shouted back. He stood up and followed her inside to the bar, but when she handed him the receiver, the line was dead. He frowned.

"Whoever it was, they've gone," he explained and then frowned again. Who could possibly know that he was here? He shook his head and walked back to the visiting bikers, but as much as he tried to forget it, the incident left a nagging worry in the back of his mind.

"Well I'm telling you, I've spent my last TT in Douglas," one of the men he was drinking with announced to the crowd, "Peel's the place where it's all happening; it's got atmosphere, presence and character and it hasn't turned into a collection of yuppie flats." His companions agreed with him heartily; many of them were seasoned Island visitors and bemoaned the fact that their former hotels and guesthouses had all gone. Now it seemed to be a choice between homestay and camping, unless you were lucky enough to have a local friend.

"Or you're rich enough to be able to stay in one of those posh places on Douglas Promenade," another man added and Price said nothing, being one of those rich people himself.

The sun seemed now to be plummeting toward the western horizon and many of the drinkers began to make tracks for the sea front. It was but a short walk along the quayside and having come this far and stayed this long, Price felt he should really do the same. He reached the promenade just as the red globe hit the water and to his surprise discovered that Peel beach really was the place to be. A rock band was playing Deep Purple and the tantalising smells of a barbecue wafted through the air. He bought himself a juicy looking hamburger and found a perch in the corner; this was far better than what he had seen in Douglas, it was only a shame he had to return.

The sun had long-since set, but the party showed no sign of easing when Price glanced at his watch and noticed the time. It was after eleven and he needed to find a taxi; in his modest experience of the Island such a task could be sometimes rather difficult. He knew none of the local telephone numbers so made his way back to *The Creek*. As he expected the pub was still serving, but then again the Island had long since abolished licensing hours and at this time of year most places would stay open until the last person left. He found the pleasant young woman who had called him for the 'phone call still serving and asked her if she knew a reliable taxi firm. She gave him a number and he called it on his mobile; fortunately this year he had remembered to request *global roaming* from his cellphone service provider and the telephone worked. He spoke to an operator who sounded tired, but helpful and she told him a cab would be along in half an hour or so.

"But do you mind sharing back to Douglas," she asked, "only we are rather busy and there have been one or two calls from people like yourself."

"Not in the slightest," Price replied, "I'll be waiting outside *The Creek*." When Price thought about this statement later, he realised that it could have saved his life. A couple of revellers arrived from the beach party and at half-past eleven a dark blue Mercedes drew up outside the pub. It bore none of the usual taxi accoutrements, but the nearside electric window slid down silently and a hoarse voice croaked.

"Taxi for Price, to Douglas." The doctor who was now more than a little tipsy, walked over, opened the door and climbed into the front seat, but the two revellers from the party decided to join him, opened the door behind him and tried to climb in the rear.

"Don't worry mate, operator said we could share with you," one of them said, getting in, but the jovial remarks were short lasting, "bloody hell, get out mate, there's a fellow in here with a gun." The two revellers piled out of the car even quicker, if that were possible, than they had got in and Price, who thankfully had not been *that* drunk or incapable dived back out onto the pavement having not yet closed the front door. The Mercedes shot off, it's tyres screeching and Price pulled himself up from where he was lying, feeling suddenly a lot more sober than he had been a moment before.

"You all right mate?" one of his would-be companions asked, looking rather pale and a little frightened at what he just seen.

"I'm okay, really," Price replied, "I thought that was our taxi; what did you see?"

"It was pretty dark, but there was a man in there with a handgun and he didn't seem too happy when I got in. Is there someone around here who's got it in for you mate, 'cause that looked like a set up to me."

"Are you sure? I mean it was pretty dark in that car," Price responded.

"Sure as I am standing here," the man replied, "come on, I'll get you a drink at the bar."

Chapter Twenty One

Monday Morning – Late May – Practice Week

Price was tired when he awoke the next morning. It had been a long night and he had consumed far too much beer. He had called the police from *The Creek*, but when a uniformed constable finally arrived, the time was well after one, the pub was closing and the men who had tried to share the bogus taxi were long gone. He had asked them to stay and make statements, knowing that he had witnessed little, but when he mentioned the word 'police' they both became rather nervous and drifted inside to the bar. He never saw them again and the constable seemed less than impressed by his story, based as it was almost entirely on hearsay and made by a man who freely admitted to have been drinking for several hours. The constable spoke to the bar staff, but they had seen nothing; he took a note and promised Price that he would make enquiries, but he seemed less than interested in the whole affair. As a result of waiting for the police, Price had missed his taxi which arrived shortly after the dark blue Mercedes had shot off into the night. When the policeman left, Price had rung for another taxi, but this time the operator had been distinctly unfriendly and had advised him that all cabs were busy and in future he should take the one that had been sent for him. He tried a few more numbers and eventually managed to summon a taxi, but it was based in Douglas and, of course, charged him for the entire round trip. He finally fell into his bed at half-past three and thanked the organisers of the races for having done away with early morning practice.

Breakfast had long since been cleared away by the time Price made his way down to the hotel's dining room and it was almost time for lunch. He settled for a cup of coffee and tried to ring Louise, but there was no reply from her office and her mobile 'phone was switched off so he left a brief message on her voice mail asking her to call him back. Price had to sign on as a race doctor so a trip to Nobles Hospital was in the offing and then, he thought, it would be about time for a blast around the Course, but first he had to get back to Peel and pick up the bike. After his experiences with taxis the previous night, he had pretty well been put off the things for life so he pulled on his boots and leathers, grabbed his helmet and made his way out of the hotel. He seemed to recall seeing some bus stops down near the old harbour and was pretty sure he could catch a bus from there to Peel. Being in no real rush to get there, he started walking along the promenade towards the centre of town. A minute or two later he heard a sound that was familiar: it was the staccato 'clip-clop' of the Douglas Corporation Horse Tram coming up behind him; he stopped in his tracks for a moment, then decided to jump aboard. The horse tram showed no sign of stopping, but was moving at little more than walking pace, so he broke into a jog, leapt onto the running board and sat down. The tram continued slowly and sedately on its way, shaking ever now and then, with its wheels and primitive suspension emitting the occasional rattle and bang. After a few minutes, the conductor came and took his fare. Price ventured a question:

"Does Lester still work on the horse trams? Little ginger-haired guy with glasses?"

"Naa," the man said, "hasn't done since last summer; someone told me he's moved out of Douglas, but I dunno where he's gone." It was the end of the conversation, but Price remembered that the men who worked on the horse trams were generally a rather taciturn bunch so he left it at that, sat back on the hard wooden slatted bench seat and enjoyed the ride.

Although Price knew nothing about it, a news conference had been hastily arranged for that morning to deal with the growing rumours that were circulating about the forthcoming Presidential visit and, as his tram drew past the Villa Marina, Price realised that something was going on. Half a dozen police cars were parked outside and he could see a man holding a video camera and another with a large woolly microphone. The logo on a van next door to the police cars confirmed the presence of the BBC. He thought about going to investigate, but decided against the idea. Inside the building the Chief Minister was just bringing his announcement to a close: he had told the press that the rumours were indeed true and that President Shrub would be staying on the Island for a couple of days the following week and had been asked to present the trophy at the conclusion of the Senior TT. The President, he explained, would be a guest of the Lieutenant Governor and although security would, of necessity, be tight, it was hoped that there would be an opportunity for the President to meet some of the competitors and even, perhaps, be taken on a trip around the course.

"The President has discovered that he has distant Manx ancestors," the Chief Minister added, "and has found out that they originally hailed from near Cregneash so we are hoping to arrange some sort of visit to take in that part of the Island." It was a comment that the reporters found perhaps less newsworthy than the rest of the announcement and so it never made its way into the papers or the evening television bulletin which, given what eventually happened, could be said to have been a rather major oversight.

The journey to Peel was unexciting, but took far longer than Price had expected. The buses seemed desperately infrequent and he realised, albeit belatedly, that this was because he was trying to catch one on a bank holiday. When he eventually arrived in Peel, Price quickly located the yellow Triumph. He climbed on board, fired up the motor and smiled at the engine note. The sun was still shining and the bike sounded particularly good so, rather than head off back to the hospital, he decided to tackle the mountain course. He thought that he knew the roads on the Island well enough now to dispense with the need for a map and reckoned he could follow the coast road to Kirk Michael then join the Course. It was a slow trickle at first through the narrow streets of Peel, but his speed picked up when he hit the open country and the enjoyment factor went up and up. The road was undulating and twisty, just the sort of challenge that he loved and followed a contour which lay just above the cliffs beside the sea. The traffic was light going in the direction of Kirk Michael and at first pretty well the same coming the opposite way, but as he drew nearer the village he began to notice that the number of oncoming vehicles had started to pick up. At first it seemed only a trickle, a few minutes later that trickle was approaching a flood. He passed the turn off to Glen Wyllin and its campsite and some of the bikes travelling in the opposite direction started to flash him and wave in warning so he slowed down and prepared to stop.

The coast road joined the TT Course just before Kirk Michael at a place called Douglas Road Corner which lay at the beginning of the village's main street. The bikes flashed through the village in the races at speeds in excess of the ton, but the rest of the time, a 30mph speed limit was strictly observed. When Price arrived at the corner, after making the short climb from Glen Wyllin he found the place solid with stationary traffic. Nothing was moving in the Course direction and most of the bikes were either turning round or pulling off to take the road from which he had just come. It didn't need an expert to work out what had happened: an accident somewhere further down the road through the village, so Price turned right and took the road back towards Douglas. Traffic seemed to be moving fairly freely in this direction until he came to Barregarrow when, once again, it ground to a halt. He inched forward up from the bottom of the hill until he reached the crossroads by the little chapel at the top, but as he came over the brow, he could see that the queue stretched out ahead of him for what seemed miles so he decided to turn left and follow a little lane which he had never tried before.

It was a route with which he was completely unfamiliar, so he kept a careful look-out and took his time. The road was fairly narrow and climbed steeply up into the hills, but seemed to be heading in roughly the right direction. Every now and again, bikes shot passed him, their riders evidently more in a hurry than he, but Price had no desire to play follow-my-leader. The road opened out onto empty moorland and after a few miles he came across a junction where a branch forked off to the right. By his calculation and the little he could remember of the local geography, the road he was on joined the mountain road at the Brandywell, right by the highest point on the Course, but the side road would take him back to Douglas. He stopped for a moment and thought about what to do. Two bikes flashed by him heading for the Brandywell and the mountain and that made up his mind. He turned right and followed the fork up a moorland slope, round to the right and then down. He felt straight away that he had made the right decision. It was a quiet little lane and, for the first time in what seemed ages nothing passed him in either direction. The lane descended from the open moorland into a thickly wooded valley and narrowed. At the bottom of the hill, a tightening off-camber hairpin exercised his skills in machine control, but then the road seemed to flatten out, although it remained rather twisty and ahead of him he saw the glint of light reflected on water through the trees. The trees suddenly opened out to reveal a reservoir and Price suddenly felt the urge to stretch his legs. He pulled the bike into the side of the road and stopped. It was a beautiful spot, but when he took off his helmet, he realised that the Island's famous racetrack was far nearer than he had first thought. He could hear the whine of powerful engines and drone of exhausts bouncing and echoing down the valley and reckoned that the section of road that went past Windy Corner would be a mile away at the very most.

"Crack.....Crack." The doctor froze. The sounds were not those of an engine backfiring. They came from somewhere in the trees ahead of him and were distinctly close at hand. The land around him seemed like good sporting country, but gunshots are fairly distinctive and Price knew that the ones he had just heard did not come from a shotgun being used to hunt game. There could, of course, be an innocent explanation, a local gun club or some such thing, but his experiences of the night before had made Price ultra-cautious so he put his helmet back on, started the Triumph's engine and began to crawl slowly along the lane. At least, he reasoned, he would have more chance of getting away on the bike than on foot. He rounded a sharp corner and saw a turning leading from the road up to the right into the trees. Following the track with his eyes, he observed that it ran but a few yards before coming to a blind end in a clearing. What he saw in that clearing caused his heart to miss a beat: a dark blue Mercedes saloon car stood close to a black Transit van. The Mercedes looked just like the one he had got into the previous night and the Transit could well be the one that Louise told him Roy Love had observed. Worse still, a shape that could only be a body lay on the ground beside the van and above the body stood a hooded monk holding what appeared to be, no, what definitely was a handgun. Two other hooded figures emerged from the open rear door of the Transit, climbed down and seized the body. They picked up the shape, then moving quickly, thrust it into the van. Suddenly one of them let out a shout and pointed; he had spotted Price. The figure with the gun turned.

"Crack...Crack" The sound seemed quiet and deceptively harmless compared to the boom and roar of the motorbikes echoing down the valley from the mountain road above, but Price saw the flashes from the muzzle and recognised the nature of the threat. The man with the gun was probably sixty yards away; it was long range for a pistol, but Price had no plans to test the accuracy of the gun or ability of the shooter. He muttered a four-letter word beneath his breath, opened the throttle wide and dropped the clutch. The three-cylinder engine burbled then roared, the front wheel lifted and the bike took off.

The Triumph shot past the dam and the Reservoir-keeper's lodge, down a short hill and then up the other side. It was a narrow, twisty road, bounded by high banks and hedges; certainly one that only an idiot would take at high speed, but the circumstances of the moment took over and, although he could see no further than the next corner, the doctor kept hard on the gas. It was difficult riding, but the machine handled impeccably and kept him out of the trouble he should have got in. After what seemed a dozen miles, but was probably no more than two or three, he reached a decently long straight, eased off the throttle and chanced a look back. The road appeared clear…but no it wasn't: the Mercedes and the black transit were still behind him, well back, but moving as if being driven by demons; there was no choice but to tuck in and light up again. He reached a T-junction a minute or two later and without touching the brakes turned left. As he shot past the cottages of a little village, he glanced at his speedo: it was hovering around the 70mph mark, but the road was straight again now and he opened the throttle sending the reading up to over the ton. Another village was fast approaching and a sign by the roadside announced *Strang*. There were plenty of parked cars and the threat of children so he piled on the brakes and sat up. Glancing in his mirror, he saw that this time the road behind him appeared empty, but he was not about to take any chances. He reached a mini-roundabout and at last got a bearing on where he was: the road joining from the right came from Union Mills and Noble's Hospital lay directly ahead. He debated whether to go straight on to Douglas, ride up to the police station and tell them what he had seen, but the events of the previous night still hung heavily in his mind: the policeman had not believed him then so why should any of them believe him now. In any event, he argued, the hospital was a good place to hide and one that the malicious monks, if they were still behind him, would be unlikely to suspect that he would go.

Louise Templeton had been working since daybreak on the undertaker's defence. It was a bank holiday and her office was officially closed, but bank holidays had little meaning to the self-employed and she had spent the time productively, having had no distractions from clients or visitors or continually having to answer the 'phone. The Defence was starting to fit together rather well and she thought, for the first time, that her client had a pretty good chance. Professor Clarke she knew would make a good expert witness and the jury would warm to him rather than the arrogant Dr Stopps, but the best news she had received since she had taken the case on was that her two petty thieves Darren Finch and Jason Quiggan had agreed to give evidence. It had taken rather a long time to persuade them, but she had managed to get an assurance from the Attorney General's Chambers that they would not be prosecuted for any related offence. She had taken statements from them the previous week and filed them with the Court and now her witness list was complete. She glanced at her watch and found it hard to believe that it was nearly six pm. It was time to put her pen down and close the loose-leaf pad on which she had been scribbling her notes. She had done enough for the day. It was a fine, warm evening and the evening practice session beckoned, but first she turned on her mobile and checked her voicemail. There were a handful of unimportant messages and two from Jonathon Price, but the doctor's voice sounded different on each occasion. The first time he sounded tired and a little bored, but the second time…were her ears deceiving her, or did he sound just a little scared? She called the number he had given and it was answered by the third ring.

"Price," the doctor's voice answered sharply.

"Jonathon," she began, "sorry for not ringing you back; I got your messages, but only a minute ago. I've been working all day and I've only just turned my mobile on."

"We need to talk urgently," Price replied, "I don't want to say anything more over the phone. I've just arrived at the Creg; I'm race doctor for the practices this evening can you get up here in the next half an hour?"

"Not a problem," she said, "the course may be closed, but the back road's always open; I'll see you there shortly."

Chapter Twenty Two

Monday Evening – Late May – Practice Week

The course was closed by the time Louise left her office and Douglas was thick with traffic. A ferry had just docked and was disgorging its cargo of two and four-wheeled vehicles onto a promenade which now served as the only link between the south of the Island and the north. Fortunately, the advocate was on her motorbike and was able to move up the outside of the row of stationary vehicles until she reached Summerhill and the road up to Onchan. Once she had passed through the village, the traffic rapidly thinned out. It thinned again when she took the turn off to Creg Ny Baa.

The car park behind the pub was full to overflowing and the large field beside it was getting that way, but Louise managed to find a space somewhere amid the mass of cars and bikes, parked the R6 on its sidestand and made her way into the bar. It was heaving with people, even though the first bikes had only just set off and were not expected past the pub for nearly a quarter of an hour. She had been to the place more times than she cared to remember, but had never seen it so crowded, even on the busiest race day. If that evening was anything to go by, it was going to be a phenomenal TT. The advocate stuck at her mission, struggled through the throng and, as expected, found Jonathon with the rest of the marshals standing outside the front of the building. The road was quiet, but rather than chatting to his fellow race officials, the doctor was standing silently on his own.

"Jonathon," she called. He turned to face her and she realised immediately that something was wrong. He walked over until they were standing close together, separated only by the bars of a steel cage. It was a health and safety feature, which had in recent years been erected for the TT fortnight, to protect members of the public who were enjoying a drink outside the bar. The pub itself lay on the apex of a right-angled corner which formed the end of a fast downhill straight. There was a lane on the side of the building which provided a safe run off for any racer who happened to get it wrong and for the best part of a century spectators had sat happily outside the front protected only by a low row of straw bales. Louise had never heard of a spectator being injured, other than by excessive sun or excessive beer, but some nameless official had ruled it all far too dangerous and this caged monstrosity was the end result.

"What's up?" she asked. The doctor shook his head.

"I'm not happy, Louise," he replied, "that's what's up. When the Chief Medical Officer wrote to me in the winter inviting me to act as a race doctor at this year's TT, I told myself that last year's little drama was down to a freakish set of circumstances and could never happen again in a million years. I was arrested, trapped in a mine and someone tried to kill me, but I saw enough of the races themselves to know that I wanted to come again and thought I was going to really enjoy myself this year. I've been here for barely two days and I'm already beginning to experience a sense of déjà vu. I didn't mind helping you with your investigation, but I'd not planned on taking a major role. After the last twenty-four hours, I'm in two minds about whether to ride down to the harbour, get on the boat and go straight back home."

"What's happened, Jonathon?" the advocate asked calmly and the doctor seemed on the point of spitting it all out, when a travelling marshal sped past and he realised that he had a job to do.

"Not here," he replied, "the racers'll be with us in a minute or two. I really need to go through what I have to tell you slowly, but in this job I have to keep a close eye on the road." Louise nodded. She had no idea what he was going to tell her, but agreed that this was hardly the best place.

"I'll wait here and watch the evening practice. When it's over, follow me and we'll go back to Douglas and find somewhere quiet where we won't be overheard."

The Island was bathed in golden sunshine for the early part of the evening, but the blue skies and glorious weather were not forecast to last. Dark grey clouds were gathering on the western horizon and the advocate could feel that the air was cooler than earlier in the day. Fortunately conditions stayed dry for the practice session and there were no serious incidents at Creg Ny Baa. A couple of riders slid off, but although the doctor ran over to examine them, Louise could see that his mind was elsewhere and she felt a sense of relief when the *roads open* car flashed past. Price appeared beside her and seemed a little happier than he had been when she arrived.

"Come on," he said, "let's get out of here."

The Course was now open, but a uniformed policeman had

materialised from somewhere and was standing in the middle of the road in a brave, but perhaps foolhardy, attempt to stop the hordes of motorbikes coming down off the mountain and let out the traffic from the pub. A traffic jam had been created which was backing up the hill at the rate of a dozen yards per second and the stretch of tarmac which had been empty only a minute or two earlier now resembled a parking lot. The advocate pointed to the back road which led east towards Laxey and Onchan.

"Best go that way," she advised, "it'll be snarled up here for half an hour at least." They walked back to their machines and Louise noticed that Price seemed to examine his rather carefully, before putting in his key and turning the engine on. She said nothing, but pulled on her helmet, thumbed the starter and set off down the lane. The dark grey clouds were now overhead, the sun had disappeared and it began to rain, at first so lightly as to be unnoticeable, but the clouds were ominous and threatened rather more than drizzle so Louise opened the throttle and took the bike along the winding country road at a pace which Price struggled to maintain. They had almost made it back to Onchan when the heavens opened and a sudden, almost winter gloom enveloped the scene. The rain came down in torrents, droplets seemingly as big as cherries bouncing off the tarmac then coalescing to turn the roadway into a broad moving stream. Irritatingly, the traffic lights in the centre of the village seemed to linger on red and Price, who had opened his badly misting visor began to feel tiny rivulets of cold water creep down his back beneath his leathers as he stood there waiting for the red to change to green. The lights changed, but the traffic ahead of them moved infuriatingly slowly and they were still some yards away from them when the green had changed back to red. The rain was growing, if anything, heavier; Price pulled his machine alongside that of his companion's and shouted across.

"This is ridiculous, Louise. This traffic doesn't seem to be moving at all."

"It'll be all the bikes coming down off the mountain and funnelling through Governor's Bridge," she explained, "the police always have somebody on duty there and they tend to give priority to the mountain traffic. We'll try turning left and going down Royal Avenue to Port Jack, but the promenade will probably be a nightmare with the traffic, the horse trams and the rain." Her comments made Price's mind up.

"Let's pull in somewhere and shelter."

"Where do you suggest?" she asked.

"I dunno; you're the local. Anywhere dry, preferably where I can get a coffee," came his terse reply.

"Okay, we'll try Onchan Pleasure Park," she suggested.

The lights ahead of them finally changed to green and the advocate followed by the doctor turned left onto a long straight road which ran down a hill. The road was thoroughly suburban in character and bordered by neat semi-detached dwellings with well-kept leafy gardens. They could see the sea some way ahead of them, but at the bottom of the hill, Louise turned right and pulled her machine in beside the entrance to a park. Price followed her and they ran towards a building on the far side of a boating lake. When they reached the building, she pushed a door open and both of them fell inside.

"What's this place?" he asked, panting.

"Onchan Stadium," she replied, "where they have the stock car racing...and the purple helmets...you mean you've never seen them?" Price shook his head and looked around. The room he had fallen into seemed to be a small café or a bar, but it was deserted apart from a rather bored-looking woman sitting behind the till. Most importantly it was warm and dry. Louise ordered coffees and they sat down at a table by the window. Outside, the rain continued to fall heavily and a premature dusk seemed to have fallen, suggesting that the rain clouds would not now lift before the following day.

"We can talk here," Louise explained, "What's happened?"

Price told her. It was a lengthy narrative, but she allowed him to make it without interruption. When he had finished, he looked a little more cheerful, unburdened, perhaps, by getting the whole story off his chest. She frowned and in the dim light of the café her dark eyes smouldered as she tried to make sense of what she had just heard.

"So the driver of this Mercedes asked for you by name?" she demanded, "Who knew that you were there?"

"That's just it," Price replied, "Nobody; I didn't make any plans to go anywhere until after you'd left. Somebody must have followed me from Cregneash, but if they did, I didn't notice them so they must have been good. And..."

"And if someone followed you, how could they know what you were called?" Louise continued, finishing his sentence for him. "Did you tell anyone your name when you got to Peel?"

"Told a couple of the people I was drinking with my first name, but I don't think I told...no, hold on, I told the landlady of the pub and, of course, the taxi operator."

"Who else knows you're here?"

"What, here, as in on this island?" Price replied, "I haven't tried to keep it a secret; I didn't see any need, but I don't think I've told many people my surname. The Chief Medical Officer, my hotel, the ferry company, you, Boroweski..."

"I think we can exclude most of those. Somebody seemed to know your name within twenty-four hours of your arrival; are you sure you didn't mention it on the ferry to anyone?" Price was about to answer in the negative, but on reflection realised that he had."

"At least I didn't tell him myself; but he heard Boroweski address me as Dr Price." He told Louise about the man with the green Kawasaki and the bunch of German bikers.

"Not much to go on there, I'm afraid," was her response and she moved on. "You're sure it was the same Mercedes you saw out near Ingebreck?"

"That's the name of the place with the reservoir, is it? Well it was the same colour and model, but I never got a look at the plate when I saw it in Peel. I've got it now though," he added, "and the van; I took a note of them both when I arrived at the hospital." He produced a slim notebook from inside his leathers and passed it to the advocate who examined both numbers carefully before passing it back.

"English plates," she confirmed, "and...I'll have to check, but that does look like the number of the van Roy and I saw by Cronk Ny Arrey farm on the night Quilleash was killed. You say you saw someone being shot; are you certain?"

"I didn't see them being shot," Price explained, "I heard two shots then I saw a body lying on the ground and someone holding a gun standing over it. It was a fairly simple deduction to work out what had happened, but they saw me and the man with the gun started shooting so I took off."

"And they were dressed as monks?"

"I swear it; all of them. They wore brown habits with the hoods up so I couldn't tell you what they looked like, what they looked like under the habits, I mean. They came after me, but I managed to get away, turned into Nobles hospital and hid there until I thought it was safe enough to risk riding to the Creg.

"I wonder who it was they shot?" the advocate asked. It was a rhetorical question, but Price thought it had been directed at him.

"How the hell should I know," he replied sharply, "I didn't see much of a future in going across to take a look."

"Did you report this to the police?"

"No, I thought about it, but I didn't. Like I said, I called the police after that incident in Peel, but I didn't have any witnesses to back me up and I got the distinct impression that the copper who came out to see me thought I was barking mad. If I told them about seeing murderous monks, then I think they'd send for the local psychiatrist and probably lock me up."

The advocate thought for a few minutes in silence before finally giving him the benefit of her advice.

"You got problems, Jonathon. I can't even guess who is after you or why, but you're going to have to make yourself a lot less conspicuous than you are at present. These people know your name and what you look like and now they know what sort of a bike you ride. I suggest that you keep a careful eye behind you at all times and don't tell anyone else who you are. Get hold of some less distinctive clothing as well; the leathers look great, but I haven't seen anyone wearing anything remotely similar and they do stand out a mile."

"Okay," Price agreed. "What are you going to do?"

"This must have something to do with the murders back in February, although I can't see a possible link."

"But I wasn't even here in February," Price protested.

"I know," the advocate replied, "that's why I can't see any possible link, but what else could it possibly be?" the doctor shook his head.

"I haven't a clue. Richard's trial starts soon, doesn't it?"

"Next week, I've been in my office finalising my defence and the good news is that I have two witnesses who are prepared to give evidence that they saw Ernie's dead body before Richard returned to the house."

"Great," Price replied, "but if these hooded monks have got

anything to do with it make sure you keep the identities of your witnesses secret."

"I'm not allowed to do that, Jonathon," she retorted, "I've had to disclose their names and their evidence to the Prosecution and the Court, but," she added cautiously, "I'll give them both a ring and gently warn them to take extra care."

Chapter Twenty Three

Tuesday – Practice Week

Tuesday broke with squally winds and heavy rain and the forecast was distinctly unpromising for the rest of the day. For once Louise Templeton was glad that it was her turn on the rota to act as duty advocate at the court of the High Bailiff; after the soaking she had received the previous evening it would make a welcome change to stay inside and keep warm and dry. She arrived far too early, as usual, but the security guard saw her waiting outside the door and let her in.

"Morning Miss Templeton" came his cheery greeting, "can't keep you away from this place can we, what'll it be today?"

"High Bailiff, Duty Advocate," she replied with a smile. She enjoyed her sessions as Duty, provided the lists didn't go on too long. It was quick fire stuff, acting for clients who turned up without their own representation and there was precious little time to prepare, but she found it a refreshing contrast to the cases she had which dragged on for what seemed an eternity, where nothing happened for so long that everything began to seem stale.

The prosecuting sergeant was already sitting in Court Three with an ominously large number of files piled in front of him. His face wore its usual mournful expression, but when the advocate entered the otherwise empty courtroom she remarked that his colour, normally relatively healthy, was a decidedly unpleasant shade of grey.

"It's this bloody presidential visit," he explained, "practically everyone's already working double shifts, but I think that somebody wants me to work triple."

"Never mind, George," she teased him gently, "think of the overtime! What have you got for me today?"

"Take your pick, Louise," he replied waving casually at the pile of paper, "usual rubbish; nothing that'll set the earth on fire. I've had a quick glance, but what with this and that and everything, I haven't had the chance to properly prepare." The advocate shook her head.

"The High Bailiff won't like that, George and it's not like you. What have you been doing?"

"Like, I said, it's this visit," he replied, "we're short staffed, and as prosecutors, our jobs are supposed to be here. In theory, we *should* have nothing else to do, but does that count for anything? No, we've still got to take our turn down on harbour duty, checking bikes and visitors and anything else that the Chief Constable is minded to throw our way."

"What are you actually looking for?" she asked, curious at the immense amount of searching and checking which seemed to have taken place over the previous few days."

"God knows?" the sergeant replied, his hang-dog expression replaced momentarily by a wry smile, "I certainly don't; I suppose anything out of the ordinary, but that's one of the reason's why this court is so big today. We've searched every single visitor coming to the Island and so we've found far more people carrying, er, things that they shouldn't be, than usual and every single one of them has had to be processed and charged in the normal way. What with that and the speeding and drink driving, I wouldn't be surprised if this court goes on all day. Here, take a look at the list." He thrust a sheaf of A4 sized papers towards the advocate.

"Hmm, see what you mean," she said flicking through the papers, "they're not all visitors, though, I can see one or two of the usual suspects down here...Hold on a minute," she stopped at a couple of names that were extremely familiar, "Darren Finch and Jason Quiggan; what have they been doing?" the sergeant leaned over wearily and pulled out a file from near the bottom of the pile.

"Section three, public order, why, are they clients of yours?" The advocate frowned and replied testily,

"I had asked them to keep out of trouble, they are defence witnesses in the trial of Richard Quayle."

The court lasted even longer than the sergeant had gloomily predicted and it was after seven when, her last case duly dealt with, Louise Templeton finally made her escape. It was still raining heavily and she assumed that the evening practice had been cancelled, but worries about something far more important than the TT races were now gnawing at her mind. Her two key witnesses had failed to appear in court. The prosecuting sergeant didn't seem in the slightest bit bothered about it, but the advocate was rather concerned. She had represented them many times before and had never known either to abscond. It wasn't as though the crime they had been accused of would have attracted a heavy penalty; there were no aggravating circumstances and with a good plea in mitigation, they would both walk. She turned on her mobile as she walked down Prospect Hill and was unsurprised to find a text telling her that she had voicemail; more problems, she thought, it had been that sort of a day. The messages could be checked a little later, she told herself, once she had got back to the office and out of the rain.

The tiny office that the advocate was renting was only a short walk away. Her secretary-cum- receptionist, had shut up shop and gone home nearly two hours earlier, but Louise had to go through her post and dictate her letters before she could relax and call it a day. She turned her key in the lock, opened the door and walked through the empty reception area to her room. She desperately needed a coffee so flicked the switch to turn the kettle on, then sat down and began to leaf through her in-tray. Glancing to her right, she noticed that the red light on top of her phone was shining disapprovingly. She sighed and tapped the button to play the messages: there were three of them, but two had been left by the same caller. It was Roy Love, the private detective and he wanted her to call him: it was urgent, he insisted; he had tried her mobile and left the same message there. Louise picked up the 'phone and punched in his number; the detective must have been waiting for her call, because he answered straight away.

"I've had those registration numbers you gave me last night checked," he explained, "by a friend in the Met who has access to the PNC. Both of the numbers are genuine which surprised me a bit, but the disturbing news is that the blue Mercedes is carrying diplomatic plates and the entry on the computer carries a Special Branch notice. It's registered to the embassy of the Democratic Republic of Iszbechisztan and so is the Transit."

"Where is that?" the advocate enquired.

"Impoverished former Soviet republic," the detective replied, "isolated, secretive and…wait for it…thought to be the current abode of the disgraced former billionaire Vladimir Illosovich."

"So that's the connection," Louise muttered, half to herself.

"It certainly is," Love said, "I'm coming over; we need to look at that Petromax bike again."

"I think you'll find that extremely difficult," the advocate warned, "from what I've heard, all the flights and ferry crossings are fully booked for the next week because of the centenary TT."

"Don't worry, I've managed to track down Mike Smith at Pinkertons; I filled him in with the latest developments and he wants me to follow this up. He's flying to London tomorrow and he instructed me to charter a private plane; I've got one booked for Friday morning from an air taxi firm here in Cardiff so we should be with you by Friday lunchtime. In the meantime, stay away from those vehicles and stay away from Cronk Ny Arrey Farm and you'd better tell my old friend Jonathon to do exactly the same."

Louise found the doctor sitting in a corner of his hotel bar. It was around about the time when early doors drinkers had departed, but the late shift had yet to arrive and the place was almost empty. Price confirmed that Practice had indeed been cancelled, but he seemed far more cheerful than he had been the previous evening and, instead of talking about the races or himself, wanted to know about her day.

"I've just been talking to Roy Love," she said quietly and looked around to make sure no-one else could hear what was being said before she repeated the conversation of an hour or so before. The doctor grimaced when he heard the name Iliosovich, but remained silent until she had finished speaking.

"He's here, I know it," he said.

"We don't have any evidence to suggest…" the advocate began, but he silenced her with a wave of his hand.

"Roy says that the vehicles belong to the embassy of the Democratic Republic of Iszbechisztan. That may be true, but doesn't necessarily mean that all of the people in them are embassy staff. When do you think someone from Iszbechisztan last paid a visit to the Island? I'd say never was a pretty safe bet, but whoever's driving those vehicles, or more likely directing where they should be driven, knows their way around this place and they know my name. Take that reservoir, for example: I doubt if you'd be aware of its existence unless you knew the Island pretty well. Illosovich had a house here, didn't he? And he used to visit all the time. He's here; I don't know why, but I'd guess that there's something here that he wants so desperately that he's prepared to take an immense risk. The fact that he's involved this obscure country's embassy suggests there's something in this for them as well."

"What do you think it is?" she asked. Price shook his head.

"I really can't even begin to guess, but whatever it is, it involves our friend the undertaker and the farmhouse down in Cregneash. Talking about Richard, did you remember to tell your witnesses to keep their heads down?" She told him her second piece of news and a cloud passed over his face.

"That doesn't sound promising, Louise; I hope they've simply done a runner, but with this news about Illosovich, I really do fear the worst. Have you tried to contact them yourself?" The advocate explained that she had tried to ring them both, but their mobile phones were dead.

"I managed to get hold of Darren's mother, but she hasn't spoken to him for weeks," she said, "they're both in breach of their police bail conditions so if they're on the Island, they'll be picked up soon enough. It just doesn't do a lot for their credibility as witnesses if..."

"...if they're still alive, Louise," Price interrupted, "if Illosovich had gone to the trouble of setting Richard up and framing him for the murder, he wouldn't want your two petty thieves coming along and spoiling it, would he?"

"But how would he know, I mean only the police and the Prosecution..." her voice tailed off as she realised what she had said.

"Precisely," Price responded; he said no more for they both knew exactly what he meant.

"Roy should be here by lunchtime on Friday," the advocate began again, "and he really would like you to stay out of sight. I know you've signed on to be a race doctor, but do you have to, I mean would they miss you if you just didn't turn up until say early next week."

"Yes they would, Louise," Price replied a little sharply, "I'm here for the racers and I'm certainly not about to let them down. Anyone would think I had something to be ashamed of, not Illosovich or his cronies. I won't wear those blue and white leathers and I'll try to keep my head down, but there's absolutely no way I'll back out of my duties. Anyway, I can't see them trying something when there are plenty of people around. The danger with those sort of characters is when you come across them alone in some dark and empty place. My best form of protection is company and I don't think there'll be any shortage of that this year. Don't forget, Illosovich doesn't know that I'm on to him and forewarned is forearmed, as they say, so I think I'll manage. What about you?"

"He doesn't know me," the advocate said dismissively, "so how could he possibly constitute a threat?"

"Your name is pretty well common knowledge," Price replied, "you seem to be in the local paper almost every week; it's a matter of public record that you did the inquest on that racer last year and you're defending the undertaker next week. If he can do the things we think he has, then ascertaining your identity would, to him, be a piece of cake."

Chapter Twenty Four

Wednesday – Practice Week

Douglas seemed to have filled to almost overflowing whilst Price slept on Tuesday night. When he awoke and looked through his hotel room window on Wednesday morning, the promenade quite literally resembled a sea of bikes. The small groups of machines that two days earlier had stood rather forlornly about the place had multiplied, coalesced and joined together to form one continuous, seamless chain. When the doctor appeared in the dining room for breakfast, a crowd of unfamiliar faces told him that the hotel had filled up too and a brief chat with a friendly waiter revealed the reason for the sudden change: the Island always filled up noticeably on the Thursday of Practice week, but this year the ferry operator had chartered two extra ferries to cope with the expected extra load. The boats had been supposed to arrive the previous weekend, but had been delayed and had only started to make crossings on the previous night. With five boats now in continuous operation the large backlog which had built up was rapidly expected to clear and it was looking certain that the Island would have far more visitors for the centenary of the races than on any previous year.

The rain had stopped, but it was still dull and rather cold for late May and Price, heeding the warning he had been given, pulled a set of waterproofs over his leathers before he set out from the hotel. The waterproofs were of a popular make and design and he noted almost immediately that many other riders were wearing identical ones so they disguised him quite well. He had been told to stay away from Port Erin, Port St Mary and the South, so he pulled out of the hotel car park and turned his yellow Triumph motorcycle the opposite way. He had a notion to visit Laxey and followed the coast road up through Onchan towards Groudle passing the undertaker's house on the way. In the cold grey light of the morning, the rambling house and overgrown gardens looked even gloomier, if such were possible, than they did on a bleak winter's day. Price shuddered; the house had a sinister air about it and, from what Louise had told him about the murder in the workshop, it was now well deserved. He rode on, passing over the bridge which spanned the deep ravine of Groudle Glen and alongside the electric tramway for a mile or so before reaching the main road by the Liverpool Arms hotel. It was busy and he was forced to wait for several minutes before he was able to turn right. When a gap in the traffic finally appeared, he pulled out, but decided almost immediately to turn off the busy highway and meander along the quieter back lanes. A little way further on, he spotted just the sort of route he was looking for and turned left into the countryside. It was a single track which ran between high banks and hedges in the general direction of the hills and as he rode along admiring the scenery and abundance of wild flowers, something in his subconscious stirred and a submerged memory slowly took form.

The lane wound upwards for a mile or so then opened onto a wider one which Price recognised as the back road to Creg Ny Baa. He followed it for a while, then took a fork to the right, then another to the left. As the heather-clad uplands of Snaefell loomed up in front of him, he remembered clearly now when he had taken the road before; it had been dark at the time and foggy, but he recognised the road as that which led to the Petromax mine. Sure enough, the lane grew narrower again and then plunged into a belt of woods; he saw the unmade track dropping down from Windy Corner and after a short steep descent crossed a ford. The place had changed little since the previous year, although the stream had fallen to little more than a trickle and the stagnant mere which had surrounded the old mineshaft had disappeared. Price parked the bike by the side of the road and decided to take a look around. He had been warned to stay away from possible danger, but this place had been sealed by Illosovich when he flooded it, something the man would hardly have done if he had left anything of value at the scene. Sure enough, what little remained of the old buildings seemed completely derelict, their rotting timbers and crumbling masonry now only home to the weeds and fungi which flourished in the damp Manx air. He reached the site of the old shaft and saw that it had been capped by a platform of rough, but well-maintained wooden planking. A new sign stood beside the shaft which was similar to the one which had been there the year before.

Keep Off
Deep Mineshafts

As Price stared at the sign a voice behind him spoke.
"Good morning Doktor Price; you think the same as me." Price

turned and saw Mikael Boroweski standing a few yards away beneath the trees.

"Hello Mikael," he said, "yes I was curious to see this place again. I see that someone's put a cap on the shaft, but other than that it doesn't look like it has been touched for a year." The tall Russian walked slowly over to him.

"Not everything is as it seems," he said grimly, "let me show you." He kicked the seemingly solid planking and it moved several inches to one side. When he kicked it again, it moved a good deal further and a gaping black hole appeared. "This wood for show, only," he explained in clipped tones, "you see heads of nails and think it firmly in place, but look." He seized the plank, pulled it upwards and turned it over. None of the rows of nails which could be seen on the outer side of the plank passed through the other side."

"But, why?..." Price began. Boroweski interrupted him.

"Last year this mine flooded, yes?" Price nodded. "Look now," the Russian commanded and pointed down the shaft. There was no sign of water and to make the point, he seized a large stone that was lying beside them and dropped it down the shaft. It was a good few seconds before they heard a faint splash.

"Well, I suppose the floodwaters must have receded," Price suggested, but the Russian shook his head.

"It is possible Doktor Price, but this is very wet place; streams from the hills would keep mine full of water. Maybe, I think, it has been *drained*; there are signs that someone has been here."

"What...recently?" Price asked. Boroweski shrugged his shoulders.

"Not so recently and yet not so long ago; look here." He pointed at some rutted tracks in the woodland clearing and followed them back to the road. Price could see that they had been made by the tyres of some large plant or machinery, a tractor or excavator perhaps. They seemed, as the Russian had said neither fresh nor particularly old.

"These tracks were made last winter," he continued, "grass has grown in them this spring." Price noticed the thin green wisps of vegetation rising from the soft brown earth and remembered what Louise had told him about Roy Love's trip to the Isle of Man three months earlier.

"I think Illosovich came to the Island in February," he said, "could the marks have been made then?"

"It is possible," the Russian replied.

"But why? I mean the mine was empty; I was down there and could see that nothing had been left behind."

"Can you say that for certain, Doktor?" Price thought for a moment, before admitting that he had only examined one chamber of what may well have been extensive workings, but if something valuable had been left there, why had Illosovich flooded the mine? Boroweski laughed.

"Better than a lock and key," he replied.

"We must examine the Petromax machine," Boroweski announced suddenly, "and we must do so immediately; you have access to the house where it is kept?"

"I don't, but I can get it; you want to go now?"

"I do; we must waste no more time." He put two fingers to his lips, whistled shrilly and two men appeared from out of nowhere. Price recognised the bearded figure of Boroweski's giant companion, Peter, but the other man he was certain he had never seen before. They were dressed, as was their leader in fairly modern biker's clothing, not quite state of the art, but far removed from the gear they had worn the previous year and the machines, he discovered when they led him to them were Japanese and of recent design. The motorcycles were parked back close to the lane; Price realised that he had passed them and must have seen them and something about his puzzled expression led Boroweski to explain.

"We learn from our time here last year; Russian motorcycles okay in Russia, but too conspicuous here. This year, at least some of us must try to blend in with all the other visitors. We go now; you lead, we follow."

Price thumbed the starter button and the Triumph burst into life. He moved off down the lane and the three Russians followed in single file, Boroweski bringing up the rear. The road was narrow and winding, but after a few miles dropped down from the wooded slopes into open country and gateways to large and expensive houses began to appear. They were approaching Laxey and, on turning a corner, suddenly caught sight of the great Wheel. After a short steep descent, they reached the main road through the village and turned right towards Douglas. The road was busy in both directions, but no one gave them a second glance and after an uneventful ten minute ride they turned off onto the undertaker's driveway. The courtyard beside the house was hard to see from the road so Price thought it unlikely that their presence would attract any untoward attention, but he made sure that the bikes were parked in the most concealed spot and then rang the advocate for the key.

Fortunately Miss Templeton was not in court and answered her mobile straight away. She seemed a little unsure about taking Boroweski's help, but Price had no doubt it was the right thing to do.

"He and his men know what they're doing, Louise and they're already here. It's okay you suggesting that we wait for Roy and the American, but they won't arrive for another two days. That may be too late."

"Okay, okay, I take your point; just keep your eye on them and don't let them take anything away. You remember what they did last year?" The conversation came to an end and Price wandered back to the Russians who were standing by their bikes talking in low voices in their native tongue. When Price got back to them, Boroweski looked up; his raised eyebrows asked the unspoken question. Price nodded.

"She's coming," he said, "ten minutes."

Louise took half-an-hour longer than expected and looked rather hot and flustered when she arrived. Perhaps rather foolishly she had used her car rather than her bike and had been reminded that two wheels were the only way to make any sort of progress along Douglas Promenade during the TT.

"Worse than ever," she said when describing the traffic and explaining the reason for the delay, "and those horse trams don't help; they really should put them in some sort of special lane all on their own and out of everyone else's way." She produced the key from her handbag and unlocked the door.

The house was dark and smelt musty, but as Louise explained, such was to be expected, given that it had been unoccupied for over three months. The curtains were still drawn as the undertaker had left them and the whole place needed airing and a good clean. Apart from her visit with Roy Love in February, she had not been near the place and after hearing of the murder, Richard's cleaner had refused to set foot in the house again. The advocate led them to the Blue Room and after a glance or two at the other motorcycles in the collection they walked over to the black and gold Petromax machine. Boroweski looked at his companion, the one Price had never seen before; he was a slightly built rather studious-looking type who, whether because of a natural reticence or inability to speak English had remained silent until now.

"Сергей, время для работы!" Boroweski said sharply and the words had the air of a command.

"это будет машиной?" the man said pointing at the Petromax.

" да"

The slightly built man pulled a large rucksack from his back and put it down beside the black and gold machine. From the rucksack he withdrew a black case which he opened to reveal a wide range of tools. The man behaved unhurriedly and Price could see that he knew precisely what to do. At first he thought him a mechanic, but something about the man's general demeanour just did not fit with that particular trade. Although unhurried, his hands moved skilfully and he began to dismantle the motorcycle with apparent ease: the fairing came off, then the tank, then the cylinder head. Price looked on with interest; he had seen nothing yet which would give him cause for concern, but the man stood up suddenly and spoke to Boroweski in Russian. The words came out rapidly and Boroweski's face darkened as if he had just received bad news.

"What is it, Mikael?" Price asked. Boroweski shook his head.

"Not good, Doktor; Sergey, he tells me that this is just ordinary motorcycle."

"What do you mean?" Price asked again, this time a little bemused.

"What I say," the Russian replied, "it is genuine Petromax motorcycle; all engine parts are normal. It will no doubt run if you put petrol and oil in it. This is not the motorcycle which your friend the undertaker bought in the auction last year. That was a special machine constructed, we think to conceal and transport engine parts which were very special indeed."

"You mean the bikes have been switched?" the advocate said, latching onto the conversation, "but when and why?" She bent down and started to inspect the bike rather more closely than she had done before.

145

"Maybe on the night Ernie Quine was murdered?" Price ventured, "he could have come across them doing it and they killed him in here and then put his body in the workshop; your pathologist did say it looked rather stage managed and…"

"No," the advocate said loudly and emphatically, "this isn't the bike I saw in February; it looks ever so slightly different and the marks Roy showed me aren't here. Someone had taken it apart and put it together then, but they've swapped it for a real bike since."

"Hold on a minute," Price was thinking out loud, "didn't Roy say that he saw shapes that looked like motorcycles in the back of that Transit on the ferry. Maybe one of the shapes was this Petromax?"

"And they planned to get the fake one off the Island in exactly the same way," Louise continued, "that makes a lot of sense, particularly if they time their exit for the end of the TT when there'll be thousands of vans and motorcycles flooding onto the ferries. Is that how you read it, Mikael?"

"Perhaps, Miss Templeton," the tall Russian replied, "I think, yes, Illosovich still had very special engine parts at the bottom of that mine and those parts were removed and put in the other Petromax which has since been removed, but what Illosovich is to do with it, of that I am not clear…Still, there is but one course of action now open to us. We must find Illosovich and the machine."

"Isn't he in Cronk Ny Arrey Farm?" Louise asked, rather surprised at what Boroweski had just said.

"No Miss Templeton," he replied, "we have watched the farm closely, but no-one has gone near it since the day my men arrived."

Chapter Twenty Five

Thursday Morning – Practice Week

Thursday had traditionally been set aside for afternoon practice and Price had expected this year to be no different to any other, but when the day arrived and he checked his instructions, he discovered that the afternoon session had been moved to the evening and so he had a few hours of unexpected free time. He had spent the previous evening on the mountain, but it had been windy and cold and miserable and from the relatively slow speed and unadventurous lines of the riders, it seemed that most of them had felt exactly the same way.

Price was unsure about what to do. The news that their adversary's location was unknown made the earlier advice to avoid the south of the Island redundant; in fact, he thought, it could be argued that the south was exactly the place to go. He had decided to take no more part in the advocate's investigation, reasoning that there was no need for amateur meddlers now that a whole host of professionals were involved. In the end, after toying with various ideas, he left the bike behind at the hotel and went for a walk up towards the paddock area behind the grandstand.

The weather had improved from that of the previous two days, but still looked unsettled and although most of the sky was now blue, banks of dark grey cumulo-nimbus hung threateningly close at hand. Rather than take the risk of a complete soaking, Price pulled a paddock jacket over his shoulders and started up the road behind his hotel that led up to the top of the cliffs. There was an old funicular railway which once ran to a hotel above the one he was staying at. The hotel had long since been turned into offices, but the rusty remains of the old railway could still be seen and as he climbed the rather steep hill, Price wished, not for the first time that it was still running. When he reached level ground, he paused and looked back at the broad expanse of Douglas Bay. It was completely empty of vessels for the moment, but from what he had read, it was not likely to stay that way: an armada of tall ships and cruise liners was due to arrive at the end of Practice week and stay for several days. He turned and walked on to the end of Palace Road then turned right onto Victoria Road, passing by the prison's main gate. His thoughts suddenly turned to his friend, Richard, the undertaker who was still inside those walls, incarcerated and awaiting trial. He turned left and had started up the short road that ran by the side of the gaol when someone shouted his name. Surprised, he looked around; his name was shouted out again and he was able to see from where the shout came. There was a figure at one of the windows on the upper floor of the prison; the window was open, but bars ran across inside it and partially obscured the figure's face.

"Jonathon!" the figure shouted again and this time Price recognised the voice.

"How are you doing, Richard?" he shouted back.

"Great," the man replied, "get to hear them going past the grandstand and right down Bray Hill; don't see a lot, but seeing's not everything and even the food in here is okay. What about Rorletski? Is he doing well or what? Colin Desmond will be absolutely furious if Rorletski wins again, particularly if he does it on my bike!" The conversation went on like this for several minutes and was enough to convince the doctor that any sadness or sympathy he had been feeling for his friend was misplaced. The undertaker sounded far happier than his usual miserable self and had not even mentioned his forthcoming trial.

Nobles Park had undergone a dramatic metamorphosis. For most of the year it served the same functions and purposes as that of any other park in any other small or medium sized town, but for the two weeks of TT races, the tennis courts, crazy golf and football pitches were overshadowed by and in some cases submerged beneath a temporary metropolis of race transporters, vans, old buses and legions of tents, large and small. The hard standing area immediately behind and below the Grandstand became the centre of it all, with stalls, marquees and temporary retail outlets selling everything from tee-shirts, tyres and helmets through to videos and beer. The amateur rugby club known as *Vagabonds* found themselves ejected from *The Mike Hailwood Centre* which formed their club-house for most of the year and *The TT Supporters Club* moved in serving tea and refreshments to the riders and spectators. It was all most interesting and Price wandered around lazily taking in the sights and sounds. His attempts to remain incognito, however, were proving rather unsuccessful.

"Doktor Price! Doktor Price!" It was the second time his name had been called out in under half an hour and Price wondered if he should give in and have his name emblazoned on the back of his jacket like most of the racers seemed to do. He might as well have done so if his attempts to blend in with the scenery were going to have this result.

"Doktor Price!" a man came running up to him and grabbed him by the hand. Price was lost for a moment, but then managed to put a name to the face.

"Andre, Andre Rorletski," he exclaimed, "good to see you again; I've just been speaking to your sponsor and he's rather pleased with your practice times." The tall young Russian glanced momentarily towards the prison then turned back to face Price and smiled.

"Yes I know, I go there every day and report on how the machine behaving on each corner of every lap."

"What, they let you go in and see him?" Price asked.

"Yes, Prison Governor is great fan of TT Races and he wish to give me all the help he can. He say that because Richard on remand, he allowed special privileges and because Richard have no family, the prison, it treat me as his son." Rorletski sounded enthusiastic and asked Price to come over to see the race bikes. He pointed out where exactly his team had set up their base in the paddock and Price promised to pay a visit a little later on. On that note, the evidently very busy young Russian said goodbye and dashed off.

"Hello Doc." It was another voice that Price vaguely recognised. He turned and saw that it was the man he had met in the queue at Liverpool; he remembered the face, but could not recall the name. "Des," the man helpfully reminded him, "how you getting' on?"

"Pretty well," Price responded, "at least I haven't had to deal with any accidents yet."

"Good," Des replied, "let's hope it stays that way, eh?" He wandered off into the crowd and Price frowned; something about the man seemed familiar, he'd seen him somewhere other than at the dock in Liverpool and on the ferry, but he couldn't quite remember where. He wandered around the stalls for half-an-hour or so then made his way over to the paddock. A bored-looking security guard asked him for his pass which was rather inconvenient as he had left it back at the hotel, but he managed to talk his way past the man without too much trouble and into the area bounded by a tall steel and wire fence. The fence was a temporary measure, he later learned, to keep out unwelcome visitors and reduce the growing problem of theft from competitors vehicles, but judging by the number of gaps Price could see in it, compounded by the ease with which he had got passed the security guard, it could be little more than a token offering.

Rorletski's team were based in an old single-decker bus that had been converted into a bike transporter and mobile home. It was life on a much more humble scale than the grand black and gold Petromax race transporter of the previous year, but the man himself seemed far happier and beamed in delight when the doctor appeared. Rorletski insisted in showing Price around the vehicle, pointing out with great pride every minor home-spun piece of alteration or conversion, before finally unveiling the brace of Hondas which he was campaigning that year.

"How are they?" Price asked.

"Very fast," the Russian replied, "as fast, maybe even faster than the Petromax and they handle much better. Richard spend plenty of money on setting them up; they as good as the works machines." Price knew that they would have to be good for Rorletski, despite his formidable talent, to stand much of a chance against the array of super-trick machinery wielded by the mighty factory teams. Blessed with almost unlimited budgets, they used motorcycle races in general and the TT in particular to promote and sell their road-going bikes. The centenary races seemed to dangle an almost irresistible carrot before the likes of Honda, Suzuki, Yamaha and Kawasaki, with the victorious manufacturer almost assured of dramatically increased sales over the forthcoming year. It was no surprise that they had wasted little time in signing up the world's greatest road racers to help them achieve that aim with no fewer than six former race winners returning to the TT, some after an absence of several years. The only surprise was that Rorletski, the previous year's double winner had chosen a privateer outfit rather than the glamour, kudos and undoubted big pay cheque that went hand in hand with riding for one of the household names. Price asked Rorletski why?

"Richard ask me first," came the simple and honest reply, "and he arrange for me to come and live in the Island and get me a job. When Petromax sack me, I have nothing, but now I am Comeover; one day I will be Stopover...see I even learn Manx words!" He smiled triumphantly and the doctor laughed.

"I'm glad you like it here." He could see Rorletski's mechanic hovering in the background and took that as his cue to leave. With only one mechanic and little else in the way of assistance, the young Russian had to take a far more hands-on approach to everything than many of his rivals, but in some ways that had its own advantages. Price recalled that the great Joey Dunlop always worked on his own machines; on a course as demanding as the Mountain Circuit course knowledge and mechanical sympathy went hand in hand in the battle to achieve ultimate speed. He said goodbye, but all the talk of bikes had started to make him miss his so he decided to return to the hotel, put on his leathers and do something he had yet to do that year: take a lap around the Course.

The road was even busier than Price had imagined possible when he filtered onto the Course at St Ninian's crossroads and began the descent of Bray Hill. Happy memories of his ride on closed roads the previous year were now rapidly fading and what he recalled had been a plummet down the hill at breakneck speeds was today reduced to an asthmatic crawl. The traffic backed up seamlessly from the twin roundabouts of Quarter Bridge, but even after he had left that particular bottle-neck well behind, things did not improve dramatically and he realised that it was going to be a long, slow haul. The speed limit signs appeared to have migrated since the previous year with far less of the Course unrestricted than he remembered, but the sheer volume of bikes, along with cars, wagons, buses, tractors, cyclists…the list was endless, using the road meant that even forty mile an hour was an unrealistically high speed to try to achieve. Things might improve over the mountain, he thought, but he doubted it and couldn't face the prolonged crawl that would be necessary just to test out the hypothesis so took the road straight on at Ballacraine traffic lights and headed out to Peel.

The road became noticeably quieter once Price had left the Course and after he had passed through the sleepy hamlet of St John's and left the ancient Tynwald Hill behind him, he struck one of the few unrestricted stretches of tarmac that still remained on the Island. The speedometer climbed rapidly for a few seconds, but remembering the blind entrance to a quarry some distance ahead on the right, he thought better of releasing any pent up frustration in that particular way and shut off the throttle. A wagon appeared at the entrance as if to endorse his decision and the doctor braked, then carried on sedately until the hilltop cemetery on the left of him heralded the beginning of the thirty zone in the ancient city of Peel. He had no particular plans so rode down to the harbour and parked the bike by the *Creek*. Taking off his helmet, he glanced at his watch and noticed that it was a shade after one. He had heard that the pub was noted for its sea food and, as the evening would be spent at the practices, he thought a midday meal would serve him well and set him up properly for the rest of the day. It was, of course, an ordinary working day and the pub was far quieter than when he had visited on the previous Sunday so he went inside, took a seat at an empty table and, feeling a need to spoil himself, ordered lobster. The blond-haired lady was not present, but one of the barmaids remembered him and within a few minutes he had placed and paid for his order and was sitting back relaxing, in contemplation and eager anticipation of the dish he was to be served.

Looking out through the window at the traffic passing along the quay, he noticed a figure on a green motorcycle draw up alongside his machine. Both the figure and the motorcycle looked familiar and in flash he remembered that he had seen them before when he had been sitting outside drinking four days before. The number plates were English and Price wondered whether it was a visitor staying in Peel, when the figure removed his helmet allowing Price a clear view of his face. It was the fellow from the queue for the ferry: the cockney who said his name was Des. Price inched back from the window; something about this man concerned him and he felt it would be better if he were not seen. The man was quite clearly looking at the doctor's yellow Triumph motorcycle and after a few seconds he produced a mobile 'phone and started to make a call. Price thought for a moment: the signs did not look good; had this man been following him and if so, why? Coincidence was one thing, but the 'phone call implied something more. The man put the cell 'phone back in his pocket, pulled his helmet on and rode off just as Price's lobster arrived. It was exquisitely presented and he had no doubt it would taste superb, but what he had just witnessed had taken his appetite away; he had to get away from that place without further delay. Without saying a word to the barmaid, he walked out of the front door, fired up the three cylinder motor and decided to make his way back to Douglas by the least obvious possible route, conscious that contrary to the advocate's sound advice, he was wearing his conspicuous leathers and stood out a mile.

Price trickled through the narrow streets of the centre of the town and took the road back towards Glen Helen, turning off to the right just before he reached the Course and then meandering through St Johns to Foxdale and back to the Island's capital by a succession of minor roads. He kept his eyes peeled for any possible tail and when he eventually arrived at his hotel could say with reasonable certainty that he had not been followed. He parked the bike and went to his room; although he had told himself not to get involved in this case, the man on the green Kawasaki was important news and he really needed to tell Louise. He rang her office and spoke to the pleasant secretary-cum-receptionist who explained that the advocate was out on business and would probably not return much before the end of the working day. He left a message asking her to contact him, then tried her mobile, but it was switched off so he left voice mail and sat down on the edge of his bed wondering what else he could do. His schedule had him timetabled for May Hill in Ramsey that evening; quite fortunate, he thought, as much of the Island seemed to rapidly be becoming too dangerous for him. There seemed nothing connected with Illosovich, murderous monks or Petromax up in Ramsey, but he would go there in ordinary clothing and just to be on the safe side, he would leave the bike at the hotel and travel by the electric tram.

Chapter Twenty Six

Thursday Evening – Practice Week

The Manx Electric Railway was probably a pleasant way to travel, Price reflected, on a gloriously hot and windless midsummer's day, but as the open sided antique tramcar jolted and rattled along its tracks to Laxey and thence past Dhoon and Ballaglass Glens to Ramsey, a biting easterly wind was blowing straight off the sea and the grey clouds had spread and darkened blotting out the sun. When he eventually arrived at the terminus in the northern town he felt glad that the journey had ended and resolved to return to Douglas by other means. He was chilled to the bone and felt a little bruised and battered by the combination of unsprung wooden seat, primitive suspension and ninety minute journey, but the views of sea, glen and mountain had been spectacular and the end of the line was conveniently close to where he had to be.

The corner was a sweeping uphill right-hander which looked fast and rather dangerous. A large house stood beside the road right on the apex of the corner; it was built in the gothic style and looked as though it would be more at home in a horror film than beside a racetrack, but Price soon discovered that the family who lived in it were enthusiastic supporters of the meeting and kept him and the marshals well supplied with regular cups of coffee and tea. Bikes flashed past at breakneck speed, but although one or two of them got the corner wrong, the session progressed without major incident until just before eight when the light faded badly and the first few spots of rain began to fall. Messages soon came down from the marshals up on the mountain that conditions had deteriorated so much that it was unsafe to continue and the session was brought to a premature end. The marshals he was with untied the ropes between the Course and the side roads and the *Roads Open* car flashed past. The crowds of spectators cleared rapidly and within five minutes the doctor found himself standing by the roadside on his own, just as the dark black clouds crowded in and the light earlier drizzle changed into persistent heavy rain. He walked quickly back towards the centre of the town, looking for somewhere warm and dry to take cover and possibly get a bite to eat, but no restaurants seemed to be open. There were, however, plenty of public houses which seemed to be doing a roaring trade, so rather than stay out in the rain searching for an alternative, he dived into one of these. It was crowded with bikers and locals, as he expected, but he managed to squeeze forward to the bar and order a pint. Hopes of a more solid form of sustenance were dashed immediately by a sign advising that food was only served until eight; that time had now passed and the doctor accepted rather philosophically that he was destined for a diet that particular day.

He found a perch in a corner and, feeling a little too tired to break into the conversation, sat back and watched and listened. At first the talk was of the practices and the hopes for the coming week, but after a while he heard something which caused him to prick up his ears.

"I see that Russian fella, Rorletski's riding for Honda this year."

"It's a privateer outfit, though, not a factory team."

"Shame, you'd think one of the factory teams would have made him an offer, after he did the double last year."

"What about that Russian team he raced for; they don't seem to have entered. I've not seen any of their machines listed in the programme or go past in any of the sessions so far."

"The bikes are here though, I saw one the other day in the back of a van."

"You sure?"

"Yeah, they're pretty well unmistakeable with that black and gold colour scheme, but the bike wasn't in that fancy transporter they brought over last year, just in a plain black Transit van."

"Excuse me," Price interrupted, "but, this van, where exactly did you see it?" The group of bikers turned to face the doctor and the one who had seen the Petromax replied.

"Down near Port St Mary, outside an old house in Perwick Bay. Why?" Price showed him his race doctor's pass and made up a story about wanting to contact someone in the Petromax Team. Fortunately, none of this particular group of bikers seemed to know about the demise of Petromax or its shadowy former owner or even the absence of a Petromax racing team at that year's TT. Anxious to help, the man pulled an ordinance survey map from his pocket and pointed out the exact location of the house in Perwick Bay. Price thanked him and made a mental note of the coordinates. Roy Love and Mike Smith were due the following morning; he would pass this on to them. In the meantime, seeing as he wasn't driving or riding, there could be no harm in having another beer. He asked the group of bikers if they minded his joining them and spent an enjoyable couple of hours before finally deciding that he really ought to make tracks for his hotel. There were a couple of taxi numbers pinned up beside the bar and Price turned his mobile on to give them a ring when the 'phone bleeped, telling him that he had text and voice mail.

It was Roy Love and by the tone and terse content of the message he was worried. Price rang him back and the private detective answered immediately.

"I've been trying to get hold of Louise all day," he explained, "but she's not answering. Her secretary said she should have been back in the office by five, but she wasn't. I've tried her mobile and her home land line, but all I get is the answer-phone. Mike Smith and I are flying over tomorrow and Louise knew I was going to call her today to finalise the arrangements. Can you check out her apartment and make sure she's okay?" Price said that he would, just as soon as he got back from Ramsey and told the detective that he would call him again later. He had a few things to tell his old friend, but a crowded public house was hardly the best place to do it. He rang off and tried one of the taxi numbers. Wary of his experience in Peel, he used a false name and, as luck would have it the operator told him that one of her cabs was just dropping in Ramsey and could pick him up in less than five minutes. A minute or two later a car horn sounded and Price, who had already learned that this was the standard way in which Manx taxi drivers announced their arrival, said goodbye to his drinking companions and went outside.

He stared at the vehicle a little warily, but it had all the necessary accoutrements of a bona fide taxi. The driver gave the name of the doctor's assumed identity and Price nodded and gave Louise Templeton's address in Douglas. They took the mountain road which darkness and rain had now completely cleared of traffic and had reached their destination in little under fifteen minutes. Price paid the fare and then pressed the button for the third floor apartment. Looking up, he could see that the place was in darkness, but it was after eleven now and the advocate could have had an early night and gone to bed, although knowing her, he very much doubted it. The place looked rather secure, but also rather empty; no lights were showing anywhere and curtains only hung at a handful of windows. Price recalled the advocate telling him that she had been the first to move in when the block had been completed. If external appearances were anything to go by, few had followed and as yet she had virtually no neighbours. He tried a few of the other buzzers in the vain hope that someone would let him through the front door, but no one answered. Standing there in the pouring rain, he knew that he looked a rather suspicious character, but could think of little he could do when suddenly he recalled the story Louise had told him about the apartment's underground garage filling up with water. Turning to one side of the entrance, he immediately saw the ventilation grills which ran at just above pavement level. He bent down to look inside and fortunately the lighting was working. He immediately recognised the advocate's motorbike, but could see no sign whatever of her four wheel drive. As there was nothing he could do to find out more, he hurried back to his hotel and made the promised call.

"Maybe she's still out on business?" Price said when he had reported what he had found, "she does have rather a lot of work on at present and with no assistant, she has to do it all herself." He put the possibility to Love more in hope than in honest belief and the detective dismissed the suggestion immediately.

"She knew I would call, Jonathon," he said. "If she was out on business, she would have kept her mobile on or she would have returned my calls. This doesn't look good."

"What do you want me to do?" Price asked.

"For the moment, nothing, but I'd like you to check her apartment again first thing in the morning to see if she's returned. If she hasn't, then go round to her office, speak to that secretary of hers and find out if she knows where Louise went. After that, I leave it to your judgment, but from what you've told me, someone's on to you so take care. Mike and I should be there by lunchtime, but as we've chartered a plane I can't give you a definite time. That'll be down to whatever plan the pilot files with air traffic control. Let's meet in your hotel at three tomorrow afternoon; that should give us plenty of time and we can take things on from there."

"I do have commitments in the evening, the practices…" the doctor began.

"Cancel them," the detective said brusquely, "if Louise is still missing, we're going to need every man we've got and get hold of Boroweski, if you can."

"That'll mean going down to the south of the Island and after what's happened..." Price voiced his thoughts out loud. There was silence at the other end of the 'phone for a long minute before Love replied:

"Someone knows your name and the identity of your motorbike and that information's easy to pass on, but whoever we're dealing with may not know exactly what you look like. They called out your name and you got into the car, didn't you?"

"Illosovich and the guy with the green Kawasaki do."

"We don't know for sure that Illosovich is there and even if he is, he'll be lying low and getting others to do his work for him. As for the other fellow, I dunno; you say he's definitely English?"

"Definitely."

"Well I haven't a clue who he is, but I doubt if he works for Illosovich; that guy only tends to employ his own kind." There was another period of silence as Love thought again for a while before continuing, "tell you what, do what you did today. Dress in ordinary clothes, put on a pair of shades, wear a baseball cap or something and go by public transport."

"I'll see what I can do, but the dark glasses might be a bit over the top, particularly if the weather's anything like today. I'll find out what time the 'bus goes; taxi fares over here seem a little steep."

"Whatever you think best, Jonathon, but don't forget there's also a steam train."

Chapter Twenty Seven

Friday Morning/Early Afternoon – Practice Week

Price awoke early, even though he had gone to bed relatively late. The little sleep he had managed had been troubled by disturbing dreams and had been interrupted by the sound of shouting and then of sirens at some dark hour of the night. When he looked at himself in the mirror his face seemed drawn and thin; either worry or lack of nourishment was beginning to exact an unpleasant toll on him. He showered and chose clothing that he thought would fit in with his new disguise: he would adopt the role of a tourist cum trains potter with absolutely no interest in motorbikes.

Down in the hotel lobby, he sensed an atmosphere laden with tension amongst the usually friendly staff; something had happened in the night, but no-one seemed eager to bring him up to date. Even the chatty Italian waiter seemed reticent and quiet, so after he had several cups of black coffee, Price took the plunge and asked him outright.

"Bad, bad things happen, Mr Price," the waiter replied, "men come into hotel late in night; the police think they want to rob Casino. The night manager, he challenge them and ask for ID. When they refuse to give it, he say he call police. There is fight and one of them produce knife and stab him. He is in hospital and the doctors, they fear for his life." Price felt a cold tingle travel slowly down his spine.

"Were they locals?" he asked, "I mean had anyone seen them here before?" The man shook his head.

"No," he said, "the manager think they Russians, but they get away before the police arrive so no-one really know who they were."

Price found his appetite, until then ravenous; disappear for the second time in as many days. So, the police and hotel staff thought it had been an attempt to rob the casino; he had other ideas. That they had traced him, he was in no doubt. How they had done so was an academic point, but he distinctly remembered telling Des that he was staying in a hotel on Douglas sea front at some time on the boat. He guessed a simple call to each of the promenade hotels asking whether a Dr Price was staying with them would meet with an honest reply. Once they had found the hotel, a quick look around the car park would confirm the presence of his bike. How they would ascertain his room number, he did not know, but he assumed they had a plan. He debated again whether to go to the police and tell them everything, but he still had no real evidence and without that his cries for help were likely to fall on deaf ears. He suddenly remembered the advocate's predicament and reprimanded himself for his selfish thoughts; she was missing and could be in danger or something even worse.

When Price stepped outside the hotel, he discovered that the rain and cold winds of the previous day had gone, but it was still far from warm and Price felt sorry for the thousands of visitors who were camping, because they were unable to find an affordable hotel. Camping, to his way of thinking, was just about acceptable on a well equipped site somewhere in the South of France in the middle of July. He had not paid a visit to any of the sites he had seen by the roadside here, but suspected that facilities were rather more basic and, as for the weather so far that year, it had been variable, but with rather more emphasis on the fresh and bracing than anyone would have liked. As he walked down the promenade towards the centre of the town, he could see thin wisps of sea mist curling over the headland and the harbour fog-horn began its eerie boom. It brought back memories of journeys made the year before and, he shuddered; at least making this trip by public transport meant nothing could go wrong.

The first job was to visit the office of Louise Templeton, Advocate and he was standing on the doorstep well before the secretary arrived. He remembered the lady well: her name was Frances and she had been Louise's secretary for years, choosing to stay with her and not remain with Bradley when Louise set up on her own. He explained that Louise had not returned the previous evening and was still not answering her mobile 'phone. He had checked her apartment again on the way there, but it still looked unoccupied and, of the four wheel drive, there was no sign. What he wanted to know, if she could tell him, was the nature of any appointments or business the advocate had the previous day. If they could retrace her steps, they may discover what had happened to her and that could lead them to where she was now. Frances checked the advocate's diary, but shook her head: nothing had been written down and Louise had said nothing about where she was going, just that she would be back before the end of the day. Price was on the point of leaving when the lady remembered something.

"Wait a minute," she said, "Louise had been going on about those two witnesses in the Quayle case. I don't know if she told you about them, Darren Finch and Jason Quiggan."

"The two petty thieves who have both gone missing?" Price replied, "yes, she told me about them the other night; why? Do you think she might have gone looking for them?" The secretary nodded.

"She told me that if they told the jury what they had told her and didn't budge under cross-examination, Richard would be acquitted, but if they didn't…" she left the sentence unfinished, but Price got the drift of what she was trying to say.

"Pretty important witnesses then; have you got anything that I can start on?"

"Wait a minute," she replied, "I'll get the file."

Ten minutes later, Price walked out of the door armed with a list of names, addresses and telephone numbers. They were everything the advocate had managed to glean about the contacts of the two missing men. The contacts would have to be spoken to and quickly, but Price needed help before he began. It was quarter to ten; he had already discovered that the first train left Douglas in fifteen minutes so he made his way along Athol Street towards the Victorian railway station.

He had ridden past the place a number of times and, intrigued by the imposing red brick archway with its gold minarets, had often meant to pay a visit and maybe even take a trip on a steam train. He had never managed to get around to it before, but today the time had come when he would have his wish and camera in hand like a proper tourist, he hurried down the flight of steps beside the archway and into the building. He was looking forward to the whole experience far more than he would have cared to admit, such was the attraction even to ageing schoolboys like himself of the enigma that was steam.

The booking office was open and before it stood a lengthy queue. Price was surprised to see that besides the ubiquitous Japanese tourists and expected train spotters, quite a few bikers were making the trip; perhaps they had grown weary of the Mountain Course, or perhaps they just wanted a change. He joined the line of figures and when his turn finally came, bought a return ticket to Port Erin and walked through the doorway to the platform. He was pleased to see that the little engine had already built up what appeared to be a respectable head of steam and sure enough, no sooner had he climbed on board when the guard waved his flag and blew his whistle, signalling that it was time for the train to leave. He heard the satisfying thud of old fashioned carriage doors closing, then, with a piercing scream of its steam whistle followed by a laboured, drawn out chuff, the engine and its carriages began to move slowly forward; the journey had begun.

It had been a bit of a rush to make it, what with the walk from the advocate's office and the unexpected queue, but now he could sit back and relax, or so he was thinking until he looked around the antique compartment and realised who he was sharing it with. He saw the coarse brown weave of a monk's woollen habit and his heart missed several beats, but then the face of the elderly man within it smiled benevolently and Price felt the tension ease. This was not the face of a cruel assassin, but could it be sheer coincidence that the man was heading south? A question was brewing within him, but first he needed to introduce himself.

"Good morning," he said, holding out his hand "Jonathon Price; I take it you're a fellow enthusiast?" It lacked originality, but was a good an opener as any he could think of at the time. The man shook his hand.

"Brother Michael," he replied, "I am afraid that I have little interest in steam trains, but my journey takes me to Port Erin and I thought that this would be a more stimulating form of transport than the bus."

"Port Erin," Price mused thoughtfully, rubbing his forehead, "now I did see some people wearing the same, er, rather distinctive clothing as yourself, quite near there the other day."

"Hardly surprising," the man replied, raising his voice above the *chuff chuff* of the engine as the little train gathered speed, "a number of us are to meet for a week of prayer and meditation in a house on the Calf of Man."

"A number of monks?" Price enquired, "pardon me for asking, Brother, but are you all from the adjacent Isle?"

"Yes, Jonathon," Brother Michael responded, "we are indeed all monks, but although most of us do come from monasteries in England, a number will be attending from further afield."

"Quite unusual, I would have thought to have a collection, group, whatever you call it of monks on the Calf of Man."

"The correct word, I'm afraid is *abomination*, sadly a most unfortunate term, but we do hold such meetings on a regular basis in quiet, restful spots where we can be alone. I do believe, though, that this is the first time we have gathered in this particular one." Brother Michael evidently did not hail from a silent order and was becoming distinctly chatty as the journey progressed. Price interrogated him gently and by the time the train wheezed into Port Erin station, he had found out a good deal. Most importantly, he now understood that men wearing habits would be a common sight in the south over the coming days. Brother Michael had told him that although the house on the Calf owned by Manx National Heritage was to be their base and venue for meetings, the numbers coming meant that most would lodge out in Port Erin or Port St Mary and be ferried to the tiny island every day. The choice of attire of the mysterious group of strangers Love had seen on the *Ben My Chree* now seemed to make a little more sense. There would be plenty of similarly clad figures they could blend in with and who would think ill of a monk?

Price stepped off the train and wished the elderly monk a pleasant and rewarding time on the Calf of Man, then strode down the platform and out of the station onto Port Erin's main street. He knew that it was a fair walk to Cregneash and had no time to loiter. It could be a wasted journey; he could not be certain that Boroweski would be there, but the Russian had told him that his men kept a permanent eye on the nearby farmhouse so at least Price would be able to get a message to him.

At half-past twelve precisely a single-engined Cessna Caravan touched down at Ronaldsway Airport and taxied to the apron under instructions from the tower. The engine cut and even before the propeller had stopped turning, Roy Love and Mike Smith were out on the tarmac and heading for the Arrivals hall. The security checks were far more rigorous than either man had expected, but after an hour or so they were through. They knew that transport on the Island was going to be a problem; Love had called every car hire firm he could find listed, but had received the same polite, but unambiguous reply.

"A hire car in TT week this year without giving three months notice?" followed by "I'm sorry, Sir, but everything we have was booked up long ago."

Standing in the lengthy queue for a taxi seemed rather a let down after making the trip from Cardiff in a private plane, but there seemed no alternative, or so it appeared until they saw the Douglas-bound 'bus approaching. Love looked at his companion who nodded; the queue they were in showed precious little signs of movement, but the 'bus would at least get them to where they wanted so they ran over to the stop and climbed on board.

The 'bus itself was almost empty and the journey took less time than they had feared. The American, amazed by the amount of two-wheeled traffic on the road and transfixed by the crazy stunts of the riders, supplied a running commentary.

"Geez, look at that guy…he's goin' past on one wheel…he's not goin' to make it…hell that was close," seemed typical of most of what he had to say as at times the 'bus appeared to be moving backwards through a sea of motorcycles, such were the numbers trying to overtake. Eventually they arrived in Douglas and made their way from the Lord Street terminus to the hotel. Love had booked their rooms by telephone a few days earlier, but when they gave their names at reception, they met with a blank stare. The receptionist shook her head, then called the manager who appeared after some delay.

"I'm sorry gentlemen," he began, "but there seems to be some mistake; we have been fully booked up for months. Do you have a reference number so that I can check who made your reservation?" Love handed him a piece of paper and the manager's face clouded over. He whispered something to the petite oriental receptionist and then turned to face the men. "I must apologise," he said, "this reservation has been made in error. I have asked Miss Chan to 'phone around and try and locate you a room in another hotel; in the meantime, could I please offer both of you a complimentary drink?"

There seemed little point in arguing. Someone had been incompetent, but fully booked was fully booked so the two men ordered coffees and sat down in the lounge to wait. After an hour, the manager returned, his red face and embarrassed manner told them that the news he bore was not good.

"I am sorry gentlemen, but we have contacted every single hotel in the Island. All are completely full, but the Tourist Board have informed me that there are still one or two homestay places left. You are over for the races, I take it?" The American was about to correct him and say that they were over on business, but Love replied first.

"We are, what is available?" He explained to Smith a little later that the homestay scheme did not extend to business visitors.

"There is a house over near Hutchinson Square where they could put you up, if you don't mind sharing a room, that is?" Although the manager's words came out calmly, his face bore witness to his distress; his particular establishment was four-star rated and prided itself as being one of the Island's best so to have to turn away customers in such circumstances and then offer such an alternative was something that he did not enjoy.

"We'll take a look," Love said, "can you give us the address?" The cloud lifted from the manager's face and he told them that he would take them there himself.

The house itself was a large modern affair and sat on one corner of a crossroads. The hotel manager tried the front door bell, but although they could hear it ringing inside the house, no-one came to the door so they walked around the corner to try the back. A high stone wall ran down the side of the house and in the middle of the wall was a tall solid-looking wooden gate. This seemed at first less promising than the unanswered front door bell until they heard the sound of voices on the other side of the wall and a racing motorcycle engine crackled into life. Love hammered on the wooden gate and the engine suddenly cut; a bolt shot back and the gate opened.

"G'day," a voice welcomed them with a pleasant antipodean twang.

"These are the two gentlemen for homestay," the hotel manager began to explain, but the Australian interrupted.

"Yeah, Grant told us to expect you, but he's had to pop out; what are your names, guys?"

Love and Smith introduced themselves and told the hotel manager that they would be okay. The man was anxious lest the accommodation prove unacceptable, but Love told him that he was sure it would be fine. With his face now a little happier, the manager turned to go back to his car, but added, almost as an afterthought, that if they cared to return to the hotel anytime and let him know when they were coming, he would make sure that they would have a complimentary meal and drinks.

Chapter Twenty Eight

Friday Afternoon/Evening – Practice Week

The two private detectives picked up their bags and followed the Australian through the open gate into the wide, paved courtyard which stood behind the house. Two men in red overalls were crouching beside a racing motorbike which was mounted on a paddock stand in the middle of the yard. They had been locked in an earnest debate about something or other, but when the Australian introduced himself and them, they stood up, held out oil-stained hands and gave Love and Smith a grin.

"I'm Don," said the man who had let them in, "and this is Graham and Mitch. Grant said to show you around; he'll be back later on."

It turned out that they were a racing team from New South Wales and it was their very first time on the Isle of Man. They had managed to get there on a shoestring budget; it had been difficult, Don explained, but they had made it. Trouble was, they had given no thought at all about where they were going to stay. Fortunately, Grant, the owner of the house, was a fellow countryman and when an appeal had gone out on Manx Radio for help, he had stepped in with an offer of accommodation and room to work on the bikes, all for absolutely free.

"Great place, too," said Don, the rider, "and so convenient. We're just down the road from the Grandstand so we don't need to move from here until it's time to take the bike through scrutineering. Come one, I'll show you 'round the house."

Love and Smith had feared the worst, but were pleasantly surprised at the size of their room and facilities on offer. It boasted en suite and, to be honest, was better than many hotels Love had experienced over the years.

"Do your own thing, guys," Don told them, "cook what you want for breakfast; Grant's cool about that sort of thing."

"What does he do?" Love asked, but the Australian merely shrugged his shoulders.

"Something for the Isle of Man Government," he replied, but he doesn't talk about it and we don't really want to know."

Love glanced at his watch and then looked at his companion.

"Mike," he said, "it's after half-past three...When do you think

Grant will be back?" he asked the Australian, "only we'd arranged to meet someone and we're already over half-an-hour late."

"No worries," Don responded, "like I said, he's cool. Shall I tell him you want to stay?"

"Definitely. We'll leave our bags in the room and catch up with him later tonight." He asked Don for directions to Price's hotel and to his surprise found, firstly, that the Australian knew it at all and, secondly, that it was quite nearby.

"Nearest Pub," Don said by way of explanation, "go down this road, over the main road, then down the little lane by the Daihatsu garage. Follow the steps down to the bottom, down the hill and you're on the promenade. Can't miss it from there."

It was ten to four when they arrived at the hotel and found Price sitting in a dark corner of the bar. The place was fairly quiet, but, for some reason best known to himself, he seemed anxious to leave and go somewhere quieter still. Love suggested the doctor's room, but Price responded with a brief shake of his head so after a moment or two's discussion, they decided to walk along the promenade and find another bar.

"Preferably one that's small, dark and quiet," Price requested, "so that when we're in there we're not as much on view."

A few hundred yards down the road, they found a simple doorway underneath one of the less salubrious hotels. A sign beside it suggested a bar, or maybe even a small nightclub so they took a chance and walked in. It fitted their requirements perfectly: it was empty, there were no external windows and plenty of dark little corners where they could sit and talk in relative privacy; moreover they could see anyone entering without themselves being seen from outside.

"What's the problem with the hotel?" Love asked when they had bought drinks and sat down. Price told him about the incident in the night and how he was now convinced that their antagonist knew where he was staying.

"I can't stay there," he explained, "I've even started to wonder whether they've got a bug in my room, but I've checked all the other hotels and there's no space anywhere; what do you think I should do?" Love looked at Smith who nodded, then turned back to face Price.

"We've found digs in a private house up there," he said, pointing vaguely above and behind them, "it's convenient, quiet and private and there's a large concealed courtyard where you could keep your bike. We'll need to speak to the owner, but from what we keep hearing about him, I don't think he'll object. Do you need to do Practice this evening?" The doctor shook his head.

"No, I managed to get out of it, but I don't think they'll run it anyway. The mountain's been covered in mist and low cloud for most of the day and I don't think it'll lift in the next couple of hours."

"Good, tell us what else has been happening then we'll go back up the hill and see Grant."

Grant turned out to be an unusually laconic Australian who took Love's story of multiple double bookings with a wry, but genuinely sympathetic smile. He did have another room available, if Jonathon was desperate, but it was a little basic, he was afraid...Price looked at the room and told Grant it would be fine. The next problem was to move his motorbike without being seen.

"Don't check out of your room," Love advised, "and take the bike out for a long run. Keep your eyes on your mirrors for anyone following and when you're certain no one is, make your way back here by the most circuitous route you can find. In the meantime, Mike and I will move your stuff. The main thing is for the hotel to think you're still staying there so if anyone asks, that's what they'll be told. We'll leave enough of your gear in the room so that the hotel don't think you've skipped without paying, just tell us what to bring and what to leave behind."

Price did exactly as he was instructed. The evening practice was, as he had predicted, cancelled, so he was able to escape from Douglas and ride until the mist caused a premature dusk to fall. When he returned to the house, the two private detectives were waiting; the heavy wooden gates slammed shut behind him and the steel bolts rammed home. The owner and his Australian guests had gone out so Price, Love and Smith had the large kitchen to themselves. It was time to talk, Love explained and time to decide what to do.

Roy Love began with the background, told them about his visit in

February, the murders and the arrest of Richard Quayle, then it was the doctor's turn to bring them up to speed on the developments in the case and his experiences on the Island since he arrived the previous Saturday afternoon. Both men had plenty to say and Mike Smith, the American, was experienced and patient enough to let them say it without interruption. When Price had finally finished speaking, he looked at the brief notes he had scribbled down and began.

"Quite a few little problems there gentlemen, so I think we're gonna have to prioritise. Finding out who's behind those murders sure is important, but it ain't as important as making sure there ain't any more. Firstly, we're gonna have to find Miss Templeton and secondly we're gonna have to figure out what the bad guys have in store for the President and stop, whatever it is, from happening."

"So you really think that's what this is all about?" Price asked, "an attempt to kill President Shrub?"

"I think we've got to assume that, until proven otherwise," the American replied. "Your Russian friends have had intelligence that there's gonna be an incident here on the Island and I can tell you that we've heard pretty well the same. With all due respect, I think the President's visit has got to be the biggest thing that's gonna happen here this year."

"What about the motorbike, the Petromax, that's been taken from Richard's house?" Price demanded, eager to know ho this could fit in with the American detective's view of things. Smith shook his head and looked uncertain.

"I dunno," he admitted, "but we know it's been modified to carry radioactive materials without detection. I think they just want to use it to get their remaining plutonium off the Island...or maybe..." he left the sentence hanging, but Love completed it for him.

"...they're planning to release radioactive material and contaminate the President, is that what you're saying?"

"It's possible, but I think unlikely. A dirty bomb is not a very selective weapon; good for mass terror, but not for targeting an individual. We think they'll try something far more orthodox: a bullet, or a bomb."

"It's going to be virtually impossible to guarantee protection against those," Love said, "with all the people that'll be here when he comes."

"I think you'll find that his advisors will keep him wrapped up in cotton wool," the American answered "They weren't all that keen on him coming in the first place and if they think that the threat level's significantly increased, you won't see ol' President Shrub walkin' around and meetin' the crowds."

"What about Louise Templeton," Price demanded, a little sharply, "President Shrub's got advisers and secret servicemen to protect him and more than that, he knew the risks before he took the job. Louise is out there somewhere and we've got to find her. Where do you suggest we start?"

"Have you tried all of that list of contacts?" Love asked. Price nodded.

"Not all of them answered, but those that did were no help. Darren Finch and Jason Quiggan seemed to have disappeared off the face of the planet and the more I think about it, the more I'm sure they've been killed."

"But why? I mean if you think Illosovich is behind this, why would he jeopardise his master plan, if that's what it is, of killing the president, by murdering two petty thieves?"

"I don't know, Roy," the doctor replied, "but if they're still alive where are they now?"

"That's easy enough to work out, Jonathon, they got cold feet at the thought of giving evidence and skipped the Island rather than face court."

"I don't think so, Roy, not from what Louise told me, but this argument is getting us nowhere." He turned to the American, "Mike, what do you think and more importantly what should we do?" The American scratched his head before he began speaking.

"What I think is largely conjecture, but it fits the facts, so here goes. Illosovich came over here in February and his plan, at that time was to recover the remaining plutonium. He arranged the first murder; we don't know how, but he got Ernie to the house whilst Richard was out. I don't believe that Ernie misinterpreted Richard's text. I think it's far more likely that Illosovich's men lured him there: maybe they flagged his Landrover down somewhere and forced him to drive to Richard's house. We'll probably never know for certain, but his aim was to get Richard out of the house...long term. He wanted that bike for its unusual properties, but if he'd simply stolen it, then Richard would have raised the alarm so he framed Richard for the murder simply to keep him out of the house for months. He saw you, Roy, on the ferry and thought you'd recognised him; you were with him, of course, in that mine…"

"It was dark and I hardly saw him," Love objected, but Smith dismissed the objection with a wave of his hand.

"…he thought you recognised him and when you knocked on the door of his cabin, he must have feared the worst. They drugged you with ether or chloroform and no doubt had every intention of putting you over the side, but something stopped them. Maybe a member of the crew…"

"One of them knew I was in there," Love interrupted.

"..Maybe a member of crew knocked on the door and asked if everything was alright," Smith continued, "Illosovich would have said something to get rid of them, but couldn't take the risk of doing anything to you. Some time after he gets here, admittedly several months later, he finds out that you're on the Island, Jonathon. You are someone else who has seen him before, so he tries to have you kidnapped or murdered, fortunately without success."

"But, what about Louise?" Price repeated, "she's never seen Illosovich in her life."

"She's not seen him," Smith replied, "but she has seen and can identify the Petromax bike. That's why I'm sure getting the bike off the Island was his primary objective and assassinating President Shrub was a rather later plan. He suddenly saw a window of opportunity and plans to take it, but he still wants to get the bike and the plutonium off the Island and away to his friends in Iszbechisztan. That's why he needs Richard and Miss Templeton out of the way."

"I don't quite understand," Love began, "I mean, he could have taken the bike away at any time since February. Why leave it so long?"

"I see," Price interrupted excitedly, "it's the old proverb about hiding a body in a graveyard. He could have tried to get the bike away at any time, but there was always a risk he'd be seen and the machine recognised; far less chance of that at the end of the TT when it would be one of more than ten thousand and the police and the port authorities just want to get rid of them all."

"Jonathon's got it in one," the American confirmed, "as for what we do, well that's pretty obvious; we search for Miss Templeton, Illosovich and the Petromax bike. We haven't many men, but this is a pretty small island so I think we have a fair chance. I don't really want to have to trust your friend, the Russian secret agent, but we have no other choice. I take it that he will help?"

"He'll help," Price replied with a certain amount of conviction. "He may not have a great deal of love for your President, but he wants to nail Illosovich, I'm absolutely certain of that."

Chapter Twenty Nine

Saturday Morning/Afternoon – Race Week

The Saturday of Race Week began early for the Chief Constable of the Isle of Man Constabulary. The week was invariably a busy one and, as usual, all leave had been cancelled with senior officers recalled from their management courses on the adjacent island, but the headache he faced this year was far more painful than simply handling the antics of fifty thousand bikers. In four days time, President Herbert T. Shrub of the United States of America would make an official visit and, by way of preparation for that momentous occasion, a team of the President's official advisers were due to arrive that very morning to inspect and approve the security arrangements he had put into place.

The whole idea had, in the Chief Constable's eyes, been from the very outset preposterous and he had counselled against it, but the new Chief Minister had ploughed on with his grand plans, turning a blind eye and a deaf ear to the obvious difficulties such a visit would entail. There had been a general election in the Island the previous November and the Chief Minister had a personal mission to thrust the Island and his own image onto the world stage. The Chief Constable's resources, already stretched, showed signs of breaking up completely unless he ordered his men to ruthlessly prioritise their work and put anything that could wait on hold for a week, at the very least. At five am that morning, he held an emergency meeting with his Deputy and senior officers to finalise their plans for the next few days.

"We've put the two murder investigations on hold for the moment," the Deputy Chief confirmed, "not that they've gone anywhere in particular for the last few weeks. We're still no nearer identifying the body that washed up on Douglas beach and Seth Quilleash has not been seen by anyone since he left the Bay Hotel on the night of his brother's death. We've got the Quayle trial starting on Tuesday and listed for three days. A few officers will be called to give evidence, but the Attorney General's Chambers have said they'll try and get their evidence out of the way on the first day. Other than that, everything's been put on hold until after Race Week and we've allocated everyone who's firearms trained to a newly formed special unit just to guard the President."

"*Everyone?*" the Chief Constable asked, raising his eyebrows.

"Er, well, I know some of them are not very good shots," The

Deputy Chief admitted, "but it's all for show anyway; it's not as if they'll actually have to do any shooting, is it?"

"We have to look complete professionals," the Chief Constable warned sternly, "with the eyes of the world looking on, so make sure that you only have highly trained marksmen in that unit. I don't want to see people like Jones from Traffic on Presidential guard duty; I know he's supposed to be firearms trained, but I've seen him shoot."

At eight o'clock a private jet touched down at Ronaldsway. It had been given priority clearance with all other expected flights put on hold. The 'plane taxied to a reserved area of the apron and its passengers were met on the tarmac by the Chief Constable himself and a small delegation of his senior men. Words of welcome and thanks were briefly spoken, then without further ado, the President's men were led across to waiting cars. The usual formalities such as searching were, of course, on this occasion forgotten. The cavalcade of limousines had an escort of police outriders and made their way out of the airport onto the main road. The Manx police had hoped to ferry their guests to Douglas, without delay or upset, but unfortunately race week had just begun. A high performance bike roared past the cavalcade, its rider paying scant regard to the flashing blue lights, then another and another until within minutes the limousines had been separated from each other and from their escort. The President's chief security adviser turned around anxiously. He was sitting beside the Chief Constable in the back of the first car and seemed taken aback with what was happening. He instinctively reached for what the Chief Constable took to be a concealed weapon, but when no attack seemed to materialise, put his hand nervously down by his side.

"What's happening?" he demanded.

"Nothing to worry about," his companion reassured him, "just a little over-exuberance on the part of some of our visitors. The roads will close for racing in a couple of hours and some of the visitors want to get to their vantage points in plenty of time."

"You mean, this is, er, normal," the American asked.

"Quite normal for this time of year, Sir, in fact it will probably get quite a lot worse."

They carried on through Ballasalla and up the hill, at times accelerating, then braking as yet another bike passed and cut in to avoid the oncoming traffic. The plan had been to follow the main road through Santon back to Douglas, but when they reached the bridge over the steam railway, the road ahead was blocked by stationary vehicles. The driver radioed control and immediately discovered the reason: an accident minutes earlier some way ahead had effectively closed the road. Officers were attending, but the Chief Constable and his visitors would have to use another route. They turned right onto the Old Castletown Road, at first followed and then engulfed by a growing throng of two-wheeled machines. The President's advisor said nothing, but the Chief Constable could see the man shaking his head and mentally taking notes. The Old Road was twisty and bumpy and hardly designed for speed at the best of times; the volume of traffic on it that morning reduced their rate of progress to little more than twenty miles per hour.

When they reached Douglas Promenade, things were little better, but the Chief Constable knew they were going to get an awful lot worse. It was only quarter to nine on a Saturday morning, there were no commuters about, roads had not yet closed and the horse tram had not yet begun.

They finally reached Police Headquarters at a little after nine. A journey that should have taken under twenty minutes had taken nearly an hour. The President's chief security advisor shook his head as he got out of the car.

"You say it's always like that?" he asked in tones of amazement.

"Well, at this time of year, pretty much so, yes."

"Sheeeez, we can't put the President through that, Chief. The security risks are unacceptable. We're gonna have to..." The Chief Constable had all his fingers mentally crossed...*call off the visit?* he silently mouthed "...find a better way of getting here from the airport. Do you guys have a helicopter?" At that precise moment, the noisy clack of helicopter blades announced the arrival of just such a machine. It swept over the police station and slowly descended onto the rugby pitch beyond.

"Perfect," the American said, his face, a moment before creased with worry, now wearing a triumphant smile.

"But...I mean you can't use that," the Chief Constable tried to explain, "It's the emergency chopper, strictly for use in the races and anyway it wouldn't be big enough for the President and all his men."

"No matter, we'll get on to the US military," the security advisor responded, "they'll let us have something suitable. It'll be useful for ferrying the President around this little island, given the terrible congestion you seem to have." He had made up his mind on the matter and was not going to back down. "Now let's have a look at your security plans and then we'd better check out where the President's gonna stay; what did you say the hotel was called?"

"He will be staying in the Lieutenant Governor's residence."

"Strange name for a hotel, but we'll check it out and see if it's suitable."

The Chief Constable sighed; it was going to be a very long week.

The crowd at Ballaugh Bridge was far larger than even the oldest marshals could recall and Price was glad he had made an early start. He had guessed that the roads would be busy; record numbers of visitors had already arrived on the Island and, with it being a Saturday, many of the locals would be out to see the race. Dawn had broken with just the slightest wisps of mist on the mountain, but the sun had soon broken through and the sky was now deep blue from horizon to horizon. The first race of the meeting, the Superbike, looked as though it would take place in perfect conditions, but although he felt he should be looking forward to it, Price wished he was elsewhere. He had spoken to Love and Smith before he left the house that morning and knew that they, along with Boroweski and his men would be scouring the Island for the missing lawyer. He had wanted to withdraw from his duties as a race doctor and help them, but Love and Smith had counselled otherwise.

"One more pair of hands won't make any difference to what we have to do," they had said, "and your skills are better suited to the job you came over here for. We'll be in touch if anything happens; if not, we'll see you back at the house." He had reluctantly agreed with them and made the seventeen mile trip out to Ballaugh whilst the road was still quiet. Now that same road was closed and tension mounted; Radio TT had covered the start a few minutes earlier and heads were craning forward, eyes straining and ears listening expectantly for sight or sound of the first racing bike.

The two private detectives' first problem had been transport, but that little difficulty had been overcome almost immediately, for when they had spoken to their host, Grant, that morning, he had offered them the use of his car, not just for the day, but for the whole week.

"I've taken the week off to help Don," he explained, "and I'll be in pit lane with Graham and Mitch. We'll be going up in the van with the racing bike, but it's walking distance anyway, if I have to pop back. I don't need the car so you two guys be my guest." The car turned out to be a rather nice piece of machinery: a shiny red BMW sports coupe with low profile wheels and all the kit.

"Christ," Love said when he saw it, "good job there's no speed limit on this island; I reckon this thing won't half shift."

"Just keep a close eye on the road for all those darned motorcycles," the American advised, a little nervously, "I have plans on getting off this island under my own steam and not in a pine box."

They had arranged to meet Boroweski in the south of the Island. When they had called him the night before, it had looked like they would be using public transport so the rendezvous had been set for somewhere easy to reach. Love had suggested Castletown Square and the Russian had said that he would meet them there at ten. The loan of Grant's BMW had taken some of the pressure off the two private detectives and, restrained by the wishes of his companion, Love motored south at a leisurely pace. They came across the aftermath of the accident that had occurred earlier, but the traffic was now moving freely and they reached Castletown well before the scheduled time.

The square beneath the white limestone walls of the old castle was surprisingly empty and the town itself rather quiet. Love wondered if the entire population had decamped to watch the races with the weather now being so good. He pulled into an empty parking space and the two men got out, prepared, if necessary, for a lengthy wait. Fortunately, after less than five minutes, a large black motorcycle pulled into the square and stopped. The rider, a tall figure clad in black leathers, black helmet and dark visor killed the engine and climbed off. Love knew it would be the Russian; he did not recognise the bike, but Price had told him that Boroweski had moved forward and was now riding a modern Japanese machine. Sure enough, when the rider pulled off his helmet, the private detective recognised the well-worn, but familiar face beneath. He offered a handshake, but the Russian seized him with both arms and gave him a bear hug.

"Good to see you Meestar Love; you look well, better than last time I saw you." Love laughed.

"Was that after I'd been entombed in a flooded mineshaft, or shot at by Illosovich's men?" he replied. The Russian laughed with him and then turned to face Mike Smith.

"Meestar Smith, is it not?" he offered his hand and the American took it.

"Good to meet you Mr Boroweski; I hope we can work together on this."

"So I hope too," Boroweski responded, "we go to the house now; you have transport or shall I call my men to take you on their motorcycles?" Love pointed at the car.

"We have transport, thanks, Mikael; you lead and we'll follow."

They followed the road to Port St Mary and climbed the hill to Cregneash. Love, of course, had been there before, but his companion had not and looked around with growing interest. When he saw the radio beacon, even though he had been told about it, his attention was transfixed.

"You say this house, the one we think Illosovich has bought is near that?"

"You'll see in a minute," Love replied, "it's just the other side of the hill."

"Can't be sheer coincidence," Smith muttered shaking his head. He said nothing further and minutes later they turned left and drove slowly through the village and up the narrow bumpy lane to the single storey flat-roofed house which stood at the end.

They parked outside the house and Boroweski led them in. Love had expected to find the Russian's men inside, but the place was empty with no sign of anyone.

"Where are the others, Mikael?" he asked.

"Out looking," came the terse reply and Boroweski walked over to a sturdy wooden table which stood in the middle of the room. A large scale ordinance survey map of the Island had been spread out on it, held flat by a number of empty mugs. They were old, cracked and chipped, but contained dregs of what looked like coffee and were evidence, if such were needed, that the Russian was not alone. He pointed to their location.

"We are here, in extreme south of Isle of Man. We know this place of importance to our enemy, but why, we are not yet sure. We search for Miss Templeton, but first we must find her car; once we find it, there may be clue as to what happened to her. If she has been taken by our enemy, they will try to hide or destroy her vehicle, but they will do this far from here so that if it is located, it draws no suspicion or unwelcome attention to this place. That is why my men are searching all places here, here and here." He pointed to the northern tip of the Island, an area Love knew to be a sparsely-populated plain. "There are isolated farms, fields and empty beaches," he continued, "where car could sit for many days unnoticed. I have teams of men looking; if it is there we will find it before the end of the day."

"You refer to *our enemy*, Mikael," Love said, "surely you mean Illosovich, don't you?"

"I mean Illosovich and worse people who are with him," he hinted darkly, "I think they, not Illosovich, give the orders now."

"You agree that this is probably a way of smuggling the remaining plutonium off the Island and getting it back to Iszbechisztan," the American asked bluntly. The Russian smiled.

"It may be, Mr Smith, but plenty of plutonium already in Iszbechisztan, left behind in nuclear reactors built in the days of the Soviet Union. Why go to all this trouble to bring some more?"

When Price returned to the house that evening, he found the gate open, but the courtyard empty. Of the bright red BMW, there was no sign, so he assumed that Love and Smith were still out doing whatever they were doing, parked his yellow Triumph and went inside. He was feeling tired and more than a little deflated: Rorletski had been leading the race until he broke down and went out on the very last lap. A well-known English rider had taken the laurels, with another couple of factory riders making up the top three. There had been a number of incidents at Ballaugh, with the helicopter attending each time. Thankfully he later discovered that no-one had been seriously injured, but what with the stress of dealing with the crashes and the underlying worries about Louise, he felt far from his normal self. He went straight to the 'fridge and pulled out a can of beer, then wandered over to the kitchen table and sank wearily into a chair. As he did so he noticed a scrap of paper bearing his name and those of Roy and Mike sitting in the middle of the table-top. Curiosity taking over from weariness, he picked it up, unfolded it and read.

Guys

Don came tenth in the Superbike and won a replica so we're partying. Come down the British Pub by the old harbour and let your hair down.

Grant

Price laughed. He had wondered how the Australian had done as the radio commentary had only given the first six finishers home. Tenth was a brilliant result for them and he felt genuinely cheered. Roy and Mike had told him to avoid his old hotel, but he couldn't recall them ordering him to stay inside. To hell with it, he thought, he was on holiday. He would go down and join them. What could be wrong with him having a couple of beers?

Chapter Thirty

Sunday Morning – Race Week

When the two private detectives arrived back in Douglas, it was well after midnight and, as the house was in total darkness, they assumed that their host and fellow guests had already gone to bed. Exhausted from a day spent hunting through every hidden nook and cranny on the Island, they did the same and within moments were fast asleep. Smith slept the night through in dreamless slumber, but at some time in the early morning, the sound of a door closing caused Love to wake. Glancing at the luminous dial of his watch, he saw that it was it was ten to five. He heard muffled voices, but silence soon prevailed and he went back to sleep. When he woke again, the sun had risen and was streaming in through his bedroom window. He blinked and looking around the room saw that the curtains had been pulled wide open, Mike Smith's bed was made and the man himself was up and dressed.

"Time to get up, Roy," the American said with a laugh, "it's after eight and we still have half an island to search. I've had a text from Boroweski; his men have found the four wheel drive and he wants us to meet him at a place called the Point of Ayre. I've had a look at the map and…"

"I know where it is," the Welshman said a little gruffly, "extreme northerly tip of the Island. When did you get the text?"

"It was waiting for me as soon as I awoke. I reckon those Russians have been searching all night."

"Good for them, at least they've got a result. I'll be ready in a few minutes, why don't you go and wake Jonathon, I'm sure he'll want to come with us on this." The American left the room and Roy Love stepped into the shower, the powerful stream of hot water bringing him rapidly to life. When he stepped out again, Smith was standing there waiting with a worried expression on his face.

"Jonathon isn't there," he said. The Welshman shrugged his shoulders.

"It's a nice day," he replied, "he's probably gone out on his bike." Smith shook his head.

"His bike's outside and his bed hasn't been slept in." Love felt the colour draining from his face.

"Go and wake the others," he commanded, "I think I heard them coming in earlier on this morning. Maybe they know where he's gone."

A few minutes later they were standing in the kitchen with Grant and Mitch whom Smith had managed to awake, albeit with a certain degree of difficulty. His best efforts had proved entirely unsuccessful with their friends Graham and Don. With their red eyes and wild hair, the two Australians looked a less than pretty sight and it didn't need a detective to see what they had been doing for most of the night.

"Wh.. Whaat's the problem guys," Grant stuttered, his speech still a little slurred.

"Where's Jonathon?" Love demanded.

"Dunno, isn't he, isn't he in bed?" their host replied.

"No, his bed has not been slept in and his bike's still outside. You guys have obviously been out partying; did he go with you last night?" Grant looked at Mitch.

"Yeah, he did, well I think he was with us earlier on, wasn't he Mitch?" he said.

"He met us down at the first pub," Mitch confirmed, "and he stuck with us for part of the crawl, but I don't remember him in the nightclub or the casino. He was getting pretty hammered so I just guessed he'd had enough and gone home."

"I remember now," Grant added, "A guy spoke to him in that last pub and he turned white as a sheet. He rushed outside and I thought he was gonna throw up so I went to make sure he was alright. People were packed in that place like sardines, I mean it was really hard to move and by the time I got outside he was nowhere to be seen so I assumed he'd gone home."

"Which pub was that?" Love demanded, "and who was this bloke who spoke to him?"

"Sheez, now that's a question, I mean we went to quite a few," Grant explained, "I think it was that little place on the quayside called the Saddle, but after all those beers, I really can't be sure. As for the guy, he was a pretty ordinary sort of guy, but I think I heard him say his name was Des." Love looked at Smith.

"That sounds like the man I told you about; the one who Jonathon swears has been following him."

"Sounds like Jonathon's been right then, doesn't it?" the American replied. "Can you describe him, Grant?" Their guest tried, but his talents, whatever they were, did not include visual memory or powers of graphic description and the best he could do was precious little use.

"Middle aged, white, average height, average build and greying hair…and you think he had an English accent," Smith repeated what their host had said. "Thanks Grant. I think you and Mitch had better get some more sleep, but if you remember anything else then give us a call."

"What are you gonna do?" Grant asked.

"Well, we're gonna have to go look for him," the American replied and then turned to Love, "after all, we've already got one missing person, so we'll just add our doctor friend to the list."

The pretty little red and white lighthouse at the northerly tip of the Isle of Man had long been an automated station, but the buildings beneath and around it were far from uninhabited and the Point of Ayre was a popular spot for visitors, whether they be tourists or locals, at just about any time of the year. Vehicles belonging to residents, fishermen, walkers or campers could nearly always be found parked there, sometimes for several days at a time. Louise Templeton's four wheel drive had been there since first thing Friday morning, but the man who Love spoke to had not seen it arrive. He lived nearby and took his dogs for a walk there every morning and evening; the vehicle, he confirmed, had not been there the previous evening, so it must have appeared on Thursday night. Further discreet questioning of the people living by the old lighthouse disclosed no information that was of the slightest value in the case.

Unfortunately, the car revealed nothing, even to the closest expert examination by Love, Smith, Boroweski and his men, but its location did suggest that Boroweski was right when he somewhat perversely said they should now turn their full attention to the south. Love and Smith had told him about the missing doctor, but he seemed less concerned about the mysterious *Des* than they felt he should. When they suggested the man might be somehow connected with Illosovich, he snorted with derision.

"Whoever this man is, I do not know, but Illosovich and those from Iszbechisztan would not have an Englishman in their employ," he said. When they pointed out the chain of what must otherwise have been sheer coincidences, he shrugged his shoulders and gave them a curious look. "The good Doktor Price can look after himself," he said a little callously, "we have more important things to do than search for him. We must find the lady lawyer and we must find Illosovich before this American President arrives. Come, let us return to the south, we have little time and much to do."

The assorted collection of motorcycles burst into life and, led by Boroweski, filed off down the narrow lane. Although their leader and his trusty lieutenant's bikes were Japanese and modern, the rest of the men still rode Soviet era Cossack and Ural machines. Judging by the clouds of acrid smoke which hung in the morning air, emission tests had not yet made it to Russian roads and both Love and Smith coughed violently as they walked over to the car. They had no real choice, but to follow the Russians. If Price was in danger, then without any leads as to where he was, there was nothing they could do.

Love took the wheel and drove the BMW down the narrow lane. Fortunately, it was otherwise free of traffic and he was able to keep up with the line of two-wheeled machinery ridden by Boroweski and his men. They passed through the village of Bride with its picturesque parish church then turned left and, rising out of a hollow, saw the town of Ramsey and the Island's central mountainous mass looming dead ahead. Love had hoped that the Russians would take the coastal road, but somehow knew that they wouldn't and, sure enough, when the line of bikes reached the northern town, it turned neither left nor right. Traffic lights had sprouted in Parliament Square since his visit the previous year, but as luck would have it, they were on green and within a minute they had begun the mountain climb.

"Hold on tight," he said to the American sitting beside him and gritted his teeth. The lights would hold up the bikes coming along the Course behind him, but not for long, he was sure of that.

"What's up?" Smith enquired, "this is the quickest road back to Douglas, isn't it?"

"It is, but…" Suddenly a bike flew past them. A 30mph sign told them that a strict speed limit was still in force at that point, but as they rounded Ramsey hairpin, the bike was closely followed by what seemed like a thousand others, all charging manically uphill on both sides of the road.

"…it's Mad Sunday, I forgot to warn you," Love said.

They drove on up past the Waterworks, Tower Bends and the Gooseneck, engulfed in a tidal wave of bikes. There were red bikes, blue bikes and green bikes, all buzzing angrily like a swarm of hornets released from their nest. Easing off the accelerator had no effect whatsoever, for every bike that went past was simply replaced by one more, so Love kept his pedal on the floor and his eyes on the road ahead of him. When he got to the end of that road he could relax, but certainly not before. Suddenly, the mobile phone in his pocket began to ring.

"Can you get that," he said to his companion, "as you can see, I've got my hands full." Smith reached across and took hold of the mobile.

"Hello, Mike Smith answering for Roy Love…Yeah, he's driving at the moment and can't really speak…Oh it's you Grant…can I help….yeah…yeah….what?...are you sure?...look we can't…we've got to go somewhere. Look we'll get back to you as soon as we can." He pressed the 'end' button to terminate the call.

"What's up with Grant?" Love asked. The American was silent for a moment, then slowly spoke.

"He's just got up and discovered that someone's ransacked the house, well, the downstairs bit of it anyway."

"What, whilst he and the others were sleeping?"

"Yeah, must have happened pretty soon after we left."

"What were they looking for?"

"Christ knows, but it must have something to do with Jonathon. Grant's pretty pissed; he wants to know what the three of us are up to. I can see his point, but he says if we don't explain everything right now, he's going to the police. What do you want to do?"

"We better make a detour to the house and calm him down. We know where Mikael and his men are going so we can catch them up later, but the sooner we get back to Douglas, the better. It's a pretty good road and it's one way only so I'm going to put my foot down, if you don't mind." The American nodded silently and gripped the sides of his seat. His face was wracked with tension: it was evident that in the State of America he came from, no-one drove at these speeds.

The BMW leapt forward, but bike after bike still came streaming past. On the mountain mile the speedometer was reading over one hundred and Love threw a quick glance at his passenger, but saw that Smith's eyes were tightly shut. They sped through East Mountain Box and the Verandah, past Bungalow Bridge and Hailwood's Rise. A bunching of traffic forced them to slow at the Brandywell, but the road grew clearer as they began to descend from its highest point. Love took the car through the refashioned Windy Corner, tyres screeching in protest at the speed, then on through the fast, but smooth Thirty-third milestone, the right then left-hander at Keppel before Kate's Cottage and the awesome drop down to the Creg. At the bottom of the hill a queue was forming and Love realised it was the end of the unrestricted one-way section so he trod on the brakes and the car slowed so quickly it felt like glue had been applied to the road. Mike Smith opened his eyes and smiled with relief to find that they were now travelling at safe and sane, rather than insane speeds.

"I'll turn off here," Love said, "and we can take the back road to Onchan and Douglas. The Course gets horrendously congested when it gets close to Douglas and it'll be quicker, even though longer to take the country lane.

When they arrived at the house, Grant was distinctly unhappy. Love tried to placate him, but it was no use, their Australian host was extremely upset. He showed them around and pointed out the damage and disorder; he had lived in that house for over six years, he said, but nothing like this had ever happened until they arrived. Who the f**k were they, he demanded and who the f**k was their friend Jonathon Price.

Love looked at Smith, but the American had no easy solutions. He shrugged his shoulders and said:

"Better tell him the truth." So the Welsh private detective launched into a detailed explanation which involved, by necessity, a Russian billionaire, smuggled plutonium and secret agents, plans for the assassination of the US President and a handful of murders to date. Now, on top of that they had a couple of missing persons including an advocate, Miss Templeton and the doctor, Jonathon Price. Grant's eyes opened wider as the tale unfolded, but curiously, he allowed Love to continue until he had finished what he had to say.

"So Louise Templeton is involved in this?" he said when the Welshman had finished speaking.

"You know her?"

"Strewth, yeah, I know her, in fact Louise and I go way, way back. This got anything to do with that business last year?"

"We think so," Love responded and the Australian grinned; at last they had him on their side.

"She told me about the rider who was killed and mentioned something about radiation poisoning, but she wouldn't go into details and, from what I can remember the Coroner gave an Open verdict. The stuff you've just told me is so far out you couldn't have invented it and if Louise is in danger, count me and the boys in. We'll help you in whatever way we can."

Chapter Thirty One

Sunday Afternoon – Race Week

The house had indeed been turned over, the two private detectives agreed, but who had done it or why, they could not even begin to guess. Grant and his friends had heard nothing, but freely admitted they had been dead, or as good as dead, to the world for most of the morning. The only thing that any of them could think of was the disappearance of Jonathon Price, but as Love pointed out: what could there possibly be of his that anyone would want so much as to take the risk of burglary in broad daylight? They looked carefully around the house, but Grant eventually declared that nothing seemed to be missing, even though every drawer and cupboard seemed to have been searched. Reassured that none of his or his guests' possessions had been taken, the Australian sat down and for a few moments seemed deep in silent thought.

"I suppose there *could* be a connection with what I do," he suggested eventually, "but I can't see how this guy Illosovich found out who I am or where I live."

"What do you do, Grant?" the two private detectives chimed in unison.

"I, er, work for the Isle of Man Government," he ventured cautiously, "in the investigation and prosecution of Financial Crime."

"You're a policeman?" Love asked.

"No, an advocate," he replied, "that's how I came to know Louise, but I've long been out of private practice. I've worked for the Attorney General for a number of years."

"So you know about Illosovich?" the American enquired.

"I know about the American and the Russian investigations and I know about the worldwide restraint orders freezing all his assets, in fact I was the man responsible for enforcing them on the Isle of Man. Do you think that could have something to do with this burglary?" Smith nodded.

"Seems possible, maybe even likely; is there anything you have that he might want?" The Australian thought again for a few moments then shook his head.

"Everything I have connected with Illosovich is in my office; I hardly ever bring anything like that home, except, of course, my laptop, but that was the first thing I checked and it's still locked in a secure cabinet in my bedroom. I suppose he could have been after that, but how would he know it even existed, never mind what it contained?"

"Does it hold anything he would consider useful?" Smith asked.

"Yeah, I reckon it does," Grant replied, "a file full of e-mails and documents detailing the evidence against him and an indexed summary of all the restrained accounts. If he had that he would know who had given evidence against him and what they had said. He'd discover the full case against him and be able to work out which of his assets, if any, the authorities knew nothing about."

"Sounds like the sort of thing a desperate man would risk murder for, never mind domestic burglary," Love advised, "he'd be able to interfere with witnesses and access any funds you had no knowledge of without the risk of being caught. Does anyone else know about this laptop?"

"Well, it's hardly a state secret," the Australian replied, "I suppose everyone in the Attorney General's Chambers would be aware of it and of course, the people in the FCU."

"What's that?" the Welshman asked.

"Financial Crime Unit," Grant explained, "it's a division of the Isle of Man Constabulary which deals with what its title suggests…They're a sound bunch of people though," he added, "if you're trying to suggest one of them is on the take."

"I'm not suggesting that for one minute," Love said, "if they were, then I suppose they could have got to you long before now. The laptop's safe, you say, for the moment. I suggest you put it somewhere safer still."

"I'll go straight down and lock it in my office; what do you propose we do then? Like I said, I want to help and Don, Graham and Mitch are up for that too."

"What, no races to prepare for?" the Welshman asked with a smile. Don, who along with the two others had been standing there silently listening, took the question as one meant for him.

"Naa, we're not out racing now until the Senior on Friday; only got the one bike, you see. I'll probably have a practice lap on Monday and another on Wednesday, but she's runnin' like a beauty so why change anything. We'll come with you; sounds like great sport."

"It could be dangerous," Love advised.

"Even better," Don replied with a smile.

Fifteen minutes later, the team had been assembled. The house, their host explained, could be tidied up later; now, there really was no time to lose. With the two private detectives leading in the red BMW and the four Australians bundled into their old van behind, they drove to the Chambers of HM Attorney General where Grant hurriedly locked away his computer, then set off for the south of the island.

They had arranged to meet Boroweski by the harbour in Port St Mary, having already called him on his mobile and explained the reason for their delay. When they got there, the Russian was alone and pacing around impatiently. His men, he said, were searching the nearby hamlet of Fistard which lay on the hillside above Perwick Bay. Grant, as an officer of the court and employee of the Attorney General found Boroweski's statement rather hard to take.

"But you don't have any rights of search or entry," he protested, "if your men are going into properties under any pretence whatsoever, then I'm afraid they're breaking the law." The Russian commander laughed.

"My men break no laws," he replied, "they simply visitors to Isle of Man TT races who looking for somewhere to stay. Most times, the local people friendly and invite them in for cup of tea; if they see or hear anything they think suspicious then they report back to me."

"Sounds a good idea," Grant said, nodding with approval, "just the sort of trick a wandering, homeless Aussie racing team could try. How about it guys?" Don, Graham and Mitch gave the plan an enthusiastic thumbs up and Boroweski spread his large scale map out on the bonnet of the BMW.

"We must cover all this area," he explained, "then here, then here." His long, thin fingers darted rapidly about the map and the others crowded around to see. When he had finished, Grant led his fellow Australians over to the van.

"Better get started," he said as a parting shot, "it's gonna take us most of the rest of the day to get through that little lot." The diesel engine coughed into life and, followed by an unhealthy-looking cloud of black smoke, the tired and battered old van headed off down the street. Love looked at Smith and then at Boroweski.

"Those guys can get away with a story like that," he said, "they just look the sort of people who would turn up on the Isle of Man without bothering to find somewhere to stay...well," he suddenly remembered, "that's exactly what they did do, isn't it? But I think Mike and I might have problems trying to use the same ploy; we, er, just don't look the part." Boroweski looked at the two private detectives; they were casually dressed, in as much as they weren't wearing suits, but their attire was, well, a little too smart to convince anyone that they were a couple of itinerant bikers looking for accommodation.

"I think, perhaps, you are right," he agreed, "and for you, I have other plans."

Boroweski wanted someone to pay a visit to the Calf of Man and it looked like the two private detectives had inadvertently volunteered. A cover story was necessary for, as they all knew, the tiny island had become the focal point of a gathering of monks who, presumably would not take too kindly to being disturbed. The sophisticated cameras which he had noticed both men carried had given him an idea. It would be accepted by any boatman as a perfectly good reason for wanting to travel to the Calf and would, he hoped, prove acceptable to those who were already there.

"Bird-watchers," Love spat out the word in disgust after the Russian had explained, "but I don't know the slightest thing about ornithology; do you Mike?" The American shook his head.

"Nothing, but I can see Mikael's point. It gives a perfect excuse to go wandering around with the long range lenses taking pictures of anything we want. Do you really thing there is anything over there that could help us, Mikael?" The Russian shrugged his shoulders and held out his open palms in a gesture which indicated he was unsure.

"Our original intelligence suggest incident on small island to south of Isle of Man, but we think intelligence not quite accurate. We think incident will be on Isle of Man itself, maybe house by radar beacon, but we must check other island just to be sure. Can you do this?"

"We'll try, any ideas how we get there?" the Welshman asked. Boroweski nodded.

"We have discovered that there are two boatmen who have licenses to take passengers to island. One here, in Port St Mary, one in next village, Port Erin. The boats make trip every morning, but perhaps, if you ask them nicely, they make extra trip today?"

"It's worth a try. Come on Mike."

Boroweski told them the name of the boat and that of it's skipper, and although unsure of its exact departure point, thought it somewhere close at hand so Love and the American wandered along from the harbour car park to the collection of low buildings at the foot of the breakwater. It seemed the obvious place to start looking and within minutes, their quest seemed about to succeed. They found a small wooden hut, presumably a little kiosk, bearing a sign which informed passers-by that trips to the Calf departed every morning from the end of the jetty at ten-fifteen. Unfortunately, the time was now well after three; the shutters had been pulled down over the front of the kiosk and its door was firmly locked. They carried on walking and in time reached the end of the jetty, but every boat moored alongside it appeared deserted and, apart from a handful of children fishing, no-one seemed to be about.

"What now?" Smith asked.

"I think we'll try that little pub I discovered back in February. It's called the *Bay View* and it's just along the road; come on, let's go back to the car."

"Why go to the pub?" the American asked, seemingly mystified by his companion's response, "shouldn't we drive over to Port Erin and try and find the boatman there?"

"We will, if we need to," Love explained, "but in little places like this you can usually find out everything you need to in the local pub. In fact, I wouldn't mind betting that's where everyone is."

Roy Love's speculative suggestion proved uncannily accurate for although the village streets were empty, when they had parked the car outside the pub and opened the door, they were met by a wall of sound. It was the sound of laughter and talking and shouting and singing, all at the very same time. The *Bay View* was obviously the place where it was all happening that Sunday afternoon, for the little public house was packed to the roof. It took the two men all their time just to squeeze in through the door and worm their way to the bar. Fortunately, the landlord recognised Love and welcomed him as a long-lost friend; the Welshman shook his hand and suspected, on the strength of the warmth of the welcome, that the landlord might well have had rather a lot of drink.

"What are you two fellas up to then?" he asked, after Love had introduced Smith and he had poured them both drinks which he insisted were 'on the house', "Still investigating old Ken Quilleash's death, are you?" The Welshman smiled.

"Sort of," he replied, "but what we really need at the moment is to find someone who'll take us to the Calf. I hear that there are a couple of boatmen who make the journey and I just wondered if you know either of them?" The landlord, who was a hearty, stout and red-faced fellow roared with laughter.

"Know 'em?...I'll say I know 'em...when they're not out on their boats, they spend most of their time in here. They're both here now...Alf, Bob," he shouted, "come over here; got some business for you." A wiry little man of, Love guessed sixty or so, waved from a nearby table. Judging by the number of empty glasses in front of him and his fellow drinkers, rather a lot of the local ale had already been consumed and there was precious little evidence to suggest that this particular pattern of behaviour was soon about to stop. The little man stood up and made his way rather unsteadily over to join them. "These fellas want to go over to the Calf," the landlord explained, "when can you take 'em, Alf?" The boatman scratched his head then shook it.

"Not this week," he replied, "maybe next weekend?"

"What?" the landlord roared, "not until next weekend? Why the hell not?"

"S'all these monk fellas," the boatman explained, his speech just a little slurred, "they've got me and Bob chartered takin' 'em backwards and forwards every day. Neither of us are takin' any other visitors 'till they've packed up and got off home."

"He's right," added a younger and much taller man who was now standing beside them at the bar. He seemed far less in drink or more able to take it than the other and Love discovered that he was the boatman who made the trip from Port Erin. "I'm fully booked, same as Alf. Can't help you until next weekend either."

"We'll make it worth your while," the American offered, producing a fistful of Manx notes, but although the men looked at the money wistfully, both shook their heads.

"Can't do it, I'm afraid," the younger man said, "one of the conditions of the charter. The Brother who booked us said that they'd come for a week of prayer and meditation and didn't want disturbing by anyone else. They won't allow us to take anyone not from their number, with no exceptions; trust me, I did ask."

The two boatmen had returned to their friends and their drinking, leaving the private detectives in a pretty fix.

"D'you think we could hire a boat and get over there ourselves?" the American suggested, but Love shook his head.

"Don't know the first thing about boats and the waters around the Calf look pretty rough. I should think that you'd need to have a certain amount of experience and local knowledge before attempting a crossing like that, even on a flat calm summer's day."

"I'll get you over there," a voice cut into their conversation, "but it can't be today and it'll cost."

Love and Smith arrived back at the house in Douglas several hours before Grant and his guests and when the Australians eventually walked in, their tired and dejected faces spoke of a long afternoon which had brought little success. Grant opened the large refrigerator which stood in the corner of the kitchen and pulled out two four-packs of beers. Throwing a can to each of his friends and the detectives, he slumped into a chair and briefly recounted his and his friends' afternoon.

"Met plenty of nice people," he said, "some of them offered us a room so we had to make excuses why we couldn't take it, but no sign of any Russians, apart from Boroweski and his men and absolutely no sign of anything suspicious. If Illosovich is holding Louise or Jonathon, he's not doing it anywhere we've been today. It sure as hell is tiring knocking on doors, but we told Boroweski we'll help him again tomorrow morning. What about you guys?" Love told them.

"You trust this guy then?" Grant asked, frowning, "I mean does he know what he's doing?" Love shrugged his shoulders.

"Don't see as we've any alternative. We're meeting him in Port Erin harbour at six o'clock tomorrow morning. He's going to take us over to the Calf and then come back for us when we call him."

"But, when these monks see you they'll throw you off the island, won't they?"

"I don't think they can," Love replied, "I mean it's not their island. If they want to put a clause in a contract with a boatmen preventing him from taking other people there, then that's different. The guy who's taking us has nothing to do with either Alf or Bob, but he's going to drop us in some little bay he knows, well out of sight of the house the monks are using so they shouldn't see us arrive. From then on, we'll keep out heads down until we leave."

Chapter Thirty Two

Monday Morning – Race Week

At six am on Monday, an early morning mist hung over Port Erin, partially obscuring Bradda Head and the far side of the bay. Love stared at the mist anxiously and hoped it would quickly lift for although he was unable to see their destination from where they now were standing, it looked as though visibility deteriorated quite markedly further out to sea. It was a windless morning, but there was a damp chill in the air which suggested that the days of warm dry weather were drawing to a close. The change in temperature had brought the mist, but without wind or strong sunlight to blow or burn it away, the mist could linger or even worsen as the day wore on and Love feared their boatman might use it as a reason not to put to sea.

The two private detectives had been up since long before dawn and were waiting by the quayside impatiently, eager to get to the Calf, but although a fair number of boats were moored beside the jetty or lying at anchor in the bay, none seemed to display signs of activity and pangs of doubt about the reliability of the man they had met in the pub in Port St Mary, until that time entertained by each of them, but not voiced openly, began to surface.

"D'you think he'll show?" the American asked.

"Your guess is as good as mine, Mike, but for the price he's going to charge us, he'd be a fool not to," Love replied.

"If he's got a boat," Smith added, "it could just have been the drink talking."

Suddenly, the whirr of a starter motor cut through the still air, followed by the cough and hesitant beat of a diesel engine drawing breath and coming to life. The beat grew stronger and more confident as the seconds ticked by and the two men on the quayside could see that it came from a little blue and white boat moored beside the stone jetty a short distance ahead of them.

"Come aboard mateys," a voice rang out. Their boatman had appeared from nowhere and seemed keen to be underway.

The two men walked along the jetty and looked down at the boat. The tide was almost fully in and the vessel floated just below their feet requiring no more than a few steps down an iron ladder to gain the sanctuary of its deck. Mike Smith was down in a second, but Love eyed the rusty, barnacle-encrusted, ladder warily and tested each rung carefully with his feet before trusting it with his full weight. Once they were on board, their skipper, in a sudden burst of energy, leapt up onto the jetty, cast off the bow and stern lines, then leapt back down and seized the helm. The engine's lazy beat quickened and the little boat moved off into the bay. Love had time to look around the vessel and saw that, although small, it seemed extremely well equipped. The skipper seemed preoccupied with something or other, so Love had wandered forward and put his head into the small cabin which lay at the front of the boat. He was amazed by the amount of high-tech electronic equipment that seemed to have been crammed into such a tiny space. He thought he could see radar and sonar as well as a sophisticated VHF radio and the almost obligatory GPS. Why someone should invest so heavily in expensive technology, for such a little boat, set his mind wondering, but the skipper was now aware of what he was doing and spoke.

"Stay out of the cabin; some expensive gear in there and I don't want it touched."

"I can see that," the detective said, "what sort of a boat is this anyway?"

"Peel inshore fishing boat," came the reply, "some people call 'em Peel Pigs, 'cause of the distinctive snout."

"What do you use it for?" Love asked.

"Fishing," the skipper replied tersely, "that's what all that gear's for; means I can find all the best marks, night or day and it means I'll be able to get you to the Calf of Man even in this fog." Love looked up and realised that they were now a good way from the jetty and had moved out of the confines of the horseshoe-shaped bay. Ahead of them, rather ominously, banks of thick white fog were rolling slowly in from the Irish Sea and the soft, mournful hoot of a foghorn sounded from somewhere in the distance.

"Shouldn't we, er, be sounding a foghorn or something?" Love asked. The man shook his head.

"Thought you said you didn't want anyone to know what you were doing," he said. "Fancy cameras," he continued, pointing at the long-lensed photographic equipment which both his passengers carried slung around their necks. "Bird-watchers, hmph, pull the other one; never seen bird-watchers like you two before." Love opened his mouth to protest, but could think of nothing convincing to say. "This fog will keep your visit nice and secret, provided you stay out of sight when you're there," the skipper said, "I'll pick you up from the same place I'm gonna drop you: a landing place I know over on the far side of the island. It's out of sight of the house so even if this fog lifts by the time we get there which I don't think it will, no-one should see you arrive." Love said nothing; the man was quite obviously a local smuggler and nowadays that meant drugs, but he was taking them where they wanted to go and was probably very used to finding away around the Manx coastline in conditions of poor visibility. Customs and Excise probably expected drug smugglers to use high-speed rigid inflatables and would pay scant attention to a little fishing boat like this. He made a mental note of the name of the vessel and decided to tip Grant off about this fellow when they got back to the house.

The fog deepened as they moved further from the harbour and by the time they were a couple of miles out, neither Smith nor Love could see land, even though, as their skipper pointed out on his GPS, they were motoring fairly close to the shore. The sea was flat calm and all they could hear above the dull chug of the inboard diesel engine was the distant hoot of a foghorn and the screech of gulls. Love was beginning to find the experience strangely relaxing when suddenly a shape appeared ahead of them and his heart missed a beat. A large triangular fin cut through the water, then a huge open mouth appeared on the surface a few yards in front of the boat.

"What the hell is that?" he shouted.

"Basking shark," the skipper replied, "plenty of 'em around this part of the Island at this time of year. Harmless enough, unless you crash into 'em; best give it a wide berth." He swung the helm round and the boat turned to starboard, passing the giant fish on the port bow. As they did so, Love could swear that it gave them a look of sad curiosity before sinking silently beneath the surface and disappearing from sight. "We're past the Sound now," their skipper explained. "Need to take her 'round The Stack and Caigher Point before I pull her in. The light over to your left is the Calf of Man lighthouse. We'll be passing under it very shortly. Make sure you're ready to jump ashore when I give the word, 'cause I don't plan to tie her up or hang about, I've other things to do." What others things? The Welshman wondered, but said nothing and the man turned the wheel to port. The boat must have rounded a headland for another, more distant light appeared, flashing intermittently through the fog.

"What's that?" the American asked.

"Chicken Rock lighthouse," their skipper replied, "we've rounded The Stack and in a few minutes I'll be taking her in."

When the boat pulled in, the mysterious boatman was true to his word; he told them to jump out and scramble up the rocky shore. When they did so and turned to look back, the little boat had already disappeared.

"Rum fellow that," Love commented, "d'you think he's a…"

"…Drug smuggler," the American finished his sentence for him, "let's just hope he comes back for us before he gets caught." His companion nodded, "not a very trustworthy sort," he said, "but he'll come back; we haven't paid him yet. Get out the map; let's see where we are and where we've got to go." Smith pulled the large scale ordinance survey out of his bag and spread it out on a flat rock.

"This fog is even thicker now than it was earlier," he said, "good job I've got my hand-held GPS." Love stared at the American's latest piece of kit and shook his head in disbelief.

"I didn't realise they made those things so small; is it accurate in a place like this?" Smith smiled.

"It's differential GPS and accurate to about five yards which is about what visibility is so we should be okay."

"Going to be bloody hard seeing anything in this fog though," Love grumbled, "and well-nigh impossible to use the cameras. We might as well have left them in the car."

"Should be okay with this though," his companion said, pulling yet another piece of equipment from his seemingly bottomless bag.

"What is it?"

"A high-resolution infrared camera, it'll cut through this fog like it wasn't there; look!" He pressed a couple of buttons, then passed the sophisticated device to Love. "Point it anywhere you like and look at the LCD display," he directed and the Welshman did as he was told. To his amazement, the display showed the landscape around him as clearly as if it were a bright and fogless day.

"Where do you get all this stuff, the CIA?" Smith shook his head.

"Nope, we field test it for the manufacturers, then they sell it to the CIA."

Grant had been toying with the idea of getting expert help for the best part of a day, but a morning spent trudging around a foggy Port St Mary had made his mind up: he would act now and contact the police without any further delay. The only real question on his lips was who he should inform; ordinary police investigations were somewhat outside his sphere of expertise, but he was well aware that two branches of the detective force existed: proactive and reactive CID. One of the guys in the FCU would probably be able to point him in the right direction so he pulled his mobile from his pocket and tapped the familiar number on the keypad of the 'phone. After several rings, the call was answered.

"Financial Crime Unit, Detective Constable Liszt speaking." It was the one officer within the Unit that Grant had never really trusted or liked, but now he had taken the plunge, he did not feel like backing down.

"Hi Richard," he began, "it's Grant from the AG's. Are any of the others around?"

"Sorry Grant, I'm afraid I'm on my own this morning. Who is it you're looking for?"

"No-one in particular; I just need to pick someone's brains about something that might be nothing. It's not a financial matter, but I'm not sure whether I should go to proactive or reactive CID."

"Why don't you tell me?" Detective Constable Liszt asked, "I should be able to point you in the right direction." He sounded friendly and helpful and the Australian wondered whether he had misjudged the man in the past so he launched into an abridged explanation of the disappearance of one of his guests. He had already decided to keep the story simple so avoided any references to Russians, private detectives or plutonium and kept it as a straightforward missing person. Liszt listened without a word of interruption until Grant had finished his tale, then spoke so quietly the Australian got the distinct impression he was afraid of being overheard. "Doesn't sound the sort of thing CID would really be interested in, Grant," he explained, "I mean, you don't know for certain that there's been any crime at all; this home-stay guest of yours could simply be staying elsewhere. He's a grown man on holiday at the

TT and he's only been missing for just over a day. You said he was pretty drunk when you last saw him so I'd guess he probably crashed out somewhere. Mark my words he'll turn up in a day or two at the very most, with a very sheepish grin on his face. Everyone is so busy with this Presidential visit, on top of the TT that you wouldn't get any thanks at all if you tried to foist your missing doctor on anyone in CID."

"You're suggesting I do nothing?"

"Nothing more than you've already done," Liszt replied, "you've told me and I'll look into it, but I don't think we need to trouble anyone else, for the moment, do you?"

As morning wore on into afternoon, the banks of white fog rolled slowly, but relentlessly in from the sea. The day's races which had already been postponed for several hours were finally put off until the following day. Grant and his fellow Australians had been listening to the little radio in the dashboard of their van since leaving Douglas many hours earlier and were in some respects pleased and in others disappointed that they would not need to dash back for Don to get his practice lap. They had been asked by Boroweski to go back to Fistard and revisit a house that his men had been to the previous day. On that occasion, the Russians' knock on the door had gone unanswered, but the householders had, in all probability been away. A further check was needed, Boroweski explained, lest their enemy slip through their grasp. Bored and rather tired with it all, Grant turned into the little lane as instructed. The farmhouse was like a dozen others they had visited that day: small, a little ramshackle, but neatly whitewashed and he knew before he even drew up to the house that it would prove another false trail. Suddenly though, as he approached, he saw something that made him think again: a black Transit van stood outside the house and the van had English number plates. A quick glance at his notebook confirmed what he had both hoped and feared: the van's number plate matched that which Roy Love had given him the previous day. They had found one of the things they had been looking for, but was this harmless-looking Manx farmhouse, Illosovich's secret lair?

Chapter Thirty Three

Monday Afternoon/Evening – Race Week

Whilst his friends had been searching the Island for signs of him or Miss Templeton, Jonathon Price had spent an uncomfortable thirty-six hours sitting in a spartanly furnished room in the company of a group of grim-faced, sinister-looking men. They had not spelt out exactly who they were or represented, but the barrage of questions they had fired at him proved that they knew far more about Illosovich than even Mike Smith. Certain elements of their attitude and behaviour suggested that they were British Army officers, and others that they were police, but the combination together with those elements of subterfuge they had used to ensnare him, could only mean one thing: Military Intelligence or whatever name those in the murky, clandestine world of the British Secret Services went by in 2007. The man on the green Kawasaki who had told Price that his name was Des, was, of course, one of their number. He must have slipped something in the doctor's drink, for Price recalled suddenly feeling unwell and when he had gone outside that the *Saddle* for some fresh air, he had been unceremoniously bundled into the back of a waiting car and spirited away. His memories of the car journey were a little vague, but he was sure it had not been a long one and was certain that the house he had been held in was somewhere close to the centre of the Island's major town.

They had forced mug after mug of black coffee down his throat and bombarded him with endless questions, phrased in such a manner and put to him in such a tone as to suggest they suspected him of some sort of collaboration with their enemy, despite his protests that things were really the other way around. The man Price had known as Des dropped his phoney cockney accent and spoke in cultured Oxford tones, but his voice carried a hint of menace and Price was extremely careful about what he said. They had been watching him very closely, the man told him and wanted a convincing explanation for his movements as well as the names and true identities of all of those he had met. It was hard to judge exactly how much they really knew about what had happened on the Island, although their knowledge of Illosovich and his activities elsewhere seemed profound, but Price told them about the motorbike in the undertaker's house, how it had been used the previous year and how it had now been switched for another. Explaining his association with

Boroweski could have proved tricky, but fortunately his interrogators seemed to have only seen the Russian when he was wearing his biking clothes and presumably assumed he was just another biker. Price remained silent on that score and told them that his detailed knowledge of Illosovich and Petromax came from the Pinkerton man, Mike Smith, which, of course, was largely true. When he had told them everything else he either knew or guessed or thought and when he was beginning to fear that they would keep him in that empty windowless room for ever, the man he had known as Des stood up and told him he could go.

"That's all, for now Doctor," he said, "but we're not leaving town. Do not tell your friends about this little meeting and do not tell anyone else either; I leave it to you to think up a reason why you deserted them for nearly two days, I'm sure you've got sufficient imagination for that little task, but remember, we are watching you. Illosovich and his men are our business, so please do not mention anything about him to the local police. I will give you my number and if you hear or see anything new about this matter, you must call me immediately."

And that was it. Price was led blindfold out of the room, down some stairs and pushed into the back seat of a car. The car started and drove for ten or fifteen minutes, no longer, then stopped; the door opened and he was pushed out. He struggled to pull the blindfold from his eyes, but by the time he had removed it, there were no moving cars in sight and he saw that he was standing alone on the pavement in Hutchinson Square, just a stones throw from Grant's house. He walked back to the house and let himself in. The place seemed deserted, but that was only to be expected: Don would be out in the Superstock race and Grant and the other Australians would presumably be up at the pits; as for Roy Love and the American, they could be anywhere, but he guessed they were still looking for Louise. He glanced at his watch, then pulled his mobile from his pocket. He would call the others shortly, but first he needed to 'phone the Chief Medical Officer and apologise for his absence from duty that day.

"They were postponed until tomorrow Jonathon," the man explained, "because of the mist. I'm sorry you've been ill, but I'm glad you're feeling better; now are you sure you'll be okay for the morning?"

"I'll be fine. Where do you want me?"

"Place called the Waterworks, between Ramsey Hairpin and the Gooseneck. If you come along the coast road from Laxey, just before you get to Ramsey, there's a little lane that runs up the hill to your left. It's signposted *Ballure Reservoir*, but if you take your bike up there you can park by the reservoir and walk up the footpath to the Course. It means you won't be stuck there waiting after the races until they re-open the road." Price thanked him and said he would be at the allotted spot well before the races began. The next call he made was to his friend, the Welsh private detective, but strangely, Love's 'phone was turned off so he left voice mail and tried the American, again without success. He didn't know any of the Australians' numbers, but guessed that even though the day's racing had been put back until tomorrow, all four of them would still be somewhere up behind the Grandstand, so he pulled on his leathers and boots, grabbed his helmet and gloves and walked out to his bike.

There was no sign of the old van anywhere, even though Price had looked everywhere it could conceivably have been parked and his enquiries with the other riders and mechanics revealed that not one of the Australians had been seen since Saturday. He discovered that Don had not entered the race that had been scheduled to take place that day and although that helped allay his fears a little, he felt sure that the man would have wanted to get some more practice in and, if the racing had gone ahead, would have taken part in the later practice session. Perhaps he was beginning to feel a little paranoid, but it was hardly surprising, given the events of the previous few days. Miss Templeton had disappeared and now it seemed that a number of others may have joined her. He decided to go back to the house and try the 'phone numbers again and if there was still no answer...If there was still no answer, what would he do? Not for the first time, he thought about calling the police, but he remembered what the secret serviceman had said. Should he call that man and ask him for help? In his mind he could see the secret serviceman's face quite clearly: it was cold and hard and purposeful, but Price rather doubted if that purpose extended beyond the narrow confines of his mission. Capturing or killing Illosovich was, no doubt, his aim, not saving lives or rescuing hostages; he would consider them expendable.

Price walked back to the Triumph still wondering what he should do. He had parked the bike by the tennis courts half-way down Nobles Park so he had plenty of time to think whilst he was walking, but no brilliant ideas or clever solutions to what was fast becoming an insoluble mess came into his head. Out of the corner of his eye, he caught sight of the Isle of Man Prison and thought of his friend, the undertaker. Christ! He suddenly remembered that the murder trial was due to begin the very next day and the Defence advocate was missing. They would have to adjourn the whole thing, but what possible excuse could they give to the Court? If they told the truth, then the police would surely get involved, assuming that anyone would believe such a fanciful story.

The fog still shrouded the Calf of Man and the Southern tip of the Island, but a wind picked up in the late afternoon and rapidly began to freshen. The two private detectives had covered most of the island over the course of the day and with the aid of Smith's sophisticated equipment had managed to find their way amongst the slopes and rocks and heather. They had also managed to observe the community of monks without giving away their presence, but had seen nothing of Miss Templeton, Illosovich or anyone who looked in the slightest bit suspicious. There was just one more place they needed to visit before they called the boatman.

"Over here," Smith explained pointing at the map, "remember that light the boatman pointed out on the way here." Love nodded.

"What about it?"

"Well I did a little bit of research before we came over here today and I found out that there are actually three lighthouses on that headland. A modern, automated one and two old ones. The old ones were built way back in the early nineteenth century to provide leading lights, warning vessels that they were approaching Chicken rock. One tower is above the other and the idea was that if you were on a collision course with the rock you'd see one light above the other and they'd get nearer and nearer to each other until they appeared to fuse. When that happened you'd be right on the rock itself."

"Very interesting," Love said, "but I'm not quite sure of the relevance…"

"Don't you see," Smith explained excitedly, "the new lighthouse is fully automated, so it's totally unmanned and although the old ones are apparently a bit dilapidated, they're buildings that no-one goes to…ever.

Just the sort of place someone who wanted to hide something or somebody would find extremely useful."

"Good idea. Let's check it out, but we'd better be quick, the fog's lifting."

They had avoided the rough tracks that ran across the little island for fear of running into any of the legitimate inhabitants, but it had been heavy and slow going through the bracken. Now that the mist was rapidly disappearing, they decided to take a chance and use the track which led directly to the trio of lighthouses. The track allowed them to move much more quickly, but windows of clear air had started to appear between the creeping white fingers of fog and within a very few minutes visibility was approaching normal. They looked up and saw the nearest lighthouse twenty yards ahead, without the need for infrared vision. As they did so the last vestigial wisps of fog melted away and the late afternoon sun shone brightly upon them. The American tensed and stopped dead in his tracks, motioning for his companion to do the same.

"Freeze, don't move," he whispered hoarsely, "there's a guy on that lighthouse tower training a gun on us."

"Where...are you sure?" Love whispered.

"Take it from me, bud," Smith replied, his accent suddenly becoming far more noticeable, "I can see the sunlight glinting on the sights. He's wearing a brown habit, but if that guy's a monk, I'm a cardinal."

Price had one more person to try and that, of course, was Boroweski. The Russian answered his 'phone within four or five rings and when the doctor spilled out his fears, he was supportive.

"Mr Love and Mr Smith have gone to the Calf of Man," he explained, "and I do not expect to hear from them until later today. You were missing. We were all concerned; what happened to you?" Price repeated his carefully rehearsed story about sudden illness and taking refuge in a friendly Samaritan's house, but he knew the Russian did not believe him.

"What about Grant and the Australians?" he asked, but Boroweski seemed surprised at his question.

"Is he not with you?" he said, "he and his friends, they went to the south this morning, but they should have returned long ago. I have not heard from them for many hours and assumed that they found nothing."

"Where exactly in the south?" Price demanded.

"They were checking out places my men had earlier visited," the Russian explained. "There were a number of such places and as they did not call me, I have no knowledge where, exactly, they went."

"They haven't returned, Mikael, so I think you should take this rather seriously. I can't think of anything else I could do tonight and, to be honest, I do feel rather tired. I'm duty race doctor at a place called Waterworks tomorrow, but you know my mobile number and if anything happens, you must give me a call."

Chapter Thirty Four

Tuesday Morning – Race Week

Monday evening brought with it a dramatic change in the weather as a violent summer storm swept in from the south. It started as a distant rumble, but by midnight was directly over Douglas and the rolling crash of thunder and flashes of lightning continued until just before daybreak. When the roar and boom of thunder eventually faded, having managed to keep Price and most of the town's other inhabitants awake for most of the night, it was replaced by the hiss of heavy rain which carried on until the doctor finally fell asleep. He awoke early, still feeling exhausted, for in truth he had hardly slept a wink and when he looked out of his bedroom window, he could see that conditions looked particularly bad. Rain was pouring incessantly from a leaden grey sky and to his untutored eye, the heavy clouds showed few signs of lifting, and the bad weather looked set to continue for the rest of the day.

He got out of bed and wandered downstairs, but there were no signs of life anywhere in the house. All of the rooms were empty and, as he had feared and yet suspected, none of the others had returned during the night. He checked his mobile for missed calls or voice mail, but of either, there were none so he made himself a cup of instant coffee, sat down at the kitchen table and tried to figure out what he should do. After his call to Boroweski the previous evening, he really had thought his house-mates would be back by now. He would ring the Russian again later, he decided, but first he needed to check with race control. He very much doubted whether there would be any racing that day: the rain was bad enough in Douglas and he dreaded to think what it would be like out on the mountain road. The man he spoke to gave him the official line which was "listen to the radio for announcements" and then the unofficial, but rather more accurate, "absolutely no chance today," so he made up his mind not to even think about riding out to Ramsey. He wondered whether he ought to ride south and look for the others, but then remembered the undertaker's trial.

Price knew that the trial was due to commence at ten in the Isle of Man Courts of Justice on Bucks Road. He had been there before and guessed that it was no real distance from where he was staying so he decided to walk. In any event, riding a motorcycle in the pouring rain had never been an experience he had found enjoyable, so he pulled on the one waterproof coat he had brought to the Island and set off down the road. His route to the courthouse took him down Broadway, through the Villa Marina's grounds, then up Finch Road and Mount Havelock. The morning rush hour had subsided, but the roads were still busy with two and four-wheeled traffic and throughout his short journey, the rain continued to fall. Water welled up from roadside drains that had been overcome by the deluge, turning the town's streets into either shallow lakes or fast-flowing rivers and when he reached the glass-fronted building, Price was soaking wet from head to toe. Thankfully, it was after nine when he got there and the front doors were open so he went inside. He had to pass through a metal detector and undergo a search, but that was normal practice everywhere these days and as the security staff wore friendly smiles and went about their jobs in a sympathetic manner, he could hardly complain. A visit to the reception desk told him that the trial would take place in Court Three which was on the next floor so he walked up two flights of stairs to the concourse at the top. Court Three was easy to find and was the only courtroom where another set of searches were taking place. Once he had made it through those and taken the very last free seat in the public gallery, he looked around to see who was about.

The courtroom was the same one as had been used for the Taylor Inquest the previous year, but then he had been giving evidence and had neither the inclination nor opportunity to take in the atmosphere or the scenery of the place. This time things were rather different, but although Price was not on trial himself, he felt for his friend the undertaker and hoped against hope that Miss Templeton would miraculously turn up. Of the Judge, Jury and Defendant, there was still no sign and the rows of seats between the Bench and the Dock were as empty as the public gallery was full. The door opened and a solitary figure walked into the room. He wore a horsehair wig and long black gown and made his way to the front of the Court where he took a seat on the extreme left hand side of the front advocates' bench. Price took him to be the Prosecutor and could see that a collection of files and papers had already been arranged before his seat. Of the Defence advocate, there was no sign at all.

Suddenly, a bell rang somewhere and the court usher told them all to stand up. A grave-faced, elderly Acting Deemster clad in wig and gown walked slowly to his seat in the middle of the Bench, bowed and sat down. Price and all of the others took this as their cue to do the same and a man on the other side of the courtroom began to speak.

"I fence this Court in the name of our most gracious sovereign lady the Queen. I charge that no person do quarrel, brawl or make any disturbance and that all persons answer their name when called. I charge this audience to witness this Court is fenced. I charge this audience to witness this Court is fenced. I charge this whole audience to bear witness this court is now fenced."

Price had no knowledge of the purpose of that little speech, but correctly guessed that it stemmed from some ancient Manx tradition. When the man had finished speaking, the Deemster addressed the Court.

"Thank you Coroner…The Crown against Richard Quayle…can we have the Defendant please?"

"Errm," the Prosecutor cleared his throat.

"Yes, Mr Kneale," the Deemster said, looking down from the Bench, "what is it?"

"We don't appear to have Defence counsel, Your Honour." The Deemster stared at the empty advocates' benches, then fumbled through the pile of papers which lay at his side.

"Who, er, is on record for the Defendant," he asked, "I don't quite recall…"

"Miss Templeton, Your Honour," the Prosecutor replied, "might I suggest a short adjournment?"

"Miss Templeton, ah yes, I remember now. Well, she's usually most reliable. Probably been delayed by this dreadful weather, I suppose. An adjournment? Yes, I suppose that would be in order, but let's get the Defendant in so I can explain why there'll be a short delay; can't keep the fellow out there waiting, can we?" The door at the back of the room opened and one of the court ushers hurried forward. The usher whispered a few words to the Deemster's clerk who scribbled furiously on a piece of paper, then passed the resulting note to the bewigged and gowned elderly man sitting above and behind her. The Deemster took the scrap of paper and frowned as he read, then reread it.

"It would appear, Mr Kneale," he said at last, "that Miss Templeton has not been seen for several days. Her secretary has informed the police that she has gone missing. Are you aware of this development?" A loud murmur of excitement swept through the public gallery. Its occupants had come expecting drama, but not at such an early stage of the trial. The Prosecutor shook his head.

"It's the first I have heard of it Your Honour," he replied. At that precise moment, the door behind the dock at the back of the court swung open and, flanked by two uniformed prison officers, the Defendant, Richard Quayle, appeared. He walked forward and stood in the front of the dock whilst the Deemster addressed him.

"It would appear, Mr Quayle, that your advocate, Miss Templeton, is not here. I have just learned that she has been missing for several days and must therefore order an adjournment. It may be that she resurfaces later today, but if she does not then I will have to seriously consider vacating this trial and discharging the jury. Do you understand?"

"But that'll mean I won't get out in time for the Senior!" the undertaker exclaimed and a murmur of suppressed laughter rippled through the court.

"I'm afraid that would be the case," the Deemster agreed. "You would be remanded in custody until a new trial date could be set. I'm sorry, but if Miss Templeton fails to appear, then there really would be nothing else I could do."

"Yes there is," the undertaker replied, "What if I were to represent myself? We could get started now, couldn't we, if I did that?"

"You...want...to conduct...your own defence?" the Deemster uttered the words slowly, as if unable to comprehend what the undertaker was saying. "Mr Quayle, you face a charge of murder, please consider carefully what you are suggesting." The Prosecutor leapt to his feet.

"Your Honour, I really must protest; this is a complex case with conflicting expert evidence which will require careful consideration and analysis of matters concerning both law and fact. The Defendant is completely unqualified to deal with such issues and if he is convicted under such circumstances, then an Appeal would quite naturally follow...." He carried on speaking for a few more minutes, but the Deemster's face had already turned an unhealthy shade of pale when the word "Appeal" was mentioned and seemed to no longer be listening.

"I really must agree with Mr Kneale," he said, addressing the Defendant firmly, "this is not a case for you to defend yourself; you must await the return of Miss Templeton or instruct another advocate."

"It says here that I can," the Defendant argued loudly, brandishing a thick red book above his head. "I quote: *a defendant has the right to conduct his own defence R v Woodward [1944] K.B. 118, 29 Cr.App.R, 159*" The citation seemed to flow quite easily off his lips. "You'll find it at page three hundred and fifty-one of the latest Archbold, Your Honour," he continued, "and it says that if I choose to exercise that right, I cannot later hold out my lack of knowledge or experience as grounds for an appeal."

The Prosecutor grimaced and exhaled loudly, then took a sharp intake of breath through a row of gleaming, but tightly clenched teeth. He shook his head gravely, but said nothing, as there really was no argument he could use to counter the undertaker's bold statement of the law. He was fully aware of the cases, but prosecuting a Defendant in person was an experience he had undergone more often than he wished and it was one of those experiences he really did not like. The Deemster frowned and looked at the relevant page of the authoritative book, wondering whether he should order a brief adjournment so that he may fully digest its wording, but the paragraph the undertaker had referred to seemed clear enough and as the Deemster read it, he recalled hearing such arguments before. He could see no good reason why he should or could prevent the Defendant from conducting his own defence so he ordered that the jury be brought into the court. The trial would begin without further delay.

Some miles to the south of this unfolding drama, Mikael Boroweski was taking counsel with his men. He had heard nothing further from the doctor that morning so had to assume that the others were still missing and that could only mean one thing: the private detectives and the band of Australians had stumbled upon something important and appertaining to Illosovich; that or they had found the criminal's den. He had a list of places that the Australians had been due to visit and Roy Love had told him about the boatman who had agreed to make the short voyage to the Calf of Man. Time was passing quickly and the American President was due to arrive the following day, but Boroweski and his men had still discovered nothing about their enemy's suspected plot so the tall Russian barked out a series of orders and when he had finished, he and his men left the flat-topped house above Cregneash and climbed onto their waiting motorbikes.

Boroweski and one of his men rode down to Port Erin and began to look for a little blue and white boat. Love had sent him a text shortly after setting out the previous morning so he had brief descriptions of both the motor vessel and its owner. It was still raining heavily when they reached the harbour, but as luck would have it, a vessel matching the description Love had given was coming in. It chugged slowly around the jetty and came to a halt just as the Russians were getting off their bikes. Two coils of rope flew up onto the quayside, then a balding head appeared, followed by the shoulders and upper torso of a well-built man. The man pulled himself up the final rung of the ladder and stepped onto the quay. He picked up the ropes and lazily threw them around nearby bollards, tied a couple of knots and made the boat fast. The tall Russian approached him.

"Your boat is called *Sealion*?" he asked.

"Yeah," the man replied with a scowl, "who wants to know?"

"You take my friends to Calf of Man yesterday morning?" Boroweski enquired, knowing full-well that he had.

"Your friends," the man exclaimed angrily, "I waited all day for them, but they never called me back and I'm still bloody waiting to be paid. Where are they? Got someone else to take 'em off the island, did they?"

"I do not know where they are," the Russian explained calmly, "but I suspect they are still on Calf of Man. Can you take me there, I will pay?" The man stared at him through cold, hard eyes, but the lure of money was something he was unable to resist.

"Hundred quid, each way," he demanded, "in advance."

Back in the courtroom in Douglas, tempers were already fraying, even though little progress had been made in the trial. The jury had been called in to be seated and the Deemster had slowly explained their role and his. When he had finished, the Prosecutor got to his feet and began his opening speech. It was the part of the trial when the Prosecution simply outlined what they hoped to prove and the Defence were expected to simply listen and take note, but the Defendant had rather different plans forcing the Deemster to intervene more than once.

"Mr Quayle," he said in tones that should have conveyed to anyone his increasing exasperation, "I have already told you not to argue with Mr Kneale. He is setting out his case and you will have your chance later. Now please sit down."

"But he's talking rubbish," the Defendant protested, "and I need to make it clear to the jury…"

"Mister Quayle, sit down or I'll hold you in contempt of Court," the Deemster shouted. Scowling with anger, the undertaker reluctantly resumed his seat, but he sat there like a coiled spring, poised to shoot up again at the slightest provocation. Price looked at the protagonists in this fascinating battle and had great difficulty in determining which of the three of them, Defendant, Prosecutor or Judge, was going to lose their temper first. Fortunately Richard managed to hold his tongue for the remainder of Kneale's address and, as it was by then nearly one pm, the Deemster decided that it was a convenient time to rise for lunch. The Defendant was, in a sense, therefore, saved by the bell, but the afternoon would bring fireworks, Price guessed, as the prosecution would call their first witness and Richard would be allowed to cross-examine.

Chapter Thirty Five

Tuesday Afternoon – Race Week

When court proceedings resumed that afternoon, Price detected a certain degree of tension on both the Deemster's and the Prosecutor's faces. The Defendant facing them, in contrast, looked quite relaxed and far from intimidated by either the venue or the proceedings to date. The doctor could feel a thrill of silent anticipation amongst those sitting around him and felt sure that it would not be long before that anticipation was satisfied.

"Yes Mr Kneale?" the Deemster began.

"The Crown would like to call its first witness, Your Honour, the pathologist Dr Stopps."

The tall, thin figure of the forensic pathologist entered the courtroom and made his way to the front. He stepped up into the witness box and, holding the testament firmly in his hand, took the solemn oath. When he had finished speaking he looked across at the jury and the Prosecutor began.

"Could you please tell the Court your name, profession and professional qualifications?"

The motor vessel *Sealion* had long since left the confines of Port Erin Bay and was chugging slowly forward through choppy seas towards the Calf. The earlier torrential rain had ended and the skies over this part of the Island were now blue, but the wind, if anything, had grown stronger and Boroweski, who had no great love of boats or the sea, was beginning to feel rather sick.

"How much... longer will... journey take...we are...in hurry?" he asked, taking gulping mouthfuls of air between each couple of words. The boatman cast him a sideways look of sneering resentment, then noticed the Russian's colour and laughed.

"Can't take her any quicker in this sea and it'll be worse when we go round the Stack. Winds blowing from the South South West so we're sheltered by the land at the moment. When we get to the other side of the Calf, it'll be a lot, lot rougher; might even be too rough to take her in."

"Can we...can we...not land...somewhere nearer," Boroweski gasped.

"Could try the Sound," the man replied, "but that's not where I dropped your mates. They didn't want anyone to know they were there, see, so I assumed you felt the same way, but if you're not bothered..."

"Just land...nearest place," the Russian replied, his face now as green as the sea around him, "how long...will it take?" The boatman pointed to the line of cliffs to the left of them.

"Follow these cliffs along for another mile and then in. We're making about four knots so fifteen, twenty minutes longer but I warn you it won't be as comfortable as this when we hit the tidal rip that cuts through the Sound so get ready to hang on tight."

"So Doctor Stopps, your conclusion was?"

"That the victim was stabbed with the knife labelled 'Exhibit One', that the knife entered the pericardium, but did not puncture the myocardium and that the stab wound rapidly resulted in death from cardiac tamponade."

"And at what time, approximately, would you estimate death to have taken place?"

"On the basis of core temperature readings taken by the police surgeon when he first attended the scene, I would say between three and four am, but estimation of time of death is not an exact science, there are rather too many variables that have to be thrown into the equation."

"Thank you Dr Stopps." The Prosecutor sat down and the Defendant was already on his feet.

"Do you have any idea how long it took me to drive back from the bottom of Richmond Hill that night?" he blazed angrily at the pathologist.

"Mr Quayle," the Deemster interrupted wearily, "you are supposed to cross-examine Dr Stopps on the expert evidence he has just given, not to ask him to indulge in speculation about matters outside his field. Kindly ensure that you ask questions that are relevant to..."

"But it is relevant," the Defendant objected loudly, without allowing the Deemster to finish his little speech, "I want members of the jury to be aware that I couldn't possibly have got back to the house before half-past four and actually it was nearer five, with all that snow and..."

"Mr Quayle, I've told you before; DO NOT INTERRUPT WHEN I AM SPEAKING," the Deemster virtually screamed, "and now is not the time for you to give your evidence. You will have plenty of time for that later, but for the time being confine yourself to the witness' evidence."

"Witness evidence?" the undertaker said, frowning and evidently puzzled as to what to ask next. Suddenly his face brightened as if he had remembered something important and he launched himself forward on another attack. "What is your explanation of the bruising on the arms of the Deceased?"

"As I explained earlier," the pathologist replied frostily, "there are a number of possible causes, the most likely, in my opinion, being fingertip pressure. If someone had forcibly gripped the victim's upper arms and pushed him backwards that would have resulted in marks just like those found on the body."

"Gripped by the murderer?" the Defendant enquired.

"Presumably," Stopps replied.

"But, how did I then managed to knife Ernie through the heart, doctor?" the Defendant demanded triumphantly, "I mean, are you suggesting I was holding the knife with one of my feet?" A ripple of laughter spread through the public gallery and Price saw faint smiles on some of the jurors' faces, but such feelings did not extend to the judge.

"Mr Quayle," he warned.

"I did not presume to suggest that the murderer was holding Mr Quine's arms at the same time as he inflicted the wound," the pathologist replied in the most condescending tones he could muster, "obviously one came before the other, he either gripped Mr Quine, pushed him forwards, released him, grabbled the knife and stabbed him or stabbed him and then gripped him. It's as simple as that."

"Would you be surprised, doctor, if I were to tell you that we have an expert report that says they were done at the same time and that there were two people involved, one holding Ernie down whilst the other stabbed him."

"I wouldn't be surprised at all," Stopps replied without batting an eyelid, "I've seen the Defence expert report prepared by Professor Clarke and he's entitled to his opinion, but that's all it is, his opinion and on some of the points he has raised we take entirely different views." The Defendant looked so surprised and downcast to see what he had expected to be a demon ball hit so easily for a six that even the Deemster looked at him sympathetically.

"Full disclosure, Mr Quayle," he explained, "your advocate was required to disclose the substance of your expert's report to the Prosecution, even though we have not heard his oral evidence yet."

The tidal rip through the Sound was even faster than the boatman had imagined and he had to hold the throttle fully open to make any headway at all. The narrow channel between the two islands had a dark and gloomy history of shipwreck and disaster and for a few moments the man thought it touch and go whether they would make it to the landing point or be swept onto the rocks. The engine shook and juddered violently as it screamed in protest at the revolutions it was being forced to maintain, but the little boat carried slowly on through the heavy seas until its progress suddenly grew easier and the boatman visibly relaxed.

"We're out of the tidal stream now," he explained, "we'll be landing in a minute and you can get off. I'll give you two hours to find your friends and get back here. I want to get back to Port Erin before the tide changes so I'm not waiting a second longer." Boroweski, who had spent the last fifteen minutes hanging over the side of the boat, overcome by that peculiar combination of smell and motion that only a fishing boat could produce, looked up and managed to produce a thin, sickly smile.

"Thank you; we will find them. I too do not wish to go against that current again."

In Court Three, the case of the Crown against Quayle had proceeded a little more rapidly than the motor vessel *Sealion*, but not much. The Prosecutor had begun to call the various police witnesses and the Defendant had cross-examined each in turn on just about every conceivable point he could think of except, as the Deemster repeatedly pointed out, on the evidence they had just given. The courtroom clock had just turned four when the Deemster, who seemed to be aging by the minute, decided he had heard enough.

"I think, Mr Kneale," he said, "that the jury have had a rather long day. Would now be a good time to rise?" The Prosecutor leapt to his feet.

"An excellent suggestion, your Honour," he said, "is your Honour minded to sit from ten tomorrow morning?"

"Yes, I don't think we need to begin any earlier, unless you, er?"

"Ten would be fine, your Honour; I should be able to finish the rest of the prosecution case before four."

"Mr Quayle," the Deemster addressed the man in the dock at the rear of the court, "will you be ready to begin the case for the Defence tomorrow afternoon if Mr Kneale finishes early?" The Defendant frowned.

"I thought I'd already begun it," he said.

"Will you be ready to begin calling your witnesses?" the judge explained.

"Oh yes," the Defendant replied confidently, but without really knowing who those witnesses would be.

The jury and then the judge rose and the first day of *R –v- Quayle* was over, but from where Price was sitting, it had been one-way traffic; if Miss Templeton was not rapidly located, the case was lost. As he filed slowly out of the courtroom, the doctor's thoughts turned to the advocate and the others. So many people could surely not go missing in such a small island in such a short space of time. Where the hell were they all?

The Calf of Man was rapidly becoming another mystery which Boroweski's considerable intellectual powers seemed incapable of deciphering. When he and his slim and silent companion had landed, they had expected to find the place populated by a gathering of clergymen, but of monks, either clad in habits or otherwise, they found no sign anywhere they looked. The house in the middle of the little island had been the first and most obvious place to look, but it was empty, although showed signs of recent occupation so the two Russians proceeded along the rough track to the next place on Boroweski's list. He had a small tourist guide book which outlined the Calf's main attractions and in it he found several pages devoted to the cluster of lighthouses on the headland above the Stack. One of these was new and still in service and the other two old and now redundant, but all three were buildings that he and Sergey needed to search. In addition the book spoke of outbuildings and of ruined keepers' residences: all places that could be used to hide someone or something. He muttered a few words to his companion in their native tongue and Sergey unslung the rucksack he had been carrying from his back and produced a pair of small, but powerful electronic binoculars. He handed them to Boroweski who focussed carefully on the buildings ahead. There were no external signs of life so Boroweski waved his hand forward and they set off again.

They approached the trio of lighthouses with a degree of caution that bordered on trepidation, but both men had good reason to fear what they knew they might find: Boroweski from his role and long experience as a Russian secret agent and Sergey, because he had once been one of Illosovich's men. Every minute they expected to hear a shout, or a shot, or feel the cold pain of a bullet, or feel nothing, but suddenly just cease to live, but none of these things happened and when they reached the first lighthouse and made their entrance, they found it empty and derelict with no signs of recent life. The second was a modern, automated tower with locked doors which had not been opened or tampered with for some time so, with hearts sinking at the thought of yet another unsuccessful journey they carried on up the hill to the third and final lighthouse.

The door was open and the two men tensed. Boroweski produced a small pistol which had been concealed somewhere on his person and in a sudden flash of movement sprung through the doorway and dived onto the floor. He had the area in front of him covered with his gun, but when he saw what was there he relaxed. Three bodies were chained to the foot of an iron spiral staircase, but although cold, wet and desperately uncomfortable, all three were moving, albeit with difficulty. All three could see that the movement they had heard outside a moment earlier did not signal the return of their captor, but rescue and Boroweski could see from their faces the flood of relief. He reached out and pulled the rough gag from Louise Templeton's mouth. She coughed and choked.

"God, Mikael, I'm so pleased to see you; I think I'm going to cry," and she did. Roy Love and Mike Smith were ungagged and Boroweski's companion started to work on their bonds.

"How long have you been gagged and chained like this?" Boroweski demanded.

"Pretty well since we got here," the American explained, "they released us one at a time when they wanted to give us something to eat or drink, but not for long and they left early this morning, before dawn."

"Illosovich?" Smith nodded.

"We've not seen the man himself, only his men, but I know enough words of Russian to have been able to work out who is in charge. From what I could gather, they were keeping us as hostages, in case their plans didn't quite work out and they needed a ticket out of here."

"So...what exactly are those plans?" the tall Russian asked slowly. Smith shook his head.

"I don't know, but they have something to do with the President's visit. Whatever it is, it's going to happen very soon; that's why they've all gone."

"It is the radio beacon," a voice cut into the conversation. It was Miss Templeton and, after gulping down the bottle of water Sergey had given her, she continued:

"They held me somewhere else until two days ago; I think it was the cellar of an old house, but I don't know where. When I was there, I heard someone talking in English once. I had been sleeping and maybe the person thought I was still asleep, but I heard this voice talking about the beacon. It said *and then Puff no beacon and no American President*. I don't know who the voice was speaking to because I didn't hear them say a word."

"When you say 'English' Miss Templeton, you mean English like you speak?" Boroweski asked.

"No, an accent, definitely an accent...a bit like yours only..."

"Go on?"

"Sorry, I hate to be rude, only rather more suave and sophisticated." The tall Russian laughed.

"That is Illosovich," he explained, "he more used than me to moving in exalted circles."

"We'd better get moving then," another voice spoke. Roy Love had taken a little longer then the other two prisoners to recover his voice and get his thoughts together. "President Shrub arrives tomorrow morning and if they intend to get him by blowing up the beacon, they'll have to do it whilst he's airborne between Shannon and Ronaldsway, but..." he stopped for a moment and scratched his head before finishing lamely, "I still can't see how that would work."

"If that's their plan, we'll have to act on it," the American asserted firmly, "Do you have a boat, Mikael? Good, the sooner we get off this island, the sooner we can start warning people."

Chapter Thirty Six

Wednesday – Race Week

The two private detectives and the advocate had all elected to stay in the house near Hutchinson Square and Boroweski had agreed that it was probably as safe as anywhere else on the Island. When *Sealion* had arrived back in Port Erin, they had found the BMW gone, but had managed to locate a taxi and, with Boroweski and Sergey riding shotgun behind them, had reached the house and an astonished, but overjoyed Price in the early evening. Boroweski insisted on leaving two of his men to guard them and for once, no-one voiced the slightest objection. They had sat up until midnight trying to formulate a plan for the morning, but eventually, overcome with exhaustion, they had agreed to sleep and rise at four-thirty. With rest might come inspiration and rest was one thing that each of them needed.

Wednesday was to be a busy day for all of them, for Price had insisted on carrying on with his duties by the racetrack and Miss Templeton would spend her time in court. That left the two private detectives and the Russians to somehow persuade the Manx authorities that an attempt would be made on the President's life. The doctor had said nothing of his earlier abduction and forced interview and of all of them, he seemed the most relaxed, for when he had heard their news the previous evening, he had instantly thought of the man he had previously known as Des. He felt rather bad about not taking the others into his confidence, but in some ways it was better that they did not know and he formulated a plan to leave the house as early as possible and then make a call from somewhere he could not be overheard.

Louise Templeton knew that she faced a long and uphill struggle in the case of *R –v- Quayle*. The doctor had described the previous day's developments and explained that, whilst failing to make any effective points in his cross-examination, her client had managed to antagonise most of the witnesses who had given evidence, in addition to the Prosecutor and the Judge. What she needed was a good performance from her expert witness and, although she had now just about given up on the possibility, one or other of her two petty criminals, Darren Finch and Jason Quiggan to turn up. It had seemed an age since the day she had spent looking for them, but every line of enquiry she had pursued then had turned a blank. There was no more time left to search for missing witnesses and, in any event, her fruitless endeavours that day had resulted only in her own abduction when visiting one of Jason's friends in Peel. The man she had gone to see had been singularly unhelpful, but something about his facial expression had told her that he knew far more about Jason's whereabouts than he was letting on. A few minutes after speaking to him, she had been seized from behind, blindfolded and bundled into a vehicle, then driven off at speed through the town's narrow streets. Whether she had been stalked beforehand or the man had given her location away, she could not tell, but she rather suspected that the man's house was being watched. If that had been the case, then it suggested that her captors were still looking for Jason and provided just a faint glimmer of hope that he was still alive and free. The abduction had led to several days of imprisonment, first in a damp and uncomfortable cellar, then in the lighthouse on the Calf of Man and throughout that time, although her overriding emotion had been one of blind terror, she had hoped against hope that her captors would release her and that one of the messages she had left throughout the Island would get through to one or other of the men. When she awoke that Wednesday morning, she found it hard to concentrate on the task before her, but although her nerves were still feeling shot to pieces, she knew she had a job to do and was not going to give up.

Roy Love and Mike Smith had taken it upon themselves to try and convince the local police that there was a clear and present danger to the visiting President's life. It would be difficult, but as detectives, albeit private ones, they both reckoned that they would stand a better chance of getting through to someone in the Isle of Man Constabulary than Boroweski or his Russians who would, in all probability, just succeed in getting themselves locked up. When they 'phoned Boroweski to tell him what they proposed to do, he made a few non-committal grunts, but voiced no objection, so they set off up the hill to Police Headquarters even though they had no real idea about what precisely they were going to say.

Roads were due to close at nine-fifteen with the first race scheduled to start an hour later. It was the event which had been postponed from the Monday and the organisers were praying for good weather as they had been forced to juggle with the programme and were now hoping to hold five races in three days. Fortunately, the cloud, wind and rain had abated and the forecast was looking good for the rest of the week. As Price piloted the Triumph Daytona along the road to Laxey, he could see Snaefell's peak clearly in the bright morning sunshine which boded well for the day ahead. He had decided to get well clear of Douglas before he made his planned call, lest it result in a further unwelcome visit from the men who had held him two days before. They would find it rather harder to find him than they had done earlier, once he had put a few fast miles between himself and the house so he opened the throttle and the three cylinder motor roared enthusiastically as the speedometer nudged past the ton. He shot past the end of the little back road to Creg Ny Baa, then tucked in behind the fairing on the long straight down to the Liverpool Arms.

In a briefing room deep within Police Headquarters, the final meeting in preparation for the Presidential visit was taking place. The officers in that room were looking at each other nervously as the Chief Constable began to speak.

"We have just heard that Airforce One is approaching Shannon. He'll be there about an hour before taking off in a private jet for the Island. Flight time from Shannon won't be more than forty-five minutes so we've got maybe two hours until he gets here. You all know your duties and those of your men, so I don't intend to go over them again this morning. The President will be welcomed at Ronaldsway by the Chief Minister and myself, then taken by helicopter to the Governor's House. He wants to see the racing so we've persuaded the organisers to put back the start for a couple of hours. They'll tell everyone that the delay's due to mist on the mountain, but not until roads are closed so that means we won't have to contend with a load of moving traffic. Everyone will already be where they were planning to be so we can concentrate all our resources on guarding our man. Anyone have any questions?"

"Not a question, Sir, more of a statement," one of the senior officers responded, "this is going to be a bit of a trial of our resources, isn't it?" the Chief Constable nodded gravely.

"The ultimate trial," he said.

"Look, we just need to speak to someone senior," Love was trying to explain to the woman behind the glass. "My colleague and I have important information which concerns the President of the United States of America and his visit here today. We think he may be in danger and that an attempt may be made on his life."

"Don't worry, sir," the woman replied politely, "all necessary precautions have been taken. President Shrub will be as safe as if he were at home." Love tried again

"But we have intelligence that we need to share with the police." The woman smiled condescendingly.

"I'll see if I can find someone who you can speak to," she said, then turned and disappeared from sight. It was a good ten minutes before she returned. "I'm afraid everyone's rather busy at the moment," she explained, "what with the races and the visit, there aren't any officers available who you could speak to, but if you were to wait or come back in an hour or so, then someone might have come back in from patrol."

"Look Ma'am," the American began, "we have vital information that could prevent an assassination; just go back through that door behind you and get someone in here now. If you don't do what I say, you'll have a murder on your hands." The woman stared at him for a moment, then turned and fled. A second later, they could hear the piercing shriek of alarm bells ringing; the door to their left burst open and two uniformed policemen wielding guns sprang out."

"Armed police," the first of them shouted, pointing his gun at Mike Smith's head, "on the floor, now, both of you and put your hands behind your backs."

Price had decided to take the Chief Medical Officer's advice and, although travelling to his allotted spot well before the roads were due to close, kept well away from the Course and approached the corner known as *Waterworks* on foot, after parking the Triumph by the little reservoir which nestled in the woods below. It was a pretty spot, he thought, a little reminiscent of some place or other he had fished for trout once, long ago, but the whine and roar of high-performance motorcycle engines echoing through the trees told him that the mountain road was not far away. Climbing up the steep footpath to the Course, he pulled the mobile from his pocket and made the call.

"Is that, er, Des?"

"Dr Price?"

"Yes, you said that I should call you if...if I had any information," the doctor slowly began.

"What can you tell me?" the voice demanded.

"An attempt will be made on the President's life today."

"How and where?"

"We think it will be an attack on his plane...there are suggestions that the ground radio beacon near Cregneash will be destroyed. I can't say how, but..." Price spoke falteringly, suddenly less confident now in the accuracy of the information he was trying to pass on.

"Explain?" the voice said curtly and the doctor found himself recounting the words he had heard spoken the previous evening by his friends. When Price had finished speaking, there was a long pause at the other end of the line.

"We will look into this," came the eventual reply, "where are you now?" Whether it was the pause or the question that had warned him all was not right, Price was unable to say for sure, but suppressed and hidden doubts suddenly materialised within him and he pressed the 'end' button on his mobile 'phone. He thought about the voice again and realised that the man he had been speaking to was not a member of the British Secret Service. He had heard the man speak before in broad cockney and in cultured English tones, but now he had heard him speak in a voice which gave more than a hint as to his true origin and he realised that a 'phone call he had thought would save the President could well have sealed his fate. He had been walking as he was speaking and had now reached the side of the mountain road. It was eight am and crowds had already begun to gather, but Price no longer had thoughts or time for motorcycle racing: he needed to speak to his friends and he needed to ride south. He strode over to the nearest marshal and showed the man his race pass.

"Jonathon Price," he explained breathlessly, "I'm one of the race doctors and I'm supposed to be here on duty today...only...something's cropped up and I can't. Can you get onto Race Control and tell them to move someone else here...It really is a matter of life and death." The man he had been speaking to stared at him blankly for a moment, but the doctor's wild eyes convinced him that Price was either a lunatic or speaking the truth and he nodded.

"Okay Doc," he said, "I'll tell 'em; you get going and do what you've got to do."

Love stared at the locked steel door of the little cell. Their plan could not have gone more disastrously wrong and time was fast ticking by. His watch had been taken from him, but he guessed he had been incarcerated for two or three hours. If so, then President Shrub would be due to land at any time and neither he nor Smith had managed to even speak to a policeman, never mind convince anyone of the imminent danger. They had been arrested, briefly told that they had committed offences against public order and then had been locked up without interview or opportunity to give a proper explanation for what they had done. Smith seemed to have been put in a nearby cell, for he had heard the man shouting loudly in protest at the treatment they had both received, but no-one had taken the slightest bit of notice and after a time the American had given up. When they had first been locked up, Love had heard sounds from the corridor outside: sounds of people talking, footsteps, doors opening; that sort of thing, but he had heard nothing at all now for nearly an hour and began to strongly suspect that the custody suite was deserted. He banged on the door in anger.

"I need to speak to someone now," he shouted, but it was no use; his shouts and cries were met by a gloomy silence.

"Good morning, Mr President," the Chief Minister said warmly, grasping the man's hand, "and welcome to the Isle of Man."

"Well, thank you kindly, Mr Prime Minister," the President replied. One of the dark-suited aides behind him leaned forward and whispered something in his ear. "What's that," the President muttered, turning towards the aide for a moment.

"It's Chief Minister," the man whispered loudly, "Prime Minister's in England." The President's face had clouded momentarily, but the beaming smile resurfaced in an instant.

"Pleased to meet you Chief Minister," he continued, "I'm sure you're doin' a fine job standin' in for the Prime Minister. Will he be coming back from England before I leave?" The aide was unable to prevent himself glancing skywards for a second, but when he reverted his eyes, he found that President Shrub had already moved on. "Heard so much about your little country," the President was saying, "and I believe you've helped people all around the world save a great deal of money…"

"Mr President," the aide hissed loudly, "if you remember what was agreed…no mention of tax."

"Okay, okay, we don't mention tax...I'm a Republican," he explained to the Chief Minister, "and we don't like to mention tax either."

"Mr President," the voice behind him hissed again, "your speech." President Shrub's eyes lit up and he pulled a crumpled piece of paper from his breast pocket, then launched into his prepared address.

A mile or so away, Price was standing beside his motorbike listening to the President's arrival which was being broadcast live on Manx Radio. He had ridden south faster than he had ever thought possible, but had run into a stationary wall of traffic in the village of Ballasalla. The cause, he immediately discovered, was a police roadblock some distance ahead. The authorities had closed the short length of road which ran past the airport and no-one would be allowed through until the President's plane had landed and his helicopter taken off. That the plane had landed safely, he knew for he had seen it for himself and after turning on his little earpiece radio, managed to catch the final words of the Presidential address.

"...so I look forward to seeing your island, meeting your Manx people and watching your famous TT races."

"That was President Shrub live at Ronaldsway," the announcer explained, "...and we currently have a two hour delay before the start of the four lap Superstock event, but don't forget the roads will remain closed for that period. Time for a little music." Price turned off the radio and frowned. Shrub had made it, so their theory had been wrong. Either that, or someone had successfully thwarted Illosovich's little scheme. Had Roy or Mike managed to convince the police to take action or had Boroweski done something or were Des and his men really who he had initially thought they were. The doctor was confused, but no doubt time would tell. In the meantime, he had to get back to *Waterworks* before the day's racing began.

When Price returned to the house that evening it was after seven. Louise Templeton was already there, but of Love, Smith or any of the others, there was no sign at all. The Superstock race had been won by the same English favourite who had taken the laurels in the Superbike and Rorletski had, yet again, failed to finish after leading for three of the four laps.

"Richard won't be happy with that," Price said to the advocate, "how did the trial go today?"

"The Prosecution concluded their case," Louise Templeton replied. "I managed to get a few points over in my cross-examination of some of their witnesses, but not enough to swing the jury. We start our case tomorrow, but it won't take long. I've only got Professor Clarke and, of course, Richard wants to take the stand."

"Is that wise?" Price asked, "you know he's liable to lose his temper."

"It's his right," the advocate said, "and to be honest, we don't have anything else, unless by some major miracle the other two witnesses make an appearance. There's not much chance of that, though, I think they've left the Island or they're dead."

"I see your point," Price agreed nodding, "but talking of appearances, where are Roy and Mike?"

"I don't know; haven't you seen them?"

"I haven't seen or spoken to them all day." The advocate's mobile 'phone started ringing. She picked it up, glanced at the display and the look of curiosity on her face turned to one of disgust.

"Police Headquarters," she said to Price in a tone of voice which conveyed feelings of weary annoyance. She pressed the button and answered the call. "Hello, yes this is Louise Templeton. What...you have who?...can you explain?" She listened in silence for a minute, maybe two, before speaking again, "well, I think you'd better apologise to them and bring them both here...they know the address and whilst you're on, we have four missing persons...oh, you know about them? Well don't you think you'd better start looking for them?...You will do, good." The advocate ended the call and turned to Price.

"That was the Custody Sergeant. They've had Roy and Mike locked up all day and only just got around to interviewing them this evening. Sounded a little sheepish, the sergeant; blamed it all on lack of resources."

"What happened?"

"It sounds like the police got their wires a little crossed and took Roy and Mike's warnings as threats, but didn't bother to find out what our two private detectives were really trying to say until just now. The sergeant didn't sound as though he believed their story, *rather fanciful* were his exact words, but the police are satisfied that Roy and Mike haven't committed any offences so they're being released and brought 'round here now. They told the police about Grant and his friends disappearing, but as to whether that sparks any action from the boys in blue, your guess is as good as mine."

Chapter Thirty Seven

Thursday – Race Week

"Well Professor, that's all well and good, but it's only your opinion, isn't it?" the Prosecutor asked as he brought his cross-examination to a close. The pathologist had to agree that such was indeed the case and Louise could see some of the jurors nodding: the case for the Defence seemed to be ebbing away and although Professor Clarke had given his evidence with confidence and clarity, she could see that the twelve stony faces to the right of her remained to be persuaded of her client's innocence. It was supposed to be a presumption, but with Manx juries, things often went the other way with the Prosecution facing a far easier burden than the Defence. It was time for one final gamble; as the pathologist stepped down from the witness box, she stood up and spoke.

"The Defence would like to call Mr Richard Quayle." The undertaker was led out of the dock and through the court to the witness box at the front. He took the oath and his advocate began to take his evidence-in-chief.

"So could you tell the Court what happened after you had spoken to Ernie Quine?"

"Well, I got dressed, went out into the garage, got into the hearse and set off for the South."

"What time was that?"

"Oh, about two; yes it was exactly two, 'cause I remember looking at my watch and thinking, I'm getting too old for this game, I should be fast asleep in bed."

"What was the weather like?"

"Terrible, snow was coming down like nothing I'd ever seen before and it was sticking. That hearse was sliding around like a pig on roller skates and..." a suppressed giggle could be heard from the public gallery, "...and I couldn't see a thing."

"How far did you get, Mr Quayle," the advocate asked.

"Bottom of Richmond Hill. That policeman was there, the one who gave evidence yesterday. He told me that the road was impassable and I would have to go back."

"And when would that be?"

"Well, I didn't look at my watch, but the policeman yesterday said two-twenty and, although I thought it was a little later, I won't argue with that."

"So what happened next?"

"I tried to 'phone Ernie, but he didn't answer so I sent him a text."

"Is this the content of that text, Mr Quayle?...Exhibit Five, Your Honour." The advocate passed a piece of paper to the usher who took it to the man in the witness box. He examined it carefully through his glasses, before nodding.

"Yes, that's it."

Louise took him slowly through the rest of the night and when she had finished sat down. The Prosecutor stood up.

"Mr Quayle," he said, leaning forward a touch aggressively, "you say you left the policeman at the bottom of Richmond Hill at twenty past two."

"I didn't say that," the Defendant interrupted, "the policeman did; I said I thought it was a little later."

"But you said, Mr Quayle, that you wouldn't argue with the time...and then you said you got back to your house at between four-thirty and quarter to five."

"Yes, that's right."

"Are you asking members of the jury to believe that a journey which had taken you twenty minutes in one direction took over two hours in the other?"

"Well, the snow was terrible, much worse than on the way out."

"Come on Mr Quayle, six times longer to cover the same distance. A little hard to believe, isn't it?"

"Well, I, er," the undertaker's face turned even redder than its normal distinctive hue, "I may have, er, er..."

"May have what, Mr Quayle?"

"Well, it was freezing cold and I needed warming up, sort of internally, as it were so I pulled the hearse into the car park down by the yacht club and had a little drink...or two." The Prosecutor frowned; this had not come out before.

"Drink, Mr Quayle. You made no mention of this in your police station interview or in your evidence-in-chief, why not?"

"Well, er," the Defendant replied nervously, "I didn't want anyone to think I'd been drink-driving, so I just, er, kept quiet about it."

"Drink-driving!" the Prosecutor exclaimed with incredulity, "when you are facing a charge of murder. What did you have to drink? I believe that the hearse was searched after you were arrested and the reports made no mention of drink being found."

"Er, Canadian Club whisky," the undertaker explained, "it's all I ever drink!"

"It wasn't found, Mr Quayle," the Prosecutor snarled, his anger rising at this new development.

"It wasn't found, 'cause I've got a secret compartment in the hearse where I keep it and when I mean secret, I mean it's designed not to be found, but it'll still be there now and if you want, I'll show you...if that's okay with you, Your Honour?"

It was most irregular, the Deemster was forced to admit, but if the Police investigation had failed to reveal the presence of the whisky, it had also failed to reveal its absence. He was not prepared to allow an adjournment in the middle of a trial to allow further searches to be made and he ordered the jury to give the Defendant the benefit of doubt. The undertaker had said he had several drinks and had fallen asleep for over an hour. He had said that he had arrived back at the house no earlier than half-past four and that was therefore the time the jury had to take into account. Richard refused to budge on any point of the evidence he had given and after an hour of fruitless cross-examination, the Prosecutor was forced to admit defeat.

"No further questions, Your Honour," he finally said and sat down. Miss Templeton had nothing to say by way of re-examination and so the undertaker returned to his place in the dock. Louise was wondering whether to ask for a short adjournment or whether to say that she had concluded the case for the Defence when she suddenly felt a tap on her right shoulder. She turned and saw it was the usher who leant over to whisper in her ear. An expression of surprise passed across her face, surprise which rapidly changed into relief.

"I'd like to call Mr Jason Quiggan, Your Honour," she boldly announced. The Prosecutor, Kneale cast a stony glare at her, then turned to the detective sitting behind him.

"Thought you said Quiggan and Finch wouldn't show," he muttered loudly enough for Louise to hear. The man's reply was inaudible, but it didn't seem to placate Kneale. He stood up.

"I'm sorry, Your Honour, but may I request a short adjournment? This witness is unexpected and I really need to confer with the police." The Deemster frowned.

"Mr Kneale, did not Miss Templeton serve a copy of Mr Quiggan's witness statement on you, as I recall it, just the other week?"

"She did, Sir, but..."

"Then this witness is hardly unexpected is he?"

"We had information, Your Honour, that Mr Quiggan had gone missing and would not appear today and because of that, I have not come prepared to cross-examine him as fully as I might."

"That, Mr Kneale, is your problem. Your application to adjourn is dismissed." Louise cast the Deemster a glance of thanks and he smiled at her for the first time in the trial. Was it her imagination, or did she sense a sea-change in court?

"So, Mr Quiggan, please tell the Court what you did next?"

"Well we'd got into the house through the side door...Darren started an apprenticeship as a locksmith..." the witness said by way of explanation, "...he never finished it, but he has quite a few sets of skeleton keys. That lock was pretty easy anyway and we picked up a few bits and pieces as we looked around the house."

"Such as?"

"Found a mobile 'phone lying in the hallway, candlesticks that looked like they were made of solid silver; that sort of thing. Anyway, we crept along this long corridor and opened a door at the end."

"Go on."

"It was a garage."

"Were there any cars in it?"

"Yeah, just one: a powder blue Jaguar Sports."

"Nothing else...I mean, did you see a hearse?"

"Naa," the witness said, shaking his head, "just the Jag."

"What did you do next?"

"Darren pointed out a door on the other side of the garage so we went and tried it. It was unlocked so we opened it and went through."

"And?"

"There was a big room with a funny sort of table in the middle and lying on the middle of that table was the body of a fella with a knife right through his heart."

Chapter Thirty Seven

"What time was this, Jason?" the advocate asked.

"Three-thirty," the witness replied.

"And did you see anything else before you left the house?"

"What do you mean?"

"Well, for example, did you see any bloodstained footprints on the floor of the corridor?" The witness shook his head.

"No. It was a wooden floor 'cause I remember saying to Darren that my uncle Pete was getting one laid down in his house and there weren't any marks on it at all."

"Did you hear anything?"

"Yeah. We were walking back along the corridor when we heard these voices coming from a room on the sea-ward side. Couldn't understand what they were saying, but it sounded like at least three men."

"Why couldn't you understand them, Mr Quiggan?"

"'Cause they were foreign, Miss. Couldn't swear which language, but I think it was Russian."

Mr Kneale's cross-examination had no discernable effect and when she heard his closing speech, Louise knew that the Prosecutor had lost his will to win the case. He tried to cast doubt on the reliability of Jason's testimony, suggesting that a self-confessed burglar may have ulterior motives for saying what he had said, but his heart was far from in it and when he sat down, Louise felt like shouting in relief. She kept her speech short, pointing out the obvious discrepancies between the Prosecution case and the facts, then sat down and allowed the Deemster to give his summing up.

"Not guilty," came the verdict after less than half an hour's deliberation and the undertaker was released to rapturous applause. The Deemster smiled and, for once, did not threaten to clear the court, but allowed the clapping to die down before he spoke.

"I am less than happy, Mr Kneale, at the way the police and the Prosecution have handled this case. In my humble view, the jury have come to the correct decision and I will go so far as to say that this matter should never have been brought to court. I trust that you will convey my remarks to everyone concerned. Thank you." He stood up and the court rose.

It was half-past four in the afternoon when Louise and the undertaker finally escaped the clutch of reporters and photographers who had gathered outside the courthouse. The advocate had 'phoned Price to break the news of Richard's acquittal and release and Price, in turn, had news that would make the undertaker's happy day, happier still.

"Rorletski won the Junior," he said, "with a new lap record for the six hundred class."

"I'll tell Richard," she replied, "look we'd better go; see you at the house."

The roads were now open and Louise and the undertaker slowly drove through the heavy evening traffic to Police Headquarters where the handful of items found on Richard's person at the time of his arrest were restored to their rightful owner. Once reunited with his wallet, his second favourite possession, he directed Louise to drive straight to Winerite so that he might be reunited with his first.

The last house in Onchan was inhabited again that evening and the lights shone brightly from its windows for the first time in months. As Richard savoured his favourite tipple, Louise, Jonathon and the two private detectives sipped ice cold champagne. It was a celebration of sorts, but a restrained one for as Roy Love pointed out Grant and the Australians were still missing and Illosovich was still out there waiting to execute some deadly plan. The undertaker knew little of any of what had happened and as they brought him up to speed in the developments to date, he revealed something which came as a total surprise to the others, but could explain quite a lot.

"Fistard, eh?" he said, "I've got a little bolt hole down there, you know."

"What!" the others cried in unison.

"Little Manx farmhouse," he explained, "at the end of a little lane beneath Cronk Ny Arrey Hill. It belonged to my father and his before him and I kept it on as a weekend retreat when I want to escape from here."

"But Richard," the advocate protested, "you never mentioned this before, even when I asked you if you knew the Quilleash family and Cronk Ny Arrey Farm."

"Didn't I?" the undertaker replied defensively, "I'm sorry, but I just assumed you knew. Anyway, I didn't know the family or the farm. My place is quite close as the crow flies, but quite a long way by road."

"When did you last go there, Richard?" Love asked.

"Weekend before Ernie was killed. Like I said, it was my weekend retreat. Not that I went there every weekend, not in the winter, anyway, but I go there a lot in the Spring and Summer. It's a lovely place, you must come down and stay there with me whilst you're around."

"They framed you for murder," Love said slowly, "knowing that you'd be arrested, charged and remanded to Victoria Road Gaol and even if you were eventually acquitted, you'd be out of the way for months and months and they'd be able to use your farm for their own purposes, whatever they are. Cronk Ny Arrey was a blind, a red herring. Whatever Illosovich is trying to do involves your place, Richard. What's it called?"

"Shrub Cottage," the undertaker announced proudly, then looked in amazement at the curious expressions which had suddenly appeared on the faces of the others. "What's up, have I said something wrong?"

"*Shrub Cottage*," Smith uttered the words weakly, "why, what does that mean?"

"A shrub's a diminutive sort of bush," the undertaker explained, "and the garden's full of them. That's probably how the cottage got its name, but I do seem to remember once my old grandfather telling me that the cottage was named after its original inhabitant, a farmer called Shrub who emigrated somewhere about a hundred and fifty years ago."

"It's the answer," Smith cried and everyone began to speak at once.

"Shhh," the American continued, "Richard, does this cottage have a cellar?"

"Oh yes," the undertaker replied, "a deep and very extensive one; very cold and excellent for storing wine. Not that I drink wine, of course, but I do like to keep it in for guests. In fact I keep my entire collection down at Shrub Cottage and just bring a few bottles up here from time to time. Parts of the cellar are run down and dangerous so I haven't visited them for years, but I did hear old stories when I was a young fella that the cellar connects with ancient tunnels and mine-workings that riddle the whole Meayll peninsular and some used to say that they even extended under the sea to the Calf of Man."

Chapter Thirty Eight

Friday Morning – Senior Race Day

Senior Race day had come around at last and dawn broke clear and sunny with a forecast that the good weather would last until at least the following week. Great things were planned by the organisers of the final event. President Shrub had agreed to start the race and present the trophy to the victor. After the Senior Race, a cavalcade of historic machines and famous riders would parade around the Course. The riders were rumoured to include every former winner of the event still alive and able to swing their leg over a bike and the fans were out at the crack of dawn to bag their positions at every possible vantage point around the historic racetrack. But the occupants of the last house in Onchan were up and about far earlier than that, for they had business to do and precious little time in which to do it. Price had 'phoned Boroweski the previous night and explained what they had found out. It could all prove to be a false hypothesis, he said, but it did explain all the facts. When Boroweski confirmed that Shrub Cottage had indeed been one of the names on Grant's list of places to visit, the doctor could feel that the hypothesis was fast becoming a theory which might withstand the sternest test.

They piled into the advocate's four wheel drive and set off long before it was light and by daybreak had reached Port St Mary where they found the Russians waiting for them on their bikes. Boroweski had brought his full contingent of men and Price could sense a thrill of battle and adventure in the air, although he had no real idea what could possibly lie ahead. The Russians rode on in front of them, a noisy, smoking vanguard passing through the sleeping streets of the quiet little town. In just about any other place of this size in the world, Price thought, twenty hard-looking, hairy bikers appearing before dawn would strike fear into the hearts and minds of the inhabitants and spark urgent calls to the police, but Port St Mary had seen it all before and those who lived there carried on sleeping as if this were just another night.

A few minutes later, they came to a halt at the end of a narrow little lane.

"Is this the place?" Smith asked and the undertaker nodded gravely as a golden shaft of early morning sunlight picked out the name plate on the wall of the whitewashed little house. The Russians dismounted and rather strangely, Price thought, seemed to be dismantling their machines. A minute or two later their actions became rather clearer as parts of frame and fairing which had been removed were reassembled and underwent a metamorphosis into guns. Boroweski looked at the doctor's startled face and laughed.

"You surprised, Doktor Price? Trust me, when you know Illosovich like we do, you not make mistake of coming unarmed."

"I have brought the key," Richard ventured, "so you don't need to damage anything." Boroweski took it from his hand and pushed it into the lock, then with his men and their artillery behind him, turned the key and pushed open the door. The Russians were inside in seconds and Price tensed, expecting the sound of gunfire to awaken the sleeping town, but the silence persisted and in a minute, Boroweski's figure appeared in the doorway.

"This place is empty," he reported, "safe for you all to come in now."

They made their way inside and looked around the little cottage with their host, the undertaker, pointing out its features and furniture with an obvious sense of pride. The place had been occupied until very recently indeed and the stench of stale tobacco smoke pervaded every room.

"Russian cigarettes," Boroweski confirmed, "Illosovich and his men here, not half hour ago. Look!" He picked up a butt from the floor and they could all see that it had not long ceased burning. "Where is cellar?" he demanded.

"I'll show you, if you just give me half a chance," the undertaker replied, noting with some annoyance cigarette burn marks everywhere. He led them through the tiny parlour to a scullery at the rear and there pointed out the iron ring of a trapdoor in the middle of the stone-flagged floor. "That's the way down," he said, "take care on the steps; they're steep and can be slippery."

Boroweski seized the iron ring and lifted. The trapdoor flew open and a dark void appeared below.

"You're going to need your torches," the undertaker explained, "because the cellar's never been wired for electricity; I've been meaning to do it for years, but never seemed to have had the time."

Louise confessed an irrational, but insurmountable hatred of tunnels and darkness and volunteered to remain on the surface in case anything needed doing up there.

"Anyway," she explained, "I've got a pretty strong feeling that I've been down there before. I was blindfolded, but I distinctly remember being led down steps and feeling terrified lest I fall. If it is the place where they were holding me, then I really don't want to go down there again." The tall Russian commander pointed out that it was essential to guard the cellar entrance, in case Illosovich or his men should return so he left some of his men with the advocate and then led the others down the well-worn, steep, stone steps into the darkness below. When they had reached the bottom, they looked carefully around and found that the dark and cold chamber beneath Shrub Cottage was far, far more extensive than even Richard had let on. Those parts which had been in everyday use lay just beside the bottom of the stair and comprised a large, arching vault full of dusty old bottles, together with several smaller vaults which seemed to have served as general stores.

"Some damn good stuff there," the undertaker remarked pointing at the dusty bottles beneath the cobwebs, "some of those bottles are exceptionally rare vintages; would bring a fortune at auction."

"What is further on?" Boroweski demanded, seemingly uninterested in the wine.

"The main tunnel goes on for quite a way," Richard replied, "some of the vaults which come off it have been used by the family to hoard all manner of junk...never throw things away, us Quayles...never know what come in useful."

"The tunnel, Richard?" Price prompted.

"The tunnel?...oh, yes, the tunnel. I've not been more than a dozen yards along it for many, many years, but I do seem to remember that it descends quite steeply and cuts into the side of the hill. There is a section where the roof looks as though it once partially collapsed; maybe it has fully collapsed by now, who knows? But I've never been past that point, so I can't tell you what, if anything, lies beyond."

"Come," Boroweski commanded and after a brief glance at each other, the undertaker, Price, Love and Smith went after him. Boroweski's men made up the rear.

The tunnel was damp, cold and low-roofed and as most of the men were over six feet tall, they had to stoop to walk along. They passed dark spaces on either side which spoke of chambers or other tunnels, but their leader moved confidently on, deviating neither left nor right from his chosen path. After quarter of an hour, the tunnel began to slope downwards and Boroweski stopped.

"Are you sure this is the right way, Mikael?" the doctor asked, "I mean, we've passed quite a few openings from this passage. Shouldn't we check them all?"

"This is right way, Doktor Price," the Russian replied, "look!" He pointed the beam of his torch at the floor and Price saw that a thick layer of dust lay on the stone flags, but the dust was not undisturbed: it bore the marks of what seemed like dozens of fresh footprints and the mark of something else as well.

"What is that?" he asked, pointing at the solid line which ran between the footprints.

"It's a wheel mark," Smith replied, "maybe they used a wheelbarrow to move something heavy?" Boroweski shook his head.

"Two wheels," he said, "one behind other, see where sometimes they step out of line...and too wide for wheelbarrow, but just right size, I think for Petromax motorcycle."

"They brought my bike down here?" the undertaker squeaked in disbelief, "how on earth...?"

"They had men, they had ropes; this thing is possible, believe me," came the reply.

"But...why?" the undertaker asked.

"That is what we are here to find out?"

"I think this is the place I told you about," Richard said a few minutes later, "where the roof once partially collapsed, but it looks like someone's shored it up since I was last here." The tunnel had dipped even further since they had last stopped, but after reaching its lowest point, seemed now to be rising and they had come to a point where the rough wooden shuttering above and beside them did not seem to bear the marks of age. They had long since passed beyond the confines of the house and for several hundred yards, the stone walls and roof of what had been a lengthy diverticulum of the original cellar had given way to the blackened timbers of mine workings, but here the wood was clean and new and the tunnel showed signs of recent activity.

"You are right," Boroweski confirmed, "be careful and quiet now; I think we are close to that which we seek."

"What exactly..." the undertaker began.

"Shhh...listen," the Russian ordered, "extinguish torches...now." The lights snapped off and they stood there in the cold darkness. They could hear distant voices and, as their eyes became accustomed to the gloom, they could just make out the faintest flickering of light from somewhere up ahead. Price sensed slow and purposeful movement from the man beside him and guessed that Boroweski had produced his gun.

"Forward, now, slow," came the whispered command and they began to tip-toe along the passage towards the dim and dancing lights.

It took longer than any of them, except perhaps Boroweski, had expected for the sounds had carried far in the silence of the tunnel and the light had been reflected some distance along its walls, but after a few more twists and turns they could hear the voices clearly and for the first time that day the Russian smiled, for he recognised their source.

"Geez Grant, it's nearly eight o' clock. They'll have already started taking the bikes through scrutineering and..."

"Will you shut up about the bloody races Don. The rest of us are a bit more concerned about our lives. I get the distinct feeling that Illosovich isn't planning on letting us out of this place; we've seen too bloody much." Boroweski stepped forward into the light.

"Mikael, Jonathon...bloody hell, the lot of you," Grant exclaimed, "I just can't begin to tell you how pleased we are to see you guys, but how did you know we were here; we thought we'd never be found." The four Australians were sitting on the floor of the tunnel which had been widened at that point and now looked as those it had been hewn from solid rock, for there were no signs of props or shuttering. Their hands and feet were tied and the men looked grimy and unshaven, but uninjured and very much alive.

"How were you taken?" the Russian asked and Grant explained.

"That copper...Richard Liszt...I never liked him and now I know he's bent. I made the mistake of calling him to ask for help and telling him where I was, when I should have called you. Next thing I know, a load of monks appeared...monks with bloody guns..." As he was talking, Boroweski suddenly tensed, for although he had been listening carefully to what Grant was saying, another sound had intruded on his ears. It was the sound of nearby footsteps, at first walking, but now running down the passage which led on from where they now were.

"Someone listening nearby," Boroweski said, interrupting the Australian, "one of Illosovich's men. He know we here and run off to tell others. We must leave now, before they return." His men had already cut their bonds and the four Australians rose stiffly to their feet.

"Might have been the other guy," Mitch suggested.

"Other guy?" Love asked, a curious expression suddenly appearing on his face.

"Some guy Mitch claims to have seen when the rest of us were asleep," Grant explained, "we think he was hallucinating or dreaming, but Mitch reckons it was some sort of deranged hermit who lives in the mine." The others laughed, but Mitch's face remained serious.

"I saw the guy once and I wasn't dreaming," he said, "he just appeared for a second and was gone, but he had long straggly hair and a thick matted beard and his eyes were wild, like the man was insane."

"Interesting, yes, but we must go," the Russian said before Mitch could elaborate.

"Lead on," Grant said and followed Boroweski down the winding tunnel back towards Shrub Cottage. The return journey seemed shorter than the outward one, but as they reached the stonework of the outer reaches of the cellar, they heard a low rumble behind them and a few seconds later felt a hot blast of air.

"Illosovich has blown tunnel," the Russian confirmed, "I saw signs at spot where roof once collapsed that he had placed explosives, but we not have time to make them safe."

"But why would he do that?" Price asked, "I mean surely he needed to keep this tunnel open. If Shrub Cottage was his target and the President really is going to visit, then he's cooked his own goose and sealed himself in the mine."

"There must be other exits," Smith suggested, "but I agree that Shrub Cottage is looking pretty safe now."

They climbed the steps up from the cellar to find an anxious Louise Templeton.

"Thank God, you're back," she said, "you've been ages. We heard what sounded like an explosion. It shook the foundations of the house and I thought for a moment…"

"Everyone's okay," Price said, "and we've found Grant and the others. They need a bit of cleaning up and a shave, but with a day or two's rest, they'll be fine."

"We ain't got time for that, Doc," Don explained, "I've got a race to run and it starts in about two and a half hours."

"You're not seriously suggesting…"

"Too right I am Doc, after what it took to get to this Island, I'm gonna make the start of that Senior."

"But you must be exhausted…it'd be far too dangerous," the doctor protested, "and anyway, they've taken your van."

"Don't need the van, Doc," he replied, "bike's back at Grant's place and I can ride it up to the start and as for feeling tired and it being too dangerous, well I'm an Australian, not a Pom and we just do that sort of thing."

"Come on," the advocate said, "if that's your decision, you're going to need to get back to Douglas fast. I'll take the rest of your team and you, Jonathon and Richard; I assume that you'll be wanting to come? As for you others, I think you may want to stay around here."

"We probably will," Love said, "but why do you assume it?"

"Because whilst you were down there, I was listening to Manx Radio and they announced that President Shrub will visit Cregneash after the conclusion of the Senior TT."

Chapter Thirty Nine

Senior Race Day – Late Morning/Early Afternoon

Louise had stopped by the house near Hutchinson Square and, as she had no plans for the rest of the day, had been roped in to help ferry such things as tools and spare wheels to the rear of the Grandstand whilst Don rushed off to find his leathers and his mates went to start the racing machine. Don would have to ride it up there on public roads, without plates or insurance, but it was the Isle of Man and no-one seemed bothered about such things when the TT was on. Richard had returned to his usual self and was sitting impatiently in the 4WD grumbling so Price wished the Australians luck and wished Richard luck for Rorletski, then pulled on his helmet, swung his leg over the Triumph and rode off to the track.

He reached his spot only minutes before the roads were due to close and had been pleased to earlier discover that he had been allocated Hilberry. It was the same corner he had been to for the Senior Race the previous year and he knew he could get to it and away again, if he so needed, without using the Course, for a narrow and twisty, but perfectly useable lane led directly back to Onchan and meant that Hilberry Corner itself was no more than a few minutes ride from the undertaker's house. The lane was lined with parked bikes for nearly a quarter of a mile, but he managed to find a gap near the front and carefully squeezed his machine in. When he reached the rope which separated the lane from the Course, one of the marshals recognised him instantly.

"Morning Doc, you're pushing it a bit aren't you, oversleep or something?"

"Yeah, something like that," Price replied with a smile. The course inspection car shot past, followed by a yellow-jacketed travelling marshal; the road was now closed and the Centenary Senior Race about to begin. Radios, until that moment silent, were turned on and the array of old-fashioned, trumpet-like loudspeakers mounted on the rickety grandstand overlooking the corner burst into life.

"The machines are all lined up now in front of us," the commentator announced, "and it's a marvellous sight. They stretch right down Glencrutchery Road, way past the side road to the police station, all sparkling and gleaming in the brilliant morning sunshine...I

244

don't think I've ever seen so many..." Price stopped listening. It seemed, from his short experience, that the commentators said pretty much the same thing every year; he distinctly remembered almost exactly the same words being spoken twelve months earlier. Suddenly, in contradiction of what he had just been thinking, he did hear something very different indeed: it was the American National Anthem. President Shrub had arrived with the Lieutenant Governor to start the race. When the music ended the intrepid, but foolhardy pit-lane commentator tried to get an interview.

"Mr President...Mr President... could you just give us a few words about how you're finding the Isle of Man and the TT?"

"Turn that off," the Island-wide audience heard a voice mutter, "turn that off. The President doesn't do unscripted interviews." There was a loud buzz and then silence and Price grinned. He could just picture two suited heavies muscling in on the hapless reporter and seizing his microphone. The loudspeakers burst into life a few seconds later.

"Andy here, back in the studio. We seem to be having a few technical problems down there at the start line, but we hope to get things sorted out in a few minutes, ready for the start of the race." A succession of chart-topping popular songs then burst onto the airwaves and continued past the time when the race was supposed to start. Around the Island, puzzled spectators scratched their heads in confusion, wondering if or why the Senior was delayed, but everyone soon discovered that the race had started dead on time, for when the commentary resumed, it was to take the leading bikes through Glen Helen and Price was pleased but not surprised to hear that one of his friends was in the lead.

"We can see a bike through the trees...yes, just as expected, it's the number one plate of last year's winner, Rorletski. He's living down in Castletown these days so I suppose we're going to have to call him the rushing Russian from Rushen. Anyway, there he goes, 'round the corner and off up Creg Willey's Hill towards Lamb Fell. There'll be a bit of a gap now, because we've just heard that the number two machine has pulled in at Ballacraine...what's that?...oh, made adjustments and proceeded...hold on, here's the number three machine of John Bass...oh, fast, so fast John...yes the fast Bass is up there...we make it one second behind Rorletski, but there are a lot of other quick men about and we'll try to slot them in just as soon as they've gone past."

Price walked over to the marshals who were standing by the wall to his left.

"Not seen it through here since they straightened out Brandish. Is it faster?" he asked. The marshals looked at each other and one of them, a woman, spoke.

"It's so fast now, it's scary. Saw that John Bass go through here the other day and I was about to dive for cover. Never seen anyone take a bike through a corner so quick, I'll swear he was absolutely on the limit."

"I spoke to him in my hotel bar a few days ago," Price told them, "and he said that he even scared himself."

"Don Campbell leading by half a second at Glen Helen," one of the marshals who had been attentively listening to the commentary cut in. Price started.

"That's the Australian, isn't it?" he asked.

"Yeah, he started number seventeen, so he's got a lot of traffic ahead of him. Rorletski's just got an open road, until he starts hitting back markers later on in the race."

"How long before they get 'round here?" Price asked.

"Rorletski'll be at Ballaugh by now," the man replied, "so he shouldn't be more than another seven or eight minutes."

Sure enough, at exactly the time the marshal had predicted, the number one machine flashed past Hilberry Corner. The doctor gave him a wave, but the Russian was going far to fast to acknowledge it and disappeared from sight in almost the blink of an eye. There was a good thirty second wait before the next bike appeared, but then heavy traffic until the end of the race. It was a peculiar type of event to watch, Price thought as he stood there, with riders starting individually at ten second intervals it meant a long wait for the first, but then an almost constant procession of machinery until the last bike went past at the end of the final lap. The staggered starts also made it hard, if not impossible, to work out who was leading without listening to the radio and as the doctor had forgotten to bring one, he was thankful that a public address system was in place.

"Rorletski and Campbell can't be separated at the end of the first lap." The loudspeakers squawked, "and, wait for it, that's a new absolute lap record from a standing start. One hundred and thirty-one mile per hour." Price shook his head in disbelief and prayed silently that neither of his friends made any mistakes. The Australian had looked a little ragged when he flew past a minute earlier and his challenge to the Russian's smoother style seemed to stem from a technique based on aggression and pure nerve. Suddenly, there was a shout in the background.

"Look out, this one's got it all wrong!" Price looked up and saw a bike fast approaching which seemed to be on completely the wrong line. Sure enough, the rider suddenly realised his error and, in a frenzy of panic braking, the machine shook its head vigorously as if in disgust. Everything then happened so quickly that Price could never later remember the exact sequence of events, but he had a vague recollection of a riderless machine sliding towards him, of someone screaming and then blackness and silence. When he opened his eyes, he saw blue sky and wondered where he was, but a worried face appeared in the blue window and he felt a dull, gnawing pain in his leg.

"Don't try to move, Doc," the face said, but Price took no notice and tried to get up. It was then that the dull gnawing became red hot agony and he knew, without even looking that he had been badly hurt.

"What...what happened?" he stuttered.

"Looks like you've got a compound fracture of your left tibia," a voice behind him cheerfully reported and the doctor turned to one side and was violently sick. When he looked up again, the owner of the voice was within his field of vision and was holding out an oxygen mask.

"Entonox," she said, for she was a first-aider and Price seized the mask gratefully and took a deep breath.

"Hold on, don't I know you?" he asked when the nitrous oxide had taken effect.

"Yep, Glen Helen last year," the woman replied, "I was filming for Greenlight. Different duties this year...looks like I've got my own back!"

"How...how's the rider," he enquired weakly

"Better than you," she said, "he's here and wants to speak to you."

"Terribly sorry, Doc," another voice seemed to be saying and a graven-faced rider now appeared in his field of view, "I've been through this corner a hundred times before, but this time I just got it completely wrong. Must be the new section of road at Brandish...it's made the approach to this bend so bloody fast." Price took a few more breaths of the pain-killing gas mixture and was starting to feel a little high. He could hear bikes still flying past in the background, but the sound of a fast-approaching helicopter meant that his part in this race was drawing to a close.

"Can you get a message to Race Control," he mumbled.

"Don't worry, Doc, it's already done."

"Could any friends of Dr Jonathon Price please contact Race Control immediately," the voice on the tannoy announced and Louise Templeton, who had been sitting in the Grandstand watching the race, frowned and got up. She knew that such announcements normally related to riders and heralded news of serious injury or worse, but Price was not a rider, he was a doctor; what could possibly have happened to him...unless...? She climbed the steps of the tower, a worried expression now upon her face and when she gave her name and said why she was up there, she really expected to hear the worst.

"I'm sorry Louise," the Clerk of the Course was saying. He was an advocate and knew her quite well, "but he was hit by a bike at Hillberry..." She swallowed. "...and he's got a bad fracture of his tibia and fibula. He's in Nobles and they expect to operate this evening...I...why are you laughing, Louise? I wouldn't have thought a broken leg is particularly amusing."

"I thought he was dead, Charles and you've got to admit that a broken leg is one hell of a lot better than that."

Price was lying on a trolley in Casualty and a glance at his watch told him that the Senior Race was still going on. X-rays had been taken and a pain-killing injection given, but, although comfortable, he was desperate for news of his friends. He pressed the button on the handset he had been given and a moment or two later a nurse appeared.

"Do you need anything, Jonathon?" she asked, her face a picture of concerned attentiveness, "don't forget you're nil by mouth, but I could get you a mouthwash or..."

"I need a radio," Price interrupted, "they'll be on the last lap by now of the Senior Race."

"I'll see what I can do," she said, smiling. A few minutes later she returned. "Here you are; just what the doctor ordered," she announced, then departed and Price turned the radio on.

"Rorletski's indicated at Cronk-y-Mona," the commentator announced enthusiastically, "so he should be with us any second, but Campbell's still got the Mountain descent. We reckon they were neck and neck at Glen Helen, then Campbell pulled out half a second by Ramsey Hairpin. Telemetry gave half a second still at the Bungalow, so if Campbell manages to maintain that, the race is his. I can see a machine in the distance...is it?...yes it is. The number one machine of Rorletski goes past us...now and takes the chequered flag. It's going to be a long wait for the Australian. He started at number seventeen so...hold on...he's indicated at Cronk-y-Mona already. That can't be right...if it is he's pulled out over a minute. Yes, it is...Rorletski must have had a problem on that Mountain descent. The Russian's coming into the winner's enclosure now so let's just go over to Geoff." There was silence for a few seconds and then a different voice came on air.

"We don't know yet whether you've won, Andre, but Campbell's already indicated at Cronk-y-Mona, so that puts him ahead. Did you have a problem coming down the Mountain?"

"Fuel empty," the Russian explained, "light come on before Ramsey, and engine start spluttering at Creg-Ny-Baa. Last few yards just coasting. Lucky I not have to get off and push."

"Hold on, Andre, we've got news of Campbell...back to John in the tower."

"Yes, sensational news here," the commentator screamed, "Campbell's through Governor's dip and on the start-finish straight but he's coasting...he's stopped. Oh, no, it looks like he's run out of fuel too...he has got off and he's pushing in. The crowd in the Grandstand are on their feet and cheering him on...Come on Don...come on...He crosses the line...now. What's the time, Norman?"

"We make it...no, it can't be...yes it is...a dead heat, down to one hundredth of a second."

"Unbelievable! It's never happened before and it'll probably never happen again. The Centenary Senior TT trophy will be shared between *two* riders......"

Chapter Forty

Senior Race Day – Late Afternoon

Price had been moved to the orthopaedic ward and found, of course, that it was almost full. The other three men with whom he shared the four-bedded bay were fellow bikers and it wasn't long before he heard graphic descriptions of their various prangs. All three now seemed on the road to recovery, whilst he still awaited the surgeon's knife. He had been told that an operation was scheduled for that evening, and there was precious little he could do until after then. The junior doctor had been to see him and he had learned that his injuries were far less severe than had at first been thought. In fact, the man had explained, it was a toss-up whether they need to operate at all. The tibia had been fractured, but could probably be treated by plaster although that would give a slightly less acceptable end result. Less than acceptable would not be good enough for his consultant, however, who was a passionate believer in nail, plate and screw so Price just had to lie there waiting and wondering what was going on in the outside world. The little radio had been taken from him, but now the doctor had gone he was able to look around. He had rather more experience of hospitals than he cared to tell his fellow sufferers and soon found that which he sought. He turned on the headset and managed to find the right channel. The TT broadcast had just ended and the local news begun.

"So after that dramatic conclusion to the Senior Race, we've just heard President Shrub presenting the Senior Trophy to Andre Rorletski and Don Campbell. The President has now left the Grandstand and is being taken by helicopter to visit Cregneash village and what is thought to be his ancestors' home in the south of the Island. We understand that no one is absolutely certain which house the President's ancestors lived in, but our Chief Minister has done some research and is pretty sure that Cronk Ny Arrey Farm is the right place."

Sh*t, the doctor thought, we were on the right track all along, but unless Roy and the others were listening to that, they won't know exactly where the President is going and they may well have been lulled into a sense of false relief.

He had already discovered that his mobile had been broken and his earlier attempts to use the ward telephone had led him to discover that the thing seemed unable to make calls to cellular 'phones. He needed to get a message to his friends and he needed to do it fast, but the more he wracked his brains in search of an answer to his problem, the further away that answer seemed to be. Suddenly, the door at the end of the corridor burst open and a grey-suited man in, Price guessed, his early forties walked onto the ward. The man was surrounded by a gaggle of white-coated junior doctors and was obviously a consultant. The fact that he walked straight past Price's bed suggested he was uninvolved in the doctor's care, but after he had visited the man in the next bed, he turned and came back.

"Jonathon Price?" he asked, staring at the name on the clipboards at the end of the bed.

"That's me," Price replied. Something about the consultant's face seemed vaguely familiar; had they bumped into each other at a medical convention once long ago?

"I was at medical school with someone called Jonathon Price; you're not a doctor, by any chance, are you?...my name's Girvan, Patrick Girvan," the man said.

"Paddy Girvan?...well, who would believe it?" Price replied, "It must be twenty-odd years since we last met." An enormous grin appeared on the face of the consultant and he reached out to shake Price's hand. His ward-round and the junior doctors around him were, for the moment, forgotten whilst he relived days gone by.

"Remember the Huntley Street Union and all the fun we used to have?"

"And the Rugby and the nurses and Brakespear's best bitter, who could ever forget?" Price replied with a smile; a solution to his seemingly impossible problem lay very close at hand.

Less than an hour later, Price was balancing on crutches outside the hospital's main entrance. He had experienced a certain amount of difficulty in negotiating the revolving door, but such things had not been designed with people in full-length plaster really in mind. A red BMW coupe appeared at the end of the road and a few seconds later, Price was struggling into the passenger seat.

"So Paddy Girvan made the call," he said, "where did you find the car?"

"The police had impounded it," Grant replied with a grin, "but when they found out it was mine, someone brought it 'round. I take it you want to go South?"

"As fast as you can. Did you hear where they're taking Shrub?"

"Mitch just told me. We'll take the St Mark's road, it'll be quieter. Hold on, we're gonna make some rubber burn!"

Grant joined the Course at Union Mills, then put his foot down and the car shot forward as if jet-propelled. Glen Lough campsite flashed by, but the Australian didn't seem to touch the brakes.

"Christ, that was close," Price exclaimed as they shot through the Ballagarey lights, "I think you just went through on red, Grant and there's a thirty limit through here."

"No worries," Grant replied, "I reckon it was amber myself, but I've got a load of mates in Traffic and they always tell me where they're gonna set their speed traps."

The police had sealed off Cregneash village on both sides with roadblocks so that no-one unwanted could possibly get through and when the Presidential helicopter landed, the Chief Constable finally smiled. The last few days had been extremely difficult, what with the races and the exalted guest, but in a few hours it would all be over and his men could get some rest. The village was not quite as empty as he would have liked, but, as the Minister for Tourism and Leisure had patiently explained, the monks' convention had been booked for over a year and this was their last event. Once he had got used to it, the Chief Constable found the sight of men in hoods and habits rather pleasing to the eye and although the village had no real ecclesiastical history, the brothers seem to fit in rather well. Even the President's minders seemed to have visibly relaxed and when the President told them that he wanted to walk to Cronk Ny Arrey Farm with the Island's Chief Minister, but without them, the men simply nodded and smiled. The place had been searched numerous times and there was no other way in or out; if the President didn't want them with him, why should they object?

It was six o'clock in the evening when President Shrub entered the house and that was a good hour earlier than had been originally planned, but the Chief Minister reasoned that the farm's new owners would have no reason to object; after all, although he had never met them, their advocate Mr Gruber had been most cooperative. The place was deserted, just as Gruber had said it would be and although the Chief Minister knew all about that dreadful murder, lightning never stuck twice in the same place.

"Quaint little cottage," the President said after he had briefly looked around the house, "reminds me of pictures I've seen of my grandfather's homestead in Texas...before he struck oil, that is. Strange, though, I can't find the entrance to the cellar."

"Cellar, Mr President?" the Chief Minister asked, a little surprised.

"Yeah, it's an old family story...the house had a deep cellar that was haunted by a ghost. As I recall it, the ghost of a little ginger-haired fellow who, legend had it, rode a horse. It is said that the ginger-haired horseman is seen by a Shrub on his death"

"Have you seen enough, Mr President?"

"I suppose so," the man said, rather sadly, the Chief Minister thought.

They walked out of the door and back towards the road. It was now quarter-past six and the Chief Minister was feeling rather pleased with himself. He had managed to get this visit over quicker than even he had hoped which left plenty of time to get back and change for the evening's banquet at the Governor's House. That was going to be *the* important event of the week, well certainly in the Chief Minister's wife's opinion and he really hoped that she enjoyed it, as the last twelve months hadn't, as far as she was concerned, been particularly good.

He had just reached the farm gate when the Chief Minister noticed yet another one of those blessed monks approaching. He frowned; he had heard what his colleague, the Minister of Tourism and Leisure had said earlier, but the village really did seem overrun with men wearing habits. If it had been down to him...

"Back to farmhouse...now!" The man hissed, spitting out the words as though they were bullets and the Chief Minister opened his mouth to protest, but when he looked down, he froze in silent terror, for the man was holding a pistol and pointing it straight at his chest. "Back to farmhouse," the man repeated, "or I kill you and President now." His eyes were as black as coals and conveyed evil intent even more forcibly than the grey metal object in his hand.

"I think we'd better go back to the house, Mr President," the Chief Minister said, turning to face President Shrub who had been a few yards behind him and the President glanced at him in surprise.

"I thought you said we'd gotta go to this banquet?...what's up?...are you alright?"

"I think he wants us to go back," the Chief Minister replied. Shrub looked at the monk and saw the gun. It had been concealed by the long woollen sleeve of the habit, but was now pointing at his head and could not be missed. The police and the President's men were down the road in the village and Shrub realised that if all of these robed men were in this together, their situation was looking rather grim.

"Okay, okay," he said, "we go back to the farmhouse," thinking frantically of ways to escape.

Suddenly, Shrub heard a shout down in the village and turned. The robed man was no longer pointing the pistol at his head and seemed uncertain of which way to look. It was the President's chance and he took it: with a leap and a bound he was off. He had been a good runner in his youth and his legs suddenly remembered what they were for. In seconds he had rounded the corner of the house and was off up the hill towards the curious looking structure at the top. He was almost there when he heard a shot. He fell to his knees and at first thought he had stumbled, for he felt no pain, but when he looked up he knew he was dead. A strange vision was standing there before him, a vision of a ginger-haired little man on a tall white horse.

"The harbinger of death!" he wailed.

"No...I'm Lester," the ginger-haired apparition said.

Down in Cregneash pandemonium reigned. Noise, smoke and confusion were all around, for a fierce gun-fight had broken out between the monks and the police. When Grant and the doctor arrived they found themselves in the thick of it, but had no real idea what was going on. As the Attorney General's man, Grant had passed through the roadblocks with ease, but as the bullets flew between the thatched-roofed cottages, both men thought that they had got there too late.

"What the f**k," the Australian exclaimed and threw the car into reverse.

"Up there, to the left," Price shouted, "the farmhouse by the beacon, that's where he is." Grant sped up the bumpy lane with the car's twin exhausts banging and scraping on the stones beneath.

"No ground clearance, these things," he grumbled, but the doctor wasn't listening.

"That's Mikael," he exclaimed, "Stop, stop." Grant brought the car to a halt by the open gate and Price pulled himself out. He staggered up the track towards Cronk Ny Arrey Farm and reached the tall Russian just as he was stepping through the front door. "Mikael," he said, "what's happening?...where is President Shrub?"

"I think the President safe, for now," Boroweski replied, "he rescued by man on horse half hour ago. Maybe we find him later, but we have more important things to do now."

"More important than the President?"

"Come, I show you."

They walked into the farmhouse together and Price saw that several of Boroweski's men were already there. A carpet had been rolled back and a trapdoor lay wide open in the middle of the floor. The tall Russian walked straight towards it and when he got there looked down.

Можете вы defuse бомба?" he said to whoever was below.

"возможно, но оно будет трудно" came the reply. The voice sounded tense, but Price thought he had heard it before. With difficulty, he followed Boroweski down the steps and found himself in a cellar which, on first sight, seemed very similar to the one he had been in only a few hours before. There was one marked difference, however, and that stood before him now. The tank and fairing had been removed, but he recognised the Petromax machine straight away. He also recognised the slightly-built man beside it.

"Richard's bike," he said. "What is it doing here? And that's Sergey, isn't it?"

"Yes, Sergey has difficult task."

"Difficult?...it was easy enough to remove the plutonium last time; I assume that Illosovich is trying the same trick all over again?" Boroweski shook his head gravely.

"No, Doktor Price, we were wrong last year. I regret we did not look at Petromax machine closely enough. We now know what it is."

"What is it?" Price asked, although he now suspected that he knew.

"It is bomb, Doktor Price; nuclear bomb. Sergey is atomic munitions specialist who, with his twin brother, once work for Illosovich. Now, thankfully, he work for us. His twin brother murdered after he arm device in your friend Richard's house, several months ago."

"Arm?" Price demanded, feelings of panic arising within him, "you mean that thing is armed…it's not going to explode, is it?"

"It has timer set for seven o' clock," Boroweski explained, "which is when American President was supposed to visit this house."

"Can Sergey defuse it?" Price asked. The Russian shrugged his shoulders.

"Who knows," he replied nonchalantly, "but he and his brother build it, so I suppose he able to take it apart." The doctor felt beads of sweat on his forehead; his watch told him that the time was one minute to seven, but he had no real idea how accurate his watch was. To escape death on the TT racetrack only to be wiped out in a nuclear explosion seemed rather a cruel twist of fate. Suddenly Sergey turned to face them.

"Я преуспевал," he triumphantly exclaimed.

On the far side of the Calf of Man, a tall man with black eyes was waiting for a boat. He no longer had use for the brown woollen habit so had cast it aside. The rest of his men had been killed or captured, but the ruthless Vladimir Illosovich had bargained on no less from the very start. He had made his escape through the tunnels to the ruined lighthouse and, if the bomb had detonated, he would have been safe enough there, but his plan had not succeeded and when seven came and went with no explosion, he cursed and shook his fist in the air. He was not yet finished, he angrily declared. He would have his revenge on this cursed Island for what it had done to his life. He looked at his watch; the boat was late and he had far to travel. Suddenly, a blue and white motor launch appeared from around the headland and Illosovich smiled. It was rather smaller than the grand vessels he had once been used to, but *Sealion* would take him off the island and under cover of darkness he would rendezvous with the freighter. He turned to walk down from the cliff top to the shore, but there standing before him was a wild-eyed stranger with matted beard and long, straggling hair.

"Who are you?" Illosovich demanded.

"My name is Seth Quilleash," the stranger replied in a voice that was hoarse and croaking from months of disuse, "and you killed my father and brother. It is time for you to die now; make peace with your god!" Illosovich smiled in contempt, and then produced a pistol.

"How do you propose to kill me?" he responded. "I, as you can see, have a gun, whilst you appear to have none."

As *Sealion* chugged lazily around the headland, its skipper looked up at the cliffs in search of his passenger. The man had paid him well and in advance, but his experiences of earlier in the week had made him rather wary. Suddenly, he saw a figure standing there, at first alone, then struggling with another. He heard what sounded like a shot ring out and moments later both figures plummeted from the cliff-top to the jagged rocks below. He turned the boat and smiled darkly, for he already had his money and now had one less journey to make.

In the last house in Onchan, a famous party was being held in aid of a major celebration. Champagne, wine and beer flowed, as well as Canadian Club, the host's favourite tipple. The music pounded late into the night and the guests danced like there would be no tomorrow.

"I thought you were supposed to be at a banquet, Mr President" Price said.

"Well, I was, young man," the President replied, "but this guy saved my life... Damn lucky for me that he's been working for a riding school down in the south of the Island and was taking one of the horses out for some exercise...He took me back to the riding school and the people he works for were coming here so I just came along with them...Great party and I've managed to give those darned CIA bodyguards the slip for the first time since I made the Oval Office. I'm gonna recommend Lester for a Congressional Medal of Honour. D'you hear that Lester?"

"Sound," came the reply from the ginger-haired little man who was standing by his side.

"Your bodyguards don't know you're here?" the doctor asked in astonishment.

"Hell, no and I don't propose to tell 'em. Richard here has kindly offered to put me up for the night so I'm gonna let my hair down and party. Do you really know what it's like to be constantly under their eagle-eyed control?... Hey Richard...how about you showin' me that collection of bikes you were talking about?"

Price made his way around the house with rather more difficulty than he cared to admit, but plaster of paris and crutches had that effect and in many ways he had cause to be thankful. He found Rorletski and the Australians in the Blue room talking bikes. Winged Mercury, the fabled Senior TT trophy, stood in the corner of the room and Richard, who walked in a few seconds later accompanied by President Shrub, explained.

"Supposed to be kept in the vault of the Isle of Man Bank, I know, but the manager's an old friend of mine and I persuaded him to let us have it here for the party. A man from Securicor's coming to collect it in the morning, but at least the winners can share it for a few hours."

"Well done, Richard," Price said, laughing, "and talking about your powers of persuasion, I was impressed by the way you talked the Deemster into letting you conduct your own defence. Where on earth did you pick up all that legal stuff?"

"The prison's got a very good library," the undertaker replied, "and I had plenty of time to read...the food's not bad either," he added.

Rorletski and the Australians seemed to be getting along like a house on fire even though they had been forced to share the title so Price congratulated them all and they him, then he staggered on into the kitchen. Louise Templeton was there with Love and Smith and Boroweski. Louise greeted him with a warm hug and a kiss and the conversation which had been going on continued.

"So how many times did Illosovich or his men actually break into this house?" the advocate asked, looking around as if unable to believe what had happened. "Three times," Boroweski replied. "First time to make sure Petromax machine still here and then, when his men have done that, to frame Richard for murder and make sure that he kept out of house for long, long time. If Richard not here, then this house very safe place to keep bomb until time come for it to be used. Second time, shortly after police have finished looking at murder scene, Sergey's brother return to arm bomb with special engine parts taken from mine. He is man who climb steps from beach below and has to take Petromax machine apart to do what he has to do." He looked at Love. "You notice, Mr Love, slight marks on machine made by this man, but unfortunately you not fully understand their significance. Sergey's brother return to boat where another of Illosovich's men kill him and throw his body in sea...I believe it wash onto beach day or two later"

"So...he was the man strangled with the plastic bag," Louise exclaimed, "but why did Illosovich have him killed?"

"If he able to arm bomb, then he able to disarm bomb," Boroweski explained "and Illosovich want to make sure that not happen...he not know that Sergey coming to Island with us."

"And, of course, the third time was when they switched the bikes and took away the special Petromax, replacing it with a standard one," Smith continued. "They could have done that months earlier, but there was always a chance they would have been stopped. Once races had begun, though..."

"The Island is suddenly full of motorbikes in the back of vans," Price finished the sentence, "but why arm the bomb back in February if he didn't want it to explode until June. He couldn't possibly have known the exact date and time President Shrub would have been at Cronk Ny Arrey Farm, could he?"

"He said arm, Jonathon," the American cut in. "Illosovich merely wanted to assemble all the fissionable components so they were all in one place and ready to explode. He didn't want to run the risk of being caught carrying nuclear explosives about the Island when the security was beefed up. He didn't turn the timer on until much, much later, did he, Mikael?"

"That is right," Boroweski said, nodding gravely.

"I've got a couple of further questions," Price said, "if we're trying to clear up unresolved problems. Firstly, who was the guy I saw shot near Ingebreck Reservoir and, secondly, who the hell were those people who abducted me?" He had already told them the truth about his abduction, but was no clearer in his own mind as to exactly whose side those responsible were on."

"We'll never be sure who was shot, unless someone finds the body," Love replied, but I strongly suspect that Illosovich had Darren Finch murdered. We know he was looking for both Darren and Jason; fortunately, he didn't find Jason. There was some sort of leak from the police after Louise had disclosed their witness statements. It doesn't take an analytical genius to work out who the leak came from and the latest we've heard is that DC Liszt has not been seen by anyone since Monday. He may have simply gone into hiding, but Vladimir Illosovich doesn't like to leave loose ends lying around so I somehow don't think we'll be seeing DC Liszt again, ever. Illosovich knew that Darren and Jason could give Richard an alibi and he didn't want that to happen, partly because he didn't want Richard turning up at this house or Shrub cottage and partly for the oldest reason in the book."

"Which is?" Price asked.

"Revenge," Love replied. "Richard screwed up his plans last year, didn't he?"

"As for the men who held you last weekend," Smith continued, "we don't know precisely who they are, but we're pretty certain they aren't British Secret Service. There are other agencies in the world who knew or suspected what Illosovich was doing, not all of them friendly. We're pretty sure that the men concerned worked for one of them, but you say 'Des' was English?"

"He spoke perfect Oxford English when he interrogated me, but he spoke with a convincing cockney accent when I met him earlier, so who knows where he really came from," Price said. "None of the others said that much...I was sure that they were British, but I'm just as sure now that they weren't. Why do you think they would want to get Illosovich, though, if they weren't on our side?"

"They not want Illosovich," Boroweski replied, "they want bomb." Price shook his head in disbelief.

"I still can't believe you're serious about that bomb, Mikael," he said. "Why would Illosovich use a nuclear bomb to kill the President? That's using the proverbial sledgehammer to crack a nut; why didn't they just shoot him?"

"Two reasons," the Russian replied, "Illosovich thought that electromagnetic pulse from bomb would send shock wave from radio beacon near house across entire North Atlantic chain of beacons. His plan to knock out all beacons so all planes which airborne lose their way and crash. Like 9/11, only worse.

"Would that work?"

"Who knows?" he shrugged his shoulders yet again, "It might."

"And the second reason?"

"Illosovich have men build bomb to new design. He need to test it and he want revenge on Isle of Man for what happen to him here."

"So that was it...a trial?"

"The ultimate trial," Boroweski replied, with just the hint of a smile.